The Dancing Life

MIKAEL CARLSON

WARRINGTON
PUBLISHING

Danbury, Connecticut

The Dancing Life
Copyright © 2024 by Warrington Publishing

Printed in the United States of America
First Edition
ISBN: 978-1-944972-40-0 (paperback)
          978-1-944972-42-4 (ebook)
          978-1-944972-41-7 (hardcover)

Book cover designed by JD&J
Edited by Mike Waitz at Stick & Stones

Novels by Mikael Carlson:

– The Michael Bennit Series –
The iCandidate
The iCongressman
The iSpeaker
The iAmerican

– Tierra Campos Thrillers –
Justifiable Deceit
Devious Measures
Vital Targets
Revealed Secrets
Decisive Endgame

– Tierra Campos Thrillers Prequels –
Narrow Escape: The Summerville Massacre

– Watchtower Thrillers –
The Eyes of Others
The Eyes of Innocents
The Eyes of Victims
The Eyes of Addicts

– America, Inc. Saga –
The Black Swan Event
Bounded Rationality
Boiling the Ocean

– The Santa Trilogy –
Banning Santa

– The Dancing Trilogy –
The Dancing Life

For all those who find enduring love and hang on tight with both hands.

The Binge

It never should have come to this. Like all my peers, I checked all the boxes and did everything they asked. I excelled in high school and stayed out of trouble. Sure, I had a few minor transgressions…but nothing that would result in a blemish on otherwise stellar college applications. I was too focused on my long-term goals to let something dumb derail me.

My grades, honor societies, and activities were good enough to get me into my choice of Ivy League schools. I chose Princeton, double-majored in finance and political science, and graduated summa cum laude. I ranked third in my class, losing to an Asian kid who always had his face in a book, and a mousy virgin named Adele. At least we all assumed she was a virgin.

When I received my degrees, the doors opened. I had the world in the palm of my hand. I landed a good career, a fat bank account, an expensive Manhattan apartment, and a blazing hot wife for what good that did me. I'm where I am despite all of that. God has a sadistic sense of humor.

Taking a pass on this remaining trip down memory lane, I force myself to roll out of bed and climb the short flight of stairs topside. The sun is evenly split between the sky and the horizon. I don't know if it's morning or evening, and it takes a moment to get my bearings and figure out which direction I'm staring at. It's west. I slept the day away again.

I'm what the locals in the Conch Republic call a "liveaboard." Many people who call Key West home drifted into town and took up residence on motor, sail, or houseboats. It's a liberating and romantic existence, but not without annoying inconveniences. Some liveaboards can motor and sail around the keys at their leisure, while countless others are chained to shore on a broken vessel that only serves as floating quarters.

This magnificent thirty-foot sailboat I rented is in far better condition than most boats in this marina. It has all the conveniences, including a full galley, running water, and an adequate bathroom. Despite the amenities, I only sleep and shower here. Sometimes, I don't bother with the latter, like now. I need a drink.

I stumble off the ship, still wearing the clothes I donned last night. And probably the night before. I've lost track. I'm not here to impress anyone. This isn't about needing a short break from life – it's about drinking myself into oblivion and forgetting everything. If I die in the process, so be it.

The pylon on the edge of a pier makes a perfect spot to rest and steady myself. I'm fit, but all the alcohol I've imbibed is taking its toll. A hundred yards to go. I push off, forcing one foot in front of the other as I keep my sights on The Drunken Lobster.

It's not dissimilar to many of the bars in Key West. It's nautical-themed, with everything from fishing tackle and nets to life-sized plastic fish on the walls. Most of the décor is ad-hoc. The walls are plastered with license plates, old currency from countless countries, business cards, and ladies' undergarments. Every inch of the joint is covered, most in multiple layers. A fire would race through this place with all the combustible material on the walls and ceiling. At least it saves on the cost of paint.

The sun is almost down, meaning the island's nightlife is about to heat up. The Drunken Lobster is just getting going. In another hour, every seat will be filled. In two, it will be standing-room only, filled with tourists in loud shirts, shorts, and flip-flops. Key West embraces the island life. Probably too much.

I stumble through the large opening that serves as a door and ease onto a barstool. The bartender notices me and excuses himself from his conversation with a group of tourists at the other end of the bar. He walks over with a grin on his face.

"Hey, Steve," I say, rubbing my temples.

"Braden Fox…you're still alive," the bartender muses, flinging the white bar towel over his shoulder.

"Despite my best efforts to be otherwise. I'll have a bourbon, rocks."

The corner of the man's mouth curls. My mind is swimming, and my judgment is questionable, but I would swear that he looks amused.

"Sure. How do you plan on paying?"

"Debit card," I say, feeling my pockets for my wallet.

I check the back of my pants and then the front. My keys and passport are there, but no wallet. Certainly, no prepaid cards or cash. I hang my head, realizing it must have fallen out somewhere on the boat. It's not a far walk to the other side of the marina. Unfortunately, in my condition, I might as well be running the New York Marathon.

Steve reaches under the counter and pulls out a worn black wallet. He holds it up in front of me like it's an artifact from an Indiana Jones movie before tossing it unceremoniously onto the bar.

"You left this here last night."

I stare at the wallet. "How much money did you take out of it?"

"You don't think much of me," Steve says, pulling the towel off his shoulder and wiping down the bar. "Why would I need to take any?   You spend it all here anyway. Besides, there's no cash in it."

I can't argue with either of those points. Key West has a ton of bars and restaurants. It offers museums, boating trips, beaches, and a golf course. Not that I would know. This is the only place I've come since I got here.

"True enough.   How 'bout you get me my bourbon?"

"Why don't you start with somethin' your kidneys don't need to filter. They could use the break. When was the last time you even ate?"

"Good question," I say, rubbing the five-day-old stubble on my chin. "What day is it?"

Steve scoffs as he starts wiping the bar again with his towel. "You have Keys Disease, my friend. I've seen you walk back and forth from your boat on the hook at the other end of the marina. Why don't you call it a night, detox a little, and visit a beach tomorrow? You look pasty."

The locals use "Keys Disease" as either a positive or a negative. Charitable usage of the term is where someone simplifies life to enjoy each day to its fullest. They shed material possessions, live for the moment, and earn a meager living compatible with their beliefs.

Steve didn't mean it that way. He used it to imply I can't resist the temptations of living in a vacation mecca. I'm partying too hard, getting burned out, and will end up homeless and destitute. He's not wrong. That's how I plan on ending up before I permanently say goodbye to this dysfunctional society.

"Why don't you stop acting like my mother and get me the drink that I asked for?" I bark loudly enough to cause some of the other patrons to turn their heads.

I pull the prepaid debit card out of my wallet and slap it loudly on the bar. The outburst has the desired effect. Steve looks at the gawking Parrotheads and frowns before shaking his head and complying with the request. He sets the bourbon down, and I down it in just a few gulps. I shake it, indicating I want another.

The wallet holds more than my money and identification. I flip it open and pull out a battered photo, not fighting the hurt it conjures. She is so beautiful. So intelligent. So perfect. Except in the ways she isn't.

I remember this day like it happened last week. We were in Central Park. She asked seven different people to take this picture, not settling until one captured the perfect shot. Kinsey's arms were wrapped around my chest while she rested her chin on my shoulder. Her sundress flowed in the light breeze, and her auburn hair caught the sun's rays like it was photoshopped. It was magical. She was magical. And now it's all gone.

All I want to do now is drink because drinking makes me forget. Life is fragile. Happiness is fleeting. Success is a mirage. Forgetting is what I need most, and after a few more of these, that's exactly what will happen. Binge drinking is good for that.

Chapter Two

Missing Persons

So far as views of the city go, this one isn't so bad. No, it doesn't offer a sweeping panorama of the Lower Manhattan skyline or a picturesque perspective of the Statue of Liberty. But there is a terrace here on the 24th Floor that runs the length of his office that his employees can step out on when they need a break or want to admire a nice view of St. Patrick's Cathedral. Not that Arden Davenport cares. He didn't lease this office for the scenery.

New York City became an important center of commerce at the end of the 19th century. During that era, most businesses were housed on Manhattan's southern tip. The banking and investment industry was dubbed "Wall Street" because it was and still is concentrated there.

Advertising agencies flocked to Midtown and set up shop on Madison Avenue. At the height of its influence, more than one in three agencies had this street address. That has changed in the decades since, with countless firms moving to other parts of the island and across the East River into Brooklyn. The hipster borough offers cheaper rents and access to a burgeoning tech sector popping up there.

None of that matters to Arden, either. He isn't the founding member of an advertising agency, even though marketing a product is a significant part of the job. Only his product is politicians, and he needs to earn a fifty point one percent market share for each to declare victory.

There are many myths in politics. One of the most egregious is that Internet-driven, small-dollar contributions matter to campaigns. They don't. It might make a quaint talking point or serve as something a candidate can point to when wooing voters, but from a financial perspective, it's insignificant.

The real power lies in the Super PAC. The Internet may have fueled Obama in 2008, but that was an eternity ago in the political world. Big contributions are the lifeblood of American politics, and political action committees are the way to circumvent campaign finance laws and feed the insatiable thirst for advertising dollars.

Super PACs can receive unlimited contributions from individuals, corporations, labor unions, and other political action committees. Then, they can spend them to support campaigns in any manner deemed appropriate. That makes men like Arden a kingmaker. He can bolster everything from television advertising to grassroots get-out-the-vote efforts. The candidates he chooses enthusiastically share his vision for America, and there is power in that.

To exercise that power, Arden single-handedly formed the American Outreach PAC. His parents were absentee landlords, and everything he learned about the world was despite them, not because of them. What they did provide was a fat bank account.

That "seed money led to endeavors that created wealth on an unimaginable scale that served to fund many of the PACs under this umbrella. He is a bank, and the politicians who come for withdrawals are as good as bought and paid for.

Not that he could do it alone. Arden surrounds himself with special advisors who help select the candidates and set the narrative. Most of them were plucked from America's top universities and had advanced degrees ranging from finance to political science to psychology. They are wizards at what they do, and the rewards for success are gargantuan.

So is the risk. Politics is a dirty business, and it's dirty work getting a candidate elected. American Outreach doesn't pay for the long hours and effort that entails. It pays for loyalty. That is the currency of this realm, and now one of Arden's best and brightest is missing.

The knock on the door interrupts his train of thought. Arden watches two of his superstars enter his office, forcing him to draw one more breath of outside air before retreating from the balcony into his large corner workspace. Travis and Ilana wait patiently for their boss to acknowledge them.

Travis Breckinridge is one of his best hires. Brought into American Outreach simultaneously with Braden, he is a first-rate geopolitical strategist. A product of Harvard, he's as sharp as they come.

Ilana Horowitz is unique because she spent a decade in the workforce before joining the ranks. Arden rescued her from a meaningless government job and gave her full responsibility over a billion-dollar campaign coffer. She is a numbers wizard specializing in forensic accounting who didn't graduate from an Ivy League school. That doesn't mean she isn't talented as hell.

"If you two are standing in my office, it's because you found Braden. Where is he?"

"Key West."

Arden scowls and turns to stare at Travis. "You two are friends. Why is Braden in Florida when he should be working at his desk?"

"I don't know, sir. He didn't say anything to me."

"Braden made a significant withdrawal from his personal account and hopped on a flight out of LaGuardia," Ilana says, having likely checked financial records and had their Russian investigation team track down the lead. "He rented a car at Miami International Airport upon his arrival. From there, he disappeared until yesterday when a paper trail emerged from a boat rental company in the Key West Bight Marina. That's where we think he's staying."

"How much did he take out of the account?"

"One hundred thousand. Braden hasn't used his card since," Ilana informs them. "We're watching it."

Arden raises an eyebrow. "That's one hell of a vacation slush fund, so let's assume he isn't craving key lime pie. Why is he there without his wife?"

"She could be joining him later," Ilana posits.

"I would know if she was. Instead, Braden's been gone for five days without a phone call to home or the office. He vanished like a fart in the wind. Is it possible that he was lured there by another outfit?"

"I don't see how," Travis answers quickly. "He's loyal. He would never leave us."

"What about the government?" Arden asks, putting his hands behind his back.

"I would be more concerned if he was in D.C. The feds aren't meeting him in a drinking town in the Florida Keys."

"All right, forget it. Whatever the reason, Braden went rogue. I don't care why. Find out if he has any information with him that can damage us. He holds a senior position here and has his fingerprints on dozens of candidates. As my senior counsel, he knows our tactics because he invented most of them. He knows where all the bodies are buried. I need to know whether he plans on using that information."

"Yes, sir," Ilana says, and Travis nods before they march to the office door. "The two of you are being paid very well. I don't want excuses. I want results. Don't fail me."

Ilana slips out of the office, but Travis stops with his hand grasping the door's leading edge. He hangs his head before Arden realizes his other protégé hasn't left yet.

"Something bothering you, Travis?"

"Sir, even if we find out why Braden left, it doesn't solve the problem. He's still gone."

"Let me deal with that."

Travis nods awkwardly and leaves the office. Arden waits for the door to close before he pulls the receiver off its cradle. He punches a button, holding the phone to his ear.

"Yeah?" a deep Russian voice answers on the other end. That's all the greeting the powerful man is going to get. It's also all that he expects. The man running this particular organization doesn't engage in small talk or unnecessary pleasantries.

"Where's Braus working at the moment?"

"Atlanta."

"Good. Get him on a plane to Miami and tell him to rent a car. "I'll double your usual fee and have instructions for him by the time he touches down. I need him in Key West first thing tomorrow morning."

Chapter Three

The Engineer

The hour is late, and The Drunken Lobster is busy. I've only moved to take a leak once in my time here. I almost got into a fistfight with a guy wearing a Hawaiian shirt and Crocs when he tried to steal my seat. The pattern is repeating. Night after night, the same barstool, same bartender, same alcohol, and same result. My advanced state of inebriation would make Susan Boyle look like Gal Gadot. Everything is blurry, and no amount of squinting clears my vision. This ought to be interesting because it's time for another pit stop.

I slip off my stool, hanging on the bar's edge like I'm about to plunge into an abyss. Steadying myself, I stumble past tables filled with boozy tourists toward the men's room. The table near the restroom door is the only unoccupied space in The Drunken Lobster.

Standing at the urinal, I get into a war with my zipper. Once freed, I try to read the writing on the wall. My vision is hazy, and my mind is incapable of processing much of anything. None of the words make sense. After a few moments, I quit trying to decipher the text and finish my business. Nothing profound has ever been written on a bathroom wall, especially at a Key West watering hole.

"Oh, I'm definitely drunk," I slur, trying to pull the zipper up without catching the skin of parts I would rather not see bleeding.

I leave the men's room, spotting an old man seated at the previously vacant table. Curious. The numerous empty pint glasses in front of him imply that he's been there for a while. I know he hasn't. At least, I think he hasn't.

I trip over my feet and catch myself on the wall, spinning and falling into the chair opposite the man. He's a weather-worn, bearded old man who stares at me with deep, knowledgeable eyes. His look isn't one of irritation or annoyance – it's amusement.

"Oh, sorry."

"No, you're not," he says in a raspy voice. "But please, keep your seat, son."

The room starts spinning a little, so I take him up on the offer and try to form a sentence in my head. "I didn't see you when I went to…I mean, how long…did you…"

"You weren't looking for me and thus didn't find me."

"Uh-huh." The grizzled man simply stares at me, his face chiseled in place and completely expressionless. "Well, what's your name, old-timer?"

"I'm the Engineer."

"The Engineer? You mean, like, you design buildings and things?"

The man smirks, causing the wrinkles around his mouth to deepen into crevasses. He holds his worn hands up for me to see. "I drive trains, son. It's telling that you choose to assume I have a higher station in life."

I'm not sure what he means. It could be the alcohol. It might be because he's making no sense.

"Okay, well, I'm heading back to the bar. Sorry to bother you."

"You don't want to leave," the Engineer says, leaning back. "You're curious and haven't asked me what you want to know."

"What's that?"

"You tell me."

I lower myself back into the chair, trying to keep my balance. I have no idea what he's talking about, so I ask the first question that pops into my mind.

"Okay. What trains do you engineer?"

The man waves a dismissive hand. "That was long ago. Now I engineer lives, Braden. I help people with their problems."

My name. I didn't say it. At least, I don't recall using it. We never made any formal introductions.

"How did…how do you know my name?"

"It's not important," the Engineer says, slightly shaking his head.

I look around The Drunken Lobster and stop when I see Steve staring at us from the bar in bewilderment. I wag a finger at the man in front of me. "Aw, Steve put you up to this, didn't he? Very funny. He's a funny guy trying to put one over on me."

"It's not funny. Your wife Kinsey and her lover are not funny. Your work at American Outreach is not funny. What's happening to you now is not funny."

I feel the smile drop quickly off my face. The Engineer continues staring at me, devoid of emotion. He can't know that. Nobody here knows my wife's name or what I do for a living.

"How do you know about my life?"

"Your life? Braden, I've been with you every step of the way. Long enough to know you have never lived."

"What are you talking about? I lived! I had a great life! I had a Park Avenue apartment, a beautiful wife, a great job…."

The Engineer leans forward. "Having a great life and actually living are not the same thing."

"That's a load of crap. It was all taken from me."

Even the whiskey my liver is marinating in can't temper the heat of my anger. I came here to forget about my life…to relieve the pain from the wounds of betrayal. Now, it all comes rushing back. I want to hate him for that.

"If it can be taken from you, it was never really yours, was it?"

"Okay, Mr. Engineer-philosopher. What things in life can't be taken from you?"

"Experiences. Adventures. Memories. Love. All the things you've never valued."

I point my finger in his face. "Bullshit. Love can be taken away. Mine was."

"Your wife wasn't taken away. She betrayed you. Love lives in your heart. That capacity cannot be removed unless you let it."

I have no idea what kind of new-age garbage this guy is spewing. I was hoping for some real advice and guidance from someone who has clearly attended the school of "been there, done that." Life experience is the best teacher. This man has had his fill. Instead, I get quotes from a self-help book on Amazon.

"Look, save the spiel. All I want is my life back."

The Engineer looks at me blankly before nodding. "Then you will have it if you listen and follow my advice."

Finally, some words I want to hear. I fight to steady myself on the chair by grabbing the table's edge. I cock my head and force myself to focus through the drunken haze. The Engineer has as much of my attention as I can muster.

"You must forget your past and focus on the future. Once you do, you'll get your life back."

"Forget my past?" I ask, confirming I heard him right.

"Yes."

"What makes you think you know anything about me? How could you know that forgetting the past will give me my life back?"

The aging man squints as he looks me dead in the eyes. "Because I am the Engineer. What do you people do when they are lost, Braden? They ask for directions. That is why you are here."

"So, you're going to help me do this?"

"No. You need to find a guide to help with that journey."

"A guide? How will I know when I meet him?"

The Engineer smirks. "Trust your instincts."

That is hopelessly vague. I stare at the man, waiting for more, but nothing comes. He remains stoic and unflinching as I plead with my eyes for more information. That's all I'm going to get without more prompting.

"I…it's just—"

"Face your demons as men do. You can roll the dice and let fate decide if you don't know your path. Or you can trust yourself to find your way. Live your life, Braden. Stop expecting to begin living at some random future date that may never come. That's the change you must make."

I can't focus well, so I close my eyes and silently repeat the words. With that committed to memory the best I can, my eyes open, and I look around the bar. Many of the patrons at this end stare at me like I just walked out of P.T. Barnum's circus tent. When I look back for the Engineer, he's nowhere to be found.

He didn't pass me. I would have seen him. He must have slipped into the men's room while I absorbed his words. I check the bar again. Nothing. I see only Steve's blurry figure approaching me, his bar towel draped over the usual shoulder.

"All right, buddy, you've had enough for tonight," Steve says, pulling me out of my chair.

"Wait…where did he go?"

"Who?"

"The man I was talking to…the Engineer."

"You've had a lot to drink already. Call it a night. Maybe go back to your boat and sober up a little."

Steve begins to walk me to the front of the bar. Everyone is staring at me as the crowd parts to make way.

"I'm not leaving," I shout.

"You aren't staying, either. You're cut off. I closed out your tab."

I jerk my arm away. "Fine. I'll find another bar and drink there!"

"Do what you need to," Steve moans. "Just do it somewhere else."

Steve turns and heads back to his post behind the bar as I stumble onto the marina's boardwalk. That's fine. I could throw a rock from here and hit three more bars. I'll wander south and find one closer to the center of town. As soon as I get my bearings.

Instead of heading straight to the boat, I turn left and start walking. Ot staggering. Whatever. Nobody cuts me off before I'm ready. After that conversation with the Engineer, I'm not ready for any of this.

Chapter Four

Braus

It was a beautiful morning for a drive, even a long one. The trip from Miami International Airport south down the Ronald Reagan Turnpike and west on U.S. Route 1 took just over three hours. Braus checks his watch – just after nine thirty. If his quarry is here partying, he won't be awake yet.

He parks the rental car in a lot situated off Front Street and steps into the breezy salt air. Key West is not a big island, and finding parking in this tourist trap isn't an easy task. Fortunately, the lot is adjacent to the marina where Braden's boat rental is moored. Or so he was told.

Braus opens his phone and selects the picture he was sent with his instructions. The boat isn't unique. Half of the watercraft in this marina have the same look and paint scheme. This ought to be fun to find.

Fortunately, the rental listing did provide some useful directions, and Braus turns left when he reaches the pier and heads for the northwest corner. His instructions were more concise than the directions to the boat. The old man is taking a vested interest in this assignment, or so his handler informed him. That means the pressure is on to deliver results. Not that it's a problem. He's dealt with men far more cunning and dangerous than a Princeton-educated finance weenie.

Nobody is milling about at this early hour. He can hear people stirring on the vessels as he checks their hull registration and ship names, but most are still below deck. Key West is a tourist town renowned for its active nightlife and inebriated fishermen. The fishing may start early, but the tourists won't be conscious until their stomachs wake them up.

After ten minutes of searching, Braus finds the vessel he's looking for. It's a sleek sailing ship, more than thirty feet long by his estimation. He's never been a sailor. He was a soldier, and soldiers like to keep their feet dry.

Braus scans the marina. All is quiet. He reaches into his pocket, pulls out a SIG Sauer P225, and screws on a suppressor longer than the weapon itself. It took him a long time to get used to using these. The added weight on the end of the barrel throws off the balance. Shooting straight with one takes patience and practice. Lots of practice.

He quietly climbs aboard and pauses on the top deck. There is no sign of activity. The only sounds he hears are the creaks and groans of the boats bobbing in the marina and angry gulls circling overhead as they search for their next meal.

It's showtime. Braus turns the knob on the hatch and eases himself down the stairs. He holds the suppressed SIG Sauer in front of him as he scans for threats. He doesn't see any. He also doesn't find what he expects. The bed is empty.

Alarmed, he checks the galley, the head, and even the boat's storage spaces. Braden could have seen him coming and decided to hide. Nothing. There is no doubt someone is living here. There are no obvious personal effects, but the clothes strewn over the floor smell like they were marinated in whiskey and brine.

"Damn it," Braus mumbles as he lowers his weapon.

It's decision time. He could wait below deck since Braden is bound to return sooner or later. Not that he has all day to wait. His boss's overlord is demanding results, and he wants them quickly. Those instructions were crystal clear.

It's early, so the bars are still closed. It's another hour before they open for the lunch crowd and die-hard alcoholics who fill every orifice of this island. Braden could have hooked up with some woman and is shacking up with her. He could have gone on a fishing expedition. He could be lying in a gutter somewhere. Despite Key West's diminutive size, there are too many variables in play to justify searching for one person.

Not that it would be a first. Braus has stalked for more elusive targets in far worse places. This is not the Donbas in Ukraine, the rugged terrain of Chechnya, or some bug-infested sub-Saharan shithole. His work has taken him around the world, and having seen much of it, Braus settled in the United States to enjoy a higher standard of living. And the easy work. Hunting an American is like stalking a turtle – they're slow, lazy, and easy to handle when they withdraw into their shells.

Bored, Braus climbs down from the boat and wanders around the marina. He removed the suppressor from his SIG and tucked the weapon into his waistband in the small of his back. He isn't dressed for this assignment and isn't blending in. He will be forced to retreat to the boat when more people begin meandering around the marina. Men in his line of work don't like to stick out. It's career-limiting.

A man unlocks a bar up ahead. Braus glances up at the sign – The Drunken Lobster. It's not the name he would choose, but it fits with other derelict watering holes here. Maybe Braden would think so, too. He will stick close to his rented quarters if he's trying to run a low profile. This is as good a place to start as any, and he steps inside.

"We're closed, buddy," a man with a towel over his shoulder says as he wipes down some tables. "Come back in an hour."

Politeness goes a long way. Braus tries to be a patient man, but nothing annoys him more than rudeness. The large opening to the street is still closed, and the bar isn't set up. Obviously, they are closed. So, why not ask if there is something he can help with?

"I see that. I'm wondering if you can answer a question," Braus says in heavily accented German. "Have you seen this man?"

The picture of Braden Fox is from his HR record at American Outreach. He's decked out in an expensive suit, which he will likely not be wearing in this town. The bartender studies it briefly before shifting his eyes back to the visitor.

"Nope. No idea who that is."

Braus squints. Lying is an art few can master. Politicians are among the elites. Lawyers have advanced degrees in misrepresentation. Public Relations people and propagandists think they're good at it but actually suck. Steve is none of those things, making him an amateur liar.

"You're sure he's never been here?"

"There are dozens of bars on Key West, mate," the barman says. "Check them."

"I would, but I don't think I need to," Braus says, stepping closer to the man. "I'm going to ask you again. This time, I suggest you don't lie to me."

"Look, pal, I said that I don't—"

Air. It's one of the quintessential human needs. Deprive someone of oxygen, and everything changes, including their attitude. Braus is quick. He hits the man with the heel of his palm in a perfectly placed strike against his solar plexus. The result is immediate.

The solar plexus contains a network of nerves within the abdomen, and a good strike causes the diaphragm to spasm. The barman is in pain and gasping for air as he begins to double over. Braus helps him along by slamming his head into the bar and breaking his nose. He pins his head against it and holds his gun an inch from his face.

"You are very rude, mister barman. I don't tolerate rudeness. Or liars."

"Okay, okay! Please don't hurt me!"

"Hurt you? No, I plan on cutting out your lying tongue and then killing you."

"No, please…please don't! I'll tell you anything you want to know!"

"Not so tough now, are you? Let's start simple. The man's name is Braden Fox. He rented a boat in the marina that's still there, but he isn't. Where is he?"

"I don't know! I swear! He comes here every afternoon and drinks until he can barely walk. Then he goes back to the boat."

"This happens every day?"

"Yes."

Braus ponders that for a moment. His instructions explained that Braden was in hiding. That doesn't appear to be true. Hiding is buying a twelve-pack and sitting on the boat all day. What the bartender described is self-destructive behavior. Whatever he's into, it's taking an emotional toll on him. Nobody goes from a workaholic to a drunkard that quickly without reason.

"What about last night?"

"He was hammered and unnerving other people, so I threw him out. He claimed he was going to find another bar. Then he left. I haven't seen him since."

"See how easy that was?" Braus asks as he releases the bartender's head and withdraws the gun. "You will not call the police and report this. If you do, I will come back here and kill you. And you won't tell Mr. Fox I was here if you see him. If you do, there will be…consequences. Understood?"

"Ye…yes," the bartender stammers.

"Excellent."

"What will you do when you find him?" the man asks, trying to stem the blood pouring from his nose.

"That's none of your business. But if you must know, we are going to have a talk. If I don't like what Mr. Fox says, I'll put a bullet in his head and feed him to the sharks."

Braus knows he probably shouldn't have said that. It doesn't matter. The bartender is terrified and isn't about to disobey him after agreeing to their arrangement. Fear is a powerful motivator. A bloody nose is nothing compared to what Braus is capable of. Nobody signs up to learn that the hard way without instantly regretting it.

It's going to be a beautiful day. Braus steps out of the "closed" bar and surveys the marina. Braden could be anywhere on this island. The German could spend the morning searching pubs and threatening bartenders, but that would be counterproductive. The only alternative, no matter how unpalatable it will be to his employer, is to be patient. Braden will return to the boat, and Braus will be waiting for him. Fortunately, a working sailboat provides him one advantage – it offers an easy means of disposing of the man's body if it comes to that.

Chapter Five

Run

I wasn't dreaming, and part of me is thankful for that. The sensation of being unable to breathe wasn't because I was being choked out after being cornered by a vampire zombie during the global apocalypse. It was something else.

My violent coughing wakes me up. Water does that when it finds its way into someone's lungs. The tide is rolling in, and ocean waves are lapping at my face. I lift my head out of the water as it retreats across the sand. That's one hell of an alarm clock.

Everything is blurry, and I squint as I check my surroundings. My vision takes a moment to adjust. Some of it is due to the hangover exacerbated by severe dehydration. The rest is due to the bright sunshine enveloping the shoreline at the southernmost point in the United States. I roll onto my back as another wave rolls up to my thighs. Everything hurts, my head above all.

My hands migrate down to my pockets. I feel the familiar rectangle of my passport and the lump of the rental car's plastic fob in my front pocket. I check the back. No wallet. I let my head crash back into the sand. That figures.

After a few moments of contemplating self-immolation or drowning to end the pain caused by my throbbing head, I climb to my knees and scan my surroundings. I have no idea where I am. I'm on the beach, obviously, but nothing else looks familiar. The only thing left to do is pick a direction and put my feet to work.

I head away from the beach, learning before long that I'm heading north. I also uncover a couple of other things. The first is that I'm on a military base. Straw Hat Beach is part of Naval Air Station Key West. I just wandered into it somehow. How nobody spotted me lying half-dead on a desolate spit of sand is something to contemplate another day.

Second, walking in waterlogged shoes isn't fun. Every step is met with a sloshing sound and water oozing from the pores in the leather. They may be getting wrung out, but they're in no hurry to dry. Wonderful.

It's just after eleven, according to the sign hung outside a bank, but The Drunken Lobster's roll-up street access gate is still down and locked. That's odd. Steve usually opens early. Maybe he knew I was coming. I do vaguely remember him telling me I'm not welcome here. I only need to know if he has my wallet.

The side door is unlocked. I don't bother knocking, and I let myself in. "Hello?"

Steve jumps at the sound of my voice. He's seated at the bar with an ice pack against his nose and tissue dangling from both nostrils. It looks like he got hit with a frying pan and should be sitting in an emergency room instead of on a stool in the darkened bar.

"What happened to you?"

"Your friend, that's what," the bartender sneers.

"What friend?"

Steve stands and points to the door. "You need to leave. Right now."

I don't have any friends who would come looking for me here. The only man I counted as one was…well…not the wingman I thought he was. That means the man who roughed up Steve was the opposite of a friend. The only question is which goon was dispatched to have a "chat" with me.

"What friend?" I ask, folding my arms and planting my feet firmly on the ground in an unmistakable signal that I'm not moving until he answers my question.

"Big guy. Real mean. Also violent and armed. I only know that because he held a gun to my head while asking questions about you. Now, get out of my bar!"

"Did he have a German accent and big eyebrows?" I ask.

"Yeah. The guy looked like the love child of Groucho Marx and Bert from *Sesame Street*."

"Braus," I mumble.

"What?"

"His name. It's pronounced 'brows,' but he spells it B-R-A-U-S. He's not my friend. Trust me on that."

I'm moving up in the world. I wish it were a compliment. Braus is among the best contractors the Russian employs, and he gets the difficult assignments. There is a reason for the reputation that I'd rather not think about.

"Look, pal, I don't know what you're into, but I want no part of it."

"Then why did you let me in?" I ask.

"I didn't. You walked in like you owned the place. But since you're here, you'll need this," Steve says, reaching over the bar and wincing. He tosses my wallet to me and points again at the door. "Now, get out, and don't come back."

"Where is he?"

"A thousand miles away would be too close. He's probably waiting for you on your boat. I've already told you too much. This is the last time I'll say it. Get out and don't come back."

I understand the reaction. Braus isn't subtle with his threats. In addition to breaking Steve's nose and putting a gun to his head, there's no doubt he leveled some choice words about consequences. That's what he does, and I won't tell Steve that the psycho will make good on them. There's no point in scaring him any further.

I knew this day was coming the moment my plane climbed away from LaGuardia International. They only found me faster than I thought, only I figured I would never see my end coming. Braus isn't this sloppy. Then again, had I not forgotten my wallet, I would be having an awkward conversation at gunpoint below deck on the rented boat right now.

My forgetfulness has provided me with a choice. Surrender is the first option. I can walk deeper into the marina, board the vessel, and resign myself to whatever penalty Arden has in mind for disloyalty. Or I can run, at least for a while. I have the means.

The hundred thousand I pulled out of my account won't be enough to disappear forever. If they found me here, it means they're watching my accounts. But it's still a decent sum. I can make it last. Maybe.

I think back to my conversation with the mysterious Engineer. "Live your life," he said. Or, at least, I think I remember him saying that. I should take his advice. Maybe it will only be extended for a day or two, but that's better than just accepting my fate. At a minimum, I should try to get off this island. Braus is an expert at tracking people, but there's no reason to make it easy on him.

Instead of walking along the marina's boardwalk, I take the side roads in town until I reach the lot with my Miami rental car. I find a corner near a building to watch it from afar. I've worked with Braus on a number of occasions. Sometimes, politicians need reminders to do the right thing, and he is one of the men Arden contracts to deliver the message. People have no concept about how messy politics is.

I learned one thing from my time working with him: Braus is not a patient man. If he gets bored waiting for me, there's a chance he could be staking out my vehicle. Or, at least, ensuring it's still here. There's no reason to believe a man with his resources doesn't know the exact make, model, color, and the company I rented it from. Hell, he probably knows the mileage.

Braus and the men who work with him are handsomely paid for their loyalty. He cannot be bargained with. We are all compensated for our staunch devotion to American Outreach more than the labor we provide. Arden once explained that the fabulous riches he promised with employment were contingent on two immutable criteria: unwavering loyalty and strict confidentiality. I have already violated that first tenet. I could easily violate the second.

It wasn't a blind choice or one made under duress. I chose to make a deal with the devil. Now, the devil is here to collect. Secrets must be protected. Braus and his ilk have killed for less. Just because we're forbidden to talk about it doesn't mean we don't know where the bodies are buried or, more importantly, who was holding the shovel.

There has been no movement in the parking lot for ten minutes. That's long enough. I walk toward the car, nonchalantly checking to my left and right. I reach my vehicle without incident and slide into the driver's seat. I start the engine, back out of the spot, and pull out of the lot like I don't have a care in the world. It was a challenge to stay that calm. I wanted to floor it like it was the last lap of the Monaco Grand Prix.

Now, the great game begins. I will have a head start, but I can't be sure how much of one or how long it will last. Braus may not have an Ivy League education, but he has skills acquired from a lifetime of experience in some of the most vile and dangerous places on the planet. That limits my options, even in massive urban areas where searching for someone is like finding a particular grain of sand on a beach.

Stopping in Miami would be a mistake. But where else can I go? This rental can be tracked. Getting a new one will leave an equally conspicuous paper trail. I need a plan that doesn't involve using credit cards or driver's licenses. I have no idea where to start. Fortunately, I have time to consider my options during the three-hour drive on U.S. Route 1. Selecting the right one will determine how long this adventure lasts.

Chapter Six

Let It Roll

The sounds of slot machines and the buzz of gamblers permeate the air. Outside of an airport, a casino may be the best place for people-watching on the planet. This building is filled with individuals and groups from all walks of life. College kids are getting fleeced at the blackjack tables, silver hairs are pulling the arms on slot machines, and degenerate gamblers are mulling around wondering how to explain to their spouses that they just lost this month's mortgage payment.

I take another sip of my ginger ale at the bar. I didn't give up drinking, but I desperately need to remove my liver, hang it on a hook, and let it dry out for a few days. The fog shrouding my thoughts has cleared. The long drive to Miami and the two gallons of water I drank along the way took care of much of that. It gave me time to think – something I had avoided doing since I left New York.

My ending up in Fort Lauderdale was more a happy accident than a well-reasoned plan. I've never been adventurous. I certainly have never been on the run before. So, after dropping my rental off at the airport, I caught a bus that took me and a dozen others directly here.

Braus will learn of the rental return soon enough. Piecing together what happened next will be more challenging. He'll know I'm still in the country when Customs and Border Patrol reports that my passport is unused. This casino won't be the last spot he looks for me, but it won't be in the first thousand places, either. I bought more time. That's it.

I pull out my wallet and retrieve the picture. Part of me wonders what Kinsey is doing right now. A bigger part of me doesn't want to know. I want my old life back…before I learned too much. I can't bury that pain. I can't live with it either.

The Engineer's advice at The Drunken Lobster rings in my head. "You must forget your past and focus on the future. Once you do, you'll get your life back." Easier said than done. If that's what he said at all. I was pretty drunk.

I do remember him saying, "Face your demons as men do. You can roll the dice and let fate decide if you don't know your path." I'm in the perfect spot for that. He might not have meant it literally, but having a hundred thousand, more or less, in debit cards won't do me any good when Braus catches up with me.

I finish my ginger ale, give the bartender a twenty for his trouble, and spend the next half hour at the cashier trying to turn plastic cards into chips. It takes some doing. The casino must ensure I'm not laundering money and confirm the cards aren't stolen. After satisfying the requirements, I walk onto the casino floor armed with eighty thousand dollars in clay poker chips.

Well, that's not entirely true. As of seventy years ago, no single compression molded chip was composed entirely of clay. Modern chips combine earthen materials like sand, chalk, and bentonite, the clay used to produce cat litter. The engineering process is an industry trade secret, as are the embedded security measures. There is little doubt that my chips have RFID trackers to prevent counterfeiting. Criminals would have a field day scamming casinos if these things were easy to duplicate.

I weave through the casino tables and get a pit boss's attention at one of the craps tables. He grimaces before walking over to me. Most of the tables are jammed with green and black chips. Twenty-fives and hundreds. Healthy wagers, but not what I'm looking for.

"Do all these tables have maximum bet limits?"

"All the tables here have limits, pal," the pit boss says, annoyed until he glances down and sees the denomination of the chips I'm holding. "If you want something else, go to the high-roller room over there."

I turn my head to scout out where he's pointing. "All right, thanks."

Weaving between banks of slot machines to the sparsely populated room, I move past the blackjack and roulette tables and stop short of the lone craps table. Craps can be an intimidating game for beginners. I play it because it offers the best odds of any game in the house. Less risk means more potential winnings, although it rarely ends up that way for me. The table seems to have about a hundred different kinds of bets. The players are barking out commands in what seems to be a foreign language, and the pace is too fast to ask questions. Everyone here is a seasoned professional. Or they ought to be, based on the amounts of the wagers they're dropping on the table.

I take a position to the stickman's right between an older gentleman with wise eyes and a younger guy dressed like he just walked out of a 1980s Bon Jovi video. He takes a drag on his cigarette and looks me up and down. His girlfriend, wearing a sequined halter top and a spit of leather that could only charitably be called a miniskirt, does the same thing.

He might not be impressed with me, but seeing the forest-green twenty-five thousand dollar chips gets his attention. He nods his approval as the new shooter starts his roll. The calls are great. This stickman must get tipped a boatload.

"Ten, perfect ten, like my ex-girlfriend until she stopped dating men."

'Five! The cocktail waitress roll…we got a pair and tray!" he says when the two and three come up.

"Eight, the easy way, ocho…suavé."

I make conservative bets, or what would be considered conservative for this table. Most shooters hit at least one point. The table is warm until it gets around to my end. The chips are collected when the last shooter rolls a seven on his third attempt.

The rocker sets a point of ten on his first roll. It won't be easy to hit, even at a hot table. I'm glad I saved my money. His next roll is a three and four. The table moans when they see the seven.

"One roll…no butter," the stickman announces, meaning the shooter is one and done after setting the point.

I place five thousand in chips on the passline. My first three come-out rolls are sevens, meaning they are winners. I kept the same bet, which doubled after each roll. I turned my five-thousand-dollar bet into fifteen thousand in a couple of blinks of the eye. There wouldn't be a fourth.

"Nein, nein cried the Fraulein. That's German birth control," the stickman announces when he sees the six and three.

The table starts making bets, and the old man turns to me as he leans against the table. "Let's see what you've got, son."

The dice are slid over.

"Dice are moving, hands high. Shooter's got 'em. Watch 'em fly," the stickman says, prompting everyone to edge away from the table.

"Four, hard four. It may be small, but at least it's hard."

I place sizable bets on the hardways. I don't place any numbers. Not yet.

"Eight, hard eight!" the stickman calls, turning to the old man. "Reminds me a bit of myself."

I roll six more times, getting another hard eight, a five, a six, a hard six, and another five. I've made more money in a casino today than ever, but it's not what I'm here for. It's time to end this, one way or another. I turn to the rocker's girlfriend.

"What's your favorite number, hun?"

Her brow furrows, and her eyes point to the ceiling. "Ummm…ten."

Okay, that wasn't the number I was expecting. At least the blonde vixen didn't say something unplayable, like thirteen. That was Kinsey's favorite. She would play it on the roulette table in Atlantic City. It was her lucky number, or so she professed. To my knowledge, she never won once.

I toss four forest-green chips into the center. "Hard ten on the hop."

The entire table looks at me. The boxman stares incredulously from his seat at the middle of the table. "What?"

The rocker beams and claps several times theatrically. "Thatsa one-roll bet, man!"

"I know."

"You really wanna risk a hundred thousand dollars on a single roll of the dice?"

I stare at the boxman. No, I don't. It goes against every fiber of my being. It's not all the chips in front of me, but it's most of them. This may be the first real risk I've ever taken. That's why I need to do this.

"Considering the odds against me, do you really want to talk me out of it?"

Naturally, he doesn't. The payouts for any bet made in the center of a craps table are ridiculous because the odds of winning are terrible. Many players call them "sucker bets" because you'll lose far more than you win.

Of those sucker bets, a "hop" bet is the worst. It's a wager where a player bets that the next dice roll will result in a specific combination. Any player could bet the next roll will be a four and a two or a three and a five. The kicker is it's a single-roll bet.

If the combination doesn't come up, I lose the wager, meaning I'll lose a hundred thousand dollars.

The boxman looks up at the bald pit boss, who nods. It's a no-limit table, and it's a legal bet. There's no reason for him to say no. The stickman slides the dice over to me. I pinch them between my index, middle, and ring fingers and my thumb. The blonde next to the rocker guy looks more nervous than I feel. I hold the dice in front of her lips.

"Blow on 'em…for luck."

She looks at the rocker for his approval before blowing on them sensually. I can't resist a smile.

"That'll do."

I bend my arm and hold the dice a few inches off the felt. My eyes focus on the target landing area on the other end of the table. Some people believe the angle of the throw, the velocity, and the landing zone can control how the dice hit the back wall and influence the outcome. Maybe it's true, and maybe it isn't. I don't have those skills, so I will let it rip. There is no real expectation that this will end well.

"Make sure you hit the back wall," the dealer announces.

"Hey! Shut up, man! You can open your trap when you bet a hundred k on a roll."

"That's uncalled for," the older gentleman says, scolding the boxman. "Keep your people under control, or I will find a new casino to play at."

I close my eyes, ignoring the exchange. The other gamblers at the table go quiet in anticipation of the toss. I take a deep breath and exhale as my eyes open. This may be the dumbest thing I've done in my life.

"Roll the dice and let fate decide."

It was part whisper, part prayer as I cock my arm back and swing it forward. The dice slip from my fingers. They hit the small green felt landing area between the passline and the back wall and bounce around before resting on the table. The chips stacked up block my vision. I look at the stickman, who cranes his neck and makes the call.

"Ten hard, a girl's best friend!" the stickman announces.

Right now, it's my best friend. The players holding their breath at the table erupt in a massive cheer that practically shakes the casino. I stare at the dice that kicked to the side of the chips at the end of the table. Two fives. I'm a numbers guy, which is why I like craps. It was a one-in-thirty-six chance and a two-point-eight percent probability.

"Whoa! I can't believe I just did that!" I say. I really can't.

"Holy shit! Oh my God, I mean, holy shit!" the rocker says, patting me on the back hard.

"You just made three million dollars, son," the older man beside me says. "The fates are smiling on you."

That they are. I pull the rest of my bets down, except for the passline. The dice are slid over to me after the dealers pay out the wagers. It's a good thing I all but called it quits. I seven out on the roll, and my turn as the shooter is over.

"Cinco-dos, adios!"

It doesn't matter. Not anymore. I made the table some money and made myself a fortune. I get an ovation as the dice tray is dumped in the center of the table to be ready for the next shooter.

"You have a serious pair of balls on you, man! Let me shake your hand!"

I shake the rocker's hand while his date makes goo-goo eyes at me. Money does that to some women. I bid the table farewell with over three million in chips decorating a tray. Security escorts me to the cashier, where paperwork awaits me. I transfer most of the winnings to an old offshore account I set up in the Caymans for fun in college. It has next to nothing in it, and it took me a while to remember the number. The best part is that nobody at American Outreach knows it exists. There is no way I'm carrying that much cash around.

The hundred thousand in cash they give me comes with a courtesy backpack emblazoned with the casino's logo. I'm surprised they didn't charge me for it. I put a serious dent in the day's profit margin with one toss of the dice.

Our business is concluded, and I head directly to the taxi stand. My mission here is accomplished. I feel invigorated. Yesterday, I was drinking myself into oblivion. This morning, I woke up on a beach…alone, and as it turns out, hunted. Tonight, I feel like I'm on top of the world. With one roll of the dice, I got the answer I sought. Now, I need a plan.

The cab pulls up, and I climb into the back as the driver twists to face me. "Where to, boss?"

Where to? Good question. Where can I go that Braus won't easily find me? More importantly, how do I get there? I look at the shape my passport makes in my front pocket. A smile creases my lips as I look at the driver.

"Fort Lauderdale Executive Airport."

Chapter Seven

The Cossack

Arden Davenport is a devout introvert forced by his station in life to do extroverted things. His wealth means he could live in solitude if desired, but that won't help him reach his ultimate goal. Being rich also buys one of life's most important things: influence.

He wants control, even if he doesn't want to be in the presence of other people to exercise it. That makes running a well-funded political action committee appealing to him. Politicians have a well-documented love affair with money. It's the lifeblood of their campaigns, and they will do whatever is needed to obtain more of it. Arden is only too happy to oblige, assuming certain conditions are met.

American Outreach is a misnomer. This PAC isn't about reaching out to the people and unifying them. Anyone who knows the name and its architect realizes it is about uniting the country according to Arden Davenport's vision. Politicians can have the limelight. He is perfectly content to stay anonymous as the vapid men and women he bought take the abuse from angry constituents, special interest groups, and an unrelenting media horde.

As an only child, Arden never learned to share. It was why his wife divorced him shortly after giving birth to his daughter. He clings to what's his and covets everything else. That includes power and influence. Arden wishes he could live in a world where people didn't need…persuasion. Unfortunately, this isn't a utopian society filled with automatons exercising collective groupthink. Unsavory tactics often have to be used to bring the unwilling into the fold.

A maître d' arrives and patiently waits for Arden to finish his piece of filet mignon. Manhattan steakhouses are renowned for their superior service as much as for their perfectly cooked meat. This establishment doesn't have the city's best dry-aged steaks, but it makes the top ten list. What they do have is a private room in the back for couples who want a romantic dinner or men like Arden who can't be bothered to deal with the mindless chatter of other patrons.

"Yes?"

"I'm sorry to bother you, sir," he says, "but you have a guest in the foyer who wishes to join you."

Arden fusses with the napkin on his lap. "Send him in."

The man disappears, presumably returning to escort his guest. He returns a minute later with a man dressed in a suit without a tie. It's an odd look for The Cossack. Whenever they spoke on the phone, Arden always pictured him wearing military fatigues. It's hard to commit war crimes in a button-down Oxford unless you're the president of the United States or some other leader.

"Do you always eat by yourself?" the Russian asks in a deep voice and fading Slavic accent.

"Whenever possible. I don't like people."

"That's strange to hear from a man in your position. Let me tell you what I don't like: being summoned like a kid late for family dinner."

"And I despise interrupting my meal to get information I should have been provided days ago. It seems we both have to learn to live with disappointment. It's been three days since your man tracked Braden to Key West. Then you inexplicably lost him with no explanation. What happened?"

The Cossack sits opposite Arden and snatches a breadstick out of the basket. His posture is relaxed. Davenport may be one of the richest men in this restaurant, but The Cossack knows he's the most dangerous one.

"He made it back to the mainland."

Arden places his fork and knife on his plate and sips his wine. "You told me that your man is the best. I instructed you to send him after an Ivy League financial guru. Explain to me how the hell such an easy target managed to make it out of Key West."

"He was either tipped off or decided to leave that morning."

"Clearly. I really don't care how it happened. Have you found Braden yet?"

"Roughly. We thought he would hide in Miami or try to take an international flight somewhere."

"And?" Arden asks, pressing for details.

"He did, just not on a commercial airline. He took a private flight out of Fort Lauderdale that landed in Buenos Aires, Argentina. His passport was processed when he arrived in the country, and he was issued a tourist visa."

According to tradition, Spanish colonizer Pedro de Mendoza established the first settlement in that area, naming it Nuestra Señora Santa María del Buen Aire. The Spanish tongue twister translates to "Our Lady Saint Mary of the Good Air." In modern times, Buenos Aires ranks among Latin America's most important ports and populous cities. It has become a center of commerce, industry, politics, culture, and technology. But that doesn't answer Arden's most pressing question.

"Why is Braden in South America?"

The Cossack leans back and rubs his beard. "You tell me."

Even if Arden unequivocally knew the answer to that question, he would never share the information with the likes of a mercenary. It's not germane to his assignment.

"How did he pay for a private plane to take him, what, forty-five hundred miles?"

"Seven thousand, one hundred thirty-two kilometers, to be exact. Mr. Fox paid in cash or via a pre-paid debit card at the airport. We assume it was from the one hundred thousand he withdrew from his account before leaving New York, as his accounts have still not been accessed."

"Then he's out of money and can't go on much longer. That flight had to cost tens of thousands. He won't be able to do it again. Find him."

The Russian snaps another chunk of breadstick off with his teeth. "There's a problem with that."

"I don't see one," Arden says, sipping his wine.

"Our agreement only covers domestic operations. An international manhunt will incur more costs."

Arden has been in a business relationship with The Cossack for years despite not knowing his real name. They know enough about each other's operations to guarantee mutually assured destruction should one ever wrong the other. That doesn't mean either man doesn't look for leverage against the other. Arden had it when the man sent to Key West failed to get the drop on a glorified accountant. Now that's reversed. Working outside the contract has handed The Cossack leverage, and now he feels like a fleecing is coming.

"What costs?"

"Additional personnel. Logistics. Bribes. You name it. Finding someone is expensive."

"You're already being paid very well for it."

The Russian shakes his head. "Our agreement doesn't stipulate—"

"Fine!" Arden says, slamming his hand on the table, stopping The Cossack's sentence but otherwise not fazing him. "I don't want excuses. I want results. Whatever it takes."

"Are you writing me a blank check?"

Arden forces himself to calm down. "No. I will wire you an additional retainer for these services in the morning, and you'll keep me updated on expenses. We'll start there."

The Russian leans back and folds his hands on his chest. He doesn't appear happy, but he got what he wanted. That's fine, so long as Arden gets what he wants. Braden Fox must be standing in his office, or his head needs to be on a pike by the time this is over.

"Very well. We have ruled out Mr. Fox's meeting with a competitor. There is also no indication he is talking to authorities about your…dealings." The Russian leans across the table. "Why is this man so important?"

Arden glares at his dinner guest. "I run my organization as I see fit, and the 'why' is no concern of yours. I contract you to handle aspects of my dealings I cannot personally be involved in. You are responsible for finding Braden and carrying out my instructions, not asking questions."

"As you wish."

"When will I see results?"

The corner of the Russian's mouth curls. "Buenos Aires is a city of fifteen and a half million people. That doesn't count neighboring cities or rural areas. Fortunately, records indicate that Mr. Fox has never been there before. He doesn't speak Spanish and has no known contacts or friends to help him that we know of. He'll stand out. Assuming everything you've told me is true, we will find him."

Arden notices the amused look and places no value in the guarantee. He's heard it all before. Politics is filled with hollow words uttered by empty men. If it were as easy as the Russian was making it sound, he would consider this a favor and not something he needs to charge more money for.

"What's the catch?"

The Cossack's eyes change as his face wears a more foreboding look. "If Mr. Fox manages to stay off the grid and leaves the city or travels to a different country, tracking him will become more challenging."

"How challenging?"

The Cossack smiles. "You may never see him again."

Chapter Eight

A Chance Encounter

Buenos Aires is an interesting city. Then again, it's new to me. I've never been here before. Despite having a passport, I've never been anywhere outside the United States. Even my honeymoon was in Hawaii. Going to a place where English isn't the primary language has always been a little intimidating.

I head southeast after taking a stroll in *Jardín Botánico Carlos Thays*. In English, it's the Carlos Thays Botanical Garden. The extent of my Spanish-speaking ability is *hola*, *adios*, and *gracias*. Hi, bye, and thank you. Unless I look it up on Google Translate, that's all anyone here will get from me.

The one thing I've learned in the few days I've been in the city is that dancing is big here. Why wouldn't it be? It's the home of the tango. On Sunday, dancers with varying skill levels flooded the San Telmo street market. An American tourist informed me that the city is filled with *milonga* or *bailes de salón*. They are tango salons featuring beautiful dances from people of every age and background. As the woman explained, tango is truly a dance of the people.

I walk around and scan my surroundings like a soldier on patrol behind enemy lines. I swear I've seen Braus a dozen times since I got here. He's hiding behind every corner, tree, and bush. That's how my mind interprets what my eyes are seeing.

It's unlikely. The psychotic German will eventually make it to the city, but the odds of his running into me are much longer than the craps roll that earned me the money that made this fish-out-of-water adventure a reality. I have another day or two before I need to move on to stay ahead of him. Or so I hope.

I arrive at my destination and look at the sign. *La Viruta* is located in the basement of the Armenian Cultural Center. The tourist told me it's a welcoming space to dance a tango, not that I have any desire to do that. I only want to sit somewhere dark where I can be anonymous and watch beautiful women dance. The alternative is walking the streets searching for a ghost. It's not a hard choice.

The tango salon is crowded but not packed. I find a table and chair that may be the only unoccupied ones in the place. The vibe is friendly, and the crowd seems to be a mix of tourists, expats, and locals. Everyone else is here for one reason: to learn how to tango. That makes me a little uncomfortable, but the encouragement of friendly teachers won't compel me to get on that dance floor. I've been down that path before and don't want to deal with the memories.

I pull out the picture of Kinsey and strain to look at it in the low light. I wonder what she would say if she could see me sitting here now. Not that it matters. None of it matters anymore. I try to slide the picture back into the wallet, and it misses its slot and flutters to the ground.

Standing to reach it under the table, I almost sit in a woman's lap after she slides into my chair. I stare at her incredulously, and not because she stole my seat. Kinsey is a beautiful woman. Her auburn hair, bright green eyes, flawless skin, and unmatched intelligence led my college friends to conclude I hit the lottery when she agreed to my marriage proposal. My wife could stop traffic, but this woman would cause a hundred-car pile-up simply by brushing a wisp of hair from her face.

Her red dress is eye-catching, but how it hugs her is beyond alluring. The V-shaped hem climbs from well below her right knee to high up on her left thigh. The dress has no sleeves and a modest neckline that bulges at her breasts. The midriff is also flared, and the exposed skin is covered by red lace.

I'm at a complete loss for words. The beauty waits for me to say something, so I utter the first thing that pops into my mind.

"You just took my seat."

I clench my jaw after the words escape my mouth. Great, Braden. Real smooth.

"Ah, but if something can be taken from you, was it truly yours to begin with? Or was it only the illusion of being yours?"

Her melodic voice has a chili pepper's spice while still maintaining the upbeat bubbliness of champagne.

"Whatever you say, Socrates." That's when it dawns on me. "You…you speak English?"

"It is the most spoken language on the planet."

"I…uh…you speak it well. It's not your native language, is it?"

"No. I speak Farsi and French."

That explains a few things. Persian women have exotic beauty, delicate features, and the sex appeal of supermodels. This woman is trim and fit, with all the right curves and an olive complexion that only adds to her beauty. Her long, shiny black hair frames a beautiful face and almond-shaped eyes with irises in a kaleidoscope of colors and flecks. The glistening pools of green and brown are protected by long lashes that don't want for curling. Kinsey had to use fake lashes to get the same effect.

I wring my hands. "You still stole my chair."

It's meant to be playful, but the woman doesn't appear to interpret it that way. It makes sense. I don't do flirting or charming well. I've never really had to develop those skills. I'm a decent-looking guy who went to Princeton. That was enough for most women until I met Kinsey and was taken off the market. Like most things on this journey, flirting is completely new.

The couple at the adjacent table stand and make their way out of the tango hall. This vision of a woman stretches out her arm, gesturing to the now-empty seat.

"See? Fate smiles at you."

I grin. That's an interesting choice of words. I pull the empty chair under me and sit. I hurriedly slide the picture into my wallet and tuck it into my pocket. I'm desperate to start a conversation but am at a complete loss as to what to say. It's never historically been this difficult. I feel like I'm in junior high again.

"A half million Argentinian women in this city, and I meet a seat-stealing foreigner."

"It's not personal. I was tired."

"What brings you here?"

She gestures around the room. Of course. We're in a tango hall. Why else would she be here? I quietly chastise myself for yet another stupid question when she cocks her head and stares at me.

"The better question is, why are *you* here? It isn't to dance."

She's right. I'm dressed smartly in the clothes I bought at a local store, but I haven't shown any interest in a lesson the instructors are offering. She probably thinks I'm here trying to pick up women. It's better than her knowing I'm on the run from a sadistic boss who hired a man to inflict severe pain on me when I'm caught.

"I was…just passing by."

"Ah, okay…you don't want to tell me why. How mysterious," she says, leaning forward. "So, what do I call you?"

"Braden Fox."

She cocks her head at me. "I call you Braden Fox? Do you always go by both your names?"

"Well, uh, no. It's just Braden. And…yours?"

"Lyla."

I reach my hand over the table, and she looks at it suspiciously before quickly shaking it. There are no rings on her right hand. I'm relieved to see none on her left, either. A wedding band or diamond engagement ring would have shattered the moment.

"A handshake. How…professional."

"Well, I didn't think…it's not…I could give you a hug."

I close my eyes at the moronic suggestion and open them in time to see Lyla shaking her head. I can't blame her. I'd be losing interest in me, too.

"I'm fumbling this introduction, aren't I?"

"It's okay. Most men do," she says, smiling. "I've been all around the world, Braden Fox. The one thing I learned is that single, straight men are all the same. They think they're masters of the universe until a pretty girl sits next to them and bats her eyelashes. Then they become blubbering fools who can't find a coherent sentence with two hands and a flashlight."

I don't correct her on the assumption I'm single. I also don't correct her about my being a blubbering fool. The evidence more than supports that.

"Don't you have a last name?"

"Of course."

"Will you tell me what it is?"

She shakes her head. "No *chance.*"

I don't understand the amused look on her face. I didn't think it would be a state secret, but I don't try to understand women. I've been married to Kinsey for three years and haven't come close to figuring her out. Now, I never will.

"Do you live nearby?" I ask because I can't think of anything else.

"That's forward of you."

"I…I didn't mean it…I wasn't…."

"See? Blubbering fools," Lyla says with another beaming smile. "I'm only visiting the city. No, I'm not staying nearby. No, you will not get to take me there."

"I wasn't suggesting…." I stop and grimace. Screw it. This is going nowhere, so I finish my drink and stand. "It was nice meeting you, Lyla."

She grabs my arm, and I feel my skin tingle at the sensation of her touch. Her hands are warm and soft. Her grip is firm but not like a vise. She looks up at me with those alluring eyes.

"What's the matter, Braden Fox? You're quitting that easily?"

"Call it a hasty retreat to hang onto what little dignity I have left."

She smiles and stands. Her red dress moves with her effortlessly. Everything about this woman is…spectacular.

"Would you like a chance to redeem yourself?"

I shrug, trying to accumulate a couple of cool points back. "What are you suggesting?"

Lyla turns her head to the dance floor before locking eyes with me. She could ask me to help her rob a bank, and I would ask if she has an extra mask. No man could say no to those eyes. She holds her hand out.

"Tell me, Braden Fox, do you like to dance?"

Chapter Nine

An Unexpected Tango

This isn't the dumbest thing I've ever agreed to. It's close, though. I'm unsure why I'm following Lyla to the dance floor. Okay, I'm not fooling anybody. No man in this room wouldn't trade places with me right now — including the married ones.

Even her walk is captivating. Lyla is holding her head high with her chin forward. That keeps her spine straight and her core engaged, allowing her to ensure her shoulders are back. It's almost perfect posture, and the walk exudes confidence. I wish I were exuding any. But I'm not.

Lyla stops and faces me, standing six inches away. I place my right hand on her toned back just behind her shoulder. She does the same with her left hand on mine. She raises her right hand to shoulder height, and I grasp it with my left. The frame should be strong. I think back to the "spaghetti arms" scene from the movie *Dirty Dancing*. This time, I get the feeling I'm Baby.

Panic is beginning to set in. I despised my lessons because they felt unnatural, even with the woman I planned to marry. Lyla is a complete stranger, and I'm beyond self-conscious. Because of the sensual nature of the tango, its practice may result in unintentional awkward moments between partners. That box has already been checked.

I don't recognize the song that's playing. Lyla waits for me to move, but instead, I look around. Other pairs dance around us, but everyone watching is fixated on her. And, by extension, me.

She taps me on the shoulder to get my attention. "Do you know this dance? I can teach you if you don't."

"I uh…took some lessons a while back," I manage to croak, my mouth going completely dry.

Her beautiful almond-shaped eyes narrow, likely in disbelief. "Really?"

"Two lessons a week for two years."

"Okay, then you've already forgotten the basics. Stand up straight and bend your knees slightly. You need to bounce up and down as you move your feet. The tango is about fluidity. You can't be fluid if your knees are locked. Good. Let's see what you've got."

A song I finally know plays after the last one ends. It was the one I requested most during the lessons because I remember it from the dance scene in *Scent of a Woman*. A "blind" Al Pacino danced with young Gabrielle Anwar in a restaurant. I remember thinking that if a blind man could do it, I could, too. Then I remembered it was a movie and anything can be made to look good with some Hollywood magic.

Por Una Cabeza is a classic adored by many as one of the most romantic tango songs. I requested it so often that Kinsey wanted to play it at our wedding. However, I learned that its lyrics aren't as romantic or enchanting as expected when translated into English. The song is about the fanaticism of horse racing and describes the relationship between women and life. It concludes with a man's love interest losing her competition with his gambling "by a head" — the distance by which a horse might lose a race. He learns nothing from the loss and would once more bet on the ponies when another woman comes along. In the end, we picked a different song.

I catch the beat and remind myself to step off with my left foot. So, naturally, my right decides to go first, and I almost run Lyla over.

"The other foot, silly," she chides.

"This is a bad idea. I'm sorry," I conclude, breaking the hold and turning slightly to pull away and retreat to the safety of the onlookers. A dozen men are panting at the opportunity to dance with her. She can find a much better partner than me.

Lyla grabs my jaw and moves my face toward hers. I stare into her eyes despite knowing I may get lost and never find my way back to reality.

"Look at me, Braden Fox. Forget your lessons. Forget your past and the world around you. We're alone in this room. It's you and me. Just dance."

I place my hand below her shoulder and take a breath. I move my left foot forward and then my right slowly. I repeat the sequence quicker and slowly move my right foot to the right and stop. Those are the base steps of the tango. I think. It's starting to come back to me, but Lyla stops me again. She touches my cheeks and moves her face closer to mine.

"Loosen up. I'm not judging you. Nobody here is. Don't think. *Feel.*"

That's easier said than done. My whole life has been lived according to a plan. Like our dance lessons, everything was choreographed down to the smallest detail. I don't know how to let it go and feel.

I start with a basic to the cross and feel her move with me. Everything comes rushing back, and I remember to shift my weight appropriately as we move. It begins to come naturally. It helps that she's a forgiving partner.

Growing more confident, I lead her into a forward *Ocho*. The move surprises her, but she gracefully steps between and perpendicular to the line between us, making a half-turn pivot to repeat a front cross with the other foot in the opposite direction. I whip her into a pair of *boleos*. Her left leg spirals out and returns to join her right leg in a flourish that makes the crowd coo. She repeats the movement with her left.

I place a foot against hers, leading her to a stop. Then she follows the *parada* with a *pasada*, stepping over my leg with her left and placing it behind me. We turn before Lyla swivels and kicks her leg back, and we move back into a basic when the music picks up.

I turn her, and we launch into a closed promenade. The other couples have vacated the dance floor, leaving us plenty of room. We move together, slow, quick, quick, slow, the last step bringing our feet together. She ends the linear movement, looking back in the direction we came, and I signal another. She faces forward, and we move again. I can't believe I remember how to do this without tripping over my feet.

Feeling emboldened, I *calesta*, lifting Lyla slightly as I dance around her while still in the hold. She sticks her leg out, sweeping the material of her red dress away as she traces circles on the floor. That will get the men watching us drooling.

I spin her out and bring her back into the hold before sending her into a *moliente*. This time, it's Lyla's turn to dance around me while I act as a pivot point. She steps side-back-side-forward using the forward and back ocho technique. She is graceful and seductive in her moves. They're captivating.

The final notes of the song play, and we end with her lowering in almost a split with only her front leg bent. I dip my right shoulder to support her, and the crowd erupts in thunderous applause. She looks up at me with those eyes.

My heart is thundering in my chest. I may not be ready for any dance competitions, but I thought it was a worthy performance for a ranked amateur. Adrenaline courses through me, causing a high that I've never experienced. I hear the enthusiastic clapping in the room and turn to see every pair of eyes in the salon focused on us. I feel…alive.

Lyla places her hand on my face. "Thank you for the dance."

"Wow. That was…we should do that again."

"Okay. Maybe I'll even let you lead next time," Lyla says with a wink.

"There's going to be a next time?"

"That's for fate to decide. Until then, Braden Fox."

Lyla kisses me on the cheek as I remain frozen in place. It's more than having cement in my shoes. They are welded to the floor as I watch her saunter out of *La Viruta* under the watchful eyes of nearly every man gathered around the dance floor.

What was it that the Engineer said to me in Key West? I asked how to get my life back, and he said I should find a guide. Or something like that. Maybe I just found her. Willing my legs to move, I rush out after Lyla, unsure how on earth I can explain this without sounding creepy.

Chapter Ten

Minor Details

I finally make it to the door of the Armenian Cultural Center and step out onto the sidewalk. I look frantically up and down the street. The vision in the red dress is nowhere to be found. Left or right? Coming to a fork in the road and making that choice is one of life's oldest metaphors. Pick the wrong path and your life goes in the wrong direction. Pick the right one, and success comes with it. If you stand there like a fool and never decide, you get hit by traffic.

My life is defined by walking the path others have chosen for me. My parents led me to Princeton. Arden Davenport led me to American Outreach. My job led me to Kinsey. Her actions led me to Key West. It's only because of me that I ended up here, about to chase a beautiful woman like some deranged stalker.

All those choices have come with a cost. So will this one. It's time to try something different. Since I have always been told I'm on the "right" path, I decide to go left and break into a run. Lyla will be around the corner, or she won't be. Fate will decide.

I weave through the pedestrians on the sidewalk like I'm fleeing a bank robbery. I don't know the Spanish words for "I'm sorry," so I don't bother being polite. I reach the corner and turn onto the cross street, expecting disappointment. Instead, I see the red dress signaling me like a beacon.

"Lyla! Lyla!"

She continues to walk without turning as I stride to catch up. I reach her side and match her gait, earning a sideways glance and a wry smile. Something tells me that I'm not the first man who has ever chased her.

"Back for more, Braden Fox?"

"Do you always leave your partners standing in the middle of the dance floor?"

"In my experience, goodbyes are less messy that way. Besides, you were already warned that you couldn't take me home."

I quietly take a deep breath. I'm not winded, but I'm also trying not to sound desperate. "That wasn't my intention. I would have settled for another dance. Even if it's promised for tomorrow."

"I'm leaving Buenos Aires tomorrow," Lyla dispassionately says, like she's at an airport information desk telling a weary traveler of a flight's departure time.

"For where?"

"I haven't decided yet. Wherever the wind blows me."

I almost stop walking. I can't imagine what that feels like. My schedule has been regimented and inflexible for most of my life. The extent of my travels was an eighth-grade field trip to Washington, D.C., and Hawaii for my honeymoon. Both were scheduled with activities down to the hour. I don't understand how she can be so…free. And alone.

"You said 'me.' You don't travel with a husband or boyfriend?" I ask, bracing myself for the answer.

Lyla smirks. "I learned long ago that men are usually more trouble than they're worth. I travel alone. I live my life alone. I don't like the distractions of excessive companionship."

"Am I a distraction?" I ask, knowing that if she says yes, this conversation is as good as over.

She turns her head to look at me for the first time. I don't return her stare.

"Not yet."

"You said you're leaving tomorrow. How will you know where you're going?"

Lyla shrugs. "I'll scratch where it itches."

"You don't have a bucket list or something?"

"That is a very American thing to ask. No. There's no list. I just let fate be my guide."

I never realized how different the world is outside my bubble. I'm used to the American way of doing and saying things. I forget that, as similar as a place like Buenos Aires is, it's very different culturally. So is Lyla. She isn't an American – she's French and Persian. She might as well be from Venus, for as much as I know about either of those cultures.

"Let me buy you a drink before you go as a thank-you."

Lyla cocks her head. "What are you thanking me for?"

"The most incredible moment I've ever had."

Okay, I have to admit that sounds pretty depressing. But it's the truth, not because of the dance or even the amazing woman who was my partner, but because I felt…something. At that moment, there was no planning for a distant future. There was no Braus, American Outreach, or even Kinsey. The world melted away. I was living in the moment instead of watching it pass me by. How do I get her to understand that?

"It was just a dance, Braden Fox."

"It's just Braden," I say with a smile. "And I know it was…to you. For me, it was much more. I'm not asking anything from you, Lyla. I'm not trying to ply you with alcohol to get you out of that dress. I'm not looking for you to take me back to your place. I do want to thank you. You need to know what that meant to me."

Don't think. Feel. It may be the best advice I've ever received. That was the first time since childhood I'd spoken honestly without planning or measuring my words. What I heard was astonishing: pure, natural sincerity. Lyla picks up on it, too.

"Okay."

We enter the small restaurant just as the nighttime crowd fills it. One drink becomes two, then appetizers and full meals. We talk about some of the places Lyla's been – places I have only imagined going to but never once bought a ticket to visit. She gushes about some of the amazing people she's met along the way and some shady characters she encountered. Best of all were the experiences. They are all the things I've missed out on. She lives more in a month than I have my entire life.

"You don't mind that I ordered dinner, do you?" Lyla asks after noticing that I got lost in my thoughts. "I haven't eaten much today."

"Not at all. I needed to eat, too. I have a question. How do you pay your way? I mean...none of this travel is cheap."

"I whore myself out."

The blood streams out of my face. My jaw hangs and quivers as I try to speak, but I'm at a loss for words.

"I'm kidding, Braden. Jeez, you really need to relax more," she says, laughing. "I have some resources. Mostly, I make friends who take care of me. I'll work odd jobs here and there for extra money."

"Jobs doing what?"

"Painting. Sometimes of tourists, but other times I do landscapes or portraits and sell them. Whatever inspires me."

"You're an artist," I conclude, pointing out the obvious.

"School-trained."

"What happened?"

She grimaces and lowers her eyes. "Life doesn't always work out how you think it will."

I'm a testament to that. Now isn't the time for that confession. This is the first time Lyla has opened up and told me anything about herself outside of her first name, heritage, and travel itineraries. I still have no idea what her family name is.

"My turn. Why do you have so many questions? Are you just making conversation?"

"Because...." I stop. It's now or never. "All right, this is going to sound weird. I was told that I would meet you...well, sort of."

"Okay, yeah, that is a little bizarre."

"Not you per se, just...look, this is kinda hard to explain. My life has taken some unexpected turns. It led me on a journey that I'm not ready for."

I explain what happened in Key West without the gory details, careful to omit the part about Braus. I describe the conversation with the Engineer in enough detail to make it sound like we were both sober. Lyla listens, not opining about how crazy this all sounds.

"That's quite a story. It's more spontaneous than I would have expected from you. What do you need from me?"

"I'd want to go with you. Wherever you're going next."

"Go...with...me?"

I press my lips together. I know this is a big ask.

"Look, I know what you are thinking, and it's not like that. I know you travel alone. I don't wish to infringe on that. But I need to do some things, and I don't know how. I need a guide. If money is an issue, I have no problem paying."

I see a flash of annoyance on Lyla's face for the first time. "Do you think money and your high-class lifestyle impress me?"

"I know it doesn't, and that's why I want your help. I have means but no ability. You have ability without the means. You keep talking about fate. Maybe that was the real reason you sat in my chair. Fate put us together for a reason."

Lyla studies me with those eyes. There is nothing more I can say. No further justifications are required. We are at that all-too-familiar crossroads. Go left or go right. Choose one path or choose the other. One will send us on a journey together, and the other will mean we go our separate ways. The choice is hers.

Chapter Eleven

Frantic Searching

Everyone makes mistakes in life. That's what Travis keeps telling himself. That would almost be an acceptable excuse if it were only one, but it wasn't. He made the same mistake over and over for months. And then it finally caught up to him, just as he knew it would.

The best of humanity takes responsibility for their actions. The rest shirk it. Travis works with politicians, lobbyists, and political operatives. They have turned deflecting blame and avoiding prosecution for their misdeeds into an art form. Nobody takes responsibility for their actions anymore. Why should he be any different? That's why he's here.

It's well after midnight, and the American Outreach office has long since gone dark and quiet. Even the workaholics check out by nine or ten o'clock, even if it's to meet a client for dinner. He has the floor to himself.

The log finally downloads off the server. Travis opens the file and reads down the entries on the print queue. Even with six months of data, it isn't more than a few hundred lines. Printing isn't as prolific as it once was. When he reaches the bottom of the list, he rubs his eyes. There is nothing, as expected.

Information technology geeks use these logs to troubleshoot issues because they're invaluable tools for understanding what was happening before a problem occurred. Cybersecurity experts use them extensively to uncover nefarious behavior. Travis knew the logs wouldn't reveal anything about Braden. He wonders if he can manipulate them.

The answer is yes and no. The logs can be manipulated. The problem is there is no easy way to edit the entries without leaving a trail. It's not as simple as importing it into a word processor and adding a line or two that point to Braden's motive for leaving. Alterations will be annotated in the file's metadata. Even an incompetent IT professional would need only thirty seconds to sniff that out.

A tired and frustrated Travis leans back in his chair. The stress is wearing him down. He stares at the paperwork on his desk and angrily swings his arm, clearing it off in one swipe. Papers float down to the ground all over his office as he shoves the keyboard away from him.

"What did your computer ever do to you?" a voice says from the doorway.

Travis jumps and jerks his head to the right to see Ilana standing at the office's threshold. Her sudden appearance takes three years off his life. He forces himself to relax.

"I didn't know anyone was still here."

"Me neither. I left for the night and had to come back. What's your excuse?"

Travis sighs. "Braden Fox."

"Ah. I thought Arden already had a small army out looking for him."

"He does."

"Then they'll find him eventually."

It's an optimistic take. Travis would have thought Braden would be rolled up in a matter of days. He was shocked to learn that he had left the country. It was a stay of execution, of sorts – one that needs to be leveraged.

"I know. I want to know why Braden left in the first place."

Ilana knows nothing about what happened. Travis is committed to keeping it that way.

"Why?" she asks. "Are you looking to curry favor with the boss?"

"No. Braden is…was a friend. A close one. I want an answer as to why he suddenly decided to walk away."

Ilana eyes the monitor glowing on the desk. "And you think that answer lies in your computer?"

"Not mine. I have admin privileges and checked network and system logs to see if he downloaded files before leaving the city."

"And?"

Travis shakes his head. "They don't show any abnormal activity on his user account."

Ilana presses her lips together and takes a seat opposite his desk. She leans forward, planting her elbows on her knees.

She isn't unattractive, but nobody would characterize her as pretty, either. She has a lean build that isn't athletic or toned. Her hair is long, not that anyone in the office could determine its length with certainty. Ilana is never seen without it pulled back into a bun. Her wardrobe consists of knee-length skirts and pantsuits, all black, gray, or navy blue. The only thing that stands out is her intelligence and uncanny ability to be persuasive. That's the kind of thing Arden Davenport finds valuable.

"Maybe he used someone else's credentials?"

Travis shakes his head again. "How much data do you think we maintain?"

"I don't know. Terabytes worth, probably."

"There aren't any downloads or data transfers approaching that level for years on any account. And no sensitive files were recently taken off the server. Either Braden downloaded the data more than six months ago—"

"Unlikely," Ilana interrupts.

"Or he didn't take anything with him at all."

"He could have printed it."

Travis points at the computer. "I just checked the print logs. Bupkus. We don't deal with hardcopy often. When was the last time you even saw someone in this office print something? I don't think paper has been added to the tray in three months."

Ilana's eyes track to the monitor. "Were you wondering if he was going to the feds?"

"The thought crossed my mind. It's the only thing that makes sense, and I know that's what Arden is most concerned about."

"Maybe. But I'm not stupid, Travis. There's nothing in these files that's incriminating. Even the accounting looks like vanilla campaign donations. Everything else is off the books."

"That's true. But data can paint a picture."

"In South America? Buenos Aires is a long way to travel for a guy who's never left the country. It makes less sense than meeting with the FBI at Key West. You're barking up the wrong tree."

It's a rational conclusion, and that's the problem. Travis hoped Braden would make it seem plausible that he was betraying American Outreach. Unfortunately, he isn't. If anything, his uncharacteristic actions make it look like betrayal is the least likely motive.

"Maybe it's something else. How's Braden's marriage?"

"How would I know? Although I think his wife would have mentioned if there were problems. She's not the shy type. I think we can safely rule that out."

Ilana shrugs. "A loyal employee up and disappears into the wind without a hint of motive. That's an interesting mystery that *needs* an explanation."

Travis spreads his hands as he gestures at the room. "Which is why I'm *still* here. What brings you back to the office?"

Ilana sighs. "Our problem child senator from Michigan needs a gentle reminder about why he won his last election."

"That was Braden's guy, wasn't it?" Travis asks.

"It's fun doing the work of two people, isn't it?" Ilana says, standing. "It's not like I didn't have a full plate before he decided to bail. I hope they find him and drag him back here. It will make it easier for me to kill him for adding more stress to my life."

She was speaking metaphorically. Or so Travis hopes. Ilana may be average by many measures, but she is ruthless. She's more than capable of offing someone, even if she would need help hiding the body.

"Get some rest, Travis. You look like hell. Tomorrow is already here, and you'll be no good to anyone if you're a walking zombie. I can't take on your work, too, if it comes to that."

Ilana pats Travis on the shoulder as she leaves his office. There's nothing more he can do tonight. He makes a couple of mouse clicks and shuts down his computer. This will have to wait. It's time to go home and stare at the ceiling while he figures out how he'll get out of this mess. Travis knows his job depends on it. Maybe even his life.

Chapter Twelve

Chances Are...

I did as I was told. Lyla said to meet her at this bus station at nine a.m. I'm certain that's what she said when we said goodbye at the restaurant. I didn't imagine it, and I wasn't drunk when the words escaped her lips. Maybe buzzed, but definitely not intoxicated.

After dinner, I went to my apartment rental, packed my small amount of clothing, crawled into bed, and stared at the ceiling for most of the night. Then I woke, showered, and got here early. And waited. And waited.

I'm still waiting. Nine o'clock has come and gone without a hint of Lyla. There is no woman in a red dress in sight, not that she would be wearing that outfit. She didn't arrive dressed in anything else, either. Lyla stands out, and there is no sign of her anywhere. I've been ghosted, and depression is starting to set in. She's not coming.

Knowing it was a long shot, I made my pitch at the restaurant. It sounded crazier coming out of my mouth than it did in my head. She could have just said thank you, no. Instead, she agreed. Then, she gave me a time and location to meet. Why do that if she had no intention of showing up? Is it a sick game she plays?

The clock in the bus station continues doing circles around the dial. There's no way I missed her. She didn't board a bus bound for some distant city without my knowing. The only question that still needs answering is how long I should sit here like a schmuck.

I hang my head. I should have left a half hour ago. There's no reason I need to leave now. What's the rush? It's not like I have any place to be.

"I was sure you weren't going to stick around," a voice behind me says.

Lyla is standing over my shoulder, wearing faded jeans and a T-shirt she must have bought in a gift shop. Slung over her shoulder is a backpack that's full but not overstuffed. She isn't wearing a hint of makeup from last night, and her long black hair is tied back. She looks…amazing.

"I thought I had missed you. Where were you?"

"Full disclosure? I've been here the whole time."

"Doing what?"

A devilish grin crosses Lyla's lips. "Watching you."

That's not what I expected to hear. How could I have missed her? Then again, I didn't expect Lyla to be doing countersurveillance like a CIA agent behind the Iron Curtain in the 1980s. It's unnecessary, so I can't understand why she would let my stomach tie into knots.

"What? Why?"

"Instinct, I suppose. I've been on my own for a long time now. It's not the first time a man propositioned me like you did. I need to be careful."

"It sounds like you've been burned before."

Lyla nods. "Something like that. So, I apologize for letting you think I ditched you. I just had to ensure your intentions were…."

"Honorable? I get it. You should know I almost left. I couldn't bring myself to."

"I'm glad you didn't," Lyla says, touching my arm.

"So, where are we going?"

She nods at the counter and leads me to an overworked clerk. We get two tickets and head to the parking area to locate our bus. Neither of us has luggage, so we climb aboard and stow our backpacks in an overhead rack.

Lyla timed her arrival at the bus depot perfectly. Seven minutes after finding our seats, the driver departs and steers us onto Autopista Presidente Arturo Umberto Illia. The window seat provides a nice view of the Atlantic as we travel along the city's eastern edge, passing the airport before turning west with the road.

She seems content. Her eyes are closed like she appreciates the moment. What that moment could be on an aging, noisy bus like this is anyone's guess.

"What's in Rio?" I lean over and ask in a whisper, wondering why she picked that destination.

"Brazilians."

I walked into that one. "Just scratching where it itches?"

She opens her eyes and turns her head toward me. "Something like that. What do you do, Braden? Other than ask complete strangers to be your travel guide."

"I work…worked in New York City for a political action committee. It's a group…well, it helps fund political campaigns."

"Ah. You buy their votes," Lyla concludes.

"No…" I say, starting to recite a well-rehearsed lie I've uttered a thousand times. "Okay, not officially, but in reality, that's exactly what I did."

"You said 'worked.' You aren't there anymore?"

This isn't a path I want to travel down. I can't tell Lyla why I left or that I'm being chased by a psychopathic German with an uncanny ability to make people do things they don't want to.

"No. It was a different life. One that I'm trying my best to forget about. It's kind of a long story I don't want to get into."

"Sounds tragic. We'll save that for another time, then."

I grimace at the thought. "And you? I know you travel the world. Where do you call home?"

Lyla shifts position in her seat. "My home is wherever I am. Right now, it's on a bus to Rio de Janeiro."

"That sounds tragic," I say, using her words.

"Not really. I like not being rooted. It's liberating. I'm free to go where I please when I please."

We spend the next hour making small talk. It's nothing serious, and I purposely avoid asking sensitive or overly personal questions. We stick to the trivial stuff and stories about some of the adventures during Lyla's travels. She seems to have an endless supply of them.

The questions she directs back at me are along the same lines. She asks about my time at Princeton, never having attended university herself. She stops talking for a couple of minutes. I almost thought she had fallen asleep. Then she turns her body in the seat to face me more easily.

"Can I make a personal observation?"

"I thought we were steering clear of those."

"We are. That's why I'm asking your permission."

I brace myself. "Okay."

"You've led a boring life."

I wish I could argue with her, but I can't. My life has been dull, if not boring. All I do is work. Before that, I was in college and spent all my time studying. A big night on the town was getting a drink at happy hour before returning to the office. None of that must sound appealing to a woman who travels the world on a limited budget.

"Why do you think I asked for your help? I'm hoping you'll change that."

"I guess we'll see," she admits.

"Now it's my turn to ask you something personal."

Lyla tenses up. I can sense her anxiety ratchet up a few notches.

"Okay. That's fair, I guess."

I smile. "What's your last name?"

She lets out a giggle as the tension releases. "Chance."

"What?" I ask.

"My last name. It's Chance. C-h-a-n-c-e. Like the English spelling."

I shake my head and smile. "That explains it. You said, 'Not a chance' when I asked for your last name. Nice pun. Except you are one."

Lyla shrugs. "It's just a name."

There is something about how she said that, but I don't press the issue. She's a mysterious woman, and she clearly has a history. Someday, maybe she'll trust me enough to share it. It won't be today, and likely not tomorrow. Lyla isn't the type to open up to perfect strangers. I change the subject.

"Are we there yet?" I moan.

"We've only been on the bus for a little over an hour."

"I know. How long is this trip?"

The corner of her mouth curls. "Two days."

"Two…are you serious?" I ask, turning to her in shock while kicking myself for not paying more attention to the details before purchasing the tickets. "We drove right past the airport in Bueno Aires. We should have flown."

"You wanted adventure, Braden Fox. You can't get that from flying in a pressurized tube at thirty thousand feet. The best part of life is the journey, not the destination. Get comfortable and enjoy the scenery."

She must not be a big watcher of YouTube videos. I've seen plenty of footage about adventurous things that happen on planes. I don't see how this bus will be much more exciting, but I don't protest.

"Is that travel advice or a philosophy for life?"

Lyla smiles. "Who says it can't be both?"

She settles into her seat and closes her eyes for what is bound to be a long drive ahead. I'm too wired to nap, so I turn to stare out the window. It's my first time in South America. It's my first time anywhere, really. There will be plenty of time to get to know the woman beside me. In the meantime, I might as well take her advice and enjoy the scenery. There are worse ways to spend two days.

Chapter Thirteen

Life's A Beach

I have always pictured Rio de Janeiro as a distant fantasyland filled with women in skimpy bikinis and drunken revelers during Carnival. It hosted the World Cup and Summer Olympics in the past decade and has a huge statue of Christ on a mountain. That's all I knew about the city. I was pleasantly surprised after our tortuous bus trip ended.

Rio and its people are much more than a sum of those parts. Lyla and I stayed away from the more touristy coast and chose a cheap hotel near the city center. I figure that Braus would start his search where most foreigners go. It was a great choice.

The downtown area, with its museums and exhumed historic sites, has a unique energy we've enjoyed over the past four days. Rio de Janeiro is lodged between lush mountains and granite monoliths jutting from the sea. Instead of viewing it from Sugarloaf Mountain or Christ the Redeemer on Corcovado Mountain, I splurged and convinced Lyla to see it with me by helicopter. It was absolutely amazing. At least, it was when I wasn't seeing the inside of dance studios for Samba lessons.

Our last lesson is in Copacabana. We finish my final attempt to master even the basics of the ballroom version of the traditional dance and step out of the studio into the moist Brazilian air. I'm not worried about running into Braus on the street, but my head is still on a swivel. I've wanted to see this spit of sand since we arrived, and this is my chance.

"You're finally getting your wish," Lyla says as we transition from the city to Copacabana Beach.

"I only knew the name from the Barry Manilow song. I didn't realize it was an actual place until I read it on the bus."

"You were right when you said you don't get out much. I didn't know there was a song written about this place."

"Technically, it isn't. The Copacabana was a club where Lola worked as a showgirl and Tony as a bartender. Then they fall in love."

"That's sweet," Lyla says with a smile.

"Not really. Tony gets shot and killed by a guy named Rico, and Lola spends the rest of her life going to the club wearing the same dress she did the night he was killed and drank herself into oblivion because of a broken heart."

Lyla stops walking and stares at me. "That's horrible!"

"But a good song. Manilow warns his listeners to not fall in love because it only leads to heartache. People would be smart to take his advice."

My thoughts drift back to Kinsey. I loved her far more than she ever loved me. There is no pain like the hurt that comes from betrayal. I wish I had listened to that song before I put a ring on her finger. It would have spared me the heartache. I turn to see Lyla studying my face.

"You have serious trust issues, Braden."

I smile. "One to talk."

"Touché. I *am* staying in the same hotel room as you. That should count for something, though."

"What? Do you think I'm going to put you in a hole and starve you so I can make a woman suit out of your skin?"

"It rubs the lotion on its skin, or else it gets the hose again," Lyla rhythmically sings in the creepiest voice I've ever heard her use.

Now, it's my turn to stop walking. "You've seen *Silence of the Lambs*?"

Lyla reaches back and grabs my arm, pulling me forward. "I travel the world, Braden. It doesn't mean I live in a cave. A date took me to see a showing of it—in Greece, I think."

"Wait! A date took you to see *Silence of the Lambs*?"

"Romantic, right? It was his first and only date," Lyla says with a smile.

"Do you go on many dates?"

Lyla sighs. "It was years ago, Braden."

"You didn't answer the question."

"Yes, I did," she argues. "I answered it in Buenos Aires when we first met. Relationships are messy."

"What would you call our relationship?"

"Complicated."

That's not what I wanted to hear. I would have settled for "new." Even something like "undetermined" would have worked. Complicated is a whole other level. Trust doesn't come easy with this woman. Then again, she isn't wrong. Not wanting to humiliate myself further, I decide to change the subject.

"Have you been to Rio before?"

"No. It's my first time here. I planned to make this the last stop on my South American tour."

"Where did it start?"

"Bogota. Then I moved onto Lima, Quito, La Paz, Santiago—"

"Buenos Aires, and now Rio," I guess, getting a laugh and a nod. "That's quite a trip."

"I've seen painted deserts, Mayan ruins, the Road of Death, the Nazca Lines…I've met a lot of great people in small villages along the way. It's been amazing."

I'm hoping I'm one of those "great" people. "And you danced."

"And I danced," she confirms.

"With a devilishly handsome partner who can adequately tango but sucks at the samba."

Lyla slaps me on the chest with the back of her hand. "You weren't that bad."

"Oh, no. I was terrible. You can say it."

"Terrible is a strong word. You need to work on your hip movement." I playfully raise an eyebrow at her, causing her to moan. "Not like that."

"A lot of people would envy your life. I know I do."

"My life comes with its liabilities. Trust me."

"Maybe, but I've only seen Buenos Aires and Rio. And Honolulu."

Lyla frowns. "Cities are nice, but there's much more to the world than urban centers. The real magic is off the beaten path. The hidden gems unvisited by tourists and the ordinary people in the countryside just living their lives make the world a special place. You get the most out of travel when you don't only see things. You must feel an emotional connection."

I don't know how to do that. I've never let myself. My life has always been about planning for the next challenge to overcome or career obstacles to hurdle. None of that requires an emotional connection unless it's fear of losing. I can't begin to relate to her on that level.

"Where would you go next if we hadn't met?"

"The same place *we're* going—back to Europe."

"You want me to go with you to Europe?"

Lyla grins. "I wouldn't be much of a guide if I left you here. Plus…."

"You don't have the money to make the trip yourself," I finish for her.

I've seen my fair share of gold diggers. They are shallow and only care about men with fat wallets and fatter bank accounts. Any relationship with them is one-sided and usually ends in divorce. I don't think Lyla fits that mold, but my tone may have come across that way.

"You make it sound like I'm a horrible person."

"That wasn't my intention. I asked you to be my guide, not vice versa. I have no problem paying our travel expenses."

"But?"

"Who says there is a 'but?'"

"Because there is," Lyla says, grabbing my arm as we stop. "Tell me."

I scan ahead at the magnificent confluence of land and sea that makes up the four-kilometer-long scalloped beach. The sunlight is beginning to wane, and the blue skies are turning shades of pink, orange, and purple. The kids playing soccer ahead grab their ball and begin making their way home, and the beach vendors are calling it a day.

I hope Lyla doesn't press me to say what's on my mind, but she won't let it go that easily. The woman is a mystery, but I know that much about her after a week together. I might as well say it and deal with the consequences.

"I'm hoping that money isn't the only reason you decided to stick around."

"You're not going to get lucky, Braden," Lyla says with a devilish smile. "I told you that."

"I know. That's not what I meant…forget it."

"There they go," Lyla says, brushing back a wisp of hair that the breeze off the ocean blew in her face as we continue our stroll.

"What?"

"Your walls. Every time you start to let yourself start to feel, you build them again. It's a defense mechanism that most men have, but yours are next level. Do you know why you struggled with the Samba, Braden?"

"Because I'm stiff and uncoordinated."

"No. It's because you didn't let go like you did during our tango."

I say nothing as we continue walking along the edge of the surf. I don't particularly appreciate being psychoanalyzed. I don't suppose anyone likes having a mirror stuck in their face and being forced to look hard at themselves. It doesn't matter if Lyla is right or wrong.

"Fine. Since you're shutting down, I'll answer your question. No, I didn't choose to accompany you because of your money. I like having a dance partner. And, maybe, just maybe, I'm learning to enjoy your company."

"I'll take it," I admit. "When are we leaving?"

"Tomorrow, if you're able to make arrangements."

"I can. What do you want to do until then?"

Lyla takes a deep breath, closes her eyes, and lets the fading sun beat on her face.

"Feel the sand squishing between our toes and the surf rolling over our feet. If I want you to learn anything in our travels, it's that sometimes you need to stop planning and enjoy the moment."

Enjoy the moment. Easy to say but harder to do when knowing my boss dispatched Braus to hunt me down. Fortunately, the German isn't here. Lyla is. I take a deep breath and make a note to heed her advice, at least for one more night.

Chapter Fourteen

Wasted Effort

It's a combination of probabilities and simple mathematics. Braden Fox is not a stupid man. Arden Davenport doesn't employ idiots. Braden knows that the moment he purchases a ticket, they will know about it. It's why he flew private down here from Fort Lauderdale and will use a private charter to leave. Assuming he can afford it, and The Cossack assumes he can. To think otherwise would fall into the same trap the head of American Outreach is ensnared in. Braden only pulled out the hundred thousand that they know about. He could have more.

Buenos Aires offers two airports for private jets. The first is Ministro Pistarini International, with the fun IATA code of EZE. It's the largest airport in Argentina and is located thirteen kilometers southwest of the city with easy connections to highways and features a new passenger terminal.

There's also Jorge Newbery Airfield, the nation's busiest airport, located on the water in the Palermo neighborhood. Both offer customs and immigration and are possible departure points for Braden. That covers the probabilities. Now come mathematics.

Braden is alone with two viable options, and Braus is the sole person dispatched to chase him. He can't cover two places at once, nor can he be available twenty-four hours a day. Help is required to babysit the charter terminals at the two airports. And since there is a chance he could risk a commercial flight, a team or two would be needed to cover the main terminals at both airports.

Fortunately, manpower was easy to obtain. The Cossack made the arrangements with a shady pseudo-security outfit in the city to conduct surveillance. Braus has multiple two-man teams assigned to both transportation hubs. They work eight-hour shifts on a rotation, so they all stay fresh. The cordon was put in place five days ago, and then it became a waiting game while Braus began a search of the city. So far, there is no sign of Braden anywhere.

The manpower requirement is a growing expense, but he's not paying the bill. Arden Davenport is likely screaming at The Cossack to get results, but that's for him to worry about. The trail is ice-cold, and until a lead comes in, they will be playing catch-up. The arrogant boss of American Outreach will just have to deal with it.

Braus parks the rental car and heads into the terminal. The team watching the commercial area in Terminal A is right where they're supposed to be. They look like they are waiting to check in for a flight and don't appear to be raising any suspicions.

He heads to the security checkpoint and converses with the supervisor before heading to the private lounge area for charter VIPs to find the second team. He strolls up and down the wide corridor in search of them. They're nowhere to be found.

The global positioning system has made his job much easier. Every phone purchased for this assignment has a GPS tracker. Braus pulls his cell and checks the locations of the devices given to each team. All are where they should be except the one that looks to be in the back room of a nearby restaurant.

Braus follows the corridor and locates the door marked "Employees Only." At least, he assumes that's what the Spanish words mean in English. He grips the knob, twists, and pushes.

"Oh, shit," one of the guys mutters after Braus swings open the door.

He stares at the airport employees, who look at him in surprise and confusion. Two men hanging in the room look to be restaurant busboys or cooks. Three others have work boots and vests, making them either airline maintenance workers or ground crew working at the terminal. Probably the latter.

"*Salte.*"

Braus watches the men intently. His cold eyes freeze the men in their seats. He may only speak rudimentary Spanish, but the tone of his voice and hard look convey "get out" as much as the word does.

No longer able to withstand his withering stare, one of the employees stands and turns to his buddies. "*Vamos.*"

The men file out of the breakroom, leaving Braus alone with his two wayward watchers, who rise from their chairs. The man has seen many horrors and has survived countless perilous situations. As a result, he learned to control his anger. Most people find his quiet simmering unnerving.

"Was anything about my orders unclear? You are to watch the VIP lounge. I'm not paying you to hang out in a back room."

"We needed a break," one of the men protests as the other dumbly looks on.

There are plenty of English speakers in Buenos Aires, but Spanish is the dominant language. One of the requirements Braus outlined to the security company is that each team needed at least one person who could communicate in English. This is the guy. The other is clueless.

"It's over, and you will not take another. Get back to your post."

"Who do you think you are? We don't take orders from you. If we need a break, we take it."

It's not the words that bother Braus; it's the tone. Insolent. Arrogant. Challenging. And utterly futile. This man thinks he's a tough guy because he grew up on the streets, and the streets can be hard. Not hard enough. The German is anything but a soft tourist who can be intimidated. He glides confidently to within arms' reach of the two men.

"Last chance."

"Or what? Whatchya gonna do?" the man says, thrusting his chest out and cocking his head in a direct challenge.

Braus grabs the man's partner by the throat. Nothing is more terrifying for a human being than the inability to breathe. It often leads to instance compliance. The other man lunges at Braus, likely intent on breaking the hold. He doesn't see Braus reach into his pocket and retrieve his Glock. He jams the barrel under the man's chin, causing him to freeze.

"I bet you're wondering how I got this through airport security. It's because I'm special. What you should be wondering is what will happen first. Will your friend die from lack of oxygen, or will I paint the wall behind you with your brains?"

"We…we will do…as you say."

"I don't believe you," Braus says. "Your words are hollow. Convince me of your dedication. Break your finger."

"What?" the man asks, his eyes growing wider.

Braus presses the Glock's muzzle harder into the flesh under the man's chin. "Pick a finger. Any finger. Reach over with your other hand and snap it in two."

"You're crazy. No way."

Braus squeezes the other man's neck tighter. He's getting no air in his lungs as he desperately tries to pry the German's hand off his throat.

"If you don't, I will choke your friend to death, and there will be no reason to let you live. Break your finger. Do it now, or you both die."

The man tries to look down, forcing Braus to slightly adjust the gun. His finger moves to the trigger in case he has thoughts of making a stand. It would be his last. Instead, he reaches with his right hand and selects his left pinky finger. It's a good option and the one Braus would have selected if given a choice. The man takes a deep breath and does as instructed. There is a satisfying snap as the thug clenches his jaw to fight the shock of pain.

Braus eases the pressure on his buddy's windpipe. He gasps as a small amount of air reaches his lungs. At least he won't pass out now.

"*Bueno*. Now, break *his* finger," Braus commands without eliciting further protests.

"*Lo siento*," the man says to his partner before doing as instructed.

The snap is a satisfying sound. The second man is more concerned about filling his lungs than the pain radiating from his newly broken finger. He doubles over, gasping for air after Braus releases the hold on his neck.

"You should both be alert now. Return to your post. If I catch you not doing your job again, I won't stop at a finger. I will break every bone in your body. Do you understand?"

"*Sí*," the man says before helping his partner to the door.

If they're smart, they will get some acetaminophen from one of the gift shops before returning to the watch. Braus will need to make a call. These men are unreliable and need to be replaced. Compliance today doesn't mean they won't try to seek revenge tomorrow.

Braus tucks his weapon into the holster tucked near the small of his back. It's useful to have American law enforcement credentials. It buys a lot of credibility, even in foreign countries. He has no idea how much The Cossack paid for the forgery, but it's a damn good one.

His cell phone rings, and he retrieves it from his pocket. "Yeah?"

"We just got a passport hit on Braden Fox. He left the country," The Cossack informs Braus.

"Not possible. I have the airports covered."

"You do, I'm sure. In Buenos Aires. He just flew out of Brazil."

"What?"

"The *Ministério das Relações Exteriores* validated his exit visa. He departed Rio de Janeiro an hour ago. A private charter, just like you said he would use."

Braus closes his eyes and curses under his breath. "How the hell did he get to Brazil?"

"Bus. Car. Walked. Who knows?" the Russian asks in his thick accent. "He may have left BA even before you got there."

"What's his new destination?"

"Unknown. The charter company wouldn't divulge that information. Client confidentiality, or some BS like that. Get up to Rio and find out. I'll send you the charter company's details. Convince them to divulge his flight plan. I'm guessing he's returning to the States, but I need to know where. I can't wait for another hit on his passport."

"I'll get a flight to Brazil immediately. I need you to cut the security company down here loose."

"Consider it done."

The call ends, and Braus pockets the cell phone. He places his hands along the table's edge and violently flips it over. So much for not displaying anger. This whole exercise was nothing but wasted time. Braden Fox is making him look like a fool. He's going to make him suffer for that.

Chapter Fifteen

It's All Fun & Games

I'm not a world traveler. That much has been established. But I've heard plenty of horror stories from friends about their flying in economy seating on commercial airlines. I'm unsure whether I could endure that after these last two flights.

The Gulfstream IV we chartered to Europe cost about twelve thousand dollars an hour. It was a ten-and-a-half-hour flight. Do the math. Needless to say, my initial one-hundred-thousand-dollar withdrawal is long gone. Arden Davenport will be bewildered about how I'm affording this. Thinking that someone with deep pockets is footing the bill will likely drive him crazy. There is no way they learned about my lucky craps roll.

Fortunately, cheap hotels have helped defer the overall cost of this trip. We aren't staying at the Four Seasons. Our arrival in Europe also opens up cheap transportation options. Hopefully, I won't have to worry about using my passport or having my name pop up on a manifest again anytime soon.

Our arrival in Madrid was uneventful. I learned that my Spanish hasn't improved any since my stay in Buenos Aires, not that the dialect is remotely the same as what I heard in Argentina. We both slept on the plane, making the flight as short as it was comfortable. Alert and energized, we exit the airport and take a taxi to a mid-priced boutique hotel. After checking in, Lyla insisted we walk around the city a little before finding a place to eat.

"I didn't think we were staying in Madrid," I say, wondering why she had a change of heart. "You told me on the plane that you wanted to avoid the big European cities."

"One night won't kill us."

"I know. But you said we weren't—"

"Oh, my God, Braden! Loosen up, will you, please? Plans change. Learn to adapt. We have no itinerary, so if we spend a night in Madrid, it's not a big deal."

That's always been my problem. Everything needs to be planned out. Kinsey is the same way. Our wedding reception was choreographed and planned down to the smallest detail. The playlist we handed to the band was arranged in a specific order. We spent months fine-tuning the seating arrangements. Even the napkins and place settings had to be arranged according to our diagram. I'm most comfortable when every contingency is accounted for.

"I don't know how to adapt," I admit, hanging my head.

"I know. That's why you have me here to give you lessons. When was the last time you did anything for fun?"

"I took dance lessons. That counts."

"The ones before we met? Be honest. Did you take them because you wanted to or because a girlfriend made you?"

Okay, she hit the nail on the head with that conclusion. I wanted nothing to do with dance lessons. I'm rhythmically challenged and, as Lyla put it, stiff. They were Kinsey's idea because she didn't want me to embarrass her during our first dance. It was all part of the meticulous wedding planning. No stone was left unturned, especially that one. Not that I can admit any of that to Lyla. Not yet.

"Fair. I, uh…." I stop and think. The pause takes too long.

"Are you serious? You've never just cut loose and acted silly? What did you do at college?"

"I had some fun," I argue, using a half-truth. "Mostly, I studied a lot."

Lyla frowns. "What about as a child?"

I take a deep breath. "My parents were accomplished. They had big careers and worked all the time. They raised me to be the same. Success isn't achieved by cutting loose and acting silly."

"Even as a kid? That's horrible!"

"It's all I know," I say with a shrug.

She stops and looks around. "Then you need an emergency lesson in having fun. Follow me."

"Where are we going?" I ask, trying to catch up to her.

"You'll see."

We walk for what feels like a mile. Lyla keeps looking around and checking street signs. I have no idea where we're going until she stops and gestures at a set of double doors. I can't read the sign, but the pictures on the windows clearly indicate what this is.

"You can't be serious. A toy store? We barely have clothes in our bags, and you want me to buy a Nerf gun?"

"Not exactly," she says, pulling the door open.

The space is about the size of an old Toys 'R" Us, not that I spent much time in one. The outer walls are ringed with aisles of toys. Unlike a big box store in America, this shop didn't cram as many products as possible within its walls. A large area in the middle of the store attracts my attention. It's a big, subdivided play area infested with dozens of kids. All of them are playing, and countless toys are strewn around the area like a claymore mine blew up in a toy chest.

"Every toy in the store is available for kids to play with," Lyla says, smiling as she watches the kids run around under the supervision of their parents.

"This is the future of retail," I say, appreciating the ingenuity. "You can buy anything online, but can't try it first. What a way to draw customers to the store. The kids get to try the toys first, and then they'll plead with their parents to buy them. It's pure genius."

"I didn't bring you here to make a business investment, Braden," Lyla groans. "Get out of your head and go on."

"And do what?"

"Play."

"Play? Uh, don't you think it's a little creepy for a grown man to play with little children?"

"Only if you're playing 'doctor.' Go on."

My legs seize up. I feel like I'm in that Buenos Aires tango salon again. I'm completely immobile and at a loss for what to do.

"I told you. I don't know how."

"It's easy," she says, picking up a plastic battle ax off the ground and handing it to me. "Take this."

I stare at the large piece of molded plastic like it's an alien artifact. "What am I supposed to do with this?"

Lyla walks over to a small group of kids wielding plastic swords and trying to pummel each other. She taps one on his Medieval knight's helmet.

"*¡Monstruo!*" she shouts, pointing at me.

The kids hoist their plastic swords in the air and scream. Suddenly, I realize I'm in trouble.

"Defend yourself, Braden!"

The kids charge at me. I roar and swing the plastic ax in a slow arc over their heads. Then I crash it to the ground beside one of the children as he deftly moves out of the way. A girl comes in, chopping at my leg with her plastic sword, complete with karate sounds every time it lands.

I howl in mock pain and swing again. A boy circles behind me and jabs his sword into my back. I collapse to my knees and roar again. It only encourages the onslaught. After three dozen more strikes and a growing bruise or two, I moan and fall to the ground, defeated.

"*¡Otra vez! ¡Otra vez!*"

I assume that means again as the kids rally ten feet away and prepare for another battle. I climb to my feet. This time, I grab a Darth Vader mask and pick up a cheap red plastic lightsaber, holding it like I remember them doing in the movies.

"I am your father!"

They charge at me again, and another battle ensues. I lose, naturally, and lie on the ground. When I lift my head, a young girl affixes a pink pompom to my helmet with a giggle. I glance at Lyla, who's doubled over laughing with the other parents.

"Very evil. So intimidating," Lyla says between fits of laughter.

So, I almost immediately learn something about children – they eventually tire of things and have boundless creativity when they move on to their next play activity. After a few more rounds of "Slay Braden *el Monstruo*," I'm given a foam dart shooter and camouflage hat. A young girl tells me to count to thirty outside the play area. One of the parents translates the instructions for me.

Eager to comply, I do as requested. When I reach thirty, I charge into an empty play area. There isn't a kid in sight. I hear a shout, and about ten kids pop out from their hiding places. Foam bullets head my way as I open fire at the targets. As I get hit, I reenact the death scene from the movie *Platoon*. It's an epic, over-dramatized death.

Lyla and I emerge from the store after another hour of playtime that saw me hiding in a mountain of stuffed animals, playing demolition derby with die-cast cars, and making dinner with the Spanish version of an Easy-Bake oven. I have no idea how parents do it. I'm exhausted, but I feel…content. It's like all the stress of my life has lifted. The feeling is invigorating.

I stand in the middle of the sidewalk and close my eyes, relishing the sounds and smells of Madrid. It's almost as if I can feel the city's energy. It's the vibe created by over three and a half million people congregated in the same area. The spirit of the city.

"Is that?" Lyla begins to ask as she moves around to my front and leans in. "Wait. I think it is. That's a genuine smile!"

I unsuccessfully try to stifle it. "Maybe. Have I loosened up enough for you now?"

"Your grinning ear-to-ear is a good start," she says, looping her arm through mine as we begin walking. "I did learn something about you. You'd be a good father."

"How do you know that?"

"You know how to deal with kids."

It appears I learned something new about myself. Until five minutes ago, I never even found kids interesting. I never imagined they could unlock my inner child. Nor did I realize I had an inner child.

"It's not a skill I thought I had. I've never even thought about having children."

"Maybe you should start considering it. That looks like an interesting place to eat. I'm going to see if there are any tables."

Lyla abruptly changes direction and enters the restaurant, leaving me on the sidewalk. I pull my wallet out of my back pocket and slide out the picture tucked into it. Kinsey would have hated today. She never wanted children of her own. She barely tolerates other people's kids.

I tuck the picture away and scowl. I don't know why my thoughts drift back to Kinsey whenever Lyla isn't beside me. She doesn't deserve a second of my attention. I wonder if she will always live rent-free inside my head.

"The food looks amazing," Lyla says, materializing next to me and snapping me back into the present. "Hungry?"

"Famished."

"Good. You're going to need your energy for this trip. And before you get any ideas, no, I didn't mean it that way."

I didn't interpret it that way, but I don't bother correcting her. Instead, I smile and follow Lyla into the restaurant, curious about what my guide has planned next and where that could possibly be.

Chapter Sixteen

A New Wrinkle

Antonio Carlos Jobim is the main international airport serving Rio de Janeiro. It features two passenger terminals and a separate one for private business aviation. That's Braus's first stop after his plane touched down and he disembarked.

That's when things stop going as planned. It isn't because of a language barrier. Many public-facing employees in the world's airports can speak passable English. The pleasant representative for the charter company is no exception. The problem is, she's by the book. Company policy states passenger information cannot be shared with third parties without authorization. Even with fake American law enforcement credentials, it's not something Braus will get. One phone call for verification and he could find himself in a Brazilian prison waiting for extradition back to the United States.

With the direct route no longer an option, Braus needs to get creative. He can't force his way to a computer in the business terminal of a major airport. There is too much security. Finding an employee to coerce or bribe would take too much time, and he's on a schedule.

Fortunately, the terminal isn't the only place records are kept. After a few discreet inquiries, Braus discovers that the charter company maintains a maintenance hangar on airport grounds. It's located off the runway to the northeast of the three terminals. He decides to walk the access route to it.

The maintenance hangar isn't part of a major complex. It's nothing more than two corrugated steel structures situated side-by-side. The closer one is the company Braus is looking for. He isn't sure what airline the other maintenance facility belongs to, but discharging a weapon in such proximity is out of the question. They will immediately report the shots. Braus will have to do this the old-fashioned way – he'll start with words and escalate from there.

He reaches the tarmac and walks straight into the hangar. A plane is parked there with an engine cowling off. It looks like a Learjet, but that's the extent of Braus's familiarity with aircraft. A lone mechanic circles the jet and begins barking something in Portuguese as he points back toward the runway.

"I need to speak to your manager."

"No. You cannot be here," the man says, switching to English. "Must leave."

"I will, once I speak to your maintenance manager."

"No talk. Company personnel can be here. Must leave."

Braus isn't about to let some aeronautical grease monkey intimidate him. However tough this man thinks he is, the German has seen and dispatched much tougher. Frustrated that his words aren't being heeded, the mechanic shoves Braus in the shoulder. He still doesn't budge. The man goes to grab his shirt with grease-covered hands. That won't do.

There are three effective ways to win a fight. The first is the Rocky Balboa approach, using superior stamina to overcome your opponent. The second is to use skill to win, ala Jason Bourne or Jet Li. The third is a Jack Reacher favorite. You surprise your opponent and incapacitate him immediately with a liberal use of force. Braus opts for option three.

A well-placed strike can bring even the most skilled fighter or biggest man to his knees. Braus loves targeting the ability to breathe. The man reaches, almost in slow motion. The pair of knuckles made by Braus's index and middle fingers fly at Mach three in comparison. The throat punch lands right on the man's larynx, simultaneously restricting his airway while depriving him of the ability to call for help.

The man crumples to his knees, gasping. Braus grabs the mechanic and drags him to his feet. In case the man gets ideas, he places the muzzle of his gun against the man's forehead.

"Take me to your manager."

The mechanic doesn't say anything, not that he can. Fortunately, he's compliant now and does as instructed. The pair travels deeper into the hangar, stopping at a battered wood door near the back. Braus opens it and shoves the mechanic into the small office. He points at the sofa, and the mechanic sits, still struggling for air.

The manager stands and barks something in Portuguese. Braus can't understand the words, but the tone is clear enough – surprise at the intrusion leading to annoyance. No doubt there were some curse words mixed in.

The German points the gun at the man's chest. The manager raises his hands as he eyes the Glock. Compliance. It's a beautiful thing.

"I need information. You will give it to me, or you won't be home for dinner tonight. Or any other night. Do you understand me?"

"Yes…yes."

"Good. Sit down and log into your computer. Do you have flight records or just maintenance records on that thing?"

"Both."

The man does as instructed. That's the beauty of guns – they instill fear. The magazine could be empty. The firing pin could be missing or damaged. In Braus's case, using it would cause more harm than good. None of that matters. Guns are scary, and putting someone in front of the working end of one often leads to instant results.

"What do you want?" the manager asks.

"I need information on a flight that left here this morning," Braus says, glancing at the first man to ensure he isn't planning anything stupid.

"What was the destination?"

"That's what I need to find out."

"We had seven departures."

"Do you have a manifest?" Braus asks, getting a nod. "Search for Braden Fox. F-O-X."

The man moves his mouse and makes a bunch of keystrokes. He studies a window and then clicks a few more times. He looks up at Braus when he finds the appropriate record.

"Mr. Fox flew from here on a Gulfstream four."

Braus presses his lips together. That's not what he expected to hear. He might not know much about planes, but most people have heard of that one. It's the Rolls Royce of the private jet world. It would seem that Braden is traveling in style. It's expensive to fly and has a long range, making it overkill for a flight to the U.S. The better question is how he can afford it, but that's for The Cossack to figure out.

"What was the destination?"

The man stares at the computer. "He and his guest went to Madrid, Spain."

Braus cocks his head. "Guest?"

"Yes. Lyla Chance. She boarded the flight with him."

Braus remains motionless as he processes that new information. A thousand questions flood into his mind. None of them have answers. It could explain how he can suddenly afford to fly on a Gulfstream or deftly evade Braus's pursuit. Or, it could mean none of those things. But the name is a lead, giving him something to chase down.

The mechanic on the sofa sits a little straighter. He shifts his feet closer to the edge, making it easier for him to stand. Braus has seen the look in his eyes before. He intends to exact some revenge for the humiliation. Braus shakes his head as a warning, and the man relaxes into a less aggressive posture. There is no element of surprise.

"Thank you for your assistance. It would be wise to tell nobody about this conversation. If you alert the authorities, I will come back and kill both of you. Then, I will kill your families for the inconvenience you caused me. Do you understand?"

"Y-yes," the manager stutters. The mechanic says nothing, but he lowers his eyes in acceptance. That's good enough.

Braus leaves the maintenance hangar and quickly cuts back along the dirt access to the main road. The warning may be enough to stop them from picking up the phone and making a report. It also might not. There's no point in taking the risk of sticking around to find out. If he hears sirens, that will be enough of a sign about what transpired.

In his business, information is king. Braus has to report what he learned and hits the redial button on his cell. The Cossack answers on the first ring.

"*Da?*"

"I have news. Braden Fox is in Spain. Madrid."

"A bold move," The Cossack says, almost sounding impressed. "He has lots of travel options in Europe. Fortunately, I have more resources there than in South America. Get on a flight. I will arrange for them to meet you at the airport in Madrid."

"Get me a charter to Brasilia and book the flight to Spain from there. I need to change airports, and Santos Dumont only handles domestic charters."

"Why do you need to change to SDU?" the Russian asks, using the airport code.

"I'm not going to be welcome at this one anymore."

The Cossack sighs. He knows better than to ask any further questions. He demands results. The methods of getting them are left up to the operators in the field.

"Very well."

"There's something more. Fox is traveling with someone. A woman."

"A woman? Contact? Lover?"

"I don't know."

"Do you have a name?"

"Lyla Chance. C-H-A-N-C-E. French passport, but it could be a fake."

Braus can hear the Russian writing the name down. "I'll look into her. Maybe Arden Davenport has some insights."

"I'll be at the other airport in under an hour. Text me the flight details. I'll contact you before I leave Brasilia."

Braus hangs up. He needs to return to the terminal and catch a cab to Santos Dumont Airport. It's the fastest way to get there. He only needs to hope there isn't an army of cops looking for him when he arrives.

A traveling companion changes the dynamic of this situation. Braus had discounted Braden selling his information to a competitor or the feds. Now, he isn't so sure. Lyla Chance. She could be anybody. Hopefully, they will have answers before he lands in Europe.

Chapter Seventeen

Paso Who?

There is nothing I would say no to when this woman wears a dress. She was a vision in the one she borrowed to tango in when we met in Argentina. This dress isn't quite as sexy, but it's equally captivating draped over her body.

I bought street clothes for our dancing lessons, and she purchased this dress. With the amount of sweating we did, we washed them every night at our small hotel. Now that it's showtime, we rented more traditional outfits.

For me, it's matador pants and a bolero jacket. I completed the outfit with a white shirt and tie. Lyla's dress is elegant yet flamboyant. The bottom is flowy red material meant to represent a cape. She is wearing high heels, making her legs look absolutely amazing. Our outfits complement each other in color and style. We passed on other popular accessories. There was no reason to don long black gloves, a matador hat, masks, or black lace for her.

We have a decent crowd gathered in the dance studio. The instructor likes to have her pupils demonstrate their moves in front of an audience. After monopolizing her time over the past three days, we wouldn't escape a dance recital to show her other students what we had learned. It's all a little intimidating, and that's precisely why Lyla agreed to it. She likes making me uncomfortable.

The paso doble became a huge hit among the upper classes of Paris in the 1930s. French for "Two Step," referring to the powerfully styled walking, it's a dramatic dance based on bullfighting. The ballroom dance originates in France but is popular in Spain for obvious reasons. The Paso Doble is also hard to master because of its complex footwork and precise movements. It's not Samba hard, but close.

The music mimics tunes played at bullfights during the bullfighters' entrance or just before the kill. Paso music is generally played at a speed of fifty to sixty bars per minute. The most common tune is the one our instructor cues up for us: *Espana Cani,* or "Spanish Gypsy."

The best part of learning the Paso for the last few days is the ego-stroking I get from Lyla. Matadors are arrogant men, and male dancers are expected to carry their bodies in a strong, masculine manner. She has done her part to appeal to my ego, giving me the confidence to make this look good. It needs to be dramatic and intense. Lyla manages that effortlessly. I find it a little harder.

The Paso Doble features quick, staccato steps with dramatic body shaping. I enter a hold and strike my feet on the ground in a movement called an "appel." It signifies the movement a matador makes to get a bull's attention. Lyla's movements are soft and large, representing a cape flowing around me. One of the intriguing aspects of this dance is my stillness, punctuated with bursts of movement. In the bullring, the matador uses stillness to show he's not afraid of the charging bull.

Outside of the appel, I don't remember any of the names of the steps or moves I'm doing. To make things easier, we choreographed this routine. Lyla wanted me to wing it, but I told her we would be here for months if that's what she wanted. I'm a quick study in most things, but I'm a slow learner when it comes to dancing.

Her steps, on the other hand, are intoxicating. Lyla moves with a fluidity that would make water jealous. She's the star of this show for good reason. First, it's because the dance is designed that way. Second, it's because Lyla is a better dancer than almost anyone here outside of the instructor.

I try to play the strong leading man and guide her into the next moves. My steps are taken with the heel forward, but I leave the back leg in place to create a long, straight leg line. My center is forward, creating an optical illusion as my body turns in different directions. To continue the bullfight analogy, the movement creates a false space for the bull to attack without goring the matador.

The dance ends with enthusiastic applause from the spectators and our instructor. All the hard work paid off, not because I plan to audition for *Dancing with the Stars*, but because I didn't trip over my feet. Or hers.

Bathing in the other students' attention and the exhilaration of the dance, we change out of our outfits into something more street-appropriate. I'm on cloud nine. It's not quite what I felt in Buenos Aires. Like sex, you can never recreate your first time. But it is close.

We thank our instructor and then leave the dance studio. Lyla hangs on my arm, still enjoying the dance's afterglow. The crowds on the street have been growing since we arrived. I'm sure this is a tourist area, but I've seen smaller waves of people leaving football stadiums after a game.

"The city is getting busy. I wonder what's going on."

"Braden, seriously, did you grow up in a cave or something?"

The ego-boosting apparently ended with that final dance. "No, why?"

"You really don't know about the San Fermín Fiesta?"

"I know '*fiesta*' means party. Should I know about it?"

Lyla laughs and explains how the San Fermín Festival is world-famous. For nine days every July, hundreds of thousands of spectators from around the globe descend on Pamplona to experience the magic and mayhem of what the city bills as the "World's Largest Fiesta." The festival begins with a rocket blast at noon and rages until a midnight candlelit singing of "*Pobre de Mí*."

I have led a sheltered life. I've heard about the running of the bulls but never paid much attention to what it was or where it was held. I had no idea people come to see the gigantic animals run the gantlet, watch matadors test their skills, and immerse themselves in this historically rooted celebration.

It's meant to be an interactive festival, welcoming visitors to participate rather than observe. The city streets become alive with dances, parties, singing, parades, and traditional folkloric events. Now I get the reason for the lessons.

"That explains why you wanted me to learn the Paso."

"Nah," Lyla says, tugging at my arm. "That was meant to let you feel like a matador. Now, you're going to actually become one."

As we walk, I stare at her, hoping that she's joking. "I'm not up for that."

Her time as my guide is over if she thinks I'm about to fight a bull. I embarked on this adventure to escape Braus's clutches, not get trampled by a two-thousand-pound walking, snorting steak.

"You would only get yourself killed. Matadors are professionals. There is no way that the Spanish would ever let a tourist try it. How about the next best thing?"

"I'm almost afraid to ask, but what do you have in mind?"

Lyla drags me into a clothing store that feels more like a tourist shop. Instead of shelves stocked with t-shirts, button-downs, and slacks, much of the space is dedicated to white outfits, most with a logo on them. The shirts and pants are white, and red sashes and bandanas are next to them. They come in all sizes.

"What's this?"

"Your outfit for tomorrow. White shirt and pants, a *Faja* you tie around your waist, and a *Pañuelo* for your neck."

"It looks comfortable. What's tomorrow?"

Lyla smiles. "Remember what you told me on the bus ride to Rio? You said you've never done anything daring in your life."

I fold my arms. "Lyla, what's happening tomorrow?"

"Remember, you wanted me to be your guide so you could experience things you could never do on your own."

"Okay, now you're really scaring me. What's…happening…tomorrow?"

Lyla smiles, and her eyes brighten. She turns and takes my hands in hers, bringing them to her chest. She looks up at me with those eyes. This is why smitten men will do anything for a beautiful woman. Nobody can say no to eyes like that.

"Braden, I would never ask you to climb into a ring and fight a bull."

"That's refreshing," I mumble, wondering if I'm about to get talked into doing something stupid.

"I expect you to be brave enough to run with them."

Chapter Eighteen

Corre por su Vida

It's a mob scene here. Thousands of people, all dressed in white with red sashes and bandanas, crowd City Hall Square. Everyone running the route assembles at the *Cuesta de Santo Domingo* until the municipal police barriers are opened. At that point, participants can move to the area of the race they've chosen to run. The access gates are closed at seven thirty, and then no one can leave the bull route. That's now in the rearview mirror. The time for second thoughts and misgivings has come and gone.

Fortunately for me, Lyla decided to join in on the fun. From a cursory scan of the crowd, not many women do this run. But she said she wanted to be at my side, maybe for comfort or maybe so I don't chicken out. Which is tempting.

We both bought running shoes to go with the white uniform and got a good night's sleep. That's one of the requirements for a successful run. There are dozens more, including not wearing anything that might fall off or get tangled while running. We don't own a cell phone or camera, so there's no need to ensure those were left at the hotel. Nobody else is carrying one either, which is a refreshing change in modern society.

"I can't believe we're doing this," I mutter.

"It'll be fine," she reassures me. "Despite the bad press, very few people die running with the bulls. The chance of being hit or gored is relatively low. The death toll since 1910 is fifteen men if you include the guy who suffocated to death in a pile-up of runners.

"Pile-up?"

Lyla looks at me with amused eyes. "The six bulls running toward *Plaza de Toros* aren't the biggest threat. It's the two-legged animals running with them that cause the most injuries."

"Wonderful. How many have been injured?"

She shrugs. "I don't know. Thousands?"

My heart rate was already in the triple digits, and my stomach was queasy before she uttered that sentence. I'm now on the verge of having a stroke, and my stomach is in my throat. I imagine that people are regularly sick from nerves before a run. I'm about to be one of them.

I focus on taking deep breaths as we begin walking the route. I thought the Running of the Bulls was a straight shot from Corralillo Santo Domingo to the bullring. I couldn't have been more wrong. There are different sections of the route, and Lyla points out the advantages and potential hazards of each as we pass through them.

The Santo Domingo segment is the first and one of the most dangerous stretches of the route and is generally undertaken by only the most experienced runners. It's short, but there is little margin for error. The bulls are running very fast, and there aren't many places to seek refuge.

We continue the walk through the City Hall section to Mercaderes, a treacherous stretch where the famous "Dead Man's Corner" is located. I stare at the hundreds of eager faces peering down from the crumbling apartment balconies that rise five stories above the alley. They are watching for the theater of it all. It must be somewhat entertaining for them to see the fear on our faces. I know how scared I must look. Of course, it's easy to judge from up there.

"Are we running here?"

"Not unless you're suicidal. Severe injuries, gorings, and tramplings are almost guaranteed in this section. We're going to *Telefónica*. It's the final stretch of the route. The bulls are tired and slower by the time they reach us."

"That's encouraging. Have you done this before?"

Lyla looks up at the sky. "Twice, actually."

We increase our gait and cover another hundred meters when the eight a.m. klaxon blares its warning that the bulls have been released from their corral. I look at Lyla with trepidation in my eyes.

"It's showtime, Braden Fox. "*Corre por su vida.*"

Run for your life. That's an accurate description of what's about to happen. I can hear the bulls stomping on the cobblestones. The crowd above my head, buzzed on morning sangria, is cheering, gasping, and screaming. What was a relatively empty street seconds before is now awash with a horde of humanity in survival mode. Then I see it. A black wave of half-ton bulls is closing in.

I launch myself against a building as my heart fires with the staccato of a machine gun. I'm no longer scared. I'm terrified. My breathing is sucking all the oxygen from the alleyway. At least, that's how it feels.

"Ready?"

"No!"

I check behind me to see men tripping on slick cobblestones as they desperately scramble away from the lead bulls. One goes down, causing one of the pile-ups I was warned about. It doesn't last long. The small mountain of bodies is cleared when a bull hurtles through it, scattering them like bowling pins.

"Braden? Braden! Run!"

Lyla grabs my hand, and we take off up the street just as a wave of runners reaches us. We are running at full speed, making holding her hand impossible. My arms pump at my sides, driving my legs as fast as they will carry me. I pass slower runners and find myself edging closer to the middle of the alley. That's when I catch a glint of black in my peripheral vision.

The ton-and-a-half bull next to me looks pissed. He would like nothing more than to pierce one of the runner's hearts with his horn before he meets his demise. Despite my best efforts, the huge animal is faster than I am. That's even despite his moving his head and trying to send the runners ahead to the afterlife.

More tired, my ass. These bulls have plenty of energy. Then I get caught up in the moment. I am running alongside a trio of bulls in the heart of Spain. The feeling is amazing. I'm doing something I never could have dreamt of doing a month ago as I lived a boring life in New York. If Kinsey could only see me now.

The feeling of exhilaration is short-lived. A man ahead of me, who is clearly a tourist, must not have heeded the advice I was given. Runners aren't permitted to touch the bulls as they make their way to the stadium. That includes smacking them in the head with newspapers. As the first three bulls pass me, he pulls one of their tails. I'm no expert, but that's a no-no.

Pastores are the bulls' green-shirted ninja bodyguards. Each carries a long, elastic willow cane to keep the herd compact and distract bulls from people who touch them or interfere with the race. One of the *pastores* sees the man's stupidity and angles himself to run beside him.

He swings with all his might and breaks the cane across the man's nose. A huge gash opens and gushes blood, causing the man to stumble and crash onto the ground in front of me. Three runners trip over him, and the course becomes a tangle of arms and legs.

Lyla manages to clear the *monton*. It's the last I see of her before chaos ensues. I'm not so lucky with my hurdle. I feel my left leg get clipped, killing my forward momentum and sending me crashing into the pile. My shoulder slams hard into the ground, and a sharp pain radiates from my ribs as two more bulls arrive next to me. I can hear the distinct sound of their hooves hitting the cobblestones. Then, panic sets in.

I remain still and weld my hands and arms over my head to protect it. The bulls are still running, so they move on quickly. I wait for another runner to touch my back to signal it's all right to get up. It never happens. I hazard a glance down the alleyway and immediately discover why.

A *suelto* is a bull that has separated from the herd. Lyla explained that a lone bull loses his herding instinct and sees runners as predators. That's why the pastores are determined to keep them together. She said, "If you see a lone bull, run."

She didn't mean farther down the course. Not that I could run now if I wanted to. The pain in my shoulder and side is almost overwhelming. She told me to find immediate safety. That means scrambling and diving under the bottom rung of the wooden barricades meant to protect the runners. At least as much as a split-rail fence will protect anyone. If you try to climb over, you'll be easy target practice for a *suelto*.

I saw the barricades on the walk here with Lyla, only there are none in this section. There are only the walls of the buildings lining the street. I slither over to one on my belly as the pastores drive the lone bull away from some poor sap who earned his undivided attention.

He charges up the alley, paying no mind to the bodies still strewn across the ground from the *monton*. Once he passes, I roll onto my back, breathing hard. I close my eyes and let my heart rate slow, if only a little. My anxiety steadily gives way to a primal relief that I'm still alive. The danger is gone. Despite the pain, I feel more invigorated and alive than ever. I cheated death and can't help but start laughing as medical teams arrive to begin treating the injured.

Chapter Nineteen

An Angel's Touch

I made the mistake of looking at myself in the mirror. My face looks like I ran into Mike Tyson's fist. The skin around my left eye is swollen and is already turning shades of dark blue and purple. I have several lacerations, none deep, but still painful to the touch. I wish that were the extent of the damage. My face may look battered, but it's my shoulder and ribs that are killing me.

There are several hospitals in Pamplona. Most of them are dealing with the casualties from this morning's run, and I couldn't tell you which one I'm at. Lyla has been with me the entire time. Well, almost. She disappeared for a while during my examination, but now that I'm getting patched up, she's right back at my side.

One of the patients in the waiting area said this was one of the worst runs they've had in a while. The *suelto* wreaked havoc on the route as they never did get him to return to the herd. There were also countless incidents of stupid behavior, one of which I witnessed firsthand, and multiple pile-ups that resulted in a myriad of injuries and broken bones. I should feel lucky.

My shirt is off, and the doctor is wrapping a bandage around my ribs. That's about all they can do for me. My shoulder and face will heal with time and only require rest and something to ease the pain. I grimace one last time as the doctor finishes.

"*Finito*," the doctor says before handing me a sling for my arm. "*Eres libre de irte.*"

"*Gracias*, doctor," Lyla says as the doctor nods and leaves the room.

The pair shares a knowing glance. Lyla is still dressed in white, so he knows she also ran this morning. He's probably amused that she emerged without a scratch while I look like the bulls trampled me.

"What did he say?"

"Run faster next time," she says with a smile.

"No, he didn't," I argue, hoping that's not what he said. I'm pretty sure that *correr* is the Spanish verb "to run."

Lyla grins. "He said you're free to go."

"Awesome."

I struggle to put my shirt on, and Lyla jumps up to help. Any twisting of my torso or movement at all with my shoulder is met with sharp stabs of pain. I know I'll live, but it will be a rough few days. She places the sling's strap around my neck, and I slide my arm in. The relief on my shoulder is immediate.

"It doesn't look like we'll be dancing anytime soon."

"That's okay. You deserve a break," Lyla says, taking my hand. "I'm sorry I talked you into that."

"I'm not."

"You got hurt. You're lucky it wasn't worse. After you went down, that bull was inches from your head. You could have been killed."

I still don't know how I injured my ribs. It could have been the bull, although getting kicked by one of those beasts would have broken them. The unfortunate close encounter with the cobblestone alley caused the rest of my various injuries. But that isn't the point.

"Yeah, I could have been," I say, squeezing her hand. "Do you know that's the first time in my life that's been the case? I've never done anything dangerous. Not even once. Unless you count driving on the New Jersey Turnpike."

Lyla presses her lips together. "Maybe that means you're smarter than anyone else."

I shake my head. "It means I'm boring. Everything I've ever done was in pursuit of a goal. I've come to realize that the goal was never that important. I've missed out on a lot in my life. Do you know what I did after I emerged from that pile and scrambled over to the building? I laughed."

"You laughed?"

"Yeah. I was in pain and legitimately feared for my life. Two things I've never experienced. So, I laughed. I felt more alive today than I ever have. That's all because of you. Thank you."

I place her hand on my chest so she can feel my heart. I know Lyla can't relate to what I'm saying. I don't know where her journey has taken her, but she has seen and experienced more than I ever will. We are from different worlds. With her guidance, I'm getting a small taste of hers. She would never want to experience mine. Nobody would.

"Well, I was worried about you."

"I wasn't worried about you," I say, the corner of my mouth curling. It earns me a playful slap on my arm. At least Lyla was conscious not to belt me on the shoulder or in the ribs.

"Gee, thanks!"

"I knew you were okay."

"How? You were face-down, chewing dirt under a pile of people. How could you know I wasn't a hood ornament on one of those beasts?"

"I don't know. I just knew. It seems like there's no situation you can't handle."

Lyla lowers her eyes. "I wish that were true. There are…. Not everything is always as it seems, Braden. Life has thrown more than a few curveballs at me."

"Like how a classically trained artist ends up traveling by herself in South America?"

My curiosity is getting the best of me. We agreed not to ask too many questions. That was then. This is now. Near-death experiences change someone's perspective. At least, that's my excuse for wanting to know.

"For starters," she says, releasing my hand. "Let's say we get you out of here. Unless you want to spend a night in a Spanish hospital?"

"Hard pass," I say, gingerly swinging my legs off the bed.

Lyla goes to retrieve my sneakers when I take a closer look at my wristband. It has my name and home country. It also has something I didn't expect to see: New York.

"How does the hospital know I live in New York? That's not on my passport. I left the address information page blank. And how did my wallet and passport get here? I wasn't carrying them on the run."

"I had to run to the hotel while you were getting examined," she says, undoing the laces enough to slide the sneakers on my feet. "They needed patient information, and your passport and driver's license were the best I could do."

I can feel the panic. The euphoria of surviving a run with bulls determined to spearfish me is replaced by a sense of dread. Lyla saw the picture of Kinsey. She must have. It's right next to my identification. I am surprised she didn't ask who the woman in my wallet was. That's a problem for another day. There's a more pressing concern.

My name was entered into a computer. By now, Braus has figured out that I'm no longer in South America. Arden will give him whatever resources he needs to track me down. With a flag on my name in the European Union, it is only a matter of time before Braus learns I'm here. He could already be in Pamplona if he was nearby when the entry was made.

"We have to go," I say as she finishes tightening and tying the laces.

"Why?"

"We just do. We should get back on the road."

There is a sense of urgency in my voice that Lyla doesn't understand. The confusion is tattooed on her face. I don't expect this to make sense to her, and I can't explain it. Not now.

"You're in no condition to travel, Braden. Besides, do you really want to miss the fiesta? After a close encounter with the bulls, you could use a few glasses of sangria."

She's right about that. I do the math in my head. Worst-case scenario, Braus tracked my flight to Madrid. There is no record of where Lyla and I went from there. We could be in the city. We could have gone west to Portugal or southeast to Barcelona. Given the festival has started in Pamplona, that would also make his list. Fortunately, Braus can't be everywhere, so he likely stayed in Madrid because it's central.

He could fly here, but a train is more likely. That would take around three and a half hours. The bus would take longer – between five and six. He won't wait that long. That means, if I'm right, he will be out looking for me tonight. Fortunately, there are over three hundred thousand residents in the metro area and another million here for the festival. That's a lot of parties to search for somebody. Or two, assuming he knows I'm with Lyla. The odds of finding us are infinitesimally small. Or so I hope.

"Okay, one night, but we really should leave tomorrow morning. I'm not a big partier."

"Braden, what's wrong?"

"Nothing."

Lyla crosses her arms. "Don't lie to me. You're acting all weird."

I don't want to lie to her. I also can't tell her the truth. No woman will want to hear that her dancing partner is being hunted, and I'm not ready to say goodbye to her. It's a moral quandary that I'm not prepared to deal with. I swallow hard, hoping this explanation is enough.

"I don't like hospitals."

I expect to get an argument from Lyla. She is a no-nonsense woman with no patience for that kind of drama. She's a loner, and I'm lucky she agreed to have me as a travel partner. I brace myself for a tongue-lashing that never comes. Instead, she nods in understanding.

"Okay," she says, touching my face with the caress of an angel. "Let's get you out of this one and hope you never need to see another."

Chapter Twenty

Overkill

Getting information in Braus's world is the easy part. The three best ways to obtain it are digital intrusion, bribes, and intimidation. Each of those tactics works equally well, depending on the circumstances. It really depends on what you're after and where.

Intimidation is the most fun, although the quality of information may suffer. People under duress will say anything to save their skins. It's why torture isn't usually the best technique to use. It may be effective at extracting intelligence, but a torturer risks being deceived if the information can't be easily confirmed.

Hacking is the newest way, but bribery is as old as time. Braus figures that even cavemen solicited each other for information about their neighbors. It's low risk with the potential for high return. The poorer the target, the stronger the appeal for a payoff. That's why third-world countries are so corrupt. For the right price, no piece of information is out of reach.

That's how they got the address of the hotel Braden is staying at. Computers alerted them to the name of the hospital. All it took to get the information he needed was finding the right nurse with access to a computer, a couple hundred Euros, and a good story. The truth doesn't work in these situations. Braus couldn't say that disclosing Braden's whereabouts would likely result in his death. Some people wouldn't care. A nurse would.

The problem is time. Braden checked out of the hospital over eighteen hours ago. Braus checks his watch. The second sextet of doomed bulls is about to make their last journey through the streets of Pamplona. It's not inconceivable that his target has already moved on, although he may have convinced himself it'd be too difficult to locate him in this mass of humanity.

Braden likely doesn't recognize the danger he's in. Most of Braus's quarry fails to understand how fast and efficient he is. Patience can be a virtue, or it can lead to failure. That's what happened in Key West. He made an assumption and didn't realize he was wrong until he dropped the rental car off at Miami International.

Given the extent of his injuries, Braden is in no condition to travel. He knows he's being hunted but is unable to do anything about it. He will likely be passed out in bed with Lyla Chance, whoever she is. Even after a few days, there's still no word from The Cossack on her backstory. That's also interesting.

The whole city was sauced last night, making the morning streets in this area of the city eerily quiet. Parties go late in the night during the Festival of San Fermín. Outside of those watching or participating in this morning's run, most people are still nursing hangovers.

That suits Braus fine as the driver pulls their van up outside the small, rundown hotel. It's probably a family-run business passed down through a few generations, with each passing one taking less and less interest in it. By its appearance, the first generation of owners was the last time any major renovations were done.

Braus climbs out of the passenger seat as the rear door opens and the team pours out. The driver will remain in the van and watch the street. The five men accompanying the German through the front door are armed and dressed for action. Body armor and rifles were swapped for shirts and handguns. They are not charging a fortified position in Ukraine. There is no need for heavy weapons.

Still, it's overkill. Chance favors the bold and the prepared. That was how the Cossack explained it when the team was dispatched to meet Braus in Pamplona. There is to be no more pussyfooting around in Braden Fox's apprehension. Arden Davenport is growing impatient. If the Cossack insists on giving him support, Braus plans on putting it to good use.

The men take their positions as Braus goes to the front desk with one of the team members. The middle-aged woman behind the counter is bored and not the least bit curious about the new arrivals.

"Good morning. I'm looking for Braden Fox."

The woman rattles something off in Spanish that Braus doesn't catch a word of. A team member turns to him to translate. He's already providing value.

"We don't disclose information about hotel guests."

It's the standard answer and not unexpected. There is no time for this. Braus draws his weapon and places the muzzle against the woman's forehead.

"How about now?"

The woman's eyes grow wide, and her body stiffens. He motions at the book on the desk with the weapon before retraining it on her. Slowly, she opens the massive volume that serves as the hotel's register. There must be thousands of names listed in there.

Small hotels don't work the same as large ones. They don't have the capital for upgrades, much less renovations. That means they haven't computerized their records yet. Braden is smarter than Braus thought. There is no digital fingerprint in a place like this.

"*Veinte-dos.*"

"Twenty-two," the translator confirms.

Braus removes his weapon from the startled woman's face. "Babysit her. Don't let her use the phone. We'll take care of this."

Three men accompany Braus up to the second floor. Room Twenty-Two is located just to the right of the stairs. There are only five rooms per floor, but it only takes frightened guests from one of them to call the *policia municipal.* They have to move quickly.

Each man knows his role. They stack along the wall, and Braus begins a count on his fingers as the breacher moves into position. When the final finger turns into a fist, the breacher leans back, raises his left leg, and violently plants the heel of his boot next to the door's lock. The door blasts inward, and Braus leads the men into the room.

Even without knowing the layout, assumptions can be made. The bed will be prominent. There will be a dresser, and maybe a small desk. The bathroom will be off to the side. Braus trains his weapon where he expects the bed to be as he charges in. But Braden and whoever Lyla is aren't in it.

"Search it."

The team does as instructed. The room is small, and the only possible hiding places are under the bed and in the bathroom. Nothing. Drawers are checked, as is the closet. There is no sign of their belongings, either. A rolling cot is folded and stowed in the corner.

"They're gone."

Braus squeezes the grip of his weapon tightly as he clenches his jaw. He turns and storms downstairs, the three men keeping several paces behind him. He strides around the counter and shoves the terrified woman against the wall. She pleads in Spanish as he shoves the muzzle under her eye. He doesn't understand her words, nor would he care what she's saying if he did.

"Where is Braden Fox?"

"*No se*," she whimpers.

"You said he was still checked in. Speak. *Habla.*"

She closes her eyes and turns her head to the side, stammering out words. Fear drips from her voice. Braus turns to the translator, who is still standing on the other side of the counter.

"No, she said that was his room number, and she just got on shift. He could have already left. She hasn't processed the morning checkouts yet."

Braus presses the muzzle harder into her face, causing her to cry. How could she not know if Braden checked out? It doesn't make sense, but he gives the woman one last chance to redeem herself.

"Tell her to find out."

She opens her eyes and points to a box next to the door. Braus removes the weapon, and she steadies herself before walking slowly back around the counter. Her legs move like they have weights attached. As a precaution, a man stands guard in front of the door to dispel any notions of running into the street screaming for help.

She opens the lock on a battered red box and raises the cover. Three sets of keys were deposited in the slot on the top. The woman retrieves them and holds them out. One has a red tag emblazoned with a white "22." Braden has already checked out.

"Damn it."

Guests emerge at the top of the stairs. It's time to go. Braus glares at them before storming out the front door and stopping on the sidewalk. Braden isn't coming back here. They were so close. How far could he have made it? How will he likely leave the city?

"How many train stations are there in Pamplona?" he asks the translator.

"Just one. *Estación de Tren de Pamplona.* The one we arrived at."

"Let's go."

It's a long shot, but it's their only real option. A bus or a rideshare could be anywhere. If Braden checked into a different hotel, they would have to cover the train station anyway while they searched the city. This just got harder.

"He may have already caught one," the translator says from the back of the van after they pile in. "Or he could have switched hotels."

"I'm aware of the options. Fox could also be sitting on a bench waiting for his train. Let's not assume anything. Maybe we'll get lucky, for once."

Chapter Twenty-One

Under The Stars

Our escape from Pamplona was a hasty one. The trip to France was easy enough. The hard part was avoiding the truth while explaining to Lyla why I wanted to leave. I don't know if Braus could track me to the hotel. I've seen the man work and assume he has the ability, even in a foreign country. If I'm right, leaving means we stay ahead of him. If I ignored that feeling and stayed…I don't want to think about what would happen if I was wrong.

Lyla is growing suspicious. She didn't understand why I didn't want to stay in Pamplona longer, but she reluctantly followed my lead. I figured the train ride would be an opportune time for her to challenge me, but it didn't come up. I only claimed to want a nice, quiet place to relax and recuperate. She only said she knew of just the spot. If I wanted secluded and off the grid, I got it in this forested area between Bordeaux and Saint-Émilion. We aren't staying in a hotel – we're sleeping under the stars.

After warmly meeting a man named Jacque, Lyla explained our situation to him in fluent French, and we were led down a path into the woods. At the edge of a small clearing are ten eco-friendly luxury bubble pods. They are self-contained tents constructed on stained wooden decks and equipped with creature comforts, including full-sized beds and bathrooms with running water, heat, electricity, and artificial lighting.

We moved past nine pods spaced thirty meters apart, seeing four equipped with outdoor Jacuzzis. They are very private but close enough for someone to respond to an emergency. We stop at the last one in the line.

Jacque explained to us the workings of the pod and brought a gourmet meal featuring French delicacies. There was foie gras, duck confit, crackers, various cheeses, and two bottles of local wine. It was all outstanding. I hadn't realized how hungry I was.

Lyla and I sip wine as the sun disappears behind the trees, and the late afternoon sky turns purple and then black. Now, stars light up the night sky, stretching across an expanse that marks our place in the Milky Way galaxy. No wonder people stay here – it's beautiful beyond compare. I don't see much of the night sky in New York City. Only the sparkle of the brightest stars finds a way through the light pollution.

"You've been here before?" I ask, taking a sip of my third glass of an amazing Cabernet Sauvignon.

"Once or twice. Why?"

"I don't know. You don't strike me as the glamping type."

"I'm not," she says with an amused shake of her head. "Most of my nights under the stars have been on the ground in a field filled with cows."

"Cows?"

"Yeah, as in moo. One time in the Netherlands, I woke up with one's head right in my face."

"That's intrusive."

Lyla grins. "Yeah, but I *was* sleeping in her field."

I'm not sure how I would react to that. I'd probably scream like a little girl, although I'm not about to admit that to her. I've never once slept outside. That trend isn't about to change. This is hardly roughing it.

"How did you learn about this place?"

She tilts her head skyward. "Jacque's son was a student at my art school. He brought me here when his father opened this place. It was long before 'glamping' was even a word. He said that, someday, rich Parisians would pay to do what most of humanity has done for millennia. He was right, except for needing to add a few modern conveniences.

"A friend brought you here? *Only* a friend?"

"Is that jealousy I hear in your voice?"

"Maybe."

"Okay, no, Sébastien was more than a friend. He was my first true love."

She tells the story of how they first met and how she really didn't like him. But he was charming and persistent, and she slowly warmed up to him. After a while, that fondness turned into something stronger. Only then could she admit that she was in love with him. By that point, they were almost inseparable.

"What happened?"

Lyla stares at the sky for several long moments. "Life got in the way."

"Sébastien moved on to something better?"

"No," she says, shifting in her lounge chair. "He died."

The revelation knocks the air out of my lungs. I didn't expect to hear that. Lyla wipes the tears forming in her eyes.

"I'm sorry. I didn't mean to drag up bad memories."

"It's okay. It was…an accident," Lyla says before falling silent for almost a minute. "I was devastated. For the longest time, I wasn't sure I could go on without him. It felt like I lost a piece of me that day."

An accident. Lyla forced those words out. I know she's holding something back, but I don't dare ask. My mind immediately thinks the worst – she killed Sébastien and has been on the run, evading law enforcement ever since. Could that be true? Could this amazingly vibrant and intelligent woman be capable of such a thing? Would she dare return to France if it was? I don't want the answer, but part of me does.

"Is that why you left art school?"

"Indirectly."

"And you kept in touch with his father after all these years."

"Not exactly. I haven't seen or talked to Jacque since after Sébastien's funeral. But he always considered me family. I knew he would welcome us here if there was space available."

"And if there wasn't?"

"He would have found some way to accommodate us. That's the kind of man he is. It's the kind of man his son was."

Different cultures. Different worlds. I can't imagine my parents doing that for almost anyone without there being some gain for them. If old, lifelong friends showed up at their doorstep, they would more likely be offered a few hundred dollars for a local hotel than clean sheets for the upstairs guest bedroom that's never been used.

"My turn. Since you now know about Jacque, what about your first love?"

"I told you that I'm boring. What makes you think I have one?"

She turns in her chair. "The picture in your wallet."

I knew this would come up. There was a glimmer of hope that my fears in the Pamplona hospital wouldn't be realized when she didn't bring the photo up at the hotel or during the train ride into France. I was beginning to think that maybe she didn't see it. I was wrong.

"Maybe it's my sister."

"Then you two are very...*close.*"

I have my arm around her, and her hands are on my chest. It's the kind of picture lovers take, not siblings. In fact, it looks like something from an engagement photo shoot. There is no way I can pass this off as anything other than what it is.

"Who is she?"

"Her name is Kinsey. The picture was taken in Central Park a few years ago. She's...well, she's the reason we met in Buenos Aires."

"Ah, she broke your heart."

"In a manner of speaking, yes."

It was far more than that. I'm hoping that is enough to drop the subject.

"How long were the two of you dating?"

I close my eyes. It's such a magical night. Everything about this journey has surpassed my wildest expectations. It was only a matter of time before the truth was revealed to Lyla. It was bound to happen. I only wish it weren't tonight. I take a deep breath and brace myself.

"We weren't dating. Kinsey is my wife."

Chapter Twenty-Two

Bad Intentions

The world stops around us. It feels like every star in the magnificent night sky is shrouded in a dense fog of uncertainty. I stare at Lyla's surprised eyes. Her mouth quivers before she swallows the words. Then, her face changes in the pale light from the electric lanterns on the wood deck.

"You're married?"

"Yes."

"You never told me that," she says, her voice low and hesitant.

"You never asked."

That was the exact wrong thing to say. I'm not good at this. Numbers have always made more sense to me than people do, so I've never pretended to be good at emotions. My political science degree was intended to help me understand the system. I should have taken more psychology classes to understand the people living under that system.

My intent isn't to upset Lyla. I didn't mean to be deceptive about this. I just have no adequate alternative. Unfortunately, I have no idea how to tell her that. She will have to live with whatever explanation I offer her, and I will live with the consequences.

"I feel so stupid," Lyla says, shaking her head. "I can't believe…why didn't you tell me?"

"There's a lot you don't know."

My jaw tightens. I stepped on another landmine. I should teach a course on things not to say to women. I would make a fortune.

"Apparently."

"My wife and I are over, Lyla," I say, trying to recover by only managing to sound desperate. Those are the words any man would say in this position. "That's why I was in Argentina."

"Over? You expect me to believe that?"

"It's the truth."

"You're lying!" Lyla shrieks, relying on her lifetime of experience with men who will say anything to get what they want. "No man keeps a photo of an ex in his wallet and stares at it every chance he gets when things are over."

"I don't do that!"

"Don't you? Isn't that photo what you were looking at when I stole your seat in Buenos Aires?"

I don't need to think that hard because staring at that photo is what I was doing. I hadn't realized Lyla even noticed. Back then, I doubt she cared. I was just a face in the crowd with some promise of being an adequate dance partner for five minutes.

"Yes, it was."

She nods slowly. I'm busted, but I didn't lie. If I had, it would have been the end of this conversation and then our agreement. We may still be talking, but the second part of that is still in jeopardy.

"Ask me why."

"It doesn't matter," she says, shaking her head.

"Ask me why, Lyla!" I shout.

"Fine! Why?"

"Because that was the life I knew. The one I was *comfortable* with. One that never saw me escape the bubble I sealed myself in. It continues to try to pull me back in. The only reason I haven't returned is you. That's why I asked for your help. That's why I still need it."

It is as honest as I can get. Lyla stares at me, measuring me for truthfulness. It's hard to read her face. I don't know how I scored. It should be a ten. But that's the problem with deceit and betrayal. Once trust is destroyed, a relationship never fully heals.

"I believe you," she admits, causing me to finally breathe. "But it's not good enough. You should have told me from the start."

"Why?" I ask, standing to burn off some nervous energy and hide my growing frustration. "What difference does it make? We're travel companions, not lovers; dance partners, not life partners. You made that crystal clear, and I have respected that decision."

She scoffs.

"Really? When? When have I ever violated the rules you set out? When have I tried to take advantage of you by stealing a kiss or worse? We have danced for hours. When have I ever done anything inappropriate?"

She can't argue with that. It's never even once happened. Any contact between us that could remotely be considered sexual was incidental and accidental. I have been the perfect gentleman, and Lyla knows it.

"You still should have told me."

Her voice is soft, ratcheting down the tension a couple of levels. I awkwardly rock back and forth on my feet.

"Everything I've told you about my past is true."

"Except for the things you leave out."

Something snaps in my head. I was trying to reconcile. I want to atone for not telling her about Kinsey. Lyla isn't accepting my explanation. That would be fine, but she set up these rules. We don't talk about the sordid things from our past. It was never an expectation, only she's forgotten that.

"It's more than I know about *you*," I say, heavy on the accusatory tone. "Why don't you tell me about your past, Lyla? Tell me some of your secrets!"

"What?"

"Tell me. Anything. You're so indignant that I don't share details about my life, so why don't you go ahead and divulge some of your own. Let's start with this: Why did you leave Paris? Why are you running?"

"I'm not running!"

"Bullshit. There are things you aren't telling me, either. What are you scared of?"

It's not the tactic I wanted to use, but that's what happens when I get upset. That doesn't mean I don't have a right to ask the question. Lyla is keeping plenty of things from me. A woman's life is a broad ocean of secrets, and she's under no obligation to tell me any of them. But that's also a two-way street.

She doesn't see it that way as she launches out of her chair. She stares off at the distant treeline, shaking her head in disbelief. When her eyes finally set on mine, they are filled with raw emotion.

"I'm done with this conversation. I'm done with you!"

Lyla storms off to the bubble tent, or whatever it is. She stops when she reaches the door. "Sleep outside tonight. I don't want you near me. We'll go our separate ways in the morning."

She enters and closes the door behind her. I'm not sure if it has a lock. It probably does, and now it's latched. None of the lights come on in the enclosure. If she's undressing, it's in the dark. Maybe that's another of her secret talents.

I'm not sure why I'm so angry. It's possible that I didn't expect Lyla to react this way. Or I did and was hoping she would be more understanding. I may have even thought that she would open up. None of that was to be.

I'm going to sleep under the stars for the first time in my life. On some level, I would be okay with that. Too bad it's an experience born from bad intentions.

Chapter Twenty-Three

Unexplained Actions

Travis watches Arden stare at the man. He's unhappy. The Cossack was twenty minutes late, and the head of American Outreach despises lack of punctuality. In his world, time is money, and wasting it is among the highest levels of disrespect.

Not that the Russian looks remotely fazed by the glaring. Travis only knows him by reputation. He is no-nonsense, as are the men in his employ. In his world, the mission is everything. That makes fanciful people like Davenport an affront to his sensibilities. Arden pays the bills, however, so he is forced to tolerate the man.

"Any time you're ready," Arden says, gesturing impatiently.

"I expected this meeting to be conducted in private. Why are your secretaries here?"

Travis's jaw clenches. He considers himself many things, but a simple clerk is not among them. He and Ilana are anything but minor functionaries. They are among the biggest cogs in this money-making machine.

"Travis Breckinridge and Ilana Horowitz are valued members of my team. While you are tracking Braden around the world and coming up empty, they are assisting in other ways."

"What other ways?" the Russian asks in a heavy accent.

"What happened in Spain?" Arden asks, not entertaining questions from someone he considers a vendor, not an equal.

The Cossack grimaces. "Braden Fox was admitted to a hospital in Pamplona."

"Admitted for what?" Ilana asks from her seat beside Travis.

"A dislocated shoulder, bruised ribs, and lacerations to his face."

"What, did he get mugged or something?" Travis muses.

"He was caught in a pile-up and almost trampled while running with the bulls on the first day of the fiesta."

"What?"

"I'm sorry. Did I stutter?"

No, he didn't stutter. Travis shakes his head. The idea of Braden running with the bulls is preposterous. The most reckless thing his friend has ever done was get a shiatsu message instead of a Swedish at the spa. There was no way he was running down narrow cobblestone streets with massive bulls chasing him.

"You're telling me Braden Fox is at the Saint Fermín Festival?" Arden asks. He almost sounds impressed underneath the annoyance and surprise.

"Yes, at least he was there. He likely took a train there after arriving in Madrid."

"Travis, does that sound like Braden to you?"

"No…no, it doesn't."

"Ilana?"

She shakes her head. "Not a chance."

The Cossack smiles. It's not broad or toothy. It isn't a smile of happiness, joy, or even amusement. Travis sees knowledge behind the grin. Arden notices it, too, but he won't ask the reason behind it. Inquiries like that show weakness.

"He wasn't at the hospital when your man arrived?" Arden presses.

"No, he had already been discharged. His injuries were not as severe as other runners. Braus tracked him to his hotel room. He was gone by the time they moved in."

Arden scoffs. "How much did that cost me?"

"Your Braden Fox is either very smart or very lucky. Braus is skilled…and determined."

"All evidence to the contrary," Travis mumbles.

It was a little too loud. The Cossack turns to Travis and studies him. He meets the Russian's stare, although he isn't as confident as he was five seconds ago. With that stare, the man could melt ice cream in the dead of winter.

"You know Braden Fox?"

"We are friends…were friends."

"Then maybe you can explain why he would travel to South America and then to Spain?"

"I don't know. The only place I've ever seen Braden go is to Hawaii on his honeymoon. He rarely leaves the city, much less does he travel around the world."

"So, it is out of character?"

"Completely," Ilana answers.

"That's why I think he could be meeting with the government," Travis declares. "He can't hope to provide them information here without us knowing. It's the only reason he would travel to foreign countries."

"I see," The Cossack says, leaning back in his chair. "This information…have you noticed any unusual activities?"

Travis can't tell the truth. The big Russian is already fishing. He doesn't want to be the first fish to take a bite at the bait.

"We're still searching."

The Cossack smiles. "That is a no. And you?"

"No," Ilana says, swallowing hard. "I've quietly enquired with all his clients. None of them seem to know anything about his sudden disappearance."

"We work with liars, Ilana. Somebody knows. Braden must have something," Arden concludes.

"Yes, he does. He has you all fooled."

The three members of American Outreach exchange glances. For Travis and Ilana, it's one of confusion. Arden's face wears something closer to anger.

"Excuse me?"

The Russian stares at Arden. "Who is Lyla Chance?"

The name. That's why he smiled at Arden when Ilana said, "Not a chance." He had been waiting to ask this question and was amused that it came out of Ilana's mouth. There was knowledge behind it, but even a poker player who knows he has the best cards will grin at the end of the hand.

"How would I know?" Arden says, returning the glare.

The Cossack shifts his gaze at Ilana, who shrugs. Travis has no idea who she is, so he doesn't need to put on a front. The name is one of millions worldwide that he's never heard.

"We don't know a Lyla Chance," Arden says, growing even more impatient. "Is she a government contact? One of my competitors?"

"No, she's a ghost. There is no current record of her. She has no address, employer, social media profile, or phone number…she doesn't exist."

"Then it's an alias," Arden offers.

The Cossack shifts in his chair and brushes some lint off his shirt. It's theatrics. While he may be no-nonsense, he does like to make a point. He doesn't believe they don't know who Lyla Chance is.

"Perhaps. However, an alias does not attend a prestigious art school in Paris. That is the last known location of anyone matching her name and age."

"It could be a coincidence. A stolen identity. What does it matter?"

"That is who Braden Fox is traveling with. According to Brazilian customs information, she boarded the plane with him to Spain. The staff at the hospital remembers him being accompanied by a woman. The clerk at the hotel confirms that information."

"They stayed in the same hotel room?" Arden seethes.

The Russian notices his odd reaction to that piece of information. Why the hell would Arden Davenport give a damn that one of his employees is stepping out on his wife? If only he knew the truth.

"Apparently, she is quite lovely."

"That's not the point! He's married!"

"Arden, marriage is tricky. Not everything is always as it appears. You're not naïve enough to believe that married men do not cheat. Isn't that right, Travis?"

He swallows hard. "I wouldn't know. I'm still single."

The Russian narrows his eyes and smiles. "Of course."

Travis's spine begins to tingle. He wants to be anywhere but in this room with this man. He doesn't know how much The Cossack has learned, but it's something. And any crumb of evidence is bad news.

"Do you know where Braden went?"

"He's no longer in Pamplona. Based on the train schedules, he may have headed to Germany or Italy. Or he could still be in Spain. Braus is searching CCTV footage at the station to determine what train he boarded. Then, we can anticipate his next move."

"Find him. Soon," Arden demands.

"Of course. We will also look into this Lyla Chance woman. Perhaps your…colleagues can do the same?"

"Naturally. Travis, Ilana…this is your primary responsibility. I want to know who that woman is and who she is working for."

"Keep me informed. I will be sure to do the same," The Cossack says, rising from his seat and leaving the office.

Travis and Ilana are both excused. She has to race to a meeting and heads to the right after walking out the door. Travis heads left and bumps into The Cossack, who paused to tie a shoe just outside the office.

"Excuse me. Apologies," Travis weakly offers.

"I don't abide liars, Mr. Breckinridge," he says in a near-whisper after standing and leaning in close to Travis. "Especially ones who lie to their boss…and to me."

The man is a walking threat. Everything about him is intimidating. He isn't to be trifled with, but he isn't a priest either. This is no time for confession.

"I'm not lying."

"You are," the Russian says with a smile. "I strongly suggest you don't let me find out about what, or any apology you offer won't suffice."

Travis watches the man walk away. He doesn't look back the way someone who lacks confidence would. That may be the most intimidating thing of all.

Chapter Twenty-Four

Surprising Verdict

I'm never awake before dawn. My job demands long hours, but that means late nights, not early mornings. I don't remember the last time I was conscious before the sun came up. My eyes clicked open at 4:30 this morning, mostly because sleeping in a wood patio chair isn't exactly a night at the Four Seasons.

Fortunately, the morning air is fresh, and everything is still. It feels like the world around me has completely stopped. There isn't a sound, even from the woods.

Waking up this early gives me a chance to sit back and witness one of the most beautiful events nature can provide. Sunrise offers a new beginning. It's a chance to start over and appreciate a new day. I'm not sure how much I will appreciate this one, but I push that thought out of my mind.

Slowly, the orange and yellow ball begins to appear above the horizon. The sky turns into a fruit salad — the colors of oranges, lemons, and grapefruit. The tall pines of this forest still block its rays. As the sun slowly creeps higher into the morning sky, the colors become even more vibrant. It's going to be a beautiful day.

I check the fire next to me. The last of the logs has burned down to glowing embers. I managed to keep the fire going for warmth through the night, and now the coals are the main source of the heat. Even in summer air, the nighttime chill compelled me to build a fire and wrap myself in a blanket to keep the morning dew off me. In a couple of hours, it will be warm enough not to matter.

It was more comfortable than I thought it would be. My back is stiff, but some light stretching when I woke was enough to get some of the kinks out. I am staring at the sky when I hear the pod door open. I hear the pattering of Lyla's footfalls before she sits in the chair beside mine. I don't bother looking at her. There's nothing to say.

The silence grows more uneasy with each passing second. I half expect Lyla to ask something stupid, like how I slept. I must look pathetic, so the question answers itself. Or she could tell me to get my things and leave. That would be mercy. It would end the awkwardness.

"I'm sorry," she says in a near-whisper.

It's not what I expected to hear. I've been playing this moment out in my head since before the sun started its daily march across the sky. In all the scenarios I imagined, not one of them began with an apology. It's thrown me off.

"Sleeping outside wasn't as bad as I thought. It was quite peaceful, actually."

"No, I'm sorry for getting angry with you. I was wrong."

I'm speechless. I've been dating on and off since I was fourteen. Despite my focus on college and a career, women seem to enter my orbit without my trying. There is one universal truth about every one of those relationships: Never once did I hear a love interest say those words. Maybe because they couldn't admit they were wrong. Maybe because they never were. Regardless, this is a first.

"Say something, Braden."

"I'm…just caught off-guard. You were pretty angry last night. You made it clear that this journey is over."

I hazard a look at Lyla. Her eyes are red and puffy from crying. Or she has allergies.

"You and Kinsey…I didn't handle that well. I guess I made assumptions about you and got a little freaked out when I found out one of them wasn't true."

"Lyla, I never meant to keep it from you."

Okay, that's a lie. I'm going to pass it off as a harmless one. I didn't want Lyla to know because I was afraid of this reaction. Right or wrong, that's how I reasoned it. The closer we got, the harder the truth was to tell.

"I know. You said that you left because of her?"

"Yes. My marriage is over. All that's left is the paperwork."

There's much more to the story, but that's all I'm willing to say. Lyla doesn't want to talk about her past. I'm not about to reveal the sordid details of mine.

"Okay."

I'm not the only one holding back. I sense that Lyla has more to say but remains quiet. It's a lousy way to end things. It's a worse way to move forward. I have feelings for Lyla. They hit me like a brick on that Argentinian dance floor and have only grown stronger since. Maybe getting out now is the best thing. Our secrets will destroy us if I don't.

I stand, willing my sore, stiff joints to work. I remove the blanket and drop it in the chair.

"Thank you, Lyla. For everything. I'll go pack my things so you can move on."

I take a step toward the pod, and that's as far as I get. Lyla leans over in her chair and grabs my arm. She looks at me with pleading eyes.

"Don't. Don't go. Please."

I want to scream. Lyla couldn't get away from me fast enough last night. I slept outside because of it. Now, when I'm ready and willing to give her exactly what she wants, she tells me not to go. What the hell? This woman is the queen of mixed signals.

"I swear, Lyla, I don't know what you want."

I sounded a little more exasperated than I meant to. Lyla stands, avoiding eye contact as she collects her thoughts. I don't rush her or try to influence her in any way. The next move is hers. I'm happy to stand here and wait for her to make it.

"Simple. I want us to continue our journey together."

"Why?"

"You asked me to be your guide," she says. "You said you needed me to show you the world. I didn't agree out of charity or because of your striking good looks. The truth is, Braden, I need a companion as much as you do."

I don't understand. I'm probably not meant to. Fate brought this woman into my life at the exact moment I needed her most. Now, it's messing with me. I desperately want to ask why she wants me to stay, but I'm afraid to know the answer. It's more important to me that she does. I choose to go in a different direction.

"You think I have striking good looks?"

"Stop it," she says, smiling as she slaps my chest. "Don't let it go to your head. You're a solid five. Maybe a six when you clean up."

"Good to know. I'll take it."

This isn't the verdict I expected. I thought I would be on my own from here on out. At least until Braus manages to catch up to me. I've learned a lot from her since that fateful tango. It doesn't mean I'm ready to travel the world on my own, but at least I wouldn't be as completely helpless as I was in South America.

I can't help but wonder if she knows what this means for us. It's going to be awkward. We aren't going to talk about the past – at least outside of the superficial stuff or harmless stories we tell to polite company. We both have secrets. That's how it looks like they will remain.

"Come on, let's not make Jacque lug breakfast all the way out here. He has the best croissants outside Paris. After we eat, we can head to Bordeaux. We have a train to catch."

"To where?"

Lyla looks at me with her enchanting eyes. "Our next adventure."

Chapter Twenty-Five

The Walls Go Up

Lyla still won't tell me where we're going. I figured we would continue heading east once we reached Zurich, but instead, we boarded a southbound train to Lucerne, the gateway to central Switzerland. Not that I'm complaining. If I can't figure out where we're heading, I assume that Braus can either. Then again, we all know the adage about assumptions.

Situated on Lake Lucerne, the small city has beautiful buildings and an impressive mountainous panorama. The breathtaking lakeside setting and nearby peaks make the town a must-see travel destination for tourists. There is no shortage of them here.

Lyla and I amble down Lucerne's cobblestone streets and past historic houses decorated with frescoes. The beautiful residences line picturesque town squares and streets in the automobile-free city. We pass a 17th-century Jesuit church widely regarded as Switzerland's first sacral Baroque building. Or so the sign read.

It's been a pleasant day, or at least as pleasant as we can make it. Things are still awkward between us. The conversation on the train rides from Bordeaux to Paris, the French capital to Zurich, and then to here was forced and uncomfortable. Thank God I slept through some of the trip. It was my only reprieve. We are both trying to get back to where we were before she learned about Kinsey, and we both are failing to find our way.

Despite her assurances to the contrary, it bothers her. I don't know why, considering she has repeatedly made it clear that there's no hope for a deeper relationship between us. I've accepted that, at least as much as I'm willing to. I still hold a sliver of hope even though it's likely futile.

We stroll to the medieval Chapel Bridge and admire its remaining gable paintings after the fire that destroyed much of the bridge a few decades ago. The rebuilt landmark is the centerpiece of Lucerne's townscape and is considered to be one of the oldest covered wooden bridges in Europe. We stop mid-span to admire the buildings lining the Reuss River's north bank. A few tourists amble past us, but we have much of this portion of the bridge to ourselves.

"This may be the prettiest city I've ever been in."

"It's one of the prettiest in the whole world," Lyla says, also admiring the view. "I should take you to Bruges, Belgium. It gives Lucerne a run for its money."

"Have you ever been here before?"

"Once, a long time ago."

I turn to look at her. "Alone?"

The question slips out, and I regret asking it the moment it escapes my mouth. How many times am I going to tap dance on the edge of that cliff before I fall off once and for all?

"No, but you probably already guessed that," Lyla says before I can take the question back. At least she did me the favor of answering with an amused smirk.

There's no point in putting the genie back in the bottle, so I return to staring at the buildings along the river and the majestic peaks in the distance behind them. Not that I'm ungrateful to Lyla for bringing me here, but I have no idea why she did. It's starting to irk me.

"Are we dancing here?"

"No. This is only a stop along the way. I wanted good chocolate."

That box got checked less than an hour after we stepped off the train. Switzerland is practically synonymous with chocolate, and some of the best is made in Lucerne. Chocolatiers in this city work with unsurpassed passion, and their labors will satisfy even the most discerning sweet tooth.

"Okay," is all I manage to say when a lone figure walking on the bridge catches my eye.

I instantly freeze up as a man approaches. He has the height, the swagger…and the hair. A surge of electricity charges my muscles. I can't make out his face, but I have a sinking feeling that Braus has finally caught up to me.

My fight-or-flight instinct kicks in as adrenaline gushes into my bloodstream. I turn to look back the way we came. I could make a run for it. I could leave Lyla standing here and make one final mad dash and hope for the best. Walking around the city might have provided me with enough local knowledge to elude him. Not that it would do any good. Braus is a tracker. How long will it be before he finds me?

I turn and watch the figure continue to approach us. The man is calm, almost strolling as the distance between us closes. It isn't the determined stride I expected. I take a deep breath. It's too late to run. Accepting my fate is the only option.

A wave of relief washes over me as the man grows close enough for me to make out his face. He could be Braus's cousin, but it isn't the German hunting me. I exhale sharply, turning to see a concerned look on Lyla's face.

"Braden, are you okay?"

"I'm fine," I croak.

"Are you sure? You look like you're on the verge of a nervous breakdown."

I force a smile. "Everything is fine. I promise."

Lyla turns to watch Braus's doppelganger walk past us without a care in the world.

"How much longer are you going to walk on eggshells around me?"

"What do you mean?"

"You know what I mean, Braden."

She's right. It was a stupid question.

"I'm sorry. I just…I don't know where I stand with you. You're flirtatious yet distant…playful yet serious. You were going to leave in France and then suddenly changed your mind the next morning."

"And I apologized to you for that."

"I know. I guess I'm on guard, waiting for the next bomb to drop."

It was an honest explanation, if not a complete one.

"What makes you think there will be one?" she asks, turning her body to stand directly in front of me.

"Because the U.S. Air Force drops fewer of them than you do. Lyla, there is a part of your life you refuse to talk about. I'm okay with that. We agreed to keep our pasts in the past. I only wonder if the things we don't tell each other will catch up with us again."

It was as vague as I could get. Unfortunately, I *know* my past will. I cannot run forever. Who knows what Lyla is running from? She has said it's nothing, but I don't believe her. At least, I don't think I do.

Lyla places her hand on my cheek. Her touch still makes me tingle.

"We all have demons, Braden. I've done my best to exorcise mine. I know you're trying to do the same. It doesn't matter what our backstories are. The person you see in front of you is me. The real me."

I look deep into her captivating eyes. Lyla inches her face closer to mine, and I do the same. She looks as if she is expecting me to kiss her, but at the same time, she seems conflicted by it. So am I. I want nothing more than to kiss this woman, but it's not a good idea. Fortunately, she pulls away before the devil on my shoulder talks me into it.

"There is another thing. Do you remember when I said we weren't going to have a physical relationship? There's a reason for that."

My heart sinks despite expecting this. "What reason?"

"I don't want you to fall for me."

"Does this have to do with your past?"

Lyla bites her lip and shakes her head slowly. "Past, present, and future. Promise you won't."

How can I make that promise? I already have. Kinsey consumed my every thought in Key West. The appeal of getting my old life back, courtesy of the Engineer, is the driving force behind this journey. But then I danced a tango.

Ever since, I think of my wife less and less. The picture has come out of the wallet rarely, if ever, since Pamplona. Time may heal wounds, but the recovery from this heartbreak should be measured in years, not weeks. Lyla is the reason for my healing because I experienced the rarest of all emotions in Buenos Aires: Love at first sight.

"Okay. But what happens if you fall in love with me?" I ask, trying to play it cool.

Lyla closes her eyes for a moment and then opens them. When she looks at me again, her eyes are pleading. There is pain behind them. And regret. It's part of a backstory I am likely never going to hear.

"Promise me."

I'm left with no choice. "Okay. I promise. But you didn't answer my question."

Lyla forces a slight smile. Again, with the mixed signals. She takes my hand and winks at me as we amble back across the bridge.

"I know."

Chapter Twenty-Six

Leveled Threats

The driver lets The Cossack out in front of a building with a regal façade of white bricks and ledges, floral relief carvings, and tall Greek columns. It's tame compared to other, more ostentatious structures on the Upper West Side that feature carved balconies and marble windowsills. He could never live in a place like this.

A doorman smiles after adjusting the cuffs of his uniform. It's another luxury that's emblematic of the entire building – everything is "form over function." He could see the utility of an armed doorman who's trained in a martial art. That would be beneficial in a crisis. Instead, this man spends his time scanning the street and sidewalk for residents returning home. Once they show up at the door, it's his job to open it. In truth, he's nothing more than a glorified Walmart greeter employed to make the people who spend a fortune to live here feel special.

The man opens the door, an activity that sums up his meager existence, and welcomes the Russian to the building. The Cossack steps into a vestibule covered in burgundy carpeting and adorned with flower bushes and a golden umbrella holder. He passes into the lobby and admires the crystal and gold chandelier as it casts a dim light over the lobby's red velvet couches and antique mirrors.

The other doorman mans a shiny wooden desk in the center of the room. He's dressed in a matching blue suit with gold finishings, with the building's address embroidered where the breast pocket would typically be. His gold nameplate reads "George," and The Cossack uses his name as he politely makes his request.

"I'm sorry, sir, Ms. Fox isn't receiving visitors. She has left strict instructions that she isn't to be bothered. I can take your name and let her know you stopped by."

The Cossack leans against the desk. "This is not a request to see Ms. Fox. This is me telling you that I *am* going to see her."

"I don't think you're in a position to make demands, sir," George says, straightening.

"And you're not in a position to refuse them."

"Very well. I'm calling the police."

George lifts the handset of his phone and is about to press a speed dial button when The Cossack deftly presses down on the plastic handset sensor in the cradle to disconnect the line.

"You don't want to do that, George. The average police response time in this neighborhood has been increasing for years. It's up to almost seven minutes, even in this swanky part of the city. Now, the muzzle velocity of my SIG Sauer P320 here is a whisper under twelve hundred feet per second," the Russian says, pulling out his gun and holding it in front of George so he can see the weapon's beautiful shape in all its forged steel glory. "What do you think will arrive first: New York's Finest or the bullet I send crashing through your skull?"

The Cossack doesn't need to point the weapon at the lowly doorman. Just the sight of it has caused him to go pale. Legal gun ownership isn't a thing in New York City. It makes having a firearm compelling. People do what you want them to.

He's keenly aware that there likely are cameras pointed at him. It would be a prudent security measure, even in one of this city's safer neighborhoods. None of the cameras are obvious to avoid offending the sensibilities of their high-class residents. Everyone wants to be protected, but nobody likes the feeling of being watched.

"I'm a simple man, George. I see things in black and white. I don't want to hurt you, but you have a choice to make. You will allow me to have a conversation with Ms. Fox, or you'll become an obstacle that needs to be removed. Which is it?"

"The safety of our residents is our primary concern," George croaks after swallowing hard.

"Of course. I understand. Then allow me to reassure you that I'm not here to harm her in any way. I'm only here to talk. You have my word."

The Cossack makes a goodwill gesture by holstering the weapon. He gives George a cold, hard look. It's the advantage of being Russian. Most people find the stare and the accent intimidating.

"I…I can get in a lot of trouble," the doorman says, fidgeting as he breaks eye contact.

"You won't. Trust me, Ms. Fox will not say a word about this. Now, do I have your cooperation?"

George nods over his shoulder. "Go on up. Seventh floor."

"Thank you for your cooperation. I will be back in ten minutes. I would strongly suggest you don't inform the authorities. They may take me out in handcuffs, but I will make bail and then hunt down you and every one of your family members. I won't be gentle with you or them. Don't let it come to that, George. I'm already a busy man."

The doorman nods. Properly leveled threats always have better outcomes than outright violence. Fear is a powerful motivator, and The Cossack is in a results-oriented business. In some respects, he wishes that were reversed. It'd be more fun to shoot the man.

The Russian takes the elevator to the floor. He already knows which residence is hers and moves directly to the door. This building didn't skimp on the woodworking. Each of the doors leading off this elevator foyer is framed by ornate wood trim and columns. It's just another example of the form over function that plagues this building…and this country.

A sharp rap on the door causes movement he can hear on the other side.

"George? Is that you?" a woman says from behind the door before opening it. She stops stone-cold when she sees the Russian standing at her threshold.

"No, Ms. Fox, it's not George."

"Who are you?"

Kinsey Fox is a beautiful woman. At least Braden has taste. Her long, reddish hair sweeps down her slender neck to her shoulders. She's thin but has curves in the right places. Her chest isn't large, but it's enough to bulge out the front of her thin floral robe that travels to mid-thigh. She also has amazing legs that must look incredible when shaped by a pair of high heels. Unfortunately, she's barefoot, so The Cossack needs to use his imagination.

"I own a consulting firm in the employ of American Outreach. May I come in?"

"Do I have a choice?" Kinsey says, crossing her arms.

"No."

He enters the apartment but doesn't travel past the foyer. He doesn't need to see the residence beyond his vision. The space is well-decorated with high-end furnishings and accents. The couple knows how to live in the lap of luxury.

"What is this about?"

The Cossack offers an incredulous look at the demand. "Are you unaware that your husband is missing?"

Kinsey lowers her eyes and stares at her bare feet. "Is he dead?"

"Would you be relieved if he was?"

"He left me…. I didn't catch your name."

That's the kind of game people play when they don't want to answer the question. It's meant to do two things: buy time and divert attention. It won't work.

"I didn't tell you my name. Answer my question."

"I would be devastated," she says, indignantly thrusting her jaw out. "But I'm angry. Braden left me and didn't give a reason why."

A wry smile snakes its way across the Russian's lips. "Perhaps he didn't need to."

"Excuse me?"

It was the type of indignant response he expected from the woman. "Despite perceptions that I'm an idiot because of my foreign accent, rest assured, Ms. Fox, I am not. You know exactly why your husband left, even if his employer doesn't."

She clutches her robe and shakes her head. "I don't."

Most people have no idea how obvious it is that they're lying. Body language is a dead giveaway. Con artists and natural liars overcome those tells, but ordinary people think their words will be taken at face value. Never listen to what someone says. Always watch their expressions and actions. There is truth in movement.

"You're lying. Normally, I wouldn't care, despite my distaste for being disrespected in such a manner."

"I'm not lying," Kinsey insists. "I resent this questioning and demand you leave."

The Cossack leans closer to her and raises an eyebrow. "Or else?"

"I will call George and have him phone the authorities."

Most people would pick up a phone and call the police themselves. He can't help but be amused at her seeming inability to dial 9-1-1. Rich people can't do anything for themselves.

"Your doorman and I had a chat about that very subject. I think you'll find him less than cooperative in that matter. In the interest of time, I will leave as you requested. Just understand something – I *will* learn the truth."

"You've delivered your message. Now get out."

The arrogance of this woman is astounding. Does she really think she can make demands? Who the hell does she think she is? Like most children of rich elites, she desperately needs to be taught a lesson on how the real world works.

The Cossack steps closer to her, causing Kinsey to retreat until she reaches the foyer's wall. He opens his jacket so she can see the weapon in its holster. Her eyes dart from the gun to the rest of the room as she frantically searches for an escape. There is none. The Russian runs his hand down her silk robe, grazing one of her breasts.

"You are a beautiful woman, Ms. Fox. There are fates in this world far worse than death. I can make most of them a reality. I know many men who would love to sample your…offerings. Don't force me to take such an extreme measure."

"I asked you to leave."

"No, you ordered me to get out. Somehow, you think your money makes you better than me…more important than me." The corner of his mouth curls. "It doesn't."

The Cossack takes two steps back before spinning on his heels and walking to the door. He stops before opening it, turning his head to the side so she can hear him. He doesn't need to stare her in the eyes to make this point clear.

"I suggest you share the truth before I learn it on my own. Your husband will be found. Whether he returns to your side or you attend his funeral is up to you. Good day, Ms. Fox."

The Cossack leaves and takes the elevator down to the lobby. George is still behind the desk and eyes him warily as he passes.

"She's safe and sound. Call upstairs to confirm that if you'd like."

The man doesn't move. He may phone her, but it won't be while The Cossack is still in the building.

The Russian climbs into the car and stares out the window as the driver takes off. Kinsey Fox handed him another piece of the puzzle. She knows far more than she's saying. She may even know the full reason behind Braden's sudden disappearance. Now, it's just a matter of extracting that information from her to prove his suspicions.

Chapter Twenty-Seven

Lions & Shadows

This place draws a crowd. The Lion of Lucerne is one of the most famous and controversial monuments in Switzerland and remains a political flashpoint two centuries after its dedication. The massive ten-meter-long sandstone monument of a lion impaled with a spear is located behind a pool of water on a hill just outside the old city. The proud animal is depicted in his death throes, resting his front paw on a shield adorned with the French monarchy's fleur-de-lis and next to a second shield bearing the Swiss cross.

The memorial honors the sacrifice of the Swiss Guards who defended the king of France during the capture of the Tuileries Palace. The event marked a turning point in the French Revolution, resulting in the eventual fall of the monarchy and the beginning of the Reign of Terror. I didn't see the problem with the memorial.

Lyla and I found a local willing to explain the controversy to us. The names inscribed on the monument are those of officers who died. The number "760" etched into the stone refers to the number of guards who were killed, and the "350" is the number who survived.

He explained that the number of victims is doubtful, but it was the image of Switzerland conveyed by the lion that stirred up the populace. The monument seemed to glorify a conservative, counter-revolutionary Switzerland. Some people saw this monument as a reminder of close ties with a foreign power at a time when they were trying to create an independent country.

I doubt any of the tourists here even understand the debate, even when a tour guide tries to explain it. Most of those who do understand won't care. All they see is a beautiful statue of a lion carved into a stone cliff in a perfect setting. I think it's much ado about nothing, but I'm not Swiss. I only want to appreciate being here.

We don't have cameras of our own, so we have some fun taking pictures of the dozens of tourists milling around. I'm useless behind a camera, whether it's a professional DSLR or a mobile device. Lyla has an eye for it, though. What I am good at is arranging fun poses. The tourists we meet are gushing about how great the pictures come out. Maybe I missed my calling.

It's a relaxing activity on a beautiful summer day. The temperature is in the high seventies, and there is a slight breeze coming off the lake. Our "Fun with Tourists" session has done its job cutting through some of the awkwardness that followed us from France. Then, it returns with a vengeance.

Lyla turns toward the benches and immediately turns her back to them, hiding her face. The action isn't what I expected, but it isn't alarming, either. It's the look she's wearing that I recognize. It's the same one I wore in Key West: fear. She saw something that spooked her.

"We need to leave."

I look over at the benches and don't see anything overly frightening. A husband and wife are sitting with a child who's eating ice cream. A pair of teenagers is on their cell phones, probably posting pictures they just took on social media. A man is sitting there, his arm extended along the back of the bench, looking as relaxed as can be.

"I thought you wanted—"

"Right now, Braden, please!"

Lyla grabs my hand and practically pulls me along as she strides back toward the park's entrance. She moves so that I'm between her and the benches. I still have no idea why she's suddenly so scared. I've never known her to be anything but in complete control. This is very new.

"Lyla, what's wrong?"

"Nothing. We just need to go."

We swiftly move out of the park. I can't get over how paranoid she is. Lyla looks behind us after every ten steps as we walk. I hazard a glance over my shoulder and don't see anything unusual. It's getting close to peak tourist visiting hours, and all I see are families and groups of friends.

"Lyla, what's going on? Tell me."

She presses her lips together before speaking. "I saw someone. Someone I'd rather not see."

"Who?"

"It doesn't matter."

We continue our walk south down Löwengartenstrasse. Feeling like we aren't in any immediate danger, I grab her arm lightly and move her behind a building to duck out of sight of the park's entrance. I check to see if we're being followed. Thankfully, it doesn't look like we are.

"Lyla, are you in trouble?"

"No, it's nothing like that. It's complicated. My family…he's someone from my past. Somehow, we always seem to end up in the same city when I'm in Europe. He feels like a shadow, so that's what I call him. That's why I was in South America. I needed to get away for a while."

"Is he dangerous?"

It's a legitimate question. I'm not scared. I already have a dangerous psychopath chasing me, so I've gotten over that feeling. It's just that I can't protect her, at least in any meaningful way. I haven't been in a scrap since that one incident at recess in fifth grade. Any hand-to-hand combat with an assailant with even basic skills would be laughingly one-sided and not in my favor.

"No. He's not dangerous. The shadow is an unpleasant reminder of things I'd rather forget."

I study her eyes and know Lyla isn't telling the whole truth. Her rule about not talking about the past now makes more sense. It benefitted her as much as it did me. I have my own secrets and am not in a rush to change that rule after what happened in France. I won't press her on this.

"We should get out of Lucerne. It's a small city. If this Shadow guy is following you, we shouldn't make it easy for him. We'll go straight to the train station."

"What about our clothing?" Lyla asks.

"It's nothing we can't replace. We have our passports on us, and I paid in advance for the hotel, so that's covered."

She nods in agreement, and we set off again. We pass the bus station, picking up our gait and making short work of the twelve-minute walk to the Bahnhof Luzern. When we reach the train station, it's a mob scene. People are everywhere. I expect this in a big city like Munich, but this is Lucerne. It feels like someone issued an evacuation order.

"Jesus," I moan. "Is every tourist in this city leaving at the same time? It's going to take two hours to get to the counter."

"Go get tickets from the machine," Lyla says, pointing at the vending machines along the wall with a line that isn't terribly shorter. "I'll see what I can do to cut this line to get to the counter."

"How do you plan on managing that?"

She bats her eyelashes at me and peers at me with seductive eyes. Point taken.

"Lyla! Where are we going?" I shout as she heads for a uniformed man near the counter. I need a destination.

"Vienna."

I join the line to use the ticket machines. When my turn finally comes, I enter the destination and go to pay. Then, the first problem arises: The machine doesn't take cash. I should have known. I don't want to use a card, even if it's a pre-paid variety. We've gotten this far using cash. I don't know what capabilities Braus has in tracking other financial means.

With no other option, I dip a debit card into the slot. I don't think this one is traceable. I can't recall if I've used it. Maybe once. We should be okay. At least, that's what I tell myself.

The machine spits out two tickets to Vienna via Zurich and a connection in Munich. Armed with the strips of paper, I head back to the massive line to meet Lyla. She comes around from the far side of the counter with a pair of tickets of her own.

"I got us two tickets. First class. The train leaves in fifteen minutes."

"Perfect! I'm impressed."

"Swiss men are like the rest – they can't resist helping a damsel in distress. Come on."

We find the platform, board the correct car, and settle into our seats. The train eases out of the station and begins to accelerate away from the city. Part of me is sad to see Lucerne go. I would have liked to have more time exploring.

"Are you going to ask me about the shadow?" Lyla asks.

I look at her for a long moment before looking back out the window. I want to. But it'd be hypocritical, and I don't know if I want to know the answer.

"No."

"Why not?"

I need to change the subject and force a smile. "I'm more concerned about what you have planned for us in Austria's capital."

Chapter Twenty-Eight

Ambush

His rumbling stomach was something he could no longer ignore. The train isn't due to pull into the station for another fifteen minutes, so Braus opts to avail himself of the takeaway foods like pastries and sandwiches sold from the kiosks on the train platform level. He skips the one selling fruit and opts for the more traditional German fare of sausage and potatoes. He loves being home.

Munich Main Train Station, known to the locals as the Munich Hauptbahnhof, is close to Marienplatz in the center of the city. The station is one of Germany's largest and provides both regional and international service, along with connections to the S-Bahn. It is one of the three stations with long-distance services in Munich and sees just under a half-million passengers a day.

Most of those travelers are roaming around like clueless zombies. They have good cause to look dazed and overwhelmed – this place is massive and confusing to navigate. Besides the trains that chug to far-flung locations, this is also a main transit hub for underground and suburban lines, airport buses, and trams. The only way to get from point A to point B is to look at the signs and not blindly hope you can stumble into where you want to be.

The station has multiple levels, with the underground trains at the bottom, the regular trains on the ground level, and suburban trains somewhere in between. Braus is on the ground floor near the big board in the middle that provides departure and arrival information. He finishes his quick meal and looks for the train from Zurich to see if it's arriving on time.

"Look alive. The train is pulling in. *Don't* be obvious."

He didn't need to issue the warning to his five-man team – they are professionals. Two men are serving as spotters, walking trainside as it eases to a stop. They have backpacks and look the part of weary tourists. The three men at the end of the platform nearest the station are more conspicuous, but by the time they are spotted, it'll be too late. They will handle Braden's apprehension. None of them are armed, but then again, they don't need to be. When he sees there's no chance to escape, he'll go quietly.

Identification should be easy enough. Like most Americans, Braden Fox will stand out. His companion has been described as breathtakingly beautiful. There's little doubt she will also be noticed, maybe before he is.

Passengers begin disembarking after the doors open. Every man on the team has a radio, but they are relying on visual cues. Braus stares at the watchers for a signal, but there isn't one yet. He tries to be a patient man, but this is testing his limits. As the seconds pass, he grows more anxious.

Braden will have to change trains to continue to Vienna. He doesn't know where the next destination for this one is, only that it isn't heading to the Austrian capital. He has to exit and pass right by them…he has to.

The number of disembarking passengers slows to a trickle. There is still no sign of Braden, and even his watchers are growing alarmed. It's possible that they were spotted, as unlikely as that seems. Maybe Braden and Lyla Chance are still on the train, coming up with a plan to avoid the inevitable. There is no hope for that, but desperate times call for desperate measures.

"Shit," Braus mumbles when the number of passengers stepping onto the platform reaches zero and holds there.

He walks up the platform with his radio held up to his mouth. "Search the train. Two cars each. Watchers, you start with the rear four cars. Everyone else, take the front. I'll keep eyes on the platform from here. Do it quickly."

The men spring into action. There are ten cars on this train, and two each seems like a reasonable assignment. They are moving in different directions as they search, making evasion next to impossible. They execute the search quickly but thoroughly. The German can see movement inside the train through the windows. Every compartment is getting checked.

One man steps back onto the platform. Then another. And another. Five minutes elapse, and his team reports that there is no sign of either Braden Fox or Lyla Chance. The leader of the five men contracted to help Braus comes up at his side. He isn't happy. Part of their payment was contingent on success. He thought this would be easy money.

"Did we miss them?"

"No. Braden and his companion weren't on this train."

It was an admission as much as it was a statement. The intelligence was excellent. Braus may not have all of Braden's income sources monitored, but he has identified some of them with The Cossack's help. Prepaid cards can still be tracked, and he used one to purchase two tickets in Lucerne. It is an undeniable fact. The question now is why he didn't use them.

"Then we can catch up with them in Vienna. We know that's where they're heading."

Braus isn't so sure anymore. Braden is always a step ahead. He's beginning to wonder if someone from American Outreach or within his own group is feeding him information. Nobody is this lucky.

"Unless they aren't," Braus sneers. "He could have bought these tickets on purpose to throw us off. He could be heading to Portugal, for all we know."

The German doesn't bother hiding his frustration. This should have been an easy assignment. He has tracked harder targets before and caught up to them quicker than this operation is unfolding. He's beginning to look bad, and that's pissing him off.

Braden isn't acting like some finance weenie, and that's the problem. All his moves seem calculated. Normal people don't buy tickets that they have no intention of using.

Spies do that. Criminals do that. Guys who work for some American lobbying firm aren't versed in that level of tradecraft. He must be getting help.

Maybe there is more to Lyla Chance than meets the eye. The woman is a ghost. The Cossack doesn't believe she works for the government or a private corporation. He thinks the idea that anyone is relaying information to them is preposterous. Braus agrees with the first part but is second-guessing the rest. She may not work for someone, but she may have superior evasion skills. This feels like the work of a trained operative.

"What do you want to do?" the hired gun asks.

Part of good leadership is not showing indecisiveness or confusion. These men are waiting for instructions from the only man who can give them. Waffling or admitting he doesn't have a plan of action will result in confidence loss. He can't have these men thinking he isn't in control.

Vienna is still the safe bet. There could be a reason Braden didn't use the tickets. Maybe he flew to a different city or found an alternate mode of transportation. Maybe something happened to him or the woman traveling with him. Either way, it's the easiest to sell Vienna to The Cossack as the next-likely destination.

That's a bigger problem – Braus's boss expects results. That's what he pays his employees for, and the German hasn't delivered. That has never been an issue before, but that's true of everything until it happens. He needs to deliver, or the micromanaging will start. Nobody appreciates having their boss look over their shoulder.

"Get six tickets to Austria. It's our best lead. Tell your men to get a bite to eat before we board. I expect we'll be busy once we get there."

"Will do."

The man moves off, gathering his four men to brief them on the revised plan. Braus checks his watch and moves to the departures board. They have plenty of time to make the train to Vienna.

Braus walks back to one of the benches in the center of the platform and parks himself on it. He stares at the gleaming train now sitting empty on the track. Part of him hopes that he will catch Braden and Lyla disembarking, thinking the coast is clear. It won't happen. The train is empty.

Hope is not a tactic. He recognized the need to change the game and has failed to do so. Braus thought this was their chance to get ahead of their quarry. He was wrong this time. He needs to ensure that doesn't happen again. He's going to catch Braden Fox. When he does, the man is going to suffer for the inconvenience he's causing. Then he's going to kill him for making him look bad. He's killed people for lesser reasons.

Chapter Twenty-Nine

A Sordid Affair

Kinsey's doorman did his job this time. George called to announce her guest, and she has been nervously pacing the floor ever since. Did he get lost on the way up here? It's not like he hasn't been here before.

She has long since showered and changed out of the robe that she answered the door in to find the big Russian standing there. She thought about changing into something sexier, but this will do. The white top closes in the front, and the short, flowy black skirt with small flowers is cut high enough to show off her legs. This ensemble should be sufficient. Add on some strappy heels, and the outfit will turn heads on Park Avenue.

The doorbell finally rings, and she rushes to open it. Standing before Kinsey is not the confident lover she usually sees. He's a shell of that man – one who looks tired and stressed. In some respects, he appears defeated. It's an awful look.

"Come in."

"I shouldn't be here," he mumbles as he crosses the threshold. Kinsey closes and locks the door behind him.

"Why not?"

"Because—"

She doesn't let Travis finish his statement. Kinsey grabs him and forces him against the same wall that the creep who came here earlier had her trapped against. It's more fun being on this side of the equation. She pushes her lips hard against his, mashing her chest into his pectorals. She feels her nipples harden as she reaches down and grabs his crotch.

"Stop it!" Travis shouts, grabbing her arms and holding them tightly.

That's a first. Kinsey's passionate kiss has been their usual greeting for months now. This was no different, except half her clothes would be off by now. Instead, he's slamming the brakes.

"What's wrong?"

"This is," he says, releasing her.

That's news to her. She has always been attracted to Travis. Even at her wedding, she imagined what he would be like in bed. Braden never had a clue that she harbored that level of lust toward another man. He was always too caught up in his work to notice much around him – especially when it came to her.

And that was the problem. Braden is a milquetoast man and unimaginative lover. Travis is neither of those things. He makes her feel like a woman because he is everything she wants in a man – strong, adventurous, capable – everything that Braden isn't.

Her flirtations only encouraged Travis to take things to another level. It still took him a while to make his move. Braden was a friend – a best friend. Their affair would be the ultimate betrayal. She knew it, and so did he. The more Travis resisted giving in to the temptation, the more she urged him to. When he showed up to collect something one night when Braden was working late, she answered the door in a black negligee that would turn a gay man straight.

Travis finally gave in, and it was the best sex of her life. Their torrid affair has been ongoing ever since. They knew Braden would eventually learn the truth. Then he did. Neither could have predicted that her scorned husband would leave the state, let alone the country. That has complicated things…for now.

"What *about* this?" Kinsey asks, pushing away from her lover, not trying to hide her annoyance.

"Do you have any idea what's happening? They suspect something is going on between us."

"So what? It wasn't like people weren't going to find out eventually," she says, sauntering over to the bar cart along the wall in the living room.

"Yeah. Except your husband is still on the run. I can't keep up the illusion that he's betrayed Arden and American Outreach. The men hired to track your husband down are starting to do their own digging."

She pours a drink from a crystal decanter as he whines, and she takes a sip of the amber liquid. Braden has a lot of inadequacies, but his taste in liquor isn't one of them. She savors the flavor and the warm sensation as it travels down to her stomach.

"I know. The big Russian came to see me."

Travis's eyes grow wide, and his mouth hangs open for a moment. "The Cossack was here?"

"He was standing right over there," Kinsey says, pointing back at the foyer to Travis's left.

"What did he want?"

"The usual – intimidate me, level accusations, make threats, cop a feel. I played the scared woman who can't defend herself, and he finally left."

Travis clams up. It's more than his physical reaction to the news. Sure, his spine straightened and jaw tensed, but it's more than that. She can sense his tension and fear.

"I should go."

"Travis!" she says, rushing over and grabbing his arm, almost spilling her drink in the process. "Relax…he's not going to do anything to us."

"He won't do anything to *you*."

Kinsey sets her drink down on a small table with a marble top. She tugs at the lapels of Travis's suit jacket before reaching up and taking his face in her hands.

"He didn't know who I was, but he'll get educated. You worry too much. Braden will be dead soon. All anyone cares about is making sure he isn't betraying American Outreach. Once they learn that, the reasons he left become irrelevant."

"Arden won't look at it that way. Appearances are everything in our business, and Braden is his golden boy. I think—"

"Shhh," she hushes, placing her finger over his mouth before kissing him. "Don't think."

"You aren't taking this seriously."

"I don't need to. You're taking it seriously enough for both of us," Kinsey says, releasing him long enough to grab her drink and lead him deeper into the living room.

"You don't understand. These men are dangerous, Kinsey. I know what they're capable of."

"That only makes things more exciting, doesn't it?" she asks, pouring the remainder of her drink onto his shirt. Travis recoils at the wet blotch covering his chest. "Oopsie. Look what I've done. We need to get you out of these wet clothes."

She unbuttons his shirt and pushes him onto the sofa. He immediately begins to struggle to his feet. That won't do. She jumps onto him, her legs straddling his pelvis. She begins thrusting her hips over his growing erection.

Her top separates at the opening that runs diagonally from her left shoulder to her right hip. She doesn't like wearing a bra and rarely needs to. While not overly large, her breasts are firm and perky, as God intended. Doctors ensure they stay that way. Now, one of them has spilled out of her top. That will get his heart racing. It always does.

She grinds harder against him. Travis feels so good. She can almost feel him inside her. He's losing his will to resist. In another minute, he'll want this as badly as she does.

"You should stop," he protests weakly.

"Do you really want me to stop?" Kinsey asks, pressing even harder against him as she rocks back and forth in his lap. "Say yes, and I will."

Travis throws his head back and moans quietly. That was all she needed to know. Kinsey reaches down and unbuttons his pants. He pulls him out and slides her underwear to one side. The sensation of skin on skin is amazing. She's already wet with anticipation. She moans as she slides his manhood back and forth between the folds of her labia. She moves her mouth to his ear, burying his face in her red hair.

"You're the only man who can satisfy me. Do you want to keep whining or go out with a bang?"

Travis yanks her top down to her waist and brings one of her nipples into his mouth. She closes her eyes and enjoys the sensation. He gets more aggressive with his hands and mouth. He is so good with his tongue, and she almost can't wait for what he does with it next. This is what she needs. It's what she's always needed.

Chapter Thirty

Practice Makes Perfect

This is more like it. I was only capable of doing a passable tango in Buenos Aires. I was horrible at the Samba and uncomfortable with the Paso Doble. Waltzes are more my style. They are simple enough, even for the rhythmically challenged. Of course, that's a simple Waltz. This is the Viennese version, and that comes with a higher level of difficulty.

The Viennese Waltz is one of the oldest ballroom dances, dating back to 16th-century France. While dancing with a closely held partner shocked the English and French sensibilities in the courts of Elizabeth I and Louis XII, the Viennese fell in love with it. By the late 18th and early 19th centuries, hosts of formal balls called for a waltz as a trendy dance highlight to the evening.

The music is my favorite part. Something clicks in my brain and allows me to keep in step with the melody. A traditional waltz ensemble is made of two violins and a bass, although orchestras add more depth to the music. The Viennese Waltz is performed in a three-quarters beat. Although a fast waltz can clock in at sixty beats per minute, I prefer the slower versions that are half that.

In the romantic slow waltz, I maintain momentum by bending my knees and then rising to the balls of my feet, generating a flowing movement through the gentle turns. The hardest part is maintaining my head's placement in the direction of travel. Now that I have overcome that challenge, our dance instructor has moved on to a different target.

"Tilt toward the floor, Braden. Sway! Sway!" she barks from the other end of the dance floor.

I get the gist, only I can't seem to master it. To get the right motion, I need to tilt my torso. Not that I'm complaining about having to practice. This requires a pair to maintain full body contact as they move clockwise across the room. Our instructor calls it a Natural Turn. I call it Heaven. Lyla has been welded to me for three days now.

"Excellent!" the instructor says, killing the music and clapping enthusiastically.

Lyla rewards me with a beaming smile. "See how good you are when you enjoy a dance!"

"You are both much improved!" our instructor exclaims. "You've picked it up very quickly. You are good students."

She would know. The waltz can be learned in any one of the city's countless traditional dancing schools. Lyla picked this one because this woman is a professional dance instructor who prides herself on teaching the basic steps in less than an hour. We've been here for three days, dancing to music from Johann Strauss, Josef Lanner, and Carl Michael Ziehrer. It's more than enough time to get it right with expert tutelage.

Not only is our instructor excellent, but she's mercifully patient. Her only flaw is that she doesn't like explaining things multiple times. The basic steps are the natural turn, reverse turn, and change figures. That's all I need to learn. The so-called American-style Viennese Waltz danced in some ballrooms adds extra figures having nothing to do with a Viennese Waltz.

Purists rail against these kinds of competitions, claiming one could win a contest in American-style Viennese Waltz without doing the Viennese Waltz. Most of those extra figures were concocted by American dance teachers in the 1900s who were inspired by swing dancing. I'm in no rush to learn those.

I take a sip of water as Lyla gets some more dance instruction. Not that she needs it. I swear, there isn't a dance on this planet that she couldn't master in a day. That's the artsy side of her shining through. I am more of a numbers guy. Maybe that's why I like music – it's all about mathematics, and that has a certain appeal to me.

"What do you say, Braden? One more time?"

She doesn't need to twist my arm. I cap the water bottle and set it down, taking my position in the center of the studio.

"Yes, again. No words or instructions from me this time. Just dance like I taught you."

I'm almost giddy. I stare into Lyla's eyes as the music starts. We step off, breaking eye contact as we move gracefully across the dance floor. I've even learned how to lead her properly. Better yet, she isn't trying to take over. That's a first.

There are different phases of learning to dance the Viennese Waltz. Learning the steps was the easy part. I started slowly, then picked up the pace to dance in time to the music. Once I had the motion down, I started dancing with my instructor as a partner.

The hardest part was overcoming the dizziness and motion sickness from the constant turning. It took five hours of practice for that to finally subside and another five for it to disappear. It took a lot of practice before I relaxed enough to dance easily and naturally. Now, I'm confident enough to move around a crowded dance floor and maneuver around obstacles.

I enjoy the sensation of having Lyla's body pressed against mine. I maintain our hold, strong in the arms and rigid in the posture, in case of an entanglement. Ladies in high heels trip on occasion, and a novice man usually goes down with her. It's why Lyla wore flats for the first half of our lessons. We've seen it happen here. As I've become more sure-footed, I'm confident enough to catch her to ensure neither of us hits the floor.

The music ends, and the dance ends with it. It was majestic, beautiful, and over way too soon. Vienna was just what we needed. The awkwardness of France and the tension of what happened in Lucerne have melted away. We are truly enjoying each other without the angst of our lives for the first time in a while.

We thank our instructor and bid her goodbye before she starts her next lesson. I give her a healthy tip. She allowed us to monopolize her time for the past three days, and I want to show our appreciation.

I follow Lyla into the changing area. All we need to do is swap our shoes for something more street-appropriate. There was no dance in front of other students like I was expecting. Now that the lessons are over, I'm wondering what she has in store for me.

"Hey, Lyla, when is the performance? I figured we would have done one."

"Look at you all filled with confidence," she says. "You usually dread that part."

"The waltz is more my style…and speed."

"It shows."

I appreciate the compliment. That was the best thing about learning the Paso Doble – she used praise to build my "matador" confidence. That went out the window with the last dance. It's nice to see the kind words return, even if they're fleeting.

"So? When do I get to display my newfound waltz skills to the public?"

"Soon enough. There is something I have always wanted to do and never been able to."

I find that hard to believe. It feels like this woman has done almost everything.

"You're not going to tell me, are you?'

Lyla smiles and wraps her hand around my arm. "You'll find out soon enough. We have to go shopping first."

I look at her warily. "The last time you said that, I almost got run over by a stampede of porterhouse steaks."

"There are no bovines involved in this. I promise. We need to get some clothes…and masks."

"Masks? Are we robbing a bank?"

Lyla giggles as we leave the studio and begin strolling up the sidewalk. She isn't going to answer the question. I regret asking because now I'm even more curious. Not that it really matters. So long as I get to dance with her close to me, I'm game for anything. Then again, those are famous last words.

Chapter Thirty-One

Cinderella's Ball

This is something right out of a fairy tale. No country holds balls as romantic and festive as the ones held in Vienna. The locals call Austria's ball season the "fifth season." Over four hundred are traditionally held in winter, although this one is a distinguished outlier. As one of the precious few summer balls, it's a highly attended event that enchants locals and guests from around the world. I have no idea how Lyla managed to get us in.

Most Viennese balls are organized by professional guilds. The Coffee Maker Ball transforms the Vienna Hofburg into a festive dance café, while the Viennese confectioners host a "ballet of pastries." I found out from the locals that the Ball of the Vienna Philharmonic Orchestra is the unofficial Superbowl of the ball season and is hosted at the Vienna Musikverein. The hardest ball to attend is The Opera Ball – the official state ball of the Republic of Austria – set in the beautiful Vienna Opera House.

Lyla brought me to the summer Edelweiss Ball, one of two with that name. While the other is hosted during the height of ball season, this one is in July at the Rathaus, or Vienna City Hall. It's an impressive place to have an event. The Rathaus is one of the tallest and most impressive non-office or apartment buildings in Vienna and looks onto a central square alongside Vienna's Ringstrassen Boulevard.

She told me that this was the one ball she had always wanted to attend. While most women like roses, she has always been partial to edelweiss. Lyla likes the flower's symbolic meaning, with the German translation of the word literally meaning noble and white. It's an appropriate description. It also has a darkness to it. According to the hosts, dozens of people die every year in expeditions to pick this wildflower.

We arrived just before ten p.m. and were treated to an evening replete with courtly customs dating back to the 18th century, including the dress code, fanfare, the debutantes' arrival, and the "midnight performance." The hands spun around the clock as we waltzed and then waltzed some more.

Balls typically go to five in the morning, which means there are only a few dances left before calling it a night. Or morning, as it turns out. The orchestra strikes up, and I start adjusting my bow tie. Lyla smiles and pushes my hand away.

"Let me."

Following the dress code is the most important consideration when attending a Viennese ball. Fortunately, Lyla made sure I didn't feel out of place, or worse, not allowed in. Highly elegant Viennese balls are white-tie, but this is the black-tie variety. In addition to a black dinner jacket, I'm wearing black trousers, highly-polished black shoes, a white wing-collar shirt, a black bow tie, and a white folded pocket square in the upper left pocket of my tailcoat. I'm wearing studs over the buttons of my distinctive diamond-shaped, waffle-textured pique shirt.

"Thanks. If I haven't mentioned it, you look gorgeous tonight."

"You may have once or twice…or a dozen times."

"Well, you do. You clean up well."

I get a well-deserved smack on the chest. The truth is, Lyla always looks amazing. She doesn't need to wear makeup, but when she does…wow. Women are encouraged to avoid wearing white dresses, as that outfit is reserved for members of the Cotillion who take part in the opening ceremony. Lyla's ball gown is a deep blue and nothing short of spectacular. Since dancing is a must at the ball, she went with shoes with a medium-sized heel.

"One more dance before we call it a night?" I ask, offering my hand.

"I thought you would never ask, kind sir."

We move to the dance floor. Couples are already rotating around, deftly managing to avoid crashing into each other. I love the waltz. It's the one dance I actually feel I have mastered. Maybe because it's the simplest or the one I've practiced most. Mostly, it's because of the closeness I feel with Lyla when we dance.

"Is there any chance we can stop time?"

"Why? Do you have a cramp or something?" Lyla asks playfully.

"No. I don't want the night to end."

She reaches up and touches my face. "Me neither."

We get into hold, and I look into her eyes. Our heads will turn soon enough, so I sear this moment into my memory. Content with the image, I ensure my knees aren't locked. I distribute my weight evenly on the balls and heels of my feet. I can feel her do the same.

We step off with the music, doing natural turns as we rotate around the dance floor. Lyla is even letting me lead, finally trusting that I won't cause an international incident on the ballroom floor. All the pressure is off. The first rule of the waltz is to have fun. It's easier when all eyes aren't on me.

I'm relaxed and thoroughly enjoying the dancing. The natural turns get infused with reverse turns, change steps, and the occasional fleckerls to spin in one spot. The first time I used it, some Austrians gushed over how well we did it. The fleckerl isn't seen often at Viennese balls, but they were adamant that it's the origin of the Viennese Waltz.

The song ends, and it's announced that the next dance will be the last of the evening. My dream has turned into a nightmare. I can't stop time, and the night is ending with the first rays of the morning sun. It would be cliché to claim it's been one of the greatest of my life. It'd also be a true statement.

"One last shot. Make it a good one," Lyla demands.

The music strikes up a faster beat, and I lead her into a traditional Viennese Waltz. I've gotten over the dizziness from all the spinning. I feel light as a feather on my feet

– confident in my movements and secure in my hold. Lyla is responsive, and we glide gracefully across the floor.

Beginners worry that if they dance too close, they might step on each other. They're wrong. I learned that we're less likely to step on each other with body contact at the waist and proper hold and position. There is nothing better than holding this woman close.

I soak up every moment until the last musical note is played. People applaud, but I'm lost again in Lyla's eyes. She holds my gaze. The world around us is a blur, and the noise becomes distant echoes. The ballroom falls away. It's just us.

Her eyes look down at my lips before returning. My head inches closer to hers. She halves the distance. I move in even closer, and she closes her eyes. I want to kiss her so badly, it almost hurts. Then I remember a pledge.

I can't ruin this. I won't run the risk. We are caught up in the moment, and that's how relationships sour. I pull back, causing Lyla to do the same. She looks embarrassed…and disappointed. I am, too, but I could be misreading her signals. Not that they are ever clear.

We awkwardly join the applause, stealing glances at each other out of the corner of our eyes. I don't know if not kissing Lyla was the right thing or the wrong thing to do. Lyla is as mysterious as her reactions. I only hope she has a favorable one to the end of this enchanting evening.

Chapter Thirty-Two

Next of Kin

Arden has lost his patience. A month has passed, and The Cossack and Braus haven't delivered results. Braden is a financial genius, not a CIA agent. It shouldn't take this long to track him down. As a result, the American Outreach staff is overworked, things are falling apart, and he's getting nervous.

It doesn't help that two of his best people were tasked to search internally for clues as to why Braden left and what he took with him. Ilana has polled every client, and there were no red flags. Travis combed through every computer file and network log to find nothing was copied or is missing. Arden checked the servers his staff can't access, with the same result. None of this makes sense.

His team is the first to arrive in his office. The days are long and the nights longer, and Arden wanted to get this discussion out of the way. This meeting is not only a status update – it's meant to determine their next moves. Nothing they've tried is working, so they need a new approach to the problem. They aren't leaving this room until they come up with one. He doesn't care how much coffee they need to drink to keep their eyes open.

The Cossack shows up a few minutes late, as expected. Arden would love to see the video of the lobby and the outside of the building. He's betting the big Russian was here early and did a couple of laps around the building to ensure he was tardy. The Cossack knows it annoys the head of American Outreach and he uses the disrespect to push his buttons.

Arden leans back in his chair and folds his hands once everyone is assembled and comfortable. "Yesterday was another day, another failure. What will make today different?"

"Nothing," The Cossack answers honestly, his face completely impassive. "The trail went cold after our plan to intercept Braden in Munich didn't work out. Our search for him in Vienna has yielded nothing. There are no leads to his whereabouts, although we are reasonably certain he is still in Europe."

"Reasonably certain?"

"Yes, as in more than seventy-five percent and less than one hundred."

Arden bristles at the condescending explanation. "What happened in Munich?"

"You tell me."

Working with politicians takes special skills. One of them is patience. Unfortunately, there is only so much supply to go around. Arden is out when it comes to dealing with this Russian.

"What the hell is that supposed to mean?" he snaps.

The Cossack leans forward in his chair. "I've been doing this for a long time, Mr. Davenport. Humans are creatures of habit unless circumstances cause them to alter their routines. Setting aside why Braden left in the first place, his travel modes are predictable even if the destinations aren't. He prefers trains to buses. The confirmation of his ticket purchase in Munich is indisputable. He is either one lucky bastard, or someone tipped him off and forced him to change plans."

"Why would someone do that?" Ilana asks from her seat across from The Cossack.

The Russian shrugs. "Maybe someone doesn't want us to catch Braden. Maybe that individual is hoping he disappears and is never found."

"Answer her question in a meaningful way," Arden demands, "or don't make the accusation at all. I trust my people implicitly, which is more than I can say for you. So, why, specifically, would someone do that?"

The Russian shrugs before turning to the other analyst in the room. "I don't know. Do you know, Travis?"

The question catches the young man off-guard. Travis's shocked look is brief, and he recovers quickly. He can lie as effortlessly as the politicians he works with. Most of the people in this office can. It's why Arden hired them in the first place. The first rule of the office is never to mislead the boss. Ever. He would hate to think Travis is breaking it.

"Of course not! I resent the…. Sir, do I need to sit here and listen to this? He's had it out for me since the moment he arrived in New York."

The Cossack shakes his head as a smile creases his lips. Arden notices and narrows his eyes.

"Travis, I'm done playing games. Apparently, our Russian friend believes he has cause. If you know something, you had better spill it, and I mean right now."

"I don't know anything," Travis snaps.

"Miss Horowitz, have you found any information about why Braden left?"

She stares at The Cossack, shifts her gaze to Arden, and then back. "No."

"No records are missing or copied?"

"Not that we can find."

"Have there been any deposits into any of his accounts?"

"No, but he could have an overseas account that we don't know about," Ilana admits.

"Maybe, but someone planning to flee the country wouldn't leave more than a million dollars in his domestic accounts. Have there been any financial transactions in or out of those accounts since before he left for Key West?"

Ilana looks around the room as she rests her hands on her thighs to keep them from shaking. "Just bills on autopayment. Nothing nefarious."

"Okay, enough of the interrogation. What are you driving at?" Arden asks, growing even more impatient at the line of questioning.

The Cossack leans back and stares at the head of American Outreach. "You haven't found answers because you've been looking in the wrong place. We haven't found Braden because your assumptions have been wrong from the beginning. He didn't flee the country to sell out American Outreach to the feds or another SuperPAC. It's something else."

Arden runs his hand over his hair as he moans. He leans back and takes a breath, trying to control his anger. He is in no mood for games. The Cossack is playing all of them at once.

"If you have answers, perhaps you'd like to share them."

The Cossack nods. "You called this meeting to come up with a new approach regarding Braden. That requires rethinking why he left to begin with. You're going to get that answer today, Mr. Davenport. The only question is, who will be the one who tells you first?"

The Russian turns and looks at Travis. Arden follows his eyes. All roads seem to lead to Braden's best friend. His assurances are beginning to mean less and less.

"Travis, our Russian friend maintains the belief that you have some insights. If you lied to me once, I don't suggest you repeat that mistake."

"I can kneecap him if he does," The Cossack offers.

Arden glances at the Russian. He's serious. When he returns his stare to Travis, his head is hung, and his eyes are riveted to the carpet. It's a tell. He's holding back, further raising Arden's ire.

"Excuse me, sir?" an executive assistant asks, poking her head in.

"What the hell is it?" Arden seethes. "I told you that I didn't want to be disturbed."

"I'm sorry, sir, but Ms. Fox insists on seeing you. She says it's of the utmost importance."

"I have no doubt," The Cossack muses. "The plot thickens."

"Fine. Send her in."

Travis begins fidgeting uncontrollably. The Cossack studies him and smirks. "You look like you're about to shit your pants, Travis."

He looks at Arden, who impassively studies him. "I'm fine."

"Yeah, well, we're about to see about that," The Cossack says as Kinsey Fox saunters into the office.

The woman may be many things, but nobody will ever accuse her of looking like a train wreck. Her makeup is perfect. Not a hair framing the sides of her face is misplaced. There isn't a single wrinkle on her white dress, which is cut just above the knee. Her high heels are buffed to a shine. Even the hat that looks more appropriate for Churchill Downs looks resplendent on her head.

She doesn't say anything as she stands just behind the assembled group in the office. She first looks at Travis and Ilana and then at the Cossack. Her eyes narrow, and Arden watches the corner of his mouth curl.

Arden doesn't bother greeting her. He only watches and waits. This is supposed to be important. She will either ask everyone to leave or just come out with it. Whatever this is, she needs to get on with it.

Her eyes make contact with his, and she exhales deeply. "Good morning, Father."

Chapter Thirty-Three

The Friend Zone

Sleep never came after our long night at the ball. Lyla and I didn't get back to our hotel until almost six in the morning. By the time we both showered, the sun was already bathing the city in the first golden rays of the day, and our stomachs signaled it was time to eat. Normally, both could be ignored in lieu of much-needed sleep. But I'm wired, and Lyla is her usual ball of energy, so we decided to venture out and explore more of the city while searching for breakfast.

Located on the Danube River, the old Roman-era settlement has grown into a vibrant city rich in history, architecture, art, music, and food. Most of Vienna's many Baroque buildings were created in the eighteenth and nineteenth centuries under Empress Maria Theresa and Emperor Franz Joseph and stand in stark contrast to the glass and steel structures of the modern era.

Today's adventure starts in the city center. We checked out some of the city between dance lessons, starting with Schönbrunn Palace, a huge 18th-century seasonal home to the Habsburgs and now a UNESCO World Cultural Heritage Site. We spent hours wandering around the grounds after the tour of the magnificent interiors. We even went to the military museum to see the car Archduke Franz Ferdinand was killed in, triggering World War I.

I insisted we visit Vienna's Riesenrad after one particularly rigorous lesson. The large Ferris wheel is an 1800s version of the London Eye, and at over sixty meters in height, it offers a nice view of the city. More importantly, it guards the entrance to the huge Prater entertainment complex. After introducing Lyla to the fun of bumper cars at the Wurstelprater, we relaxed to the sounds of nature beneath a green canopy in the park. It was another magical day on a trip filled with them.

This is likely our last day here, so we have one more thing to check off the list. After breakfast at Vienna's oldest coffee shop, we went for a long-awaited carriage ride. The fiakers are just as much a part of Vienna as St. Stephen's Cathedral and the giant Ferris wheel. Carriages are seen almost everywhere, and tourists can easily find stands throughout the city, especially in Stephansplatz, Michaelerplatz, Albertinaplatz, and Petersplatz. A ride in a two-horse carriage is a special treat. There is almost no cozier way to explore Vienna's attractions.

I splurge and contract a sightseeing tour in a horse-drawn carriage that includes a bottle of local wine and authentic Viennese cuisine on a specially equipped table. As our driver meanders through the city streets of the First District, Lyla wraps her hand around my arm and rests her head on my shoulder. This has to be one of the most romantic things I've ever done.

"You wanted to kiss me last night, didn't you?"

I was hoping that wouldn't come up. We made it through the morning and a chunk of the afternoon without Lyla uttering those words. Now, I have a dilemma. The wrong answer could ruin the moment. I hang my head. Is this something I should lie about or tell the truth? Decisions, decisions....

"Yes."

"Then why didn't you?" she asks, her head still on my shoulder.

"Just because I was caught up in the moment doesn't mean you were."

It sounded good. It's also not true. Lyla was just as caught up in the moment as I was. I may be a guy who's completely oblivious to most of the signals women give off, but I didn't miss that one. I'm giving her an out. Lyla made it clear that friends are all we will ever be. Well, mostly clear. Sometimes.

"I wanted you to kiss me."

"That would have been useful information last night. We agreed that we would keep this relationship platonic. We are traveling companions and dance partners, nothing more."

"I know," Lyla confirms. "It was my idea."

"What's changed?"

"Nothing," she says, lifting her head off my shoulder. "I just wanted you to kiss me."

"I'll keep that in mind the next time we share a romantic dance to beautiful music in an iconic building filled with people who look like they walked out of Victorian England."

"Hmm. That may be a while."

"You sound disappointed."

Lyla grins, cocking her head to one side. "Aren't you?"

Kinsey wasn't even this cryptic. That woman ran hot and cold more than a bathroom faucet. She was wildly unpredictable, and I found her moodiness infuriating at times.

For multiple reasons, this is the same...and different. Lyla is at least pure in her motives. At least, I hope she is. I don't think she even knows what she wants. Since the day we met, I have imagined what life with her would be like. I resigned myself to leaving it to my imagination because she was not in a place to commit to a relationship. I'm not even sure I could handle one with her back in South America.

I've grown since then, and it's all because of her. I would love nothing more than to explore a future with her by my side. She likes giving me a glimmer of hope. The problem is knowing whether she's still caught up in the moment or just leading me on. My heart was already crushed once this year. The pieces won't survive another attack.

"Lyla, I don't know where I stand with you sometimes," I say in a voice that sounds unmistakably frustrated. "I try to follow the rules, and then you seem to change them."

"Yeah. I'm a woman. Besides, you'd be disappointed if I made things easy for you."

Lyla couldn't be more wrong. She's giving me ulcers.

"I came close to losing you in France, Lyla. That killed me inside. I don't want to repeat that mistake."

"Okay. We'll stay in the friend zone," she says, a wry smile creasing her lips. Now I am disappointed. "Unless we find ourselves in a romantic situation like last night where a kiss is more than appropriate."

"Does now count?"

"Nah. Too many words."

It was a long shot, but one worth taking. "Will I know when that happens?"

"I don't know. Will you?" Lyla asks, admiring the old buildings as the horses clop down the cobblestone street. "You sure missed it at the end of the ball."

"I'll be sure to use better judgment next time. If there is one."

"It wasn't our last dance, Braden, and I'm sure there will be another opportunity or two down the road. The world is full of magical places. You haven't been to most of them."

I'm desperate to change the subject. My mind is melting down over how finding a romantic place to give Lyla the kiss she seems to want can coexist with "the friend zone." They seem mutually exclusive to my logical mind. I guess that's part of the problem – there is very little logic when it comes to affairs of the heart.

"Speaking of places I have never been – where are we heading next?"

"A place almost as amazing as this city," she offers.

"I find that hard to believe. Let me guess…Prague? Budapest?"

"No, something more…aquatic," she says, almost taunting me with the tantalizing clue. "I hope you like boats and don't get seasick."

I have no idea what she has in mind. That makes me part neurotic and part excited. It has become one of the best parts of this adventure, even if it stresses me out. Vienna is great, but we have to move on. I'm thinking Greece – maybe something in the Cyclades Islands in the southern Aegean Sea. That would certainly fit the bill. I'm perfectly content letting my mind grapple with that instead of dwelling on the missed opportunity of kissing the woman of my dreams.

Chapter Thirty-Four

Auld Lang Syne

I was way off. I was hoping for an island like Santorini, but instead ended up in one of the most romantic cities on Earth. The centuries-old buildings and bridges, the quiet canals, cobblestone alleyways, and labyrinth filled with small bridges and narrow alleys are the stuff dreams are made of…if there weren't so many people here. Despite the crowds, Venice is exactly how I imagined it.

We caught the last of the nine direct trains here from Vienna. The gentle rocking and rhythmic clacking of the train wheels against the tracks put us fast asleep for a healthy portion of the eleven-hour trip. There are faster trains, but we needed the rest, having not had any since well before the ball started. When the train pulled into Venezia St. Lucia, we left the train station and found a nearby hotel. I'm still leery about computer systems, but the one at reception wasn't connected to the Internet. I have to keep reminding myself that Braus is still out there searching for us. After a magical time in Vienna, I had almost forgotten.

Lyla and I begin endlessly walking around the quaint city. It is impossible to travel in a straight line here. The closest you can get is taking the water taxi down the Grand Canal that bisects the city. I was fine with walking…and getting completely lost.

The Grand Canal and Piazza San Marco are clearly the centers of tourist activity, and the surrounding winding streets are filled with stylish cafes and gelaterias, souvenir shops, boutiques, and stunning Renaissance palaces and Gothic churches. We finally break down and take the water taxi to Venice's most important and most iconic landmarks.

St. Mark's Basilica is located on the Grand Canal right next to the Doge's Palace. With their Gothic architecture, the two structures rank among the most beautiful places in Europe. It's a sight everyone must see when they come to Venice. It feels like every tourist in town is here.

We find a table at a café off St. Mark's Square out of pure luck. A couple happens to be getting up just as we walk over. We order dual espressos and savor them as we watch the throngs of people come and go. One of them is a woman in a wheelchair who loses control of her purse and dumps it onto the brick plaza. She bends down for the items, but they're out of her reach. I'm out of my chair in a flash.

"It's okay, ma'am. I'll help you."

I start picking up the items and replacing them in her purse – her wallet, a makeup compact, some candies, a brush…the typical items you find in an older woman's purse. I place the bag securely in her lap and see her beaming at me.

"Grazie! Grazie!"

"Prego," I say, kissing her hand and smiling.

I give her a wave and walk back to the table and my seat. Lyla has a strange look on her face. I have spent every moment with this woman for months and have never seen anything quite like it.

"What?"

"You've changed," Lyla observes as I sit back in the molded white plastic chair.

"How so?"

"You were very self-absorbed when we first met," she says.

"No, I wasn't."

"Really? What were the first words you ever said to me?"

I rub my chin and make a show of thinking about it. I'm not going to give Lyla the satisfaction of knowing that I remember every detail about our first encounter like it happened yesterday. It's childish, but with her, I need to savor small victories.

"You stole my chair. I remember because you did steal my chair."

"Exactly. Have you carried that chair with you since Buenos Aires?"

"No."

"Then I was right – it wasn't *your* chair, was it?"

"A fact you quickly pointed out if I remember correctly."

"I did. Because at that moment, I knew it was how you viewed the world. Everything was about you. You never noticed anything unless it directly related to you or where you wanted to be."

The truth hurts. Nobody likes hearing from someone that they think you were a smug asshat. She didn't say that, but calling someone self-absorbed is the same thing.

"And you think that's changed?"

"I know it has. The old you wouldn't have helped that woman. Her wheelchair…her problem. That was your mindset. Now, you got up and ran fifteen meters to help an elderly woman you don't even know."

"Maybe I knew you wouldn't steal my chair because you have your own."

Lyla laughs and looks around. "Fair point. Do you want to know when you really started to change? The toy store in Madrid with the children. You finally stopped worrying about appearances and connected with those kids."

"I didn't have much choice. You yelled 'monster,' and I started getting beaten with plastic swords."

"The best way to learn to swim is to jump in the water. The best way to stop drowning is to climb out. You played with those kids for over an hour when you could have left. You let go…you had fun, and that started to change you."

"Is that what you did? Jumped in after art school?"

Lyla presses her lips together. She doesn't look like she's going to answer, but then she gives me a knowing look. "Something like that. Like you, I wasn't left with a choice."

"Do you miss your old life?"

"Do you miss yours?"

"I asked first."

She stares at the tourists coming and going. "Auld lang syne."

I nod. "Old long since."

Lyla cocks her head. "You may be the first person I've ever met who knows the literal translation of that song title. Something you learned at Princeton?"

"Google," I say with a wink.

"They were 'old times fondly remembered,'" Lyla admits. "But life moves on, and so have I. What about you?"

"My old times aren't so fondly remembered. But you know most of that story."

Lyla rests her elbows on the table and her chin on the top of her hands. "Pull it out."

"What?"

"The picture of Kinsey. Pull it out."

I do as she says. Lyla watches me intently as I extract it from my wallet. I turn it around and show it to her.

"You're still carrying it. You haven't answered the question," Lyla says before sipping her espresso.

"What question?"

"'Should auld acquaintance be forgot and never brought to mind?'"

"It's a rhetorical question in the song."

"You got your money's worth at Princeton. That's what all the experts say. But is it really rhetorical, or is it a reflection of what we value in life?"

Now, it's my turn to lean forward. "My wife is having an affair with my best friend – a man I have worked with every day since I graduated from college. He was the best man at my wedding."

"I imagine that would make work…awkward."

My smile is forced. I'm trying to keep this conversation on the lighter side. "More than you know. Kinsey is my boss's daughter."

Lyla didn't know that. We haven't discussed the picture since France, and I rarely bring up my former employer. I don't know why I told her now. It's not germane to…well, anything really.

"All that being true, you're still carrying her picture around with you. Why?"

I lower my eyes briefly before raising them to meet hers. "I…I don't know. Maybe because I haven't completely found a way to move on…to look forward to a bright future instead of back at a miserable past. My journey started when a man explained how to get my old life back. I never expected to forge a new one."

Lyla shrugs. "Life can be like that."

"What about you? What do you miss most?"

"Painting. Outside of using art to pay my way on occasion, I haven't picked up a brush and seriously painted since I left Paris."

"Never?"

"Not once. I left the joy of it at art school and never looked back." She toasts with her espresso cup before draining it. "Auld lang syne."

I still don't understand why she left. I'm dying to know, but it's not the time to ask the question. Lyla will tell me when she's ready.

"The sun is getting low," Lyla says, checking the sky. "We should go."

"Dinner?"

"Not quite yet…there's something we need to do first. And it's summer, so it will likely be crowded."

"Another tourist trap?" I ask after a moan, pulling a few euros out of my pocket to pay for the espressos.

"Not exactly. Trust me."

Lyla offers her hand, and I take it. I've come to the conclusion that a smile, a bat of her eyelashes, and an outstretched hand are all it would take for me to storm the gates of hell with this woman. I can only hope that's not what she has in mind.

Chapter Thirty-Five

The Plot Thickens

The apartment door swings open. Kinsey stares at him for a moment and scowls before turning and walking away. Arden steps across the threshold and closes it behind him. He's only set foot up here a few times, and mostly to see Braden. He and his daughter have never been particularly close.

"Your doorman seems to be a little jumpy, Kinsey. He gave me the third degree before he phoned you."

"Yeah, it's his job. I'm glad he actually did it this time."

"As opposed to last time?"

Kinsey sighs. "It's a long story. What do you *want?*"

Arden is used to her acerbic tone. She wasn't raised with cherished values like politeness and respect. In that regard, she's a mirror image of her mother. While he's come to expect her contempt, it doesn't mean he likes it.

"Is that any way to greet your father?"

"Whatever. Have you calmed down, or are you here to keep screaming at me?"

He's not sure what she expected. She waltzed into the office and admitted everything that was happening. After a month of him searching for her husband, did she think his reaction would be warm and fuzzy? He yelled and screamed at her and Travis until his voice went hoarse. Why wouldn't he?

Despite appearances, he hasn't calmed down much. Arden is as angry with his daughter as he's ever been – and that's saying something. Unfortunately, verbal abuse isn't going to get the result he needs to move forward with the plan he's formulating. He needs his recalcitrant daughter to get on board one way or another.

Arden places his hands behind his back and strolls deeper into the living room. "I love what you've done with the place. It's good to see my money has been spent well."

"It was Braden's money."

"Which I paid him. Of course, he still couldn't afford this apartment, even with his generous salary. I assume your trust fund took care of that."

"It's the only thing I should bother thanking you for," Kinsey says with a sneer.

Arden ignores the slight from the ungrateful brat. "How long have you been with Travis?"

"Why do you care?"

"I'm asking the questions. You're answering them. How long?"

Kinsey folds her arms across her chest. "Is that how you think this works? I'm not a teenager anymore. You don't get to control me. I don't even *want* you in my life."

"You've made that clear."

"So, why are you here?"

Arden's eyes narrow. "You married Braden Fox."

"Ah…yes. Your golden boy."

Arden never approved of the marriage. He told Braden as much. But love is love, and his young employee was blind to his daughter's manipulations. He learned the hard way that Kinsey does what she wants. Once she sank her talons into him, there was no escaping her clutches.

"Is that why you did it? To get back at me? It sure as hell wasn't for love."

"You're a son-of-a-bitch, you know that?"

Arden grins. "So I've been told by people far better and more important than you."

"Not everything in this world is about you, no matter how warped your world perception is."

"Okay. Set me straight. Why marry Braden? Tell me with a straight face it was because you loved him."

Kinsey turns and looks out the window without answering. The question doesn't require an answer. Arden already has it. She wanted to hurt him out of spite and used Braden for those ends. It's really that simple.

"I thought so. Were there other men before him?" She doesn't answer. "How long have you been with Travis?"

"Since January."

"Over six months. Are you still with him?" This time, the question earns a sharp glare. "So, in all the time Braden was missing, you knew exactly why. You watched us scramble to uncover his motives for leaving while knowing all along. You knew he found out about you and Travis."

"Yeah, I knew. I knew everything."

The defiance and arrogance in his daughter's voice cause a surge of anger to roll through Arden. He can feel the heat in his hands and feet from the increased blood flow and his nerves firing throughout his body. All that wasted time could have been saved if she had just told the truth. But that's not her style. It never has been.

"Why didn't you tell me?" he asks, trying to tamp down his rage.

"Why do you care? Oh, that's right, it's all about your precious company, or Super PAC, or whatever you call it. It's always been the most important thing to you. It was more important than my mother was…and definitely more than me."

The words were meant to hurt, but they don't. Arden has thick armor against that accusation built up from a lifetime of having it hurled at him. And it's the truth.

"Were you afraid I would find out?"

"I was counting on it," Kinsey says, dropping her hands and going on the offensive. "I knew it was only a matter of time before Braden learned about the affair. Then you would. The only thing I didn't expect was for him to leave the country. That man doesn't have an adventurous bone in his body."

"You wanted out of your marriage."

"I wanted out of this prison."

Arden chuckles and gestures around the million-dollar apartment. "Is that what you think this is?"

"Try living here. Try living with *Braden*."

"So, you had an affair to force it to end. That was your first mistake, but not your worst. You stayed quiet about the affair and Braden's leaving, knowing the truth would eventually come out. Kinsey, your moral compass is completely broken."

"Pot, meet kettle."

"Yes. My work requires me to compromise things like ethics. That's politics. But you were raised differently. If your mother—"

"You keep my mother's name out of your mouth!" Kinsey shouts, sticking her finger in his face.

Arden has heard enough. He slides his right hand across his body and arcs it high in an effortless swing. The backhand makes contact with her cheek with a satisfying smack.

Kinsey recoils and takes two steps back. She touches her cheek to check for blood. For as hard as the slap was, it didn't open a cut.

"I've had enough of your insolence. I am your father, and you will respect me."

"Get out! I don't want you here! You're *not* my father. You *never* have been!"

He grabs his daughter by the throat and squeezes. He was a formidable athlete in his youth and has always had a strong grip. His muscle tone and strength have waned with age, but his grip still has power. She grabs at his hands as her supply of oxygen is completely cut off. It's desperate…and futile.

"Have it your way, Kinsey. My being your father is the only thing protecting you in this world. So, perhaps it's time to redefine our relationship. Because, from here on out, if you don't precisely do what I instruct, The Cossack is going to return. And this time, he's going to do far more than cop a feel of some woman whoring herself out to my employees."

Her eyes grow wide.

"That's right. The Cossack was very forthcoming about his visit to you. Consider yourself fortunate – he's capable of delivering on every threat he made. Now, I'm happy to let him. You won't be able to hide behind me because I won't help you. Your doorman won't be able to help you. The police won't help you. God himself won't be able to help you. You will truly find out firsthand how weak and vulnerable you are. Do you understand?"

Kinsey nods.

"Good. I'm going to let go of your throat. You will not utter a word or make a sound. You will sit on that white sofa and listen to every word I tell you. You will agree to everything I propose, or I will have no remorse about what happens next."

Seeing her compliance, he releases her throat. She doubles over and gasps for air. Arden watches as she recovers and raises her head to glare at him through hateful eyes. She's smart enough not to speak. Not a single word slips from her lips as she gingerly lowers herself onto the sofa. The days of sparing the rod to spoil the child are over. Kinsey is about to get a masterclass in how the real world works.

Arden moves to the bar and selects a decanter of scotch. He pours a healthy glass full and selects a chair opposite the sofa to sit in. He leans back and takes a long sip in blissful silence.

"Your husband is going to be found, Kinsey. When he is, one of two things is going to happen. One I can't control. The other depends on you. If you want to avoid learning what true misery looks like, this is what you're going to do."

Chapter Thirty-Six

Bridge of Sighs

The gondolas plying the busy Grand Canal and the smaller waterways of Venice are among the world's most iconic images. The sleek craft allows you to see the city from a different perspective and better appreciate how it functions using canals in lieu of streets.

I've discerned three things about gondolas since arriving here: They're undeniably overpriced, possibly overrated, and extremely busy because tourists don't seem to care about either of the first two observations. There is only one city on Earth like Venice, and it's the only place where someone can glide in a gondola along a canal in a more than 1200-year-old city. For most travelers, it's the opportunity of a lifetime and ranks among one of the most dreamed-about traveler experiences.

A gondola is a thirty-plus-foot-long, flat-bottomed, wooden boat hand-built in special workshops called *squeri*. Or so it was explained to me by a third-generation gondolier farther north up the canal as he was performing maintenance on his family's prized possession. It's akin to riding in a luxury car. Black is their official color, and many are ornately decorated and equipped with comfortable seats and blankets.

Most gondoliers speak at least some English. That makes sense from a tourism perspective – it has fast become the world's universal language. I've even heard some of them speak a little German or French. They all wear black pants, a striped shirt, and closed dark shoes. Very few of them sing, although I have occasionally heard songs being belted out on the canals. Lyla explained that it isn't a requirement and more a product of Hollywood romance movies than reality.

The crowd grows thicker the closer we get to the Grand Canal. I don't know how Lyla is going to manage this. We aren't the only ones with an idea of a boat ride at this hour.

She looks around, scanning the area and then looking out at the water. Suddenly, she grabs my hand and moves closer to one of the areas where the gondolas tie up. Instead of waiting in a line of impatient tourists queuing near part of the canal, Lyla leads me over to the edge away from them. We stand there, minding our own business.

"What's the plan?"

"Watch and learn."

It's chaos in the gondola area. Some boats are trying to leave as others pull in. There is nothing efficient about the operation. Lyla glances at the canal beside us. More gondolas are pouring out of the narrow channel. Most of the men steering them grimace when they see the turmoil ahead. One of them peels off and heads right for us.

He pulls alongside and begins the process of helping two people step back onto shore. I turn to look at Lyla.

"How did you know?"

"Human nature. Do you sit in traffic or try to find a way around it?"

"I don't drive. But I see your point."

Lyla steps closer to the edge after the passengers disembark. A small horde of tourists come walking over, aiming to steal our ride.

"*Buongiorno, signore. Possiamo andare al Ponte dei Sospiri?*" Lyla asks in near-perfect accented Italian.

"*Assolutamente. Il costo è di cento euro.*"

"You speak Italian?" I ask, getting a wry smile from Lyla. For as much as I know about her, she is still a vast ocean of mystery.

"Do you have a C-note on you?" she asks, holding her hand out. The gondolier grins. He's seen it before. The woman wants a gondola ride, and the man pays. That likely plays out thousands of times a day in this city.

I acquiesce and pull out a hundred-euro note. "That was a very American way of asking that question."

"Yeah, I'm clearly spending too much time with you. *Grazie, signore.*"

"*Piacere mio, bella signora. Per favore, sali a bordo,*" the gondolier says, gesturing at his majestic craft.

"After you," I say, holding my hand up for Lyla to grab to keep her steady as she steps onto the gently swaying boat.

"*Grazie.*"

"*Prego.*"

Those two words are the sum of my Italian, and even then, I still manage to screw it up from time to time. I used "*gracias*" at the train station by accident. That isn't much of an issue, but I can imagine what the man thought. I don't look at all Spanish.

A lot of people have the same idea as we do. Tourists scramble to find any open gondola. We were told at the hotel that the best place for a ride is on the quiet back canals rather than on the crowded Grand Canal. I see why. It may not be as enchanting, but there isn't bumper-to-bumper gondola traffic.

"New York rush hour isn't this bad."

"Relax. You aren't driving, not that you ever do," Lyla reminds me. It's a fair point. Not crashing is our gondolier's problem, not mine.

"Are you going to tell me where we're going?"

"On a gondola ride," Lyla says, looking at me like I'm a moron.

I walked into that one. "Okay, yes, but why this one, and why at sunset?"

"Shh," she says, pushing her finger against my lips as she rests her head on my shoulder. "Enjoy the moment."

We turn down a canal with about thirty other gondolas. Gondoliers stand up to row and use only one oar, as it's the best way to row through the narrow canals of Venice. Everyone is gawking at the sight up ahead. I look around. Most are young couples. In fact, every last gondola on this canal is filled with either a husband and wife or boyfriend and girlfriend.

"Okay, what's the deal? I feel like this is Venetian Love Connection."

Lyla smiles and points at the bridge just ahead. "We are on the *Rio di Palazzo*. That's the *Ponte dei Sospiri*. It's better known as The Bridge of Sighs."

I study the structure. Calling it a bridge is a mischaracterization. It's a work of art. The enclosed walkway spanning the canal is made of white limestone and has windows with stone bars. It's beautiful, but so are a lot of other bridges in Venice.

"Why is this one special?"

"You mean other than being one of the best-known, most photographed, and deeply admired landmarks in all of Venice?"

"Yeah, those are consequences, not reasons."

"You and your logical mind. The Bridge of Sighs connects the New Prison to the interrogation rooms in the Doge's Palace. The convicts who crossed the bridge knew they were probably seeing Venice for the last time. They weren't just losing liberty. Back then, prison terms were practically death sentences. It earned its name for the heavy sighs of the prisoners who passed over it as they resigned themselves to their fate.

The gondolier chuckles. I look back at him to see an amused look on his face.

"That's…depressing. It also doesn't explain why there are so many couples around us."

The gondolier snickers again as Lyla lifts her head off my shoulder. "People like to kiss as they go under it."

Now I understand the source of our gondolier's amusement. Any Venetian would giggle at the sight of couples kissing underneath a bridge that represents a loss of freedom and, possibly, life. In a twisted way, after my experience with Kinsey, I get it.

"Tourists do weird things."

"It's more than that. It's become a legend – if two people kiss while drifting under the bridge at sunset in a gondola as the bells of St. Mark's Campanile ring out, they'll enjoy eternal love and happiness."

I hear bells start ringing. I turn to my right to search for them, zeroing in on the bell tower, when I feel a hand on my chin, pulling my face.

Lyla brings her lips to mine, and they meet for the first time. The kiss is slow and soft…and perfect. My arms wrap around her, and the world falls away. There is no gondola, church bells, or prisoner bridge turned romantic hotspot. It is just us in the moment. I hope the legend is true as our gondola glides under the bridge. I want the love and happiness I feel right now to last for all eternity.

Chapter Thirty-Seven

Two Become One

It was just a kiss. That's what I keep telling myself. It was the slow, soft, amazing kiss that I'd been dying for since the moment I met Lyla in that Argentinian tango club. It was the realization of a fantasy, but it was just a kiss.

I try to play it cool after the gondola ride ends. I don't remember much after we passed under the Bridge of Sighs. My mind completely blanked. That's what happens when something is just a kiss. Or, so I keep telling myself.

Ditto for the dinner we have at a quaint restaurant. I can't remember what I ordered, what it tasted like, or how much it cost. Because that's what happens when a kiss is just a kiss.

We smile, talk, and laugh all the way back to the hotel. The conversation is light and airy, not that I can recall a word that was said. Because…you know. That's what I've been telling myself since our lips parted. Nothing has changed. It was the romantic moment she mentioned in Vienna. Except I missed the signal. Again. It was up to her to ensure we didn't let the moment pass.

I'm not sure even I realize how hard I've fallen for this woman. This isn't lust. Yes, I have wanted a physical relationship for a long time. But there is an unexplainable spiritual component to this. This isn't about two bodies coming together. It's about two souls finally finding each other after a lifetime of searching. At least, that's my perspective. I have no idea what she thinks. I only get glimpses into her feelings, and that's only when she permits them.

I open the door to the hotel room, and she follows me in. The sun has long since set. The tourists have largely returned to their lodgings or cruise ships. She flings her purse against the chair and turns to look at me. She stands in the middle of the room like she's waiting on me for something. Again, missed signals. I have no idea what.

"It wasn't just a kiss, Braden."

My heart leaps. That's all the encouragement I need. I stride over to Lyla and kiss her harder this time. She tugs at my shirt, untucking it before undoing the top three buttons. I start to pull at her dress when she whips me around and flings me on the bed. I slide up on it as she straddles my legs and begins grinding against me.

I sit up and move my lips to her neck, sliding my fingers under the spaghetti straps of her little dress and sliding them off her shoulders. Her top falls, exposing her perfect breasts and hard nipples the size of pencil erasers. She isn't wearing a bra. She doesn't need one.

She pushes me back onto the bed and begins rubbing against me harder, only pausing to remove her strappy heels. Lyla becomes more desperate and moans harder, bending down to give me a kiss before shimmying down my legs and off the bed. She deftly undoes my belt and the button of my shorts before pulling them off.

Lyla starts to climb on, but I have different plans. It's my turn to swing her off me. This bed is entirely too small. She almost plunges off the edge when she lands on her back. We both smile, knowing damn well that this would have continued on the floor had she fallen onto it.

"You first."

I pull her dress off, along with her panties. I begin kissing her inner thighs, working my way up her body until I reach her mouth. The kiss is hard, but not sloppy; determined and passionate without being sloppy and uncaring.

Lyla roughly pushes me off to the side. Lyla yanks off my underwear, slides up to my waist and rubs against me. It's flesh on flesh, and it feels amazing. Unable to hold out any longer, we make love, taking our time and enjoying every passing second of it.

When we finish, I roll over slightly, burying the back of my head into the pillow. It's been a while, and it was never like this. I'm too spent to even talk. I've wanted this moment for so long and resigned myself that it would never happen. Now I don't know what to think. All I know is that was the most amazing sex I have ever had.

"We never should have waited this long to do that," Lyla says, panting.

I can't suppress a smirk. Lyla makes it sound like that was a mutual decision. I was up for this back in Buenos Aires. She has to know that.

"Your idea, not mine."

She snickers. "Fine. *I* never should have waited this long."

"Was it worth it?"

That's a question that every man wants an answer to and is rarely brazen enough to ask. I've never been a player. I don't have a porn star's confidence in the bedroom. I'm half surprised the question escaped my lips. Now, I'm bracing myself for the answer.

"Oh, yes."

Lyla moves my face to hers and kisses me again until our breathing becomes too big a problem. We were already out of breath.

"Braden?"

"Yeah?"

I'm almost afraid of what she's going to say. Regret can sometimes creep in. Maybe it's my own irrational fear. Does she think this a mistake – something that needs to be ignored? Because I'm not sure I can do that anymore. That ship has sailed.

"The next hotel room you get…make it one king bed."

"I don't know," I say, staring at our bodies tangled on top of the small mattress. "I kinda like having you need to sleep close to me."

She kisses me again. This one is long, and slow, and tender. Our lips part, and she looks at me with those magical eyes.

"Who said anything about sleeping?"

Chapter Thirty-Eight

The Little Devil

The Cossack's patience is wearing thin. The man is moving too slowly, and it's beginning to piss him off. He understands his apprehension but has already explained the untenable alternative. There are only two available options: Play along and follow the instructions he's given, or get a bullet in the brain for the hassle. The choice is his, if anyone can call that a choice.

"I said, slide the noose around your neck," The Cossack orders, his voice growing deeper and more determined. "I'm not going to ask again. If it's not there in the next ten seconds, I'm just going to shoot you."

Travis stands on the chair in his living area and stares at him. The seconds tick by. Is he really thinking that this is a bluff? He must. The Cossack lifts his suppressed weapon from his seat on the couch and stares down the sights. He's deadly accurate with a handgun out to more than twenty feet. This distance isn't that far.

"Okay, okay, I'll do it."

Travis reaches for the rope and slides his head into the loop. The Cossack groans when he sees the amount of slack in the rope. He thought the arrogant young American Outreach employee was taller than that, but it doesn't matter. This will get the job done.

"Tighter. Move the knot all the way down to your neck and place it behind your right ear."

"Happy?"

The Russian presses his lips together and shakes his head. "Do you think any of this makes me happy, Mr. Breckinridge? You could have told the truth from the beginning and made life easier for both of us."

"Is that what this is? You came here to send me a message?"

The Cossack rewards him with a sinister smile. Getting into Travis's Greenwich Village loft was ridiculously easy. The building doesn't have a doorman or cameras. The door to his apartment only has a residential lock installed with no deadbolt or security bar. A toddler could have broken into this place. It has to be the least-secure residence he has ever seen.

Once he was inside, the mission got easier. It was as simple as climbing the stairs from the foyer to the bedroom in the loft and holding the rag with chloroform over Travis's mouth while he slept. He could have just as easily killed him then, but that wasn't his instructions. Pity. He could be back at his hotel watching television by now.

Instead, he had to rig the rope he brought to the railing that separates the bedroom from the living area below. He hacked into Travis's laptop with the backdoor password Arden provided and typed out the suicide note he had drafted earlier. All that was left was to wait for sleeping beauty to regain consciousness. When he did, it was to a gun in his face.

Travis has been compliant since, just slow in executing commands. The Cossack made him stand on the chair in his underwear while he read the note he composed on the word processor. The man didn't react. He thinks this is a pageant for show. He thinks he's untouchable.

"Have you received the message?" The Cossack asks, playing along.

"Loud and clear," he says, too confidently.

The Cossack leans back on the sofa and rests the gun on his lap. "You spoke to Kinsey after her sudden appearance at American Outreach, didn't you?"

"Yeah."

"She told you not to worry. She convinced you that her father would never let anything bad happen to you. Is that right?"

Travis remains quiet. Silence is as good as an admission. People don't need words to communicate. Sometimes, the absence of them speaks volumes.

"I thought so. Do you trust Kinsey? I only ask because you haven't been together that long, from my understanding. I'm guessing since around Christmas last year?"

"January," Travis mumbles.

"Ah. Close enough. Do you trust her?"

"Yes."

The answer came fast. It's like Travis was conditioned to answer that way. Kinsey Fox is a master manipulator. The Cossack almost admires that. Mr. Breckinridge is an educated man from a successful family with a high-powered job and confidence in spades, and she has him wrapped around her little finger. It's impressive. And sad.

"You shouldn't. I knew nothing about Kinsey. I had no idea she was Arden's daughter. Once I found out, I did some digging. Apparently, she married Braden to get back at her father. Did you know that?"

"She may have mentioned it," Travis mumbles.

"And you didn't tell your boss?" Again, the question is greeted with silence. "Of course you didn't. You don't have that kind of loyalty."

"That's not true. It wasn't important. There was no need to tell Arden."

The Cossack wags a finger at him. Travis knows better. The first rule at American Outreach is not to lie to the boss. An omission is as good as a lie, at least in Arden's eyes. Travis crossed a line, and this is the price.

"And you didn't want to get caught having an affair with her. Kinsey is more than the boss's daughter – she's your best friend's wife. Oof. With friends like you…."

"She seduced me."

"Says every weak man who has ever got caught in a honeypot. She used you, Travis. She used you to get back at her father and end her marriage."

"That isn't true," he says, shaking his head.

"Please tell me you aren't this naïve. What do you think it is? Love? Come on, man."

"She does love me."

The Cossack takes a cleansing breath, almost amused at this point. "Why? Because she told you so? What if I told you she said the same thing to the last five men she cheated on Braden with? Would that surprise you?"

That hits him with the force of a freight train. He probably thought he was the only one…that this was the first time she stepped out on her husband. The truth is far more sinister. Not that Travis will listen. The poor sap fell in love with her.

"You're lying."

"I have no reason to lie. Unlike you."

"Fine. You've made your point. Can I get down now?"

"Not yet," the Russian says, waving a dismissive hand. "What was your plan, Travis? I mean, you knew you were going to get caught, right?"

"Maybe."

"Maybe? No, no, no…you can't be that stupid."

"I thought Braden would just get a divorce."

The Cossack rubs his chin. "Yeah, probably. Then what? Do you think he would have stayed at American Outreach? Or were you planning on leaving?"

More silence.

"You weren't. You thought Braden would leave. Seriously? How do you think Arden would respond to that? He's the golden boy."

"Braden Fox isn't irreplaceable," Travis argues.

"No, probably not, but he isn't *easily* replaceable, either. I'm not sure if you're telling yourself that because you like the way it sounds or because you believe it," The Cossack says, standing. "Not that it matters."

"Let me down."

"Why? You're not comfortable?"

"I have a rope around my neck. What do you think?"

"That you're suicidal. You were so upset at the betrayal that you were driven to take your own life."

Arrogant men have a fascinating reaction when they realize they aren't immortal. Their confidence exits stage left and leaves a vacuum in its place. Doubt, concern, and fear all rush in to fill the void. Travis just had the revelation that he may not survive the night. He should have realized that the moment he woke up with The Cossack staring down at him.

"Nobody will believe that," he argues, almost pleading for his life.

"They'll understand when they read the note. And Kinsey will tell everyone how worried she was about you. How she was afraid you might hurt yourself."

Concern has been replaced by panic. Travis knows this isn't a game anymore. He knows his life is about to end at the end of a rappelling rope.

"Actions have consequences, Mr. Breckinridge. You never should have listened to the little devil on your shoulder whispering in your ear that it was a good idea to have an affair with Kinsey Davenport Fox. It's going to be the death of you."

Travis reaches for the rope but is too slow. The Cossack kicks the chair out from under him. He's only watched someone hang once. It's not pretty if the neck doesn't break, and Travis's didn't – the drop wasn't far enough. Instead, his body will wiggle and convulse as the rope cuts off his supply of air. It won't do any good. That's why hanging is so effective. It's impossible to escape from.

After a minute, his body goes limp. The Cossack moves the chair a little closer. He kicked it too far away for the NYPD to find it believable that Travis did it himself. Content that the mission is accomplished, he turns off the light, leaving only the desk lamp illuminated. He locks the door and closes it behind him.

Someone from American Outreach will begin ringing Travis's phone when he doesn't report to work in the morning. Maybe they'll even send someone over here. Eventually, the police will be called, and the landlord will be summoned for a health and welfare check. That's when the body of Travis Breckinridge will be found hanging from the balcony railing.

There will be tears in the office. There will be questions from the police. There will be one fewer problem for Arden Davenport to have to deal with. The Cossack hopes Kinsey lied to her father and doesn't hold up her end of the bargain. That will be more fun than this was.

Chapter Thirty-Nine

Unintended Consequences

Sleep came hard and fast. It might have to do with physical exhaustion. Our tryst wasn't a once-and-done affair. We made love three times, with each subsequent round better than the previous. We took our time to explore each other into the wee hours of the morning. When it came time to sleep, it was in each other's arms.

I open my eyes and notice the first signs of the Italian dawn are visible outside the window, letting in enough light to see the small hotel room. As my vision focuses on the woman next to me, I find her staring at me with a content smile on her face.

"Was I snoring?"

Lyla chuckles, and her smile grows wider. "No."

"Then what are you doing?"

She caresses my chest with her hand. "Looking at you."

I feel myself tingle from the electricity in her touch. It's also knowing that this slender woman with curves in all the right places is naked under this bedsheet. We're leaving today. As always, I don't know where the next leg of our journey will take us. What I do know is that this first conversation will be awkward. I'm glad we aren't going to wait for the train ride to have it.

"You probably have a lot of questions," she assumes, averting her eyes to her hand as she grazes my chest with her nails.

"No, not really."

That catches her off-guard. "You aren't wondering how we went from the friend zone to…what happened last night?"

"Do you believe in miracles, Lyla?" I ask in a near-whisper.

"I guess."

"So do I. The one thing I always promised myself is never to question one when it happens."

"You think last night was a miracle?"

It was, among other things. We had dammed up our emotions, and the concrete and rebar holding everything back finally cracked into a million pieces. The dam burst, and the deluge surged forward, leading to the most passionate night I've ever experienced. I'm hoping she feels the same way, but that's not what the miracle refers to.

"Yeah, I would call it that. You were adamant about the rules when we first met in South America. We've played by them ever since. Then they suddenly changed yesterday."

Not that I'm complaining. Not at all. But I'm worried that the tone of my voice conveys the wrong message. I don't want the statement to have unintended consequences. From Lyla's reaction, it may have.

"Relationships are complicated."

She's used that line more than once in our travels. It's the first time she has ever used it with me involved.

"Are we in one?"

"We've been in one for a while, Braden," she says, pausing to look me in the eyes. "We only consummated it last night."

"Okay. And the talk after the ball? What was that?"

"Me being in denial. The truth is, I fell for you a long time ago. I've just been too scared to let it show. Too nervous about what it could mean."

Lyla is the strongest woman I know. Kinsey pretended to be strong, but she always relied on her money to fix her problems. Ilana Horowitz has confidence but always walks around the office looking to prove herself. She may be good at her job, but she spends an inordinate amount of time convincing herself of that as she tries to convince others.

This is the first time I have ever seen Lyla vulnerable. That's what love is, or so I've read. It's a willingness to be vulnerable with someone you care about. Maybe we have finally turned a corner.

"Say something, Braden."

"Thank God. I thought my feelings were only one-sided."

"They weren't. They never were. If I hadn't felt a spark in Buenos Aires, I never would have let you take me to dinner."

I smile. "I thought maybe you wanted a free meal."

"That's not how I live my life. I don't use people, or I at least try very hard not to. There is enough of that in the world already."

That wasn't a random sentiment. There was weight behind those words – a deeper meaning that I don't understand. It has to do with Lyla's mysterious past, and it's not something I want to broach in the here and now. It's not fear over my failed marriage to a two-timing whore. I sincerely don't know how she'd respond to knowing I have a highly trained thug chasing me. Whoever her Shadow is, he isn't nearly as dangerous as Braus and The Cossack are.

"Can I ask you a question? What took so long?"

"After last night, I was wondering that myself," she says, wearing her content smile again. "I have a past, Braden. Sometimes, I let the fear of it dictate my future."

"We both have pasts, Lyla. I'm willing to put mine behind me if you can do the same."

"It's easier said than done," she complains.

"What do you want to do? Go back to the friend zone?"

Lyla lifts her head to look at me. "Would you be disappointed?"

"Disappointed? No. I would be inconsolable."

"Good answer."

She leans in and kisses me. Her breasts rub against my chest as she slips her leg between mine. It starts soft and grows harder and more desperate. Suddenly, she pulls away, but only a little.

"I want a future with you, Braden, but I don't do casual. I'm not a girl who's into flings. You have to be all in."

"You don't think I am?"

Lyla presses her lips together. "I think you want to be. Our travels together are something out of a fairy tale. But we have to face reality. You're still married, Braden."

"I'm not going back to Kinsey if that's what you're afraid of."

"Honestly, I am. I'm not what anyone would consider…wife material."

In the world of dating, there may not be a vaguer pair of words than that. What is wife material? Every person on the planet looks for something different in a spouse, even if there is a strong plurality or majority who think certain values are important. I was one of those people. Then I ignored everything I claimed I wanted and married Kinsey.

"Neither was she…and I wholeheartedly disagree with you."

"Why? Because I'm lying in bed naked with you?"

"Because you're loyal," I say, recognizing the importance of this conversation and not wanting to play games or offer cheesy quips. "You're supportive. You're feisty. Most of all, you bring out the best in me and make me want to be the best version of myself. You're everything I have always wanted in a wife…and certainly never got in my marriage."

"I'm unconventional."

"It turns out that maybe that's what I needed."

"I guess we'll find out. We have a little time before we need to go to the train station. Right now, we should take a few minutes to focus on my needs."

"Breakfast?"

I'm hoping that isn't what she means.

"You."

She pulls me on top of her. I rub my hand over her breasts and down the side of her soft but toned body. There is no need for Viagra with this woman. I'm already at full attention when she grabs my penis and slides me inside her. She moans, and I know and she is in no mood for extensive foreplay. If Heaven had a feeling, this is it.

Chapter Forty

Monte Carlo Nights

Monaco, perched on the Mediterranean bordering France's southernmost shores northeast of Nice, France, has been an independent country since the 12th century. I've read about this place and have watched the Monaco Grand Prix, always hoping that I would visit someday and never making plans to make that a reality. That all changed today.

I have always used Monaco and Monte Carlo interchangeably without recognizing there is a difference. It's a little like Manhattan and New York City – one is a subset of the other. There are four traditional quarters in the city-state. The first three are the old town of Monaco-Ville, known as Le Rocher, Fontvieille, which is a district completely reclaimed from the sea, and La Condamine, the oldest commercial quarter.

Monte Carlo is the most well-known of the four *quartiers*. That has something to do with its landmarks. In 1856, Prince Charles III of Monaco granted a joint stock company a charter to build a casino. It opened five years later, ushering in a revitalization of the economy and transforming Monte Carlo into a luxurious playground for the rich and famous.

The casino's gambling tables are open only to visitors to Monaco. It's a first stop for many tourists, even if they only poke their heads in or people-watch across the square from the Café de Paris. I decided to splurge on this visit. I treated Lyla to a Michelin-starred restaurant and a stay in the Hôtel Hermitage Monte-Carlo. I had to give my name, which means Braus will likely be alerted to our being here. It doesn't matter. We'll be gone in the morning, and the travel options are almost limitless.

The Bar de la Salle Europe is a majestic room with the sounds of chips scraping on the felt, the voices of the croupiers, and the hushed voices of gamblers. The idea was to put a bar as close as possible to the casino games. The whole room has a James Bond feel, and that's why I'm wearing a tuxedo. Life doesn't get any better than this…until it does.

I'm consumed in my blackjack game and don't even notice her come in. After winning my sixth hand in a row, I spot Lyla sitting at the bar, watching me intently. She's wearing a breathtakingly elegant cocktail dress that would make the most ardent, happily married family man question his life choices. I grab my chips and beeline over to her as smoothly as I can.

"Fox, Braden Fox," I say, sliding up beside her and pulling at my tuxedo's lapels.

"You are such an ass," she says with a smile and an eye roll. "But you do look dashing."

"Why, thank you. And you are a vision, Ms. Lynd."

Lyla closes her eyes and nods as she accepts the compliment. "Okay, I'll play Vesper, so long as you acknowledge that she dies at the end of *Casino Royale*."

"Oh, spoiler alert."

"So, tell me, Mr. Fox, are you here to play, or is something sinister afoot?"

"Ah, my love, is there any better place in the world to do this?" I ask after the bartender notices my arrival and moves in for my order. "Martini, shaken, not stirred."

"You know that movie was filmed in the Czech Republic and was meant to be in Montenegro, not Monte Carlo, right?"

I shrug. "Who cares?"

"Vodka and tonic with a twist," Lyla orders, sending the bartender off to mix the drinks.

"Actually, I needed an excuse to see you in that dress. You are beautiful, Lyla."

The shimmering blue dress has a V-neck that plunges to her abdomen and a slit that rides up to her hip. It hugs every curve as if the designer made it for her. Almost all the clothing we've worn has been left behind, but I'd be willing to pack this one and take it with us to see her in it again.

Lyla blushes and lowers her head. It's far from the first compliment I've ever given her. But we're a couple now, and the words seem to carry more weight with them. Unable to avoid my insistent stare, she looks up at me with her beautiful eyes.

"Is that your way of saying I clean up well?"

"I already knew that. I haven't seen you in a dress that sexy since we were in Argentina."

I pull out my wallet to pay the bartender. I wasn't paying attention to the picture of Kinsey. I had pulled it out and never stuck it back into the slot. I don't even remember why I took it out. Lyla isn't going to buy that explanation.

Lyla spots the picture and turns her head, trying to fight her emotions as she sips her drink and replaces it on the bar. She folds her hands in her lap. I try to pretend that didn't happen. From the look on her face, I'm not going to get off the hook that easily.

"How do I measure up?"

The question catches me off-guard. "What do you mean?"

"To your wife? How do I measure up to Kinsey?"

I am horrible at this. I've learned a lot during my time with Lyla, but one thing that escapes my grasp is how not to be cagey in uncomfortable situations. The robot from *Lost in Space* is screaming, "Danger, Will Robinson, danger!" in my head. The easy answer is that there is no comparison – that Lyla is a thousand times the woman Kinsey could ever hope to be. So, of course, I don't say that.

"Why are you asking?"

"Because I want to know. Answer the question, Braden."

"Not until I understand why you're asking it."

My combative attitude isn't helping things. Well, okay, it is succeeding in one thing: Getting Lyla pissed off.

"Why does it matter why I'm asking?"

"Because you're a walking contradiction. You tell me not to speak about our pasts, then you want to. Then we get together and say they aren't important, and now you're asking me to compare you to my wife."

"Soon to be ex-wife, or did you forget that part?" Lyla asks, turning away from me and staring blankly at a spot across the bar.

"I haven't forgotten. Have you forgotten all your rules? You told me once not to fall in love with you. Then you said you fell for me. What's it going to be, Lyla? Because, right now, I don't know which rules to follow and which to ignore."

"Forget it, Braden! Just forget I asked."

I move my head into her line of sight. "We've been playing this game from the beginning. I don't want to anymore. We are going to talk about our pasts, or we aren't. You need to decide, and that's the way it's going to be."

Lyla's face turns bright red, and she points a finger in my face. "Don't you dare presume that you get to make those kinds of demands!"

The reaction didn't match the request. It was a trigger, and I have no idea why. That's what's frustrating. Lyla won't tell me.

I outstretch my arms at my sides. "Tell me why not. Explain why we can't be honest with each other."

"I don't expect you to understand. You never will…."

Lyla wipes the tears she was trying to fight back from her eyes as she storms away from the bar. I watch her for a moment before shaking my head. Well, that went well.

"Another, sir? This one's on the house."

I nod in appreciation. The bartender was listening to the whole thing. Men are not the most sympathetic of creatures. That's about as much commiseration as you get from another guy. He's likely been there before. Most of us have.

I drain my drink quickly and make for the exit. The streets are quiet. I look around, not seeing Lyla anywhere. She couldn't have gone far quickly in those heels. Knowing she loves the view of the moored yachts, I head in that direction. It's a quick walk, and I spot her leaning against a stone railing separating the terrace from the marina below. It's a beautiful view. Behind her, the ornate, brown casino's facade is lit by exterior lighting. It's almost a postcard moment. Except it isn't.

I stop next to her and admire the view. Neither of us looks at the other.

"I wasn't sure if you were coming after me," Lyla admits.

"I will always come after you," I say, meaning it. "I needed a minute first."

"That was our first fight," Lyla whispers after nodding.

"If you don't count Bordeaux," I say, remembering that night all too vividly. "We don't have much to fight over."

I turn my head and study her face for a moment before returning my gaze to the marina outstretched below us. We don't fight much because we don't talk about things of substance. There are no political arguments or quarrels over rival sports teams. There is no financial predicament to obsess over. Most of all, there is no history before we met – except what little Lyla knows about Kinsey.

"Do we now?" I press.

"No," she admits with a shiver as the breeze picks up.

I take my jacket off and slide it over her shoulders. "Then what was that about?"

"I…I don't know. I…."

A long, uncomfortable silence grows between us. Lyla plays with her purse, and I rock back and forth on my heels. This may be as awkward as things between us have ever been. I don't know what to do or say next.

"I'm not myself right now," she finally admits.

"In what way?"

"In every way. Relationships are a problem for me. I thought I could…I need time to myself."

My heart shatters into a thousand pieces. I know I can't mask the hurt that seizes my face. I've waited so long to be with this woman. Now, it's over almost as soon as it started.

"Do you want us to go our separate ways?"

"No. I…don't know. I just…we need to tap the brakes. I need to go somewhere I can find some balance. I don't expect you to understand…or tag along if you don't want to. It's just something I need."

"Okay. Where do you want to go?"

Lyla turns to me. Her eyes are moist, and her cheeks are damp with tears. Whatever she's feeling is tearing her up inside.

"The City of Light."

Chapter Forty-One
Mistakes & Opportunities

Braus has spent most of the day walking. He needs the exercise, and exploring every corner of this picturesque old town has given him the time he needs to think. Famous for its sunny climes, gorgeous beaches, and colorful architecture, the French city of Nice is the ultimate tourist Mecca on the eastern half of the French Riviera.

After walking up and down most of the seven-kilometer stretch of the iconic, palm tree-lined Promenade des Anglais, the German finds a café and takes a seat. "La Prom," as it's known to the locals, has a commanding view of the Baie des Anges. How the Bay of Angels got its name is one of his favorite stories.

Although there are other explanations, he prefers the one about the fifteen-year-old Christian girl from Caesarea who was a victim of persecution. She was eventually killed by the Romans in 250 AD, but it took several tries. They attempted to burn her at the stake until rain began to fall and put out the fire. Then they forced her to drink boiling tar, but that didn't do the job either. Frustrated, they lopped off her head and set her body adrift on the Mediterranean Sea in a little boat. Legend has it that angels guided the boat into this bay all the way from Israel. The bones of Sainte Réparate are interred in the Old Town cathedral that bears her name.

Braus sips his espresso when it arrives. He intently watches people pass by his table as they enjoy a stroll on La Prom. When his phone rings, he barely gets the "Hello" in before his boss launches into a full-blown tirade. The Cossack's wild briefing on the events in New York is a long, run-on sentence as the man barely takes breaths as he relays chunks of information. The German's eyes may be wandering to the people along the street, but he's in "listen" mode, and his mind is locked on the implications of what he's hearing.

"So, this isn't as nefarious as it first sounded," Braus concludes when The Cossack finishes, knowing that this whole search was predicated on Braden seeking to sell out American Outreach.

"No. It was a lovers' quarrel gone wrong. Nothing more."

Braus scowls. "That would have been useful information a few weeks ago."

"A sentiment I have already expressed to Arden in no uncertain terms."

Braus would have loved to be a fly on the wall for that conversation. Arden is wealthy, powerful, and connected, but The Cossack is scary. It's not just his violent tendencies, master manipulation, or means of intimidation. He has been doing Arden's dirty work for so long that he knows where the bodies are buried. It would be a massive mistake to cast him aside. A mere tenth of what The Cossack knows would bury American Outreach and its arrogant founder under a mountain of legal troubles forever.

"Consequences?"

"Davenport is handling his daughter. Mr. Breckinridge already made his choice. He committed suicide in his loft apartment. His body was found yesterday morning after he didn't report to work."

"That's tragic," Braus says, not meaning it and not shocked at his demise. "Is there an investigation?"

"NYPD detectives stopped by Arden's office. They heard the same story from everyone in the know and seemed satisfied that Travis was working too hard, emotionally fraught, and must have sought to end the pain himself in a tragic waste of life."

Murdering someone and making it look like a suicide is an art form. There are countless shows on American television of high-profile would-be murderers who get caught trying to pull it off. Despite many common portrayals, police detectives are not stupid. All it takes is one small thing that doesn't fit to raise the alarm. Once suspicion has arisen, it never fully goes away.

"Please give my condolences to the people at the office."

"I will."

The Cossack sounds almost gleeful in his tone. He must have enjoyed what he did to Travis more than usual. The man has a sadistic side, not that Braus will shed any tears over Travis Breckinridge. He got what he deserved.

"There is another matter."

"Fox?"

"That mission hasn't changed. Finding Braden is still the priority, but he's to be returned to New York, if possible. But I was referring to Arden Davenport. The bastard lied to me, Braus."

The head of American Outreach misled both of them, not that either of them should be surprised. The man is a professional liar who operates in a world full of them. That isn't worth pointing out since the Russian is already taking personal offense to the disrespect. Knowing that Braden was married to his daughter was important information.

"It was a mistake…but also an opportunity," The Cossack continues after Braus remains silent. "Arden Davenport built an empire by shoveling dirt. It's time he learns that the same can happen to him."

"To what end?" Braus asks, uneasy about the direction this conversation is going. "We're already well-financed and shouldn't be eager to bite the hand that feeds us."

"The arrangement with Davenport has always been…tenuous. We are seen as vendors and nothing more. That means we can be replaced. It's time to change that dynamic."

"And you think blackmail will do that?"

"It's a language the old man already speaks. I will handle that detail. Your job is to find Braden Fox. Dispose of the girl and return him alive."

The Cossack ends the call. They don't do pleasantries in the course of their business. Braus sets his phone on the table before draining the rest of his espresso and summoning the waitress to bring another. He needs to plan his next move.

His team of hired guns was already cut loose. There was no need to pay the mercenaries to sit around and watch television while waiting for a lead. He has always thought their involvement was overkill, but the decision appears shrewder after learning that Braden isn't some master spy looking to sell secrets. He's a jilted husband out having a good time. It also explains the woman he's with, at least to some degree.

What Braus attributed to tradecraft was actually luck. His escape from Key West, his constant movements, the deception in Munich…at the time, it felt like he had help in avoiding capture. That appears less likely now. Maybe he has a diligent guardian angel keeping him from harm.

Braden's movements never made much sense. The world travel was perplexing when his motive was selling information or ratting out the group to federal authorities. You don't need to go to South America for that. Or Europe. In hindsight, everyone should have come to this conclusion much sooner. Now, Braus knows there isn't a specific reason for the travels.

What he has learned is that Braden is getting too comfortable. For the first time, he stayed at a hotel where he could be tracked. Nice is close enough to Monaco to monitor the principality without paying the exorbitant prices required to stay there. Where would two lovers go next from this part of the continent? The French Riviera, Paris, Spain, and Portugal are the likely choices when romance is the determining factor. They would continue north or west. There is no reason for them to backtrack.

The Cossack's call has fundamentally changed the calculus. Maybe the woman Fox is with is the key to this. They haven't found much information on her besides her name, which they assume is an alias. What if it isn't? What if she actually is Lyla Chance?

His espresso comes, and he takes a sip. It's one last taste of Heaven before heading out to do some more research on the mysterious Lyla Chance. Her file is thin, but he remembers that she was an art student in Paris before falling off the grid. That's the best place to start, and he hopes it pays dividends when nothing else has.

Chapter Forty-Two

Halls of Monet

Paris is an old city that has been around for multiple millennia. Prehistoric artifacts have been found in Paris, but the world is only truly aware of the city's history since it was called Lutetia during Gallo-Roman times. There are monuments and buildings from every era in the city since the Caesars ruled, adding character and a sense of longevity to the charming architecture.

Not that we're taking a moment to appreciate it. Lyla isn't wasting time. After disembarking from the train, we hop onto the metro and head for the Seine River near Notre Dame. Arriving at street level, I see nothing but cafés with terraces on every street corner.

"The oldest café in Paris opened more than three hundred years ago," Lyla says. "They've been brewing beans since before your country earned its independence. We can get coffee later. Come on."

"Where are we?" I ask, in what can only be categorized as a stupid question.

"Paris."

I deserved that. "Where in Paris?"

"Saint Germain. Paris has been a haven for artists and creatives for centuries, and this is its beating heart. Art is everywhere in this city, from the parks to the architecture to the museums."

"That explains why there are so many art schools."

Lyla does a twist as we walk, her arms outstretched. "And most of them are here. This is one of the great areas of the city. It has music, cinema, the best nightlife in Paris, and even places to talk politics. Jean-Paul Sartre and Simone de Beauvoir fought it out with Albert Camus in Saint Germain."

I've heard of the former but have no idea who the latter is. I'm too embarrassed to ask and I make a mental note to look it up sometime.

"During World War Two, a printing press here produced forged passports during the occupation and then printed books against Nazism," Lyla continues.

"It sounds like there is a lot of history here."

"It's the place to be in Paris. There is one art practiced above all others here: conversation. That's where all the cafés become important. It's the editorial page of the Parisian population. Do you want to know what they think about your country? What's hot or not this week? This is the place to ask."

"I'm pretty sure I already know what they think about my country."

Lyla snickers. "Don't take it personally. Most of the true Parisians I know hate anything and everything not associated with this city."

"New Yorkers are much the same. They don't believe anything west of the Hudson is important."

Lyla turns a corner and stops in front of the grand façade of a building. "This is it."

She takes a deep breath, and I follow her through the large double doors. It's not what I was expecting, even for a Parisian art school. The building has a style and décor reminiscent of Versailles. Even the furniture lining the walls looks like it belongs in a museum celebrating long-forgotten members of the French monarchy.

"This is where you studied?" I ask, looking around the cavernous building with its marble and columns.

She joins me in taking in the majesty of the structure. "Yes. This was home. *L'art Traditionnel de Paris* is one of the fastest-growing art schools in the world in terms of size and reputation. Now, it rivals Les Beaux-Arts de Paris as one of the best art schools in all of Europe. Maybe even the entire world."

"Impressive. Is it just for painting?"

Lyla smiles. "This school focuses on both theoretical and hands-on instruction, preparing students for careers related to the arts and design from drawing and painting to sculpting."

I look down at my clothes. "I feel underdressed."

"You aren't. Trust me. This is an art school, not a fashion house."

"Has it changed any?"

A girl with blue hair walks by, not paying us any attention. "Only the people."

We climb the stairs to the second level, and Lyla leads me to a room with an open door. The walls are covered in portraits, most of them looking like Monets…or Manets. I can't tell the difference. Classical music plays on an old record player, and she knocks on the jamb loudly enough to be heard over the orchestra.

"I'm busy. Go away," a man harshly barks, facing an easel with his back to us.

I look at Lyla, who's undaunted.

"If you don't want to be bothered, you should close your door. If you want airflow in this stuffy closet, buy a fan."

The man doesn't face his new visitors. Instead, he stands straight and sets his brush down. "I got advice like that once before from a woman with that angelic voice. But she became a ghost and disappeared from the Earth."

His face immediately warms when he turns and sees Lyla offering him a brilliant smile. "Boo."

"*Bonjour, ma chère Lyla.*"

They begin speaking in French as they embrace and the record reaches its end and the music stops, bathing the room in silence. He must be approaching seventy or eighty. I'm not sure. I am terrible at estimating people's ages. All I can say for sure is his weathered appearance makes him look old.

"Jean-Claude Monet, this is Braden Fox from America."

He shakes my hand, turning and speaking French with Lyla. She responds, and he seems satisfied. I'm almost certain it was about me.

"Good to meet you, *monsieur*."

"You too, sir. Did she say your last name is Monet? Like…the Monet?"

The man smiles. "He's my great-grandfather."

"The apple doesn't fall far from the tree."

"Pssh," he says, waving a dismissive hand. "I couldn't touch his work on my best day. That's why I came here to teach art history and his Impressionist methods."

"Jean-Claude spent childhood holidays at Giverny, where his great-grandfather lived," Lyla adds.

"That's where I found a large volume of his letters and photographs and developed an interest in his life. It's also why I changed my family name to match his. It's easier for people to make the connection."

"Claude Monet was a master of light," Lyla says, pointing at one of the reproductions in the room. "No matter who tries to copy his style, they never quite get it right. He was a gifted artist whose work may never be replicated."

"And many people have tried," Jean-Claude admits. "What brings you back here, Lyla?"

"Many things," she says in the vaguest possible reply.

"You don't plan to reenroll? It's a shame to let such talent go to waste."

She blushes. That's a rare occurrence and a testament to the high esteem she holds her mentor in. "It's been a long time since I've picked up a brush."

"Then, perhaps it's time to shake the rust off. If there is anything we have a lot of here, it's canvas, paint, and stressed-out art students with every imaginable hair color."

"We noticed," I say with a smile.

"You don't mind?" Lyla asks as her mentor ignores my observation.

"Most of the students are in the countryside. There is an amateur art show at a gallery in New York City in a couple of months, and only the ten best paintings are being sent. You remember how competitive this place could be."

"I do."

"Well, they are off toiling away, so we have plenty of space."

"I would love that. *Merci*."

Jean-Claude claps his hands enthusiastically. "Excellent. Then you will stay here with us, just like the old times. Mr. Fox, we do not allow our students to cohabitate during their time here. I can arrange separate quarters for you if that is sufficient."

"That would be fine. *Merci*."

The man scowls. I didn't think I mispronounced the only French word I knew. Lyla says something to him, and his smile immediately warms. He takes her face in his hands.

"Welcome home, *mon ange*."

Chapter Forty-Three

Art of the Story

I have everything I need. There is enough acrylic paint next to me to brush a mural on the side of a building. Flat, round, filbert, and detail brushes in almost every size allow me to use a wide selection of techniques. I have a traditional wooden mixing palette and knife for blending colors and a large stretched canvas on an old easel to construct my masterpiece on. I have rags and an apron to protect myself from paint splatters. There is only one problem: I have no idea what I'm doing.

Lyla and I are painting opposite each other in a space that looks like it's better suited to be a French king's throne room. Outside of the dozen or so easels and myriad of paint and brushes, this room looks like it could host heads of state or foreign dignitaries. It's bright, airy, cavernous, and rich with marble, sculptures, and detailed woodworking.

All of it is meant to inspire the students who are plying their trade within its walls. Unfortunately, inspiration doesn't translate into talent. My work isn't impressionism so much as what a toddler tripping on LSD would produce. It's been a half hour since I last asked, and the time to pose the question again has arrived.

"Are you going to let me see it?" I ask, poking my head around my easel.

"When I'm done," Lyla says, studying her canvas and not looking at me.

"I want to see it now. I need to know how it compares to this masterpiece."

I look at my canvas and frown at the abstract art. Maybe it will hang in the MOMA in New York someday. Most of the art in there makes no sense to me, either.

"You will see it when I'm ready to show you. Not a moment before that," Lyla decrees.

"That's not good enough."

"Tough. Now, stop asking."

I'm trying to pick a fight. I desperately want to see what Lyla's doing. Whatever painting this is on my canvas is a disaster. I need to see what a legitimate art student can accomplish.

"I could steal a peek."

Lyla pulls her brush back from the canvas. "Braden, if you come anywhere near my canvas, you'll need to have this paintbrush surgically removed from your rectum."

"It's long and thin. I'll be okay," I say, grimacing at the thought.

"Not when I insert it sideways."

"Ouch," I say, struggling to purge that image from my mind. "Have you ever painted in this room?"

She pauses after finishing a small brush stroke and looks around. "I spent a lot of time in here when I was a student. So much so that this room is very comfortable for me."

That's not what I expected to hear. The studio is ornate to the point of being gaudy. That doesn't seem like it would appeal to Lyla's earthy personality. It certainly doesn't mesh with the lifestyle she was leading when we met. Like everything with this woman, there is more to her than meets the eye.

"It must have been hard to leave."

"It was. I've missed painting for a while. It's relaxing and therapeutic. Painting allows me to focus on creativity instead of stressors and worries. Through art, I can express emotions that I can't convey verbally. And there's a sense of completion – making that final brush stroke is a feeling like no other. It's the accomplishment of creating something tangible that others can enjoy."

I'm not going to experience that. I'm terrible at this and only want the pain to end. The fine arts have never been my thing. Being a numbers guy, it was my least favorite subject going all the way back to middle school.

"Jean-Claude seemed happy to see you. I think he's smitten by you."

"He's like that with all his pupils."

"Even the men?" I ask, only half joking.

"Especially the men," she says with a chuckle.

"He carries quite the legacy…Monet's great-grandson. That must have opened some doors for him."

"You don't get to choose your family," Lyla says, drawing out the words slowly in a tone tinged with regret. "It did open doors, but it's also been hard on him. When your great-grandfather is the co-founder of an iconic artistic movement, people have an expectation. It wasn't until he got into teaching that he started using the last name Monet for that reason. Most people don't realize that your family's past can profoundly influence your life."

Sounds like she is speaking from experience, but I don't press. We're already in a bad place in our relationship that is only starting to mend. I'm not ripping open the wound.

"He must be a hell of a painter."

"He is, but the legacy is impossible to live up to."

"Did he try?"

"For a while. Claude Monet had an innovative approach to art. He used light and atmosphere to capture the immediate and sensory aspects of a scene rather than focusing on a precise representation. It was cutting-edge work at that time. *Impression, Sunrise* was the work that gave the Impressionist movement its name."

I never had footsteps to follow in, but I imagine that would be hard. "So, now Jean-Claude teaches and paints for fun."

Lyla nods. "You're not a painter. Did you have any hobbies before you left New York?"

"All I did was work."

"Did you enjoy it?"

"I thought so. It was what I was good at – kinda like you and painting. Beyond dealing with numbers and financial transactions, I needed good communication skills, the ability to build relationships to establish trust and credibility, and a knack for negotiation. I like structure, but this offered a dynamic element that kept things somewhat interesting. I had to force myself to be adaptable and persistent – two things I have never excelled at."

It was the only excitement in my life. Every other corner of it was dull and uninspired. I never understood how I was sleepwalking through life until this adventure with Lyla opened my eyes.

"When did you realize that you didn't?"

I don't have an exact answer, so I make one up. "The eighth drink on my second day at The Drunken Lobster."

"Excuse me…the what?"

I smile. "The Drunken Lobster. It's a bar near the marina I was staying at in Key West, Florida, before I flew to South America and met you."

"Interesting name," Lyla muses. I'm sure it offends her French sensibilities.

"It's an interesting town. After I found out about Kinsey, I did the most impulsive thing I have ever done and got on a plane heading south. When I hit Miami, I rented a car and picked a direction. I landed on Route 1, and that took me across the keys. The last stop before the Gulf of Mexico is Key West. Mile marker zero."

"And all you did was drink?"

It's my turn to laugh. "It's a party town for tourists, much like South Broadway in Nashville or the French Quarter in New Orleans, except for all the ways that it's different. It's a relaxed vibe. People fish, and then they drink. Once in a while, they eat pie."

"Pie?"

"Key Lime pie."

"Ah. I didn't know that's where it originated."

"Sort of. It's associated with the Florida Keys because the smaller and more flavorful key lime is a native plant there."

"Did you spend a lot of time at The Drunken Lobster?" Lyla asks, changing the subject.

"I knew more about the bartender than his mother did. Steve was there every day like clockwork."

"Do you miss him?" Lyla asks, concentrating on applying some paint to her canvas.

"Who, Steve? Not really. He threw me out of the bar the last time I was there."

"Why?"

"I don't really know," I say, fibbing. I was drunk as a skunk, that's why. "I was having a conversation with a guy. When it ended, he walked over and escorted me onto the sidewalk. That's all I remember. The next morning, I woke up on a beach."

"That sounds nice."

"I almost drowned because waves were crashing over me."

Lyla giggles. "Ah. You passed out."

"I was oblivious to the world up to that point. It was a reality check."

I don't mention Steve getting assaulted or the fact that my newfound respect for life has anything to do with the psychotic German my boss hired chasing me down. That was the real origin of my sobriety.

"The Drunken Lobster. Sounds like an interesting place," Lyla says.

"We should go there sometime."

"Are you welcome back there?"

It's a legitimate question. "I don't know. There's only one way to find out."

"Is that what you're painting? An intoxicated crustacean holding a whiskey bottle?"

I look at my masterpiece. It doesn't look like much of anything.

"You show me yours, and I'll show you mine," I sing out.

"You'll see it when I'm done. Have you finished?"

It's time to fess up. "I'm not sure. Once I figure out what this is, I'll let you know."

Lyla laughs, and it's good to hear it. I thought her wanting to come here was pointless, but being in this place has relaxed her in a way I never expected. She feels more grounded…and connected. That translates to how she interacts with me. Maybe there is hope for us after all.

Chapter Forty-Four

The Value of Intelligence

One key opens the door to everything. Understanding Braden's motive has changed everything. Braus assumed that the mysterious Lyla Chance was using the alias of an old Paris art student who disappeared years ago. She wasn't. Now, he knows everything worth knowing about her, not that there is that much. But what he has learned is eye-opening. Suddenly, everything makes sense.

Her past is more checkered than his. Her family saw to that. Braus knows he should have picked up on this sooner. Her Persian eyes and skin add to her breathtaking beauty. It also hints at a heritage worth exploring.

The tragic loss of her lover in Paris was likely no accident. Whoever arranged it didn't anticipate the consequences, because her sudden flight from the City of Light was unexpected. Not that she has ever been alone. Eyes are on her most of the time, whether she knows it or not. That was another of Braus's discoveries.

Braden likely doesn't know anything about who her family is or the real reason she went on the lam. It will be an eye-popping revelation when the time comes. He may or may not be keeping secrets from her, but she is definitely hiding hers from him.

The time is approaching when Braus will ask his quarry in person. He only needs to confirm the rumor. A staff member reported that two people showed up at the art school out of the blue a few days ago – a man and a woman. The woman is a former student, and the man is an American. She didn't have their names, but if it's not Braden and Lyla, it would be one hell of a coincidence.

Braus opens the door and steps into the cavernous foyer. Despite the size and echoing of his footfalls, the place is eerily quiet and completely absent the throngs of art students he expected to see. It's also very French. It's a culture that worships at the altar of gaudy opulence.

He hears voices and ducks into a room off the main foyer. It's a studio of some sort, with easels set up in a loose circle. Two of them have paintings on them covered in white canvas. He moves to the far one and sees something that looks like a cat vomited on it. If this qualifies as art, it's fallen a long way from the great masterpieces of Michelangelo, Van Gogh, and Degas. Braus moves to the other and expects the same, only this one is…breathtaking.

He drapes the linen back over the work and moves to the wall as the voices move past the door. A man and a woman. Braus waits until he hears the doors. Once they close, he slips out to follow them, hoping his chase is about to come to an end.

The German expects them to head north over Petit Pont - Cardinal Lustiger and to the island home to Notre Dame that splits the Seine. Instead, they turn left and walk along the street before descending the stairs to the riverbank. Braus picks up his pace, falling in about fifty meters behind them on the cobblestone path that follows the river.

The most impressive part of the Seine's banks is found around the two islands of Île de la Cité and Île Saint-Louis, where the river is bordered on both sides by double-decker quays. Lined above and below by poplar trees, the quays are wonderful places for walking and picnics.

The path widens before passing under the stone support arches of the Pont Neuf. The man stops suddenly on the other side. Braus ducks behind the bridge abutment and peeks around the corner. He goes to tie his shoe and looks behind him as he stands. This part of the walkway is dark enough to blend with the shadows. Braden Fox doesn't see the danger lurking.

"Gotcha," Braus whispers to himself as the couple starts walking again.

He feels for his suppressed weapon as he waits to give the couple some extra distance. His orders are clear – eliminate the girl and return Braden to NYC either willingly or stuffed in a suitcase. The method doesn't matter to The Cossack, only the result. Braden needs to be alive…at least, for now.

That's easy enough to do. There are tourists around, but not in large numbers. There are a few couples on a romantic stroll and groups of teenagers and young adults meandering about. The area is lit but not bright, and things happen quickly. It would be over before anyone could react to what they're seeing.

Braus continues walking, trying to look like a tourist out for an evening stroll. He's far enough back not to raise any attention from Braden and Lyla. They're scanning their surroundings but aren't concerned by his presence. Or the other man's.

The German saw him fall in behind the pair just as Braus was leaving the art school. He's also following along the street above, looking every bit like a visitor to the French capital. By staying above the walkway, the man can keep an eye on the pair without his presence being obvious. He's well-trained, for sure, and likely one of Lyla's shadows.

That complicates things. Braus doesn't know how this shadow will react to what he needs to do. They want her alive, or they would have killed her months or even years ago. His orders say otherwise. To the hard-boiled Russian, Lyla Chance is as disposable as a gum wrapper.

The German hurries his gait. He could take the stairs and eliminate the shadow before executing his mission, but that could backfire and get messy. Krav Maga is a mainstay with men like that. It could also get him caught, or worse, alert Braden and Lyla to his presence and send them fleeing. If they manage to evade him, he will have lost his best chance to end this.

Braus weighs his options as he continues to follow the pair. There are several opportunities to make his move and he lets them pass without action. The couple climbs the stairs back to the street level and turns right onto Pont des Arts. That used to be colloquially called the "love locks bridge" before the French dismantled them, citing safety concerns. It's a shame. The gold locks glistened in the sunlight, making the footbridge the prettiest span over the river.

The shadow has peeled off, opting to watch from afar and won't be in a position to do anything. This is Braus's chance. He can take care of Lyla and dump her over the railing into the river, spiriting Braden away before anyone is the wiser. It would be a fitting end to the chase.

He takes a deep breath, gripping his weapon before walking past the bridge. The exhale is cleansing, and the adrenaline surge begins to subside. There's no rush. Braden Fox isn't going anywhere. Braus hasn't reported to the Cossack, who will be none the wiser. There is a time and place for everything.

This doesn't have end violently or even be done their way. Screw what Arden Davenport wants and how The Cossack wants to handle this. Neither of them is here. With leverage, anything is possible, including getting Braden to willingly return to New York. That's the true value of intelligence. It can be used to make people do things they don't want to.

Chapter Forty-Five

La Vie Dansante

I was done with my painting a long time ago, but that wouldn't surprise anyone at this art school. Nor would it surprise anyone how bad it is. I tried to find inspiration from the paintings on the walls and the tips that Lyla gave me. If there is anything I learned from this exercise, it's that inspiration and talent don't always go hand in hand. I'm Exhibit A.

Lyla finally finished her masterpiece last night, not that she would let me see it. She has some plan for a reveal, but true to form, she wouldn't explain that either. Some things never change. We decided to celebrate our accomplishments by making a lunch date and concocting a plan to explore the city beyond the confines of the Fourth and Fifth Arrondissements. I'm looking forward to a day out with her. Mostly, I'm looking forward to not painting, or more specifically, not *trying* to paint.

Upon leaving my small apartment, I make my way to the main foyer area to find it filled with a few dozen people. I spot Lyla studying the room and looking just as baffled as I am. The older people are an eclectic mix of French art teachers. The younger crowd is part of the hair color mafia who are anxiously pacing around like squirrels amped up on Red Bull. In the middle of the foyer are a dozen easels, each draped with white linen. A shiver runs down my spine.

"What is this about?" I ask Lyla.

She shrugs. "I'm not sure. Let's find out."

Lyla gets the attention of one of the students who has more piercings on his face than Pinhead from the Hellraiser movies. He has the same worried and anxious look that an expectant father would have. He stops cold when Lyla approaches him. She has that effect on most men.

"What is this?" she asks.

"It's reveal day…or one of them," he advises us. "I'm sure you've heard about the big art show in New York. Instead of choosing the paintings at once, Jean-Claude likes to do an evaluation whenever there are ten or more completed works. This is the first one. After the rest come in, the faculty will make their selections."

"Why are you so nervous?" I ask.

"It's the first time we get to see the competition. This amateur art show in America is a *really* big deal. I desperately want my painting selected."

Jean-Claude Monet steps forward and gets everyone's attention. The room descends into an eerie silence. After a few remarks about the amateur show and the other art teachers present in the room, he addresses the artists. His words are kind, but he explains that the demands for this show won't be. I've never been so happy to not be an art student. Princeton isn't this rigorous…or this competitive.

"Whatever happens," Jean-Claude concludes, "know you are among the most talented painters in the world but may need to continue refining your craft. Others need far more than just refinements. To illustrate my point, I present our first entry."

He walks over and pulls the linen sheet off the first easel, unveiling my painting. It looks worse from a distance than it did up close.

The room erupts in laughter, completing my utter humiliation. Part of me is angry. Nobody likes to be mocked, least of all me. The other part wants to crawl under a rock and die of embarrassment in peace.

"Mr. Fox, I apologize for having some fun at your expense. The students here don't know you aren't a classically trained painter, much less a student here."

All eyes turn to me. "Yeah, well, when Lyla wanted to visit her art school in Paris and asked if I wanted to paint, I thought she meant someone would teach me."

"I'm not sure we can help you," Jean-Claude says, glancing back at my painting as more snickers erupt around me. "But I wanted to display your work for a reason. You see, the students are laughing because your style is absent of technique and completely devoid of nearly every artistic principle. Yet, it has what many paintings here don't: soul."

The laughter ceases immediately.

"Although the design is something most of us moved past in *école primaire*, it has spirit. Some of the great paintings I see in these halls have great beauty but lack emotion. While this is not an exemplar of great beauty, the painting is fearless. That, ladies and gentlemen, is art. Sometimes, it takes an amateur to remind us that technique may help us create a feast for the eyes, but it often fails to stir the soul. While many artists can achieve one, it is often at the expense of the other. Thank you, Mr. Fox, for reminding us that how a painting moves us is the most important part."

I look at my painting in a new light. It's not much more than a stick figure surrounded by a dark city looking up at the sun shining through a crack in the clouds. Since this place inspired me to go with an Impressionist approach, nothing is distinct. Instead, I tried to create a feeling inspired by my own life. Maybe I succeeded.

"Well done, Braden," Lyla whispers loudly enough to be heard over the applause. "That's one of the nicest things I have ever heard Jean-Claude say."

"Maybe I missed my calling. I could pioneer a new genre – abstract stickism."

Lyla laughs as he moves on to the next ten paintings. She wasn't lying. He was very critical of each of them, including the painting by the nervous man from Hellraiser who was awaiting judgment. It doesn't sound like it will make the cut.

"And our last entry is from a woman who only recently returned to these halls. I believe you all will agree that we're thrilled she did."

Jean-Claude removes the linen and unveils the painting. Nearly everyone in the room gasps, including the art teachers. The other students marvel. All the little dabs of paint up close look like nothing…the hallmark of any true Impressionist work. From a distance, they create the most beautiful painting I've ever seen.

"Whoa!" is all I manage to utter.

"I…I'm speechless," Jean-Claude says, studying the colors and admiring Lyla's use of lighting.

I remember the moment well, but Lyla managed to capture it better than any photograph could have. It's our last dance at the ball in Vienna. Using tiny strokes of paint, she captures our movement, clothing, and facial features perfectly.

"This is reminiscent of Edgar Degas in the best of ways yet has a uniqueness all its own. Look how Lyla captured this fleeting moment. It's candid and off-guard…and real. And the light and color…The softer pastels of the couple contrast the harder colors of the other dancers…it's amazing."

If I had five lifetimes to try, I could not have painted something so perfect. I imagine that most of the trained artists in this foyer couldn't have managed to. It's not the technique or the skill…it's the feeling. Lyla somehow transferred the magic of that moment onto a canvas.

"You did my great-grandfather proud, Miss Chance," Jean-Claude says with his hand over his heart and a slight bow. "This work is simply remarkable. What do you call it?"

The eyes of the people in this room tell the story. Some are soft and inspired out of appreciation for her magnificent work. Others are colored green with raging jealousy.

"*La Vie Dansante.*"

Jean-Claude wraps up the presentation with great fanfare. He steps aside as most of the art students walk over to congratulate her and ask for tips about how she painted such a masterpiece. The remainder skulk away, jealous and infuriated that they were outclassed. And they were. Not a single painting shown today comes close to rivaling Lyla's. I stare in absolute awe at one of the highlights of our journey, captured in an artistic beauty I could never have imagined.

"What do you think?"

I think this wants to make me cry. And dance. "It's…it's…."

"My journey with you," Lyla finishes. "You brought this out of me, Braden. I had never painted like this before we met. My work here was what Jean-Claude is chafed about – it was technically perfect yet soulless because I was dispassionate about my subjects. You said you needed me when we were in Buenos Aires…the truth is, I needed you just as much. I needed to rediscover who I was. Thank you for that."

"You're welcome. The title…La Vie Dansat. What is it?"

"*La Vie Dansante,*" she corrects.

"Yeah. You know I don't speak French. What does that mean in English?"

Lyla looks at me and smiles. "The Dancing Life."

Chapter Forty-Six

Famous Recreations

I'm still feeling the afterglow of the praise. Yes, my painting sucked, but it was good enough for Jean-Claude to use in illustrating a point. Maybe, just maybe, I have inadvertently inspired some young artist whose future work will grace the walls of a museum. That's a pretty cool feeling.

We cross the bridge to Île de la Cité, a small island in the Seine River that's been the historical and geographical center of Paris since ancient times. It's also one of the two remaining natural islands in the Seine within the city limits and is home to some of Paris's most iconic landmarks. Most tourists have been here, even if they didn't know that. Located on the island's eastern half, Notre Dame is one of the most famous Gothic cathedrals in the world. The cathedral suffered significant damage in an April 2019 fire, but restoration efforts have been underway since.

In addition to the cathedral is the Sainte-Chapelle, a stunning medieval chapel with exquisite stained glass windows, the Conciergerie, a former royal palace turned prison where Marie Antoinette was held before her execution, and the Palais de Justice, the city's main courthouse. Its location, iconic architecture, and historical significance make the Île de la Cité a popular destination for tourists and locals, offering a glimpse into the rich history and architecture of Paris. The only thing keeping them away today is the threatening gray skies. I should have brought an umbrella. I think we're going to need it.

Most of our walk is consumed by talking about her painting. The title was pure genius. It had obvious meaning to the two of us, but what's most impressive is how others reacted to it. That's the true meaning of art.

"Do you want to stop for an espresso?" I ask, beginning to tire from the walk and wanting to seek shelter before the sky opens up. "There's a charming little shop right here."

Lyla looks up at the café sign and grimaces. "Sure, just not this place."

"Why not? Is their coffee not 'free trade' or something?"

"Nothing like that. Let's say I have my reasons."

Here we go again – more mystery and intrigue. We continue walking. For as much as I have learned about Lyla during our months together, there is still a lot to uncover about the Paris chapter of her history. Some things I may never learn. Despite it being against my better judgment, I'm resolved to learn more. She has to learn to trust me. If she doesn't start now, she never will.

"I thought you exorcised the demons from your past."

"I did, but that doesn't mean they don't pay me a visit once in a while," Lyla confesses with a sigh. "I used to go to *that* café when I was a student here…a lot. I don't want to bring those memories back right now."

"Do you want to talk about it?"

She shakes her head. "No."

"Why not?"

I expect a sharp rebuke. Lyla gets irritated when I push too hard. I've learned that lesson the hard way on several occasions. Her reaction is different this time.

"For the same reason you don't talk about the picture of Kinsey in your wallet. You still have it, right?"

"I do," I say, eager to explain, "but not for the reason you think. It used to be a reminder of the life I lost and desperately wanted back. Everything has changed since we met. I keep it now because it reminds me of who I was and the kind of life I *don't* want to lead. The life where I was ruled by everyone's expectations instead of my own."

"I wish I could believe that," Lyla says, not looking at me.

"I can't force you to, but it's the truth. I've felt more alive with you than I have my entire life. Why would I give that up?"

"I don't know, why would you?"

I wave my hand dismissively. "You're impossible sometimes."

She tries to suppress a smile and fails miserably. "So I've been told. Mostly by you."

We cross the river to the other bank as the first raindrops start pelting me in the head. The warm summer air has been replaced with a chill and stiff breeze from the incoming storm. None of that seems to deter Lyla. She presses on, leading us down the sidewalk with the French government building in the background before stopping suddenly.

She looks back over her shoulder, recognizes the building, and smiles. "Do you know where we are?"

"Yep. Paris."

It felt good to give her that answer. I've gotten caught in that ridiculous question more times than I can count. Every single response I've gotten from Lyla was sarcastic. Now, it was my turn. Given the knowing smile marching across her lips, Lyla knew she deserved it.

"Very good, Magellan, but where in Paris?"

I look around a bit. This part of Paris looks all the same to me. The architecture is stunning, but none of the buildings stands out. I turn to Lyla and shrug.

"Behind us is the Hôtel de Ville. It's a French government building. There was a famous picture taken right about where we're standing."

"Oh yeah? Of what?"

Lyla grabs my jacket with both hands. "This."

She pulls me closer, and we share a short but sensual kiss. I wasn't sure I would ever get one again from her. Things have been that weird since Monaco. She's been aloof and lost in her own world while putting a distance between us that I wasn't sure could ever be bridged. When our lips part but our faces remain close, I think I may have been worried for nothing. It's just like Venice, except for getting pelted with raindrops that feel like they're the size of golf balls.

"The Kiss by the Hôtel de Ville," Lyla almost whispers. "It's a famous photograph that captures a couple sharing a kiss on a busy Paris street in 1950. It's an iconic representation of Parisian romance."

"Yeah, it was taken by photographer Robert Doisneau and is considered one of the most romantic images in photographic history. Its enduring popularity comes from being a candid shot against this charming backdrop," I matter-of-factly say, turning and gesturing at the building behind me. "Of course, everyone later learned that the photograph was staged using actors, but it didn't matter. The appeal is how it conveys love in the heart of a city like Paris."

"You knew?"

"I took an elective photography class during my sophomore year at Princeton."

Lyla smacks my chest. "Why didn't you say anything?"

"I was hoping for a famous recreation."

She gives me a quick, excited kiss and looks over her shoulder. "Let's get out of this rain."

We run to the entryway of a nearby building and share a long, passionate, peel-the-paint-off-the-walls kiss. When we finally come up for air, Lyla can't hide her beaming smile. Everything is suddenly right in my world. There is no rain, no Braus, no Kinsey, and no American Outreach. It is her and me sharing the experience the world has to offer. Nothing else matters.

"Where do we go from here?"

"My dearest Braden, I need to get you out of these wet clothes."

"I, uh, I meant…."

Lyla covers my lips with a finger and kisses me again. "I know what you meant. You should be more concerned about what I mean."

Lyla gives me a seductive look and leads me by the hand back the way we came.

"We're not allowed to sleep together at the art school."

"You're such a stickler for the rules. We're not allowed to *cohabitate*. That doesn't mean I can't have guests. And what happens behind closed doors is nobody's damn business."

"Even Jean-Claude's?"

"Especially Jean-Claude," Lyla giggles.

"Okay…let's go."

"No," she says, stopping. "We need to get you your espresso first."

"Seriously?" I ask, stopping. "Now you're going to make me wait?"

Lyla gives me another kiss. "Good things come to those who do. Besides, you're going to need the energy."

Chapter Forty-Seven

The Finish Line

The darkness of the room soothes Braus. There is a peace in stillness and a distinct quiet that only the night brings. He has learned to relish both. The only noise is the clanging of heating pipes and the rustling of his pants as he props his feet on the old, battered desk.

This is the right room. Braden Fox travels light, and there aren't many personal effects here. It's not if his quarry will return to his accommodation, but when. He must have gone to Lyla's room. Braus hopes his target enjoys himself because that fairy tale is about to meet its abrupt ending.

It's after one in the morning when he finally hears rustling on the other side of the door before it opens. The overhead light comes on, and it takes Braden a beat to see Braus sitting in the chair with his legs propped up on the desk. The German expected to see him freeze in fear. Not this time. It's as if his target knew he was waiting for him. Instead of running or screaming bloody murder, he simply closes the door behind him.

"Get your feet off the desk," Braden commands. "You're not at home watching Netflix in your living room."

The corner of Braus's mouth curls in amusement. He's never had someone talk to him like that, especially when his gun is resting on the desk within arm's reach.

"I don't think you're in a position to make demands."

"I'm positioned to make that one," Braden says. "This is my room."

"I figured you'd be shitting yourself," Braus admits, doing as Braden asked and placing his feet on the floor. "Instead, you're acting like I'm an old friend dropping in to say hi."

"Let's be honest – this was always going to be the outcome, whether it was here in Paris or somewhere else."

"That's true," the German says.

"I do have a question…what took you so long?"

Braus takes the question as a slight and has the urge to put a bullet through his forehead. But it wasn't an insult – it was a compliment. He has worked with Braden before and always delivered results quickly. That was what he was used to…and what he expected.

"Did you think this would happen faster?"

Braden presses his lips together before sitting on the edge of the bed. "I know you and your reputation. I honestly didn't think I would make it out of Florida."

"A reputation that you've tarnished over the past weeks," Braus says, picking up his gun and admiring it. "Do you have any idea how badly I want to kill you for that?"

"I can imagine. What are you waiting for? You've got a gun. Do what you came here to do."

Again, that isn't the reaction Braus expected. There is no hint of fear in Braden's voice. Nothing on his face or in his body language shows that he's afraid. It's like he's accepted his fate and is ready to die if it comes to that.

"It's not that simple."

"Why not? Do you want to torture me first or something?"

Braus almost laughs. "That thought has crossed my mind as well. Nobody knew why you left. I was operating under the assumption that you were looking to sell out American Outreach."

"I'm sure that's what Arden was most worried about…wait, knew? You used the past tense."

Braus leans forward. "A lot has come to light in the past week."

"You found out about Kinsey and Travis."

It wasn't posed as a question but as a declarative statement. Braden is a smart man…or an intuitive one.

"The Cossack has a way of getting information from people," Braus says, shifting his gaze between his gun and Braden. "In this case, he managed to get her to confess the affair to her father."

"So, Arden knows? I'll bet he wasn't happy. I wouldn't want to be in Travis's shoes right now."

"No, you don't, Mr. Fox. Travis Breckinridge is dead."

That was the first real reaction that Braus elicited since the man returned to his room. It was a look of surprise more than one of loss.

"Good. I hope The Cossack made him suffer."

"It was a suicide."

Braden lets out a little laugh. "Sure, it was. I hope The Cossack made him suffer."

"Do you want to know how your wife reacted to Travis's tragic demise?"

"Not really."

The German studies him. Braden Fox may work in a ruthless industry where the truth is as elusive as seeing Bigfoot walking a chupacabra on a leash down the Yellow Brick Road, but that was an honest answer. It's in his face and eyes. He doesn't care what Kinsey thinks. That confirms everything Braus heard about their relationship, not that further confirmation was needed. Another matter needs clarity, though.

"I was going to abduct you here in Paris. I even followed you and Lyla on a walk the other day."

Braden tenses. "You know her name."

"That's how I tracked you to a Parisian art school. I was behind you down by the river. I thought maybe you spotted me when you stopped to tie your shoe, but then you kept walking and took the stairs up to the bridge. I was going to grab you then."

Braden stares at the wall behind Braus. He's lost in thought, likely replaying the walk in his mind to see if he remembers being followed.

"Why didn't you?" he finally mumbles.

It's a simple but telling question. Braden doesn't know about Lyla's shadow or how that was a driving reason Braus passed on completing his mission. If he does know, he doesn't realize the scope or reason behind the surveillance. Women keep secrets, but Lyla's is a doozie that she apparently hasn't shared.

"Circumstances prevented it."

"I'm glad you didn't. It gave us the chance to reveal our paintings."

"Ah, yes…I saw the canvases. Yours must be the ugly one with a stick figure standing in a city."

Braden almost laughs. "Yeah, that's the one."

"Lyla's painting was the couple dancing? It was beautiful. She painted the two of you, didn't she?"

"At a ball in Vienna."

Braus nods. He has to hand it to Braden – he's made the most of this journey. Not only did he find a beautiful woman as a travel partner, but he seems to have worked in a lifetime full of experiences. It should bring about resentment since Braus was stuck in cheap hotels and eating on the go. Instead, he finds himself almost admiring the life Braden has been leading. It's too bad it has to end for him.

"All right. You have a silencer on that thing. Get this over with."

"It's a suppressor," Braus corrects him.

"Whatever. Just do me a favor – Lyla is innocent in all this. She doesn't know anything about what I did at American Outreach. Please leave her alone."

"She's a loose end, Braden."

"No, she isn't," he says, staring hard at Braus through serious eyes. "I don't expect you to believe me, but you're a master at reading people. Talk to her. You'll see that she doesn't know anything of value."

The German spins the weapon on the desk. His orders don't include killing Braden, but he doesn't know that. Using that as leverage along with Lyla could make this whole thing easier. This is the finish line, and how he ends the race may be more important than how he ran it.

"There is one alternative that would spare both your lives."

"What do you mean?"

"I mean that you will do what I say. It's the only way Lyla lives to see the end of the week. Whether you do depends on how closely you listen."

Braden nods. "Okay. What do you want me to do?"

Chapter Forty-Eight

Hard Sell Made Easy

I didn't expect to be having this conversation. Then again, I didn't expect to be breathing for long after Braus found me. I knew that running into him was a foregone conclusion – a matter of "when," not "if." I knew with certainty what the result would be when I did. I never for a minute thought I'd be wrong. But I was.

The day was uneventful. I wish I could say that this dinner would be the same. This is our last night in Paris, so Lyla and I dress up and head to a bistro with a reputation for excellent cuisine and a very French atmosphere. She looks stunning, not that she ever doesn't. I should be focused on her, but my mind is elsewhere.

I should be happy that Braus offered me an alternative to my fate, but this is harder than it should be. My time with Lyla is coming to an end. Every day from here on out is a gift. Then again, every day since Key West has been one. I never should have escaped my German pursuer that day. I never should have made it out of the U.S., much less led him on a chase across two continents and an ocean.

Meeting her changed everything. What started as a way to continue fleeing for my life turned into something else entirely. It wasn't supposed to happen, but I fell in love with Lyla somewhere along the way. Now, it's far too late to tell her my true motives for leaving New York. There is a price to pay for that lack of vision, and we've arrived at the cashier.

There is one thing left to do that will buy us more time. It's the only thing left for me to hope for. Time to find a way to extract myself from the situation I find myself in. Time to make things right. Time to convince Lyla that I never meant to lie to her. This is the first step in that journey. All Lyla needs to do is say "yes." That may be the hardest part of all.

"Hello? Earth to Braden," she says, grabbing my hand and shaking me into the present. "Are you even listening to me?"

"Yes," I say, causing her to cock her head. "Okay, no. I'm sorry."

"You've been distracted since last night. Is everything okay?"

Everything is definitely not okay. I thought I was hiding it pretty well, but this woman is nothing if not intuitive. She can sense my emotions before I even recognize what they are. I should have known that she would see through the façade I erected to mask them.

In some respects, her suspicions may make this proposition easier. Lyla is going to press me for details until I crack and give them to her. We've traveled that road countless times before. She is relentless when she wants answers. I have to do this, so I'm grateful for her persistence…this time.

"I'm sorry. Yes, everything is fine."

"Are you sure?"

"I am."

I croak the answer out more than speak it. From the words to the tone to the delivery, nothing about it is convincing. Lyla sets her fork down on the plate and folds her arms across her chest. Now I know I'm in trouble.

"I don't believe you. In all the time we've spent together, you've never been this detached. I'm asking for your input about where we should go next, I think for the first time. Instead of telling me where you want to go, you're thinking about something else."

There's an annoyance in her tone. I fear that I'm about to turn it into something else entirely.

"Where to go next is *exactly* what I'm thinking about. I want to go to New York."

There, I said it. I didn't know what to expect, but Lyla's reaction isn't enthusiastic. It was a long shot that she would agree without questioning my motives. She breaks eye contact, finding interest in everything about this restaurant that doesn't include looking at me.

"Kinsey is there."

"I know."

"Why would you want to go back?"

"You needed to come to Paris. I need to go to New York."

Lyla rests her chin on her hands and studies me. "Why?"

Because I've been hunted by a ruthless German employed by my father-in-law since I left New York, and he finally found me and threatened to kill us both if we don't get on a plane back to the States. That's the honest answer. They're also words I can't utter. Not now.

"Closure."

"With Kinsey?"

"No," I say, shaking my head slightly, "she doesn't deserve that. I got mine after meeting you and realizing she never loved me as much as she said she did. Closure comes in many forms – one of them is legal."

A glimmer of realization lights up her eyes. "You want to get a divorce?"

"I'm married, Lyla, at least on paper. Do you want to be the 'other woman' for the rest of our lives?"

"Braden…I don't give a damn what a piece of paper says…and I'm not the marrying type."

"I know, and I'm not asking. But I don't want that hanging over my head. That means filing paperwork, and to do that, we need to go to New York."

"And you want me there?"

"Absolutely. Have you ever been?"

Lyla presses her lips together and shakes her head. In all her travels, I can't believe she's never visited New York City. Now that I think about it, I can't believe I've never asked her if she's been there. It has come up countless times in our conversations.

"It's a great city, not that I ever took the time to really experience it," I admit.

"I don't like this."

Yeah, I wouldn't say I like it either. Truth be told, I could stay married to Kinsey forever if it means never seeing her, Braus, Arden, or The Cossack ever again. I know I won't be seeing Travis. I just don't want to meet his fate, and those are the stakes.

"I knew you wouldn't. I was preoccupied thinking of how I was going to tell you this is what I *need*."

"Braden, I don't care about your past. I don't care if you're still married."

"I do. I wouldn't ask this if it weren't important to me."

I level my eyes at her, using them to plead with her to say yes. So much rides on this decision. I don't expect her to agree, and I'm prepared to have this conversation all night until she does. It's that important. Everything rides on it…everything.

"Okay. Book the flight. We'll leave tomorrow."

"That's it?" I ask, almost stunned that she so readily agreed to the proposal.

"That's it. You followed me to Paris, no questions asked. Then, you patiently sat next to me for days while I painted. The least I can do is reciprocate. If that means a trip to New York, then to the Big Apple we shall go."

I don't want to deceive her. I was ready for the hard sell, but Lyla made it easy because she's learning to trust me. It kills me inside that I'm violating that trust, but there's no alternative. I should have told her about Braus a long time ago. She should have told me about her shadow and why he was following her. That's the problem with secrets – they lead to regrets. It's something I will have to live with. We both kept them, and now mine has caught up to me.

Chapter Forty-Nine

Mutual Respect

The public house located only a dozen blocks from the art school is quiet. Only a couple of other patrons are here, and Braus is the only one seated at a stool along the ornate mahogany bar. That doesn't mean he has the bartender's undivided attention. There is a football match on television that is soaking up most of it. Or soccer, as Americans call it, for whatever reason.

Braus checks his watch. The man is late. That doesn't mean anything. Unless it does. He's about to send a text when Braden eases onto the stool next to him. He doesn't look at the German. Instead, he studies the bottles lined up on the shelves behind the bar and acts like he and Braus don't know each other.

"We're on a flight to New York tomorrow."

"I know," Braus says, sipping a glass of scotch.

"You checked the flight records?"

"And I was sitting three tables away when you made your pitch. Very well done. I didn't think Miss Chance would be that easy to convince."

"Yeah, I didn't either." Braden shakes his head.

The bartender stops by and sets a napkin in front of his new guest. Braden orders a bourbon on the rocks, and the man moves off. Braus pegged him as the martini type. It's another misconception that has been corrected since this chase began.

"You were there in case I tried to convince her to run."

Braus turns his glass in circles on the bar. "I'm not much into American politics, but one of your leaders once said, 'Trust, but verify.'"

"Ronald Reagan."

"I figured you would know that. Mr. Fox, if I thought you would run, French police would have hauled you out of that art school in a body bag."

"No doubt."

"How did you manage to slip away?" Braus asks. "You and Lyla are rarely apart."

"She wanted to spend time with Jean-Claude before we left. I told her I was going to take a walk to admire the city one last time. Thank you, Braus."

Those are three words he has never heard in all the time he has been doing this. It's not something that results from his line of work. Any words he gets from his target are usually laced with profanity and plenty of ill-wishes.

"For what?"

Braden turns to look at him. "Not hurting her."

The words of thanks were genuine. It isn't an act.

"You must love her a lot," Braus observes, causing Braden to lower his eyes. "I don't blame you. Lyla is a beautiful woman who's full of life. She's nothing like your soon-to-be-ex."

"Kinsey is beautiful."

"She is, but that's not what I meant, and you know it. Kinsey's a snake whose loyalty doesn't extend past herself. She only married you to get back at her father. Did you know that?"

Braden scowls before taking a long sip of the drink the bartender sets in front of him. "No, but I do now. After everything that happened, I guess I'm not surprised. I should have seen it."

"You were smitten. In my experience, men don't think clearly when women are involved."

"Does that apply to me now, Braus?"

The German gives Braden the side eye. "I don't know…does it? You're going to need to make some choices in New York, Braden. Those decisions will define the rest of your life. And Lyla's."

"Yeah. I know."

This isn't the Braden Fox he knew. He was a weak man who complained, didn't accept responsibility, and didn't appreciate the world around him. Number crunching and quietly threatening politicians was all he knew.

This Braden isn't protesting or whining about his predicament. He isn't pleading for mercy or trying to make a bribe to get Braus to look the other way. He's more of a man than he expected.

"Braus…promise me you'll look after Lyla. Don't let your boss hurt her after we get to New York."

"I can't promise that."

"Please. Whatever happens to me…I need to know that Lyla's safe."

So, he is going to plead, but not for himself. That's a sacrifice most people would never make. Respect isn't something Braus has for most people. He never had it for Braden. That is beginning to change.

"Okay."

"Okay?"

"Mr. Fox, I have no desire to harm Miss Chance and don't want anyone else to, either. You should open yourself to the possibility that I'm not the monster you think I am."

He scoffs. "Steve would disagree."

"Steve?"

Braden turns his head and regards Braus with a knowing smile. "The bartender at The Drunken Lobster in Key West."

"Ah, yes. I remember. That was regrettable, but the man was being uncooperative. All I wanted was information. He could have just answered my questions. He wasn't interested in talking about you."

"That's because he threw me out the night before," Braden says, getting a quizzical look. "It's a long story."

"Can I ask you a question?"

"I wouldn't think you'd need my permission, Braus."

He cocks his head. "True. You managed to stay one step ahead of me for months. How?"

"I don't know," Braden says with a shrug. "We never stayed anywhere more than a few days and paid cash for almost everything. Other than that, I wasn't really trying. I figured you would catch up with me in Pamplona after running with the bulls. Lyla gave the hospital my information without knowing my circumstances."

"I never expected you to do anything that adventurous. It was the last place I would have looked. You checked out of your hotel before I got there and I couldn't catch up with you at the train station in time."

Braden nods. Braus leaves out the part about hiring a heavily armed team to accompany him. He doesn't want him to know that they thought he was a bigger threat than he was. It's embarrassing.

"You did a good job staying off the grid," the German admits. "I thought you were purposely trying to deceive me when you used your card in Lucerne."

Braden laughs. "The line was long. I used the ticket machine, but Lyla managed to sweet-talk a desk clerk into giving us first-class tickets on a different train that had no connection."

He's telling the truth. There's no sign of deception. Amazingly, what Braus thought was a calculated effort to avoid capture was actually due to something so simple as a long queue. This hunt has transformed from infuriating to eye-opening.

"I was waiting for you in Munich. When you didn't step off that train, I was ready to storm the gates of hell to kill you. I was convinced it was tradecraft and that Lyla was an operative of some kind."

"Sorry to disappoint you. She's nothing of the sort."

"So I've realized. I can laugh about it now, but I wasn't at the time. What about Monaco? Why did you get the fancy hotel there? You knew I could track that."

"We weren't staying long…and I wanted to stay someplace nice with her."

"She must have loved it."

Braden winces. "It turned out to be more complicated than I thought."

"And that's how you ended up here. Lyla still doesn't know I was hunting you, does she?"

"No."

It's a quiet, almost rueful admission. Braus considers telling Braden the truth about her shadow but decides against it. She should have the opportunity first – if the chance presents itself. But why hasn't she told him?

"You keep secrets from her."

"And she keeps them from me," he snaps. "I haven't told her much about my past because she hasn't said much about hers. It works well for both of us."

Braus knows he struck a chord. He needs Braden on that plane and decides not to press him further.

"You were smart to protect her. Another question – how could you afford this? You didn't pull enough out of your account to afford a private jet from South America to Europe."

The corner of his mouth curls. "A roll of the dice."

The story is something out of a movie. Braden explains his run of luck at the craps table like the whole thing happened last week. Braus listens to him talk about the old man, the crazy stick calls, and the woman who blew on the dice. He's into his second bourbon by the time he finishes the narration with the ride to the airport.

"A hard ten hop bet? That was a hell of a risk. What were you thinking?"

"That I would lose everything and wait for you to come collect me. Instead, it gave me what I needed to get out of the country. Life works that way sometimes."

Braus shakes his head. That explains a lot. "You've led a charmed life, Braden."

"Yeah, all evidence to the contrary. What happens when I get to New York?"

It's an honest question. Even if Braus knew, he probably couldn't tell him.

"I don't know. My job ends when you step off the plane at JFK. The Cossack will handle things from there."

"Okay. I guess it's almost time to find out." Braden drains the remainder of his drink. "You're buying. See you in New York."

He's a man who has accepted his fate. Whatever that is, because even Braus isn't sure. He's resolved to grant his former quarry's wish – Lyla is a bright, wonderful, and gifted woman. Nothing should be allowed to happen to her.

Chapter Fifty

Scene of the Crime

The wheels touch down on the runway, and the plane slows before veering onto one of the countless taxiways that ring the airport. The pilot welcomes us to JFK over the public address system and provides us with gate information and the current weather. I've never been much of a traveler, so taking a commercial flight from Paris's Charles de Gaulle airport is a new experience. Lyla and I splurged for a business class ticket, knowing I couldn't stomach being shoehorned into economy seating. It was a good choice.

Not checking in luggage earned us an interesting look at the ticket counter. A one-way trip with no bags is a red flag in the post-9/11 era in the United States and probably landed us on a watch list. It doesn't help that Lyla is half-Persian.

The actual travel aside, my uneasiness is more about being back in a city I've always called home. I'm putting on a brave face to keep up appearances, but I have no idea what happens after the door opens and we walk up the jetway into the terminal. Braus was vague about my fate once we arrived in New York. He claimed his mission was to deliver me home, and that may be true. Whether he was lying about not knowing what happens to me next is anyone's guess.

With no need to rush to the baggage claim, we stroll down the corridor to join the line at passport control. Lyla is on edge. Whether she's reflecting my mood or is equally nervous is a coin flip. I stopped trying to figure her out long ago.

After being officially admitted into the United States, we bypass customs and venture through the security barrier into the arrivals hall. Drivers with signs await their charges along the metal railing. I expect to see Braus holding one with my name on it. It would be something he would do as an unfunny joke, but the German is nowhere to be found. Nobody is waiting for us.

"What's the plan?" Lyla turns and asks.

"We can take a taxi into Manhattan and check into a hotel."

"Do you have a reservation?"

That's a good point. I didn't bother making lodging arrangements because I figured Arden would have other plans. That conclusion is looking short-sighted.

"No, but there are ten thousand to choose from. I'm thinking of starting with the Waldorf-Astoria. They have an amazing spa, and I could use a massage after that flight."

Lyla smiles. "Sounds good. I need to use the ladies' room. I'll be right back."

"Don't get lost," I call out as she walks away.

"I'll try not to," she says with a laugh.

I should be used to the reaction she gets just by walking. A dozen heads track her movement as she heads for the far end of the hall. One woman notices her husband gawking at Lyla and slaps him in the chest to get his attention. That's one of the milder beatings I've seen. In Italy, a woman bludgeoned her boyfriend once for staring too long and hard. Lyla ignores the attention, but I notice it. It's a reminder of what I have gained…and may lose.

I head over to a coffee kiosk. I got a little sleep on the flight, but I want to make the most of the time I have in New York with Lyla. That means being awake, and staying that way requires caffeine. Fortunately, there are options here, and I join a short line queued up in front of a register.

"You made the right choice, Mr. Fox," an ominous voice says from just over my shoulder.

He positions himself next to me, and I turn slightly to see the big Russian staring at the menu above the counter. He's dressed casually, fitting in with weary travelers and people making airport pickups.

"I was wondering who would be sent to collect me."

"The suspense is over, only I'm not here to collect you. I'm just making sure you arrived safely and aren't thinking about booking a new flight out of here."

"You don't trust Braus?"

The comment is meant to insult him, but The Cossack shows no reaction at all. "I don't trust anyone. Braus is capable, but you don't stay alive in my line of work by making assumptions that those around you are doing the right thing."

"All right. So, what happens next?"

"Nothing."

"Nothing?"

"Nothing," The Cossack confirms. "Go find yourself a hotel. Enjoy your evening."

That wasn't one of the hundreds of scenarios I played out in my head during the long flight across the Atlantic. I move to the cashier, place my order for a large coffee, and pay. The Russian steps off to the side with me after politely refusing to order with the young girl behind the counter.

"What? Are you going to make my death look like an accident?" I ask, minding my speaking volume.

The Cossack looks around. "If Arden Davenport wanted you dead, Mr. Fox, the French would have found your body floating in the Seine."

"Why doesn't he?"

"You'll have to ask him."

"I'd rather not," I mumble.

The Cossack presses his lips together before responding. "Oh, I doubt you'll have much choice in that."

That's not a conversation I'm looking forward to. Arden is more than my father-in-law. He's a demanding boss who thought I betrayed him and the company he cherishes. He cares less about Kinsey than he does American Outreach, but that doesn't mean Arden won't treat me like a threat to both. I know what happens when he does.

"Did you kill Travis?"

The Cossack scans the arrivals hall again before staring hard at me. "Do you care?"

"He was my best friend," I say before cocking my head theatrically. "He was also sleeping with my wife. So, not particularly. I just know he wasn't the suicidal type."

"Love drives people to do unexpected things. From what I hear, you should know that better than anyone. Miss Chance is a lovely woman. I shouldn't need to tell you what happens if you don't cooperate with us."

"No, you don't. Braus was very clear about that. But I expect nothing to happen to her if I do cooperate."

The Cossack shrugs. "That's not up to me."

"Yes, it is. Arden would never get his hands dirty. That's why he pays you."

"A small fortune, as it turns out. Not one I plan on losing by failing to abide by his wishes. You're not in a position to make demands, Mr. Fox. Don't presume you're calling any of the shots. From this point forward, I own you. Arden Davenport owns you. What happens to Lyla is what happens. Get used to that reality."

The girl behind the counter hands me my coffee. When I turn to respond to the Russian, he's nowhere to be found. I search the hall for him and only see excited family members, indifferent airport workers, and weary travelers lugging suitcases.

"Looking for me?" Lyla sweetly asks when I turn to see her standing in front of me.

"It took me my whole life to find you. I don't want to lose you now."

She kisses me gently on the lips. "That was sweet. Campy but sweet."

It's also more truthful than she can know.

"Are we heading out?" Lyla asks.

"Yes, ma'am. Our yellow chariot awaits out front."

We head to ground transportation to get into the line for taxis. I can hear a ticking clock in my head. The slow staccato of time passing echoes in my ear, with every second bringing me that much closer to an uncertain future.

Chapter Fifty-One

Her Father's Love

Kinsey swings the door open and scowls. Arden should be used to that reaction, but it still hurts. He would never expect his daughter to throw her arms around him out of glee. That's not their relationship. Maybe the best he can hope for is for her to open the door and not say anything.

It doesn't matter. Arden follows her into the spacious apartment after closing the door. Kinsey is a means to an end at this point. This is all about preserving American Outreach and the empire he has built. His daughter walks to the sofa and sits down. She knows it, too. Arden owns her. Her fate is in his hands.

"Are you ready?" Arden asks, standing beside the sofa.

"For what?"

"To do your part. To be the dutiful daughter you pledged to be."

"Do I have a choice?" she asks after sneering.

Arden places his hands behind his back. "There are always choices. It's the consequences that get you. It's always the consequences."

Kinsey scoffs. Acting every bit the spoiled brat, she is getting the harshest lesson he can offer about the stakes of her decisions. Nobody ever said life was fair. She has lived like a privileged member of royalty. That comes with a price she must now pay.

"You don't believe me? You were faced with a choice not long ago: Remain faithful in your marriage or fool around with your husband's best friend. You chose the latter."

"It was a loveless marriage," Kinsey argues.

"On your end, maybe. I'm certain Braden wouldn't have agreed — at least until he found out you were whoring yourself with his best friend."

"I never wanted to marry him."

"Yet you did marry him. Nobody forced you to say, 'I do.' You did it to get back at me, as I recall you saying. Regardless of your intentions, you made a vow and then betrayed it…and you betrayed him. That was your choice. This is the consequence of that choice."

Kinsey stands and walks over to the wet bar. Arden looks down at the floor, wondering if it's excessively worn from the number of trips back and forth she must make. His daughter pours herself a drink without offering him one. Hospitality at its finest. Then again, offering a beverage is something done when a guest is welcome in a home. He isn't welcome here.

"Is that how you look at everything?" Kinsey asks, taking a sip while staring at the wall. "Like an equation on a balance sheet?"

"More or less. That's how life works."

"You're wrong!" Kinsey says, turning.

Arden pushes deeper into the back of the sofa and checks the length of his fingernails. "Am I? I built an empire on the premise that you have to pay a price to get what you want. You pay a prostitute and you get laid. You pay a college and they give you a degree. You pay—"

"You have to study in college!"

"You pay with your time for that grade. In fact, time is the most valuable of all currencies. It's why people save it, make it, waste it, spend it…it's why people take shortcuts. Time is valuable. The politicians I work with want to get reelected, but fundraising costs time they don't have. So, they trade favors and access for the money I bring them."

"And screw over the American people in the process."

"Americans are unique in their lack of attention. A sizable number can't name the vice president. Most can't name a single Supreme Court justice or even their own congressman. If they get screwed, it's because they deserve it. How politicians handle that is their business."

"Making you filthy rich in the process."

"I'm a capitalist," Arden says, outstretching his arms. "There's a cost to everything. Thus, the equation."

"Let's not pretend that American Outreach is some benevolent political group," Kinsey says, pointing her index finger at him while still grasping the glass with the rest of her hand. "If you were, you wouldn't need that psychopathic Russian to threaten people who don't do what you want. You wouldn't need men like Braden to work the financial angles to make magic happen."

"Like I said, it's all part of the equation. That's the cost of succeeding. It's inescapable, even for me. To get something, you need to give something."

Kinsey refills her glass and moves to the sofa opposite the one her father is seated on. "What am I getting out of all this?"

Arden grins. The equation at work. She is cooperating and expects something in return. Her father has admitted that he isn't immune to that particular cosmic law. It's too bad his daughter is too blind to see that she is already being rewarded.

He leans forward and rests his forearms on his legs. "Your life. That's the trade."

It's a fair trade, at least in his eyes. Kinsey wanted to ruin him. She sank her talons into Braden to try to corrupt him, setting her up to do unspeakable damage to American Outreach. That betrayal can't go unanswered. It won't.

"Why won't you just die?"

The seething hatred in the tone of her voice is almost enough to peel the paint off the walls. Arden has enemies and people he despises. But he can't think of a single enemy or adversary he hates as much as she loathes him. It's not healthy. That level of angst is going to burn her up inside.

"That's not a very nice thing to say to your father. I will leave this world soon enough. But until I do, you will play your part. You know what the consequences will be if you don't. But, as always, the choice is yours."

Arden rises. He thinks about pouring a drink of his own, but his time here is done. Kinsey may find these visits agonizing, but they aren't much fun for him either. He wishes he didn't have to manipulate his own daughter to do the right thing. Unfortunately, that's not the world they live in. So, manipulation it is.

"Braden landed at JFK this morning. He is in the city. It's time to put the plan into motion. I will call you with the details. When I do, I expect you to pick up."

"The woman…the one he was traveling with that you went to great lengths in describing – is she with him?"

"Not that I think you remotely care, but yes, she arrived with him. Don't worry about her. She won't be a problem. Braden has some equations of his own he needs to worry about."

"Are you going to have your goons kill her, too?"

"I'm sorry, my loving daughter, but Travis committed suicide. If anyone should feel guilt over his untimely death, it's you. He was so lost—"

Arden can't suppress a smile. She is no longer capable of hurting him. He's seen to that.

"You're an insufferable asshole!"

"Sticks and stones, Kinsey. Sticks and stones. As I said, I've been called far worse by people way more important than you will ever be. As for Miss Lyla Chance, her future depends on the math. Keep your phone close. I'll be in touch soon."

Yes, these visits are trying, but there is a level of satisfaction to them. Kinsey thought she was queen. Now, she's finding her castle is built on salt and sand. Her father is willing to let her keep wearing the crown. Whether her head stays attached to her shoulders or rolls across the floor is the last thing that needs to be decided.

Chapter Fifty-Two

One Last Dance

When someone mentions dancing in New York City, the first thought is the trendy nightclubs that have dotted the metropolis over the past century. Manhattan has a rich history of iconic hotspots like Studio 54, The Cotton Club, The Roxy, and Paradise Garage that shaped the city's nightlife and became ingrained in its cultural fabric. While most of these legacy clubs no longer operate, their influence and impact shaped their modern successors.

Chelsea's Marquee New York has an energetic atmosphere, while Up&Down in the Meatpacking District offers a mix of music genres in a unique multi-level space. Lyla isn't into EDM or club life. Ballroom dancing has been our thing since Buenos Aires. That limits my options on this side of the pond, but fortunately, there is one spot that's right in our wheelhouse.

The Rainbow Room on the 65th floor of the Rockefeller Center dates back to 1934. Its Art Deco design creates a timeless and elegant atmosphere, complete with sweeping panoramic views of the Manhattan skyline. In addition to its fine dining, it features live entertainment. Tonight, they have an orchestra, which will allow us to make use of its dance floor in the center of the restaurant.

It also required us to do some shopping. After checking into our hotel early, we head to Fifth Avenue. I decided against a tuxedo and opted for a suit, having it rush-tailored to be done in time for our dinner reservation. It was a bad decision. After seeing the elegant gown Lyla chose, I'm going to feel underdressed. It's too late to do anything about that now.

Clothing is important in dancing. It's fine to practice in street clothes or workout attire, but the traditional ballroom attire of flowing dresses for ladies and tailored suits for gentlemen adds to the visual appeal of the dance. Given my current circumstances, I'm on borrowed time. We should at least make a statement tonight.

Having dressed to the nines, we arrive at the prescribed time and are seated next to the dance floor. The next couple of hours remind me of the best times I've shared with Lyla. We laugh, joke, and exchange travel stories over an exquisite meal. The pressure is gone. It's like the world around us doesn't exist. And in between all that, we dance.

The orchestra is excellent, and we find ourselves putting our forks down to join a half dozen other pairs on the dance floor. They are amateurs, not that I'm not one. But after a few days of intense preparation for the Summer Edelweiss Ball, I feel more prepared than I'm sure my fellow dancers are. The dance floor clears, and I have a burning desire to put on a show as Lyla finishes the last of her espresso.

"What do you think? One last dance before we head out?"

She smiles broadly. "I'd love to."

I offer my hand, and we depart our table for the dance floor as the orchestra stops to select their next song. I leave Lyla standing there to do something odd – I make a request. It takes a moment to get the conductor's attention.

"Can I help you, sir?"

"I hope so. I'm wondering if you can play 'Vienna, City of My Dreams?'"

The conductor crinkles his brow and cocks his head. Although it's a great song to waltz to, it isn't a mainstream choice like "The Blue Danube" is. It's rare at any live music venue to depart widely from mainstream favorites. That's what people always want to hear, and that's probably why a broad smile races across his face.

"You got it!"

I thank him and return to Lyla in the middle of the dance floor. Everyone in the Rainbow Room has their eyes glued to us except the conductor, who is enthusiastically informing the musicians what the next piece will be. More specifically, they are gazing at the vision in the beautiful ball gown with whom I have the privilege of dancing.

"What did you ask for?" Lyla asks.

"You'll see."

This is the most romantic waltz I know. The composition has been embraced by dancers for its enchanting melody, even if it isn't a favorite. Lyla and I get into hold. I stand tall with a straight posture, maintaining a strong frame and connection with her. It's a close embrace, and that's my favorite part of this dance. I hold her left hand with my right and place my other hand on her back while she rests hers on my shoulder.

"Everybody is looking at us," Lyla whispers.

They are absolutely looking at her. Even the women. I don't bother correcting Lyla. She isn't the self-conscious type, but why tempt fate? I smile as the orchestra prepares to play.

"Good."

We spent three full days in Vienna striving for the perfect waltz, incorporating gentle turns and twirls executed with precision and balance. Our routines were choreographed, mostly because I had no idea what I was doing. This is different. I'm going to wing it – something I never could have imagined before I boarded the plane for Florida.

The music starts slow for the first ten seconds, so instead of launching into and sticking with a traditional box step, I lead her into a series of underarm turns. Lyla immediately responds when I raise my left arm, creating a pathway for the follower to spin underneath. Her movements are slow and graceful with the music. When the beat picks up, we launch into whisks. I step forward with my left foot while turning to the right, followed by a sidestep with my right foot. She mirrors these steps, creating a smooth turning motion. It must look amazing.

Our instructor explained that the waltz is a series of gliding steps and turns, with a strong emphasis on the rise and fall motion. That's what makes the dance so mesmerizing. Steps are taken in a smooth and flowing manner, with the dancers moving in harmony across the dance floor. Dancers express emotion through their movements. It's not about executing steps but conveying a connection and chemistry between partners. I didn't understand that until right now.

For the first time, I'm not thinking about what I should do next. I'm going with it. It's the first time in my life I've just let go and allowed myself to…well, live in the moment. Lyla has pushed me to do that throughout our journey – be spontaneous without forgetting to stop and smell the roses. Enjoy the world around me instead of looking at the next task or finding an angle to exploit. This is the first moment I've managed to do that for myself.

The music changes a whisker shy of halfway through the arrangement, and I signal Lyla into a fleckerl. It's a rotational pattern where she and I weave in and out of each other. The footwork is tricky, and I mix in some natural and reverse turns, creating an intricate and visually appealing pattern. I can hear the oohs and ahs of the diners over the orchestra.

The music changes again, and I lead Lyla into a twinkle, causing her to steal a glance at me. I can't help but grin. We didn't practice this much in Austria, and I'm half surprised I remember the series of quick, small pivots that create a lively and playful element in the waltz.

"Vienna, City of My Dreams" is only a little longer than two minutes in length. The ending of the composition is as graceful and beautiful as its beginning, teeing us up for an epic closing pose. We move into a promenade, stopping to elongate our lines as we move across the dance floor. The fluid movement causes an increasing roar of applause from the room. We end in a final embrace as people rise to their feet and clap.

Lyla stares at me. Her eyes are soft and appreciative. She's breathing heavier, as am I. It's partly from the dance's exertion and partly from the exhilaration of it.

"Where did that come from?"

"It's the product of living *la vie dansante*," I explain. "Too much?"

I bring her upright. "Are you kidding? I could really get used to the dancing life with you."

We kiss in the middle of the dance floor in front of appreciative diners and incredulous dancers. It's one long, soft, passionate kiss that I fear may be our last. If it is, it's certainly going to be one to remember.

Chapter Fifty-Three
An Unwanted Surprise

It's been a magical night. Vienna was amazing, and this would be its equal if I weren't busy looking over my shoulder the whole time. I know what's coming; I only don't know when to expect it. Maybe sensing the end of the journey forced me to savor every moment a little more.

Lyla is none the wiser. At least, that's what I've been telling myself. She must know something is wrong. Despite my best efforts to mask my anxiety, like most women, she's intuitive. She knows I'm not acting like myself, even if she can't pinpoint how or why.

Not that she's acting normal, either. She's equally observant of our surroundings, likely searching for signs of her shadow. I won't ask if that's the reason. It's liable to lead to a conversation I don't want to have, or worse, an argument. If this is going to be our last night together, I don't want to spend it arguing. Of the many things in this situation that are out of my control, that is the one thing I can still influence.

Our taxi pulls up outside the hotel. I was more than willing to walk the short distance here from Rockefeller Center. She wasn't. I get it. I'm not the one wearing four-inch heels, and I have no desire to share the experience.

The Waldorf Astoria is a renowned luxury hotel brand with a history dating back to the late 19th century. The hotel was established in 1893 at Fifth Avenue and 33rd Street, and it quickly gained a reputation for exceptional service and opulence. That structure was demolished to construct the Empire State Building and the hotel relocated to Park Avenue. The Waldorf Astoria remains a symbol of luxury and sophistication. It's why countless dignitaries and celebrities still stay here while traveling to New York City.

One of them is apparently on the move. Several limousines are waiting on Park Avenue outside the hotel's main entrance as the doormen and bellhops eagerly wait at the entrance. The caravan forces our driver to drop us off farther up the block, profusely apologizing for the inconvenience. It isn't one. The rain hasn't started, and it's not like we're a half-mile away.

"How do you like the hotel?" I ask after catching Lyla staring at the lit façade and majestic overhangs as we walk back south.

"It's beautiful. It reminds me of our stay in Vienna."

I stop dead in my tracks. "That place was a dive!"

"It had character," she shrieks.

"Character? I think it was a crime scene before we rented it."

"The way you were snoring, it almost was," Lyla says, grabbing my arm and pulling me forward.

I don't think I snore, but then again, I'm asleep and can't really know. I share a laugh with Lyla at the dig as she clings to my arm. The moment is shattered by a sharp, deafening bang coming from the street as we approach the hotel's entrance. I almost jump out of my skin. Lyla looks around, alarmed. Even the doorman is on high alert.

Another loud bang pierces the night. I grab at my chest and stagger backward. Lyla desperately tries to steady me as I sway back and forth.

"Oh, he got me!" I exclaim before standing straight and laughing.

I found it hysterical. Lyla didn't. She slaps me on the chest and puts her hands on her hips. She should patent that move.

"That's not funny!"

A taxi cab sputters by, its exhaust loud from the apparent hole in the muffler. Apparently, the backfiring is the least of the vehicle's problems.

"Well, that backfire took a few years off my life," I admit.

"I hope not."

Lyla pulls me close and we share a kiss. New York is a big city. Manhattan is iconic. The hotel is majestic. Standing on this sidewalk and kissing a beautiful woman with whom I have completely fallen in love is priceless.

"I hope I'm not interrupting."

The feminine voice causes both of us to stop mid-kiss. My mouth hangs open when I see the source. Kinsey is clad in whatever five-thousand-dollar dress graced the window of some Fifth Avenue boutique. She hasn't changed a bit. Her hair is perfectly coiffed, and her makeup is flawless. Other than her eyes being puffy from tears over Travis's demise, she's a vision.

"Hello, Braden. It's been a long time."

I steal a glance at Lyla. Her eyes are riveted on the woman I once called my wife. She's seen my picture. Lord knows it started more than one argument. She knows what Kinsey looks like, but seeing her in person is another thing entirely. I feel her hands tighten around my arm as she continues her long, hard stare.

"Not long enough," I finally mutter.

"Don't be like that, Braden. You must be Lyla. It's nice to meet you."

"I doubt that."

"You're right. I wasn't looking forward to meeting the woman sleeping with my husband."

Lyla's eyes narrow. "From what I hear, you could learn a thing or two about fidelity yourself."

"Very true, Lyla…very true."

I close my eyes. I know what's coming next.

"How do you know my name?" Lyla asks, the suspicion in her voice making the hairs on the back of my neck stand up.

Kinsey grins. I speak before she can answer. I can explain it to Lyla later…along with everything else.

"What are you doing here, Kinsey?"

My soon-to-be ex-wife finally peels her eyes off Lyla, takes a deep breath, and raises her chin a bit.

"Looking for you. We need to talk."

"Make an appointment," Lyla snaps.

"I'm sorry for interrupting your evening, Lyla…well, no, I'm not. Some things need to be said between Braden and me. We should do it sooner rather than later. Wouldn't you agree?"

I have no real choice. If I decline, Kinsey's first call is to her father. Arden will call The Cossack, who will either tell Braus or handle the matter himself. I know the penalty for saying no. It isn't worth buying a couple of hours, and that's all I would get.

"Yeah, we probably should."

Kinsey looks quickly at Lyla and then back at me. I want to smack the sliver of the smile creasing her lips right off her face. Lyla has a far different reaction. Her eyes grow wide as she sidesteps and lets go of my arm.

"Seriously?"

"It'll be okay," I reassure her. And myself. "Go ahead and talk, Kinsey."

She scoffs. "In private. Come for a walk with me. I promise it won't take long."

I nod slowly at Kinsey and turn to Lyla. The look on my face must say it all. Her eyes go from being the size of saucers to dinner plates.

"You can't be serious. What's so important that it can't wait until tomorrow? Or never?"

"There's no time like the present to get this over with. I'll meet you upstairs."

Lyla's surprise turns to anger. She glares at me before shifting it to Kinsey. Then, without another word, she spins and strides through the door as the man opens it for her.

"Oh, she looks pissed."

The comment sends waves of anger pulsating through me. "Not as pissed as your boyfriend is. Assuming there's an afterlife."

"Keep the gloves up, Braden."

"You ambushed me, remember? You want to talk? Talk."

She nods up Park Avenue, and we begin walking north to Central Park. Maybe Braus or The Cossack is waiting there to kill me. It would almost be a welcome end to this misery. I despise unwanted surprises, especially when they involve Kinsey Davenport.

Chapter Fifty-Four

Ultimatums

Braden and Kinsey walk up the street, both looking straight ahead and neither of them saying anything. Braden's reaction to her sudden appearance was what she thought it would be, but it also wasn't the worst-case scenario. As they begin to walk along Central Park, it's clear he would rather be anywhere than here. Kinsey can relate. Unfortunately, she has a job to do and wants to get it over with.

"This is more awkward than I anticipated," Kinsey admits.

"What did you think it would be? Champagne and roses?"

"No, I guess not."

Braden scoffs. "I expected a visit from your father or maybe even The Cossack. I never expected to see *you*."

"I thought this was best coming from me."

Braden takes a couple more steps before turning to look at her. He was never a poker player, and today is no exception. He is wearing his resentment on his face.

"No, it's far more likely that your father thought that, and you were forced to play along."

He's right, not that Kinsey will admit it. They travel almost an entire block before she tries a different approach.

"Lyla is lovely. She seems nice."

Braden doesn't respond. He thinks the observations are a trap and refuses to walk into it. They need to communicate if they are going to get anywhere, so Kinsey decides to poke the bear.

"It didn't take you long to replace me."

"Pot meet kettle."

Kinsey nods. She had that coming. "Touché. I was wrong."

"I can think of a hundred things off the top of my head that you're wrong about. Which one are you owning up to?"

"All of them, probably," Kinsey admits. "I was wrong to agree to marry you."

"Clearly."

There wasn't the vitriol in his voice that she expected. It was completely devoid of emotion. Whatever pain he felt about her betrayal has receded. He's also absent any curiosity. It's making this conversation harder than it needs to be.

"You're not going to ask why I did it?"

"No. I don't really care."

"I'm going to tell you anyway. I—"

"Why? Why bother telling me? We're through, Kinsey. It's over. You did what you did, and I left. I've moved on. You don't owe me an explanation, and I don't want one."

At least he showed a little emotion, even if it's exasperation.

"That's just it," Kinsey mumbles. "It's not over."

"What do you mean?"

"You're a finance guy…I'm sure my father has shared his worldview with you. You appreciate equations almost as much as he does. It's why he looks at you like the son he never had. Or, at least, different than the daughter he never wanted."

"Boo hoo. You have daddy issues. Got it."

That diagnosis came quickly. Kinsey never viewed her relationship with her father that way, but it fits. At least Braden didn't say she needs therapy. It was actually a session with her therapist as a teenager where she conceived of this revenge tour against dear old dad.

"Yeah, I do. That's what led me to you. Not that anyone had to twist my arm. You're handsome, educated, accomplished—"

"Spare me your flattery," Braden interrupts.

"It's true. You're a dream guy, just not for me. We were never compatible."

Kinsey faces toward Central Park and away from Braden. A light drizzle begins to fall, making the street glisten under the streetlights.

"Everything I've done since the day we met was to lure you into marriage. I had to put on an act worthy of an Academy Award. It became too much to bear."

"Enter Travis. Was the affair your idea or his?"

"He made the first move. I honestly didn't fight it that hard."

Kinsey can feel Braden staring at her. Judging her. Questioning her. It's fair since she's lying. He probably already knows the truth or at least suspects it. Not that it matters. If they are going to fulfill her father's wishes, it's better if she doesn't confirm the truth.

Braden tucks his hands in his pockets defensively. "It doesn't change anything."

"It changes everything. When you disappeared, I thought I would never see you again. Never run my hands through your hair or kiss your lips. And now that you're back, I'm reminded of all I have lost…we have lost."

The rain picks up a little and now steadily beats against the concrete sidewalk.

"Stop playing games. You don't mean a word of that. You may have been a great actress during our marriage, but it's transparent now. We're never getting back together. Ever."

"You have no choice," Kinsey whispers, lowering her eyes. "Neither do I. If we don't, it will cost us our lives."

"What do you mean?"

"You're getting your life back, Braden. All of it. The apartment, the salary, American Outreach…and me. Everything is going to return to the way it was."

"I don't understand."

Whatever he was expecting to hear, that wasn't it. There is no more walking. They are just two people standing in the rain like a couple of kids trying to figure out how to avoid an arranged marriage.

"My father is offering us both a fresh start…. Well, that's not true. It's more like he's demanding one. That's what balances his equation. We're to return to being a happily married couple. You'll return to your job at American Outreach. If everything goes back to the way it was, we live long, fruitful lives."

"And if it doesn't?"

"You already know the answer to that. We will die in a horrific accident. So will Lyla. It's not a hollow threat. I know in my heart that The Cossack killed Travis. There's no doubt he would do the same to us."

Kinsey expects Braden to lash out – scream, yell, or throw a tantrum. He does none of those things. Instead, he starts to laugh.

"What's so funny?"

"Karma. When I went to Key West, that was my wish. I wanted my old life back."

"And now?"

He stares at Kinsey hard. "It's the last thing I want."

She understands the sentiment. Unfortunately, life isn't asking what she wants. Neither is her father. She opens her purse and pulls out a small box. Braden watches her without speaking.

"I kept this in case you ever came back."

Kinsey opens the box and pulls out a gold wedding band. Then she pulls out her diamond engagement ring and matching band, sliding the rings on her finger before taking his hand. She rotates it and sets the circular piece of gold onto his outstretched palm. He left it before fleeing New York and never expected to see it again.

"You're meeting with my father tomorrow morning at the office. If you agree to his terms, you will be wearing this on your left ring finger. It signals your cooperation. Do as he says, and we'll live a long life, Braden."

Kinsey closes Braden's fingers around the ring and kisses him on the lips. It's a quick peck devoid of passion. There won't be any of that. This will be a marriage in name only, just like it was for her before.

"The choice is yours to make for both of us."

Chapter Fifty-Five

A Secret Revealed

He should have brought popcorn for this show. He had no idea how Braden would respond to seeing the soon-to-be ex-Mrs. Fox. The look on his face when she appeared in front of him was priceless. The look on Lyla's was even better. Braus has to hand it to the man - Braden handled the ambush better than he would have. The German knows he would have punched her lights out.

Instead, they end up strolling north toward Central Park, leaving the lovely and mysterious Lyla to her own devices…and his. Braden won't look back, so Braus follows her into the hotel like he's a guest. He thought she would head straight to the elevator and up to their room. This would be easier in private. Instead, she has other ideas and heads straight through the Park Avenue Lobby and Main Lobby to the steakhouse. Braus follows her at a respectful distance. If she's used to staying alert for her shadow, it won't do to get spotted by being too aggressive.

Fortunately, none of the men tasked with tailing her are anywhere to be found. Curious. There's no doubt they're keeping tabs on her in the city. It might be that they have someone working for the hotel, maybe even in security. Braus will have to keep that in mind.

The steakhouse is dimly lit, with rich wood that creates a relaxing atmosphere. The restaurant isn't busy, and the bar is surprisingly empty outside of several couples engrossed in personal conversations. Lyla takes a seat at the bar and orders a drink. She's upset, and her guard is down. There's no easy way to do this, and there's no time like the present. This business needs to be concluded before Braden returns from the conversation with his slut of a wife. If "business" is how this can be characterized. There is only one acceptable result, and he hopes to make it quick.

"Is this seat taken?" he asks.

Lyla wipes away tears and glances at all the empty seats, likely wondering why he's choosing this one. As if that requires explanation.

"No. Go ahead."

Braus takes a seat and orders a bourbon. He's taken a real liking to the stuff, and since this is a "business meeting" that can be expensed, it's top shelf all the way. The bartender makes quick work of the pour and retreats a respectful distance away.

"I'm sorry to intrude, but you look upset. Is everything okay?"

"I wish it was."

"Do you want to talk about it?"

"I'm here to have a drink, not a therapy session," she snaps.

It's a warranted reaction. "Apologies."

"No, I'm sorry," Lyla says. "That was rude. I'm just not in the mood to be hit on."

"Is that what I was doing?"

Braus tries to play innocent. Unfortunately, he has a cultural curse: Germans are almost incapable of playing innocent.

"Wasn't it?"

"No," Braus confesses. "I would never take advantage of a woman whose lover just walked off with his wife."

Lyla's head snaps around. "How do you know that?"

The opening is complete. Here comes the tricky part. Braus needs to convey sensitive information without scaring her off. He doesn't have a good touch for this kind of thing. It's why he prefers threats. It simplifies matters.

"Because I'm the reason you're back in New York. Well, indirectly, at least."

"What do you mean?"

Braus takes a sip of his drink as he stares at the mirror on the other side of the bar. "Braden hasn't told you much about his previous job, has he?"

"How do you know his name?"

"Because I was sent to find him," he says, turning to Lyla. "I chased the two of you across two continents and an ocean. You didn't make it easy."

"You were following us?"

"Not exactly. I was tracking you. Those are two different things."

"Why?"

"Because that's what Braden's boss hired my employer to do."

Discretion is the better part of valor. Braus isn't going to give Lyla the whole truth about having orders to dispatch him if he didn't have the right answers to his questions. That was the Key West directive. Fortunately, that changed in Nice. The tracking part is true and easy enough to defend, at least.

"I don't understand. Why would he do that?"

"Because of who he is. Braden worked for a man named Arden Davenport. He's a powerful man in American politics."

"Like a politician?"

"No, they don't have any real power – it just looks that way to the masses. The illusion is created by men like Arden. Men who run groups that fund their reelection campaigns. Campaign funds are the lifeblood of elections. Money determines the winners, with precious few exceptions. With money come strings attached, and pulling those strings is my job…when I'm not schlepping around the world looking for your boyfriend."

She doesn't deny the term. "What does this have to do with Braden?"

"He's very good at his job, apparently. Arden would say he's indispensable. He wanted him back in the worst way. You didn't know any of this, did you?"

"No."

The long pause grows increasingly tense. Braus wants to fill the silence with words, but she is processing the new information. It's better if she's given time to complete those thoughts and draw her conclusions.

"He lied to me," Lyla mumbles.

"Nah, not really. It was more like a sin of omission, Miss Chance."

Her eyes grow wide at hearing her name. "You know who I am?"

"I know everything about you."

"I doubt that," she says, taking another sip of her martini.

"Don't. I'm very resourceful. If you're curious, Braden doesn't know your story. He doesn't have a clue about your past or your family."

Realization flashes across her face before she tries to mask it. "What story?"

"Where to start? He doesn't know why you're tailed everywhere you go."

"Yes, he does," Lyla interjects. "I told him."

"No, you told him what you wanted him to know. You never explained to him that the men are Mossad operatives."

The Mossad, officially known as the Institute for Intelligence and Special Operations, is Israel's national intelligence agency. Established after the creation of the State of Israel in 1949, it's responsible for intelligence gathering, covert operations, and counterterrorism. The agency is known for being efficient and effective. Anything that relates to protecting Israel's national security falls under their purview, and that's where Lyla comes in.

"I can't blame you for that," Braus continues. "I wouldn't tell my lover that I was being tailed by one of the most capable intelligence agencies on the planet. That would lead to questions, the most notable being, 'Why?' Now, that would be the start of an uncomfortable conversation."

"I have nothing to do with anything," she argues.

"I know. Like Britain's royal family, you have the curse of being born into your family. You don't get to pick it."

Lyla nods slowly. "So, you do know."

"I do. Braden wasn't the only one in your relationship who hid the past. The death of your lover in Paris wasn't an accident, and I know you know that. He was murdered. It was a message designed to achieve a specific goal – a demonstration of what can happen with one phone call. And it worked, at least for a time. Since then, you've lived with shadows always watching you."

Lyla swallows hard. "Are you going to tell Braden?"

"Do you want me to?" Braus likes answering questions with questions. It keeps his targets talking.

"No. I'm afraid they'll kill him, too."

"I understand," Braus says, taking another long sip and shifting his gaze forward. He can watch her in the mirror. "Then you know what you need to do."

"I don't know if I can."

"Miss Chance, there are specific conditions for Braden's safety now that he's returned to New York. You are not one of those conditions. You need to be out of the picture. I prefer that to be voluntary, but Arden has made it very clear that it doesn't have to be."

"Are you threatening me?"

Braus shakes his head before looking at her. "I'm pleading with you. I told Braden I would try to keep you safe, just as you're asking for my silence to keep him safe. You have had an amazing couple of months from the looks of it, but that journey is over. I know it, and I think you do, too."

"Is my life at risk?"

The German stifles a smile. He would have made a great salesman. That's a buying signal. She knows what needs to happen. She only needs to be brought along until she accepts it. He needs to push, but not too hard.

"Not if you leave, and I mean right now. At least you won't be in any danger from us. Your shadows are another issue."

"And if I don't? What will you do?"

"You don't want to find out, Miss Chance. Trust me. I'm giving you an easy out. Please take it. You have until I finish this drink to decide."

Braus takes a sip, leaving about two left in the glass. That will give the lovely Lyla about ninety seconds to determine the rest of her life. The decision is binary: She is going to make the right choice, or she won't. He has done his part to tip the scale. What happens next is entirely up to her.

Chapter Fifty-Six

Message Received

I don't know how I'm going to explain this. After leaving Kinsey, I take the scenic route back to the hotel to mull over what I'm going to say to Lyla. I have a lot to tell her, and she isn't going to like hearing what I have to say. It's the dark cloud that's been hanging over both of us since that magical tango in Buenos Aires. We have unfinished business that needs to be concluded, and that needs to happen tonight.

Traffic streams down Park Avenue, but it's long past the rush hour rush that clogs this thoroughfare when the work day winds to a close. The limousines parked out front of the gold-accented entryway are long gone. The doorman looks relaxed, no longer needing to worry about the departure of the VIPs they were previously waiting for. I nod to him as he pulls open the door.

I grasp the key tightly in my hand as I make my way through the Park Avenue Lobby. The elevator doors open with the push of a button, and I hold the card to my lips as it climbs. A lot can happen in an hour. I have no idea what mood Lyla will be in when I walk into the room. When the car slows and the doors open, I'm only a handful of steps from finding out. I take a deep breath and insert the key in the lock before turning the doorknob.

The lights in the room are off. I flip them on, expecting to see Lyla sitting in the dark or lying in bed asleep. Either way, I need to see her face for this chat – only she isn't in the room. The bed is still made up and undisturbed.

"Lyla?"

There is no answer. I look around before poking my head in the small dressing room and the bathroom, both of which are empty. Now, I'm concerned.

"Lyla? Are you here?"

I glance over at the table where she placed her bag when we arrived. It's not there. There is an envelope with my name on it resting against the bottles of alcohol perched on the minibar. That's not a good sign. I stare at it hard for a long moment before walking over, snatching it up, and pulling it open. The note inside is written on a sheet from the hotel's notepad.

You miss the beat if you close your eyes

because every night wears a new disguise.

And I live when a new surprise surrenders.

I feel it all with a willing heart

and know every stop is a place to start

Because I know how to play the part with feeling.

That's why I wander and follow la vie dansante.

But all dances end when the music stops.

-Lyla

I know the lyrics. I reread Lyla's note three times before stuffing it into my coat pocket, shaken to my core. She's gone. But where?

"Braus."

I storm out of the room and head down to the restaurants. It's a long shot, but I'm betting this is where I'll find the German. If he had a hand in this, he wouldn't have left the hotel. Not yet. He'll want to deliver a message first.

He isn't at the first restaurant I check, but I find Braus sitting at the bar at the second. I storm over to him, and he turns on his stool to greet me even before I can reach him.

"Where is she?" I demand.

Braus doesn't react. He reaches over the bar and slides a drink over to the seat next to his. The ice hasn't even begun melting in the room-temperature whisky. My nemesis was expecting me.

"Sit."

"I asked you a question, Braus."

He stares at me with serious eyes. "And I told you to sit. Don't make the mistake of confusing my kindness with weakness, Braden. You have no power here."

He's right. Demands aren't going to get me anywhere with him. He makes them, not agrees to them, so I do as he instructs. He takes a sip of his drink. That could be his first or his fifth. I have no idea how long he's been here.

"She's gone."

"By 'gone,' you mean…."

"No longer in the city." A wave of relief rushes over me. He sees my face relax and smirks. "I kept my promise. She's safe. Or, as safe as I can make her."

"Thank you."

"Do you know why…?"

"Why what?" I ask after Braus's voice trails off without completing his thought.

"Nothing. It isn't important. Where's your wedding band?"

"In my pocket. What game is Arden playing?"

He turns in his seat to face forward. "You'll have to ask him."

"I'm asking you."

"Arden Davenport is a man with many delusions. So long as I get paid, none of them matters much to me. I suspect you'll get your answers tomorrow, assuming you're wearing that ring when you meet."

I take a long sip of my drink. Braus ordered the good stuff. I'm going to need a couple more of these to get through this night. With a little luck, he poisoned it. It would spare me tomorrow's torture.

"This is twisted."

"No argument from me there," Braus muses.

I half expected the German to argue the point. He has a sadistic streak, and I thought he would find my ordeal satisfying. Instead, Braus looks almost remorseful. I would never accuse him of having a conscience, but he does seem to have a heart. Like the Grinch, it may be three sizes too small, but it's there.

"Lyla left me a note."

"I know. I was standing over her when she wrote it."

"The message was received loud and clear. It was pretty trusting of you to let Lyla say goodbye. It could have pushed me to chase her."

"I had faith that you'd do the right thing. You're a smart man, and you know the consequences of being impulsive. You won't make a move until you have it planned out. That's how you live your life, right? Carefully?"

"It *was* how I lived it."

Braus laughs. "Zebras don't change their stripes, and reformed alcoholics are only alcoholics who go to meetings. You didn't change that much in two months, no matter how much you think you did."

He's wrong about that. I have changed a lot. The old me would have been more than content to return to my comfortable apartment and familiar job. I may have even been so weak that I would have forgiven Kinsey. I asked The Engineer at the Drunken Sailor for my old life back. After a long journey, he delivered. The cruel irony is that it's now the last thing I want. I guess the adage is true – the worst thing that can happen to someone is them getting what they want.

"What will you do if I make a move?"

He shrugs. "What I need to."

I stare at my drink. That was a cryptic response. That shouldn't surprise me. The man isn't exactly forthcoming about things.

Braus drains the remainder of his drink and sets the tumbler on the bar. "I charged this to your room. After hitting on a hard ten hop bet, I think you can afford it. I'll see you around, Braden."

"I hope not."

"Oh, something tells me our story doesn't end here."

"What makes you say that?"

The German grins. "Human nature."

He slaps me on the shoulder and leaves. What does that mean? Does he think I can't handle continuing to be married to Kinsey? Does he know how miserable life is going to be? Does he understand the constant pull of wanting to search for Lyla? Or is it something else entirely? All good questions that have no immediate answers.

I pull out the note Lyla left and I read it again. Jimmy Buffett's lyrics haunt me. "La Vie Dansante" – The Dancing Life. One that I will never again experience. Regret is like a determined woodpecker – it rattles you as it pecks away at your soul and leaves a gaping hole that can never be filled. I am going to live with this one for the rest of my days.

I fold the note and hold my hands against my face as I close my eyes.

"Goodbye, Lyla."

Chapter Fifty-Seven

Into the Fold

Better times, for sure. I'm mesmerized by a picture hanging on the side wall of Arden's office. It's so captivating that I can't peel my eyes off it, getting lost in a moment that happened long ago…and recreated recently. My trance is so complete that I don't hear my former boss come in. I don't even know he's here until he touches my shoulder. I jump out of my chair when I feel it.

"Are you okay, Braden?" Arden asks.

"Yeah. I'm fine."

"Good," he says, searching for what I was so intently staring at before he gives up. "Please, have a seat."

I sneak one last peek at the framed print of the couple kissing in Paris in front of the Hôtel de Ville. Doisneau's famous picture is going to haunt me if it continues to hang in this office. It will be a constant reminder of my journey…and of Lyla.

"It's been a while, although I suspect you'd say not long enough," Arden says, taking his seat behind the desk. He stares at my left hand and the gold band on its ring finger. "You made the right choice."

"Did I?"

He presses his lips together. "You must think I'm a monster."

"No," I say confidently. "My adjectives for you are far more colorful than that."

"I can imagine."

"Why did you want me back in New York, Arden?"

"I didn't. At least, not at first. Braus had orders to find and interrogate you once we learned you had left the city. If he discovered that you betrayed me, he was instructed to put a bullet in your head and dump your body somewhere it wouldn't be found. That would have been pretty easy in a place like Key West. The Gulf of Mexico isn't small."

"Why would you think I was betraying you?"

"Why else would you leave? You were well-compensated, lived in a magnificent apartment, had a beautiful wife…. It wasn't until much later that I learned about Travis and Kinsey. I was…displeased. All my assumptions about your leaving were wrong. I should have known better."

"So, you ordered Braus to find me and return me here. Got it. So, what do you want now?"

He steeples his hands in front of his mouth. "To bring you back into the fold. I want you to return to American Outreach and do what you do best."

I rub my chin. I don't buy it. "You went through all this trouble to…what? Return to the status quo?"

Arden smirks. "I know that's hard for you to believe. For many people, it would make no sense, but there's a method to my madness. I'm not a young man, Braden. My enemies think I made a deal with the devil to live forever, but he'll want my soul sooner or later. Death is inevitable. It comes for us all. When it happens, all a man leaves behind on this Earth is his legacy. This…all this…is mine."

"I don't understand what that has to do with me."

"You're the best I have ever had. For as good as Travis was, and Ilana is, they aren't in your league. None of the others are even close. I may be the brains of American Outreach, but you are its beating heart."

He's buttering me up. He's laying the foundation for whatever he has in mind, and despite my curiosity, I almost wish there were a way I could leave this office without hearing it. If there was ever a time for the fire alarm to go off, this is it.

"I think you're overstating my value."

The corner of Arden's mouth curls. "I have thirty million dollars that says you're wrong."

"Excuse me?"

"I didn't advertise it," he says, leaning back in his chair, "but this Super PAC took a massive hit to its prestige when you disappeared. You have relationships with dozens of politicians and hundreds of movers and shakers in government and the private sector. They know and trust you. Your leaving raised a lot of eyebrows and caused quite a stir in political circles. You aren't just another employee, Braden. You're a critical part of this machine. It stops working without you. So, I'm taking measures to ensure that disruption never happens again."

"By offering me a bribe?"

"Call it a bonus, of sorts. I deposited thirty million dollars into a trust that will transfer to you upon my death, so long as you are employed by American Outreach at the time of my passing. At that point, you are free to do with it whatever you choose. If you want to retire to an estate in the Caribbean, that should be more than enough for you to live comfortably."

What the hell have I walked back into? The thought rattles around my brain like a loose tailpipe on a car hurtling down the interstate. Why would he put up anywhere near that much to retain my services? It makes *no* sense.

"You're serious about this?"

"I am. That's how much I value you, Braden."

"And Kinsey?"

Arden grimaces. "I almost forgot about that condition. I've never had a close relationship with my daughter. You know that. I can't imagine having to live with her, but I'm afraid you must remain married to her."

"Is she getting thirty million dollars, too?" I ask as sarcastically as I can manage.

Arden doesn't flinch. "She will be taken care of."

"Why?"

"Why will she be taken care of?"

I don't need to decipher the amused look on his face. He knows what I was referring to.

"Why do I have to stay married to her?"

Arden sighs. "People place value in a great many things: money, power, fame…do you know what the most valuable thing in the world is?"

"Loyalty?"

"Before you left, I would have agreed with that answer. Hell, it was the mantra around here since I founded American Outreach. Then I realized that it's *perception*. How you're perceived makes all the difference between success and failure."

That's a bunch of crap, but I don't argue. I just stare at Arden.

"Your marriage to my daughter…well, let's say it has its advantages."

"By advantages, you mean it adds to the perception that American Outreach is one big happy family."

"Now, you get it," Arden says with a nod. "I learned a few things after you disappeared. The first is that loyalty can be bought but is lost just as easily. Perceptions are much harder to change. They create a built-in bias. It's why you can have the worst president the country has ever seen, and thirty percent of the population will still vote for him…or her. They can't get past the perception."

Arden has been a fixture in political circles for decades. He knows the game. Hell, he helped invent it. His fingerprints have been on every campaign finance reform bill ever proposed…or defeated. American Outreach is the product of a system Arden Davenport helped invent. He knows a thing or two about perception and how it applies to the world.

I stare down at my hands. "Kinsey and I are miserable with each other."

"So what? The Clintons haven't slept in the same bedroom since he was the governor of Arkansas. Power couples don't stay together for love. You can both sleep with half of Manhattan if you want, so long as you remain married and are—"

"Discreet?"

"You're getting the picture."

Kinsey and Travis were discreet for a while. It didn't work out so well for that bastard.

"If American Outreach collapses once you die?"

Arden chuckles and extends his hands. "It will only add to my greatness. Everyone will realize that I was the PAC, and it couldn't operate without me."

"I thought this place was your legacy."

"The memory of what I did with it will *become* my legacy. Perception is powerful, Braden. Very powerful."

Thirty million dollars. Two months ago, I would have drooled over that number. Now, I almost find it repulsive. Three billion dollars wouldn't be worth the price of having to see Kinsey every morning. Not now. But there is another side to this coin.

"That's the carrot. What's the stick?"

"The stick," he says, pressing his lips together and tilting his head. "The stick is that I've already lost one employee to a tragic suicide. I'd hate to lose another. Accidents happen, Braden. I hope nothing like that ever happens to you."

Death may be a better option than living with Kinsey for who knows how long. With the way my luck is running, the bitch would live to be one hundred and two and her father would download his consciousness to a computer and outlive her.

"I know what you're thinking. Before you begin resigning yourself to that fate, you should think about Lyla Chance."

"She's gone," I snap, well aware that he's the man who arranged it.

"Yes, she's gone, but not dead. The Cossack is a *very* resourceful man. We found you. We can find her. Besides, we won't be the only ones looking."

I cock my head reflexively. "Her shadow?"

"That's one term for them," Arden says, leaning forward. "You really don't know, do you? Wow. I thought you were putting on an act when Braus told me that. No matter."

"Who is the shadow?"

Arden shrugs. "It's not my place to say. It's irrelevant, anyway. You'd be best served by putting Lyla Chance out of your mind. Your heart can only belong to one woman, and that needs to be my daughter. At least until I'm not around to say anything more about it."

Put Lyla out of my mind. I have a better chance of seeing a Yeti bareback riding the Loch Ness Monster in the Kentucky Derby than that happening.

"Do we have an agreement?" Arden presses.

"Am I in a position to say no?"

"That's the beauty of leverage, Braden. I know you understand the concept better than most. You worked here long enough to get an education. Of course, you can test me, but can you stomach the consequences if you do?"

"No."

Arden rises and extends his hand. "Then, welcome back to American Outreach."

I rise and button the top button of my suit out of habit. I stare at his hand for a long moment before relenting. I give it a shake. I'm at his mercy from now until his last breath. Arden owns politicians at every level of government. Now, he owns me.

Chapter Fifty-Eight

Misery Loves Company

The past two months have been the most trying of my life. Summer is marching toward autumn. The stifling August humidity has yielded to pleasant late-September breezes. It won't be long before the coffee shops have pumpkin spice lattes and pop-up Halloween costume stores occupy vacant storefronts. Two months without Lyla. Two months of doing nothing but thinking about her.

This brief retreat into the bowels of Greenwich Village has been my sanity. For an hour twice a week, I'm reminded of what I lost. The pain of her absence is punctuated by the happier memories of her presence in my life. The music, the moves, and the instruction are all the same…I am only missing my dance partner.

I considered dabbling in dances I've yet to try, but I wanted to revisit the ones I learned with her. The paso doble and tango have been my focus. I won't dance a waltz. That will hurt too much after my experiences in Vienna and my last night with Lyla in New York.

The music ends, and my partner and I strike a final pose. She's great but is no Lyla. Then again, not many women are.

"You are very much improved," my instructor says, clapping enthusiastically. "Your moves are more fluid, and your improvisation is better. We still need to work on your posture."

"Every dance instructor I've ever had said the same thing."

"They were all right!" she screeches in a high-pitched Latin accent.

"I know. *Gracias, Señorita.* See you next week?"

"Of course!"

I head to the changing area and take off my dance shoes. The oxfords I wear to work won't do for pivoting around a dance floor. I sit on the bench and am making the change when a man steps out of the adjoining bathroom. I sense him standing over me.

"I knew you traveled the world dancing, but I didn't think you were any good at it."

There's no need for me to look up. I know the voice all too well.

"What can I say, Braus? I'm full of surprises."

"You won't get an argument from me, per usual. For the record, I thought your posture looked fine."

I finish tying the laces. "You'll pardon me if I don't put much stock in your critique unless you plan on becoming a judge on *Dancing with the Stars.*"

"I don't think that's in the cards for me," he says with a genuine laugh.

"What are you doing here?" I ask, standing. "I know this isn't a social call."

"That's exactly what it is." Braus cocks his thumb over his shoulder. "Are you free for dinner?"

Is that even a serious request? The man hunted me across the globe, threatened Lyla's life to get me to return to New York, and then made her disappear like a teenage runaway. Does he really think I have any interest in sharing a meal with him like he's a Princeton college buddy who wants to catch up on old times?

"Are you asking me out on a date?" I ask, laying it on thick to hide my annoyance at his audacity. "Because I'm technically spoken for."

"Yes, I'm sure you're *so* eager to run back home to your wife," he says with as much sarcasm as a German can muster.

"I ate before rehearsal."

"Fine. Take a walk with me, then. Misery loves company, and we need to have a conversation."

I would love to say no, but that's not a word in Braus's vocabulary. Besides, if he's miserable, I want to hear why. He follows me out the doors onto the sidewalk. People are around, but the Village is hardly bustling. Nobody pays us any attention. We could be planning to overthrow the government, and nobody would offer a second look. Welcome to New York.

"How are you readjusting to married life?" he asks as we turn north toward Chelsea.

"I'm sure you already know the answer to that."

"I do," Braus says, strolling with his hands in his pockets. "I'm a little surprised you've been playing Arden's game. I would have expected you to run by now."

"To where? And why? I have no reason to leave anymore. You saw to that."

"Yes, I did. And you have thirty million reasons to stay the course."

My mouth hangs open a little as my head snaps in his direction. I shut it, silently cursing myself for rewarding him with the reaction he was looking for. I take a breath before responding.

"You know about that?"

"That's not the question you should be asking. You should want to know how I know about your rather substantial trust fund and the strings attached to it."

I nod. It takes half a second to do that math. "The Cossack."

"The man is nothing if not resourceful, Braden, and that's why I'm here. He's been plotting to betray Arden since before I caught up to you in France. His plan was always being drafted, revised, and refined. It was nothing more than a whiteboard pipe dream…until he figured out how to do it after paying a visit to Arden's legal team."

I already think I know. There was one gaping hole in Arden's plan, and it sounds like something right out of a plot-driven thriller novel. After reading the agreement he drafted, I didn't point out the one obvious loophole that the brilliant strategist never considered. The thirty million dollars transfers into my name immediately after his death. The instructions make no stipulations about how he dies.

"He's going to kill Arden. But the money transfers directly to me upon his death."

Braus turns his head and frowns. "It does, unless you're dead, too."

I stop walking. "You can't be serious."

"Oh, I'm dead serious. Agreeing to take Arden's blood money just put you squarely in the crosshairs. People kill for far less than thirty million dollars. I've seen people do it for thirty."

"What do you want me to do?"

He shrugs. "Nothing. I'm not going to tell you what to do. You already know."

"What do you mean?"

Braus smirks and shakes his head. "The files."

I was careful. I heard from Ilana that Travis scoured our internal file servers for ways he could make it look like I was betraying Arden. The servers at American Outreach don't contain any incriminating information, so he found nothing. That doesn't mean it doesn't exist on private servers that are out of reach for most employees, including Travis and Ilana. That was why Arden was so paranoid about my departure. I have the keys to the kingdom, and giving them to competitors or government entities would have been devastating. Getting my access back to those has given me what Arden believes is most valuable: leverage.

"How do you know about that?"

"I knew the servers existed and was looking for them. The mafia keeps two sets of books, so why wouldn't a political action committee? Once I found them, I knew it was only a matter of time. I saw you with Lyla, remember? There is no way you can stomach staying with Kinsey for the rest of your life. Arden may think he has you by the balls, but you're already planning your escape, just as I thought you would. I'm here to tell you that you may need to make your move sooner rather than later."

"You could just as easily be setting me up."

"I could be. It sounds like something I would do, honestly."

This man is an enigma wrapped around a mystery. I can't figure out what his true intentions are. He is either legitimately warning me or baiting the trap. I may not know which until it's too late.

"When is the Cossack planning to…?" I can't bring myself to finish the sentence. The thought that I may not be breathing next week nauseates me.

"There is no official timetable, but The Cossack isn't a patient man. He won't wait much longer. The pieces are almost in place. I've been given an overseas assignment and leave tomorrow morning."

"What? Why?"

"He knows I helped get Lyla out of the country. Those weren't my instructions. She was supposed to be feeding fish in the Hudson. He's afraid I will do the same with you. There is no such thing as trust or loyalty in my line of work, Braden. There are only common objectives."

"Are you going?"

"I have no choice. If I don't, The Cossack will know, and both our lives will be in danger. Nothing will keep him from that thirty million."

"So, this is goodbye?"

Braus smiles. "You're getting your wish to never see me again. Whether it's because you disappeared or have been planted in the ground will depend on what happens over the next couple of days. If you do leave, there is something you should know. Lyla didn't leave town because of what I told her about you."

I hang my head. That's a revelation. It's also one I'm not inclined to accept at face value.

"I don't believe you."

"You've never given me a reason to deceive you, Braden. You play it straight with me, and I reciprocate. Lyla was upset about your lack of transparency, but she left because of what I told her about herself."

"What do you mean?"

He nods up the sidewalk, and we start walking again. "How much do you know about Lyla's shadow?"

So, that's what this is about.

"He had something to do with her lover in Paris. That's all she said."

"Oh, it's far more than that. Lyla actually has multiple shadows. The one you saw in Switzerland is part of the team that focuses on Southern Europe. Mossad has agents everywhere, including the United States."

"Mossad? As in Israeli intelligence? Why would they be tailing Lyla?"

I can feel Braus studying me. "Because of who she is…more specifically, who her grandfather is. Her mother's last name was Chance. You probably knew that, and I'm assuming she never spoke of her father. He's an Iranian named Hamidreza Beheshti, a high-ranking and valuable commander of the Revolutionary Guard. His father is Sahand Beheshti, the current defense minister for the Islamic Republic of Iran. He is also one of the Ayatollah's closest confidants and a driving force behind their foreign policy. You know what that means."

"They help plan terrorist attacks," I mumble.

"Including ones against American interests in the Middle East and the Jewish state in general. The Mossad is using Lyla as a deterrent. They have made it clear to Hamidreza and Sahand through unofficial channels that any direct attacks on Israel will result in her unfortunate demise."

"That's why she's always on the run."

The information hits me with the force of a fully loaded freight train screaming down the tracks at top speed. No wonder she didn't want to talk about her past. Her life was every bit in danger as mine was. I thought that our secrets could pull us apart. I had no idea how right I was.

"I thought you should know that before…well, whatever happens, happens. Good luck to you, Braden. I wish you the best of luck. You're going to need all of it."

Braus gives me his patented pat on the upper arm and heads south. He leaves me standing in the street with more than enough to think about to occupy a sleepless night.

Chapter Fifty-Nine

Oh, No in Soho

The echo of heels clicking on the hardwood floor and hushed voices gathered around the buffet table fill the foyer. If there were a singular definition of hell, this is it. The art hanging on the walls isn't the reason for my foul mood. Thanks to Lyla, and by extension, Jean-Claude, I have a much finer appreciation for paintings than I had three months ago. No, it's the snobby, well-dressed society types milling around the spacious gallery with their cocktails that are making me miserable.

Attending fundraisers is part of the job at American Outreach. This isn't one of those, although there must be some financial connection that prompted my getting dragged to this swanky, ostentatious SoHo gallery. Considering the cost of the purses the women are toting and the dresses they are wearing, this event isn't for the one percent. The men and women decked out in designer labels are in the top one percent of the one percent.

I have no desire to make idle chit-chat. I have enough on my mind. Hearing Biff and Muffy talk about their stay in Dubai or sailing their yachts along the Amalfi Coast isn't my idea of a good time. I would take my travels with Lyla any day.

"I know this isn't your thing," Kinsey whispers as she clings to my arm, wearing her sleek black dress with a long slit up the side and four-inch heels.

It's definitely hers. Kinsey is a woman who likes to be seen. Before we were married, I'd be lying if I said I didn't enjoy being seen with her. She likes big, flashy events with fancy people. Kinsey is the epitome of style over substance.

"Then why did you drag me here?"

"My father wanted to see us out. More importantly, he wanted *others* to see us."

I look around. Everything these people do is for show. The company they keep, the clothes they wear, and the events they attend are all designed to make them look and feel superior to everyone around them. The funny thing is that society looks up to them, when in reality, it's a sad existence.

"Appearances."

"Yeah, I don't like it either, but we have to play the part," Kinsey confesses.

"Are you?"

"Am I what?"

"Playing the part?"

It's a legitimate question. Since the day Arden forced us back together, she hasn't been home much. I'm either at work or my dancing lessons, but she does neither and offers no explanation about where she goes. I can only imagine whom she's with or what she's doing. It's not that I care, other than knowing I can't be with the woman I want to be with and doing those things with her. Life isn't fair. Then again, nobody ever said it would be.

Kinsey doesn't get a chance to answer the question. The gallery owner gets everyone's attention by banging a fork against her champagne flute as she moves next to a covered easel. The hushed discussions get quashed into dead silence.

"Thank you for coming tonight. This isn't a typical art showing for us. This gallery takes great pride in procuring some of the best art the world has to offer, but tonight is a little different. All the paintings you see here tonight were created by students. We recently entered an agreement with one of Paris's most prestigious art schools to showcase the work of their best upcoming artists."

The crowd coos, and I perk up. It can't be. I look around but don't recognize any of the paintings. None of them were what Jean-Claude unveiled in the foyer that day. It could be another school, but I get the feeling it isn't. It'd be too much of a coincidence.

"This is one of my favorites," she says, removing the linen covering the painting she's standing next to. "This is reminiscent of some of the great Impressionist masters. Notice the exquisite use of lines and the contrast with colors in the background…."

I don't hear the rest of her analysis. My eyes absorb every brush stroke like I did the first time my eyes set upon it. I'm immediately overwhelmed with emotions…happiness, deep sadness, and a maddening amount of regret.

"It's beautiful!" a woman screeches. "What's the name of the painting?"

The gallery owner bends down to check the placard. I don't need to see it.

"La Vie Dansante," I announce to the group of elites. "The Dancing Life."

The guests and the gallery owner all turn to look at me in surprise. Nobody is more shocked than Kinsey, who looks at me like I just decoded an ancient alien relic uncovered in the sands of Egypt. I'm not supposed to know anything about art. I still don't, despite spending some quality time in the Parisian art school featured here. But I know this painting. I lived it.

"How did you know that?" the woman next to me asks.

"You know this work?" the gallery owner adds on.

I force a smile. "You could say that."

"Okay," she says, covering the name on the sign. This is a game to them. "Who is the artist?"

"Lyla Chance."

She removes her hand and checks the placard. "Oh, my! He's right."

"Wait!" the woman next to me exclaims, leaning closer to the painting and squinting before looking back at me. "Is that…?"

The gallery owner joins her in the comparison, as do many of the guests. Impressionist work isn't distinct. It's one of the things that gives that art movement its uniqueness. The short, thin brush strokes create a feeling, not a vibrant picture. Lyla's work does the same thing, although she captured my face with more detail than is typically seen in Impressionism. Now, it's being noticed.

I take one more long look at Lyla's masterpiece. "Please excuse me."

I make my way through the crowd gathered around the easel. My pace quickens as I stride toward the gallery's front doors. I need to get out of here. Seeing that painting brought back memories and emotions that I wasn't ready to face. Not today. Not after what Braus told me.

"Braden! Braden! Where are you going?" I hear Kinsey call out as she gives chase.

I stop and wheel to face her. "Anywhere but here."

"You can't leave. You know that. My father is watching."

"Kinsey?" a man asks, coming alongside us after entering the gallery. "It's been a while since I've seen you! How have you been?"

He moves in for a kiss. It's not the friendly one on the cheek he was looking to land. Kinsey turns her head, and his attempt catches her cheek. He pulls back, a confused look painted on his face.

"I'm fine. Giovanni, this is my husband, Braden. Giovanni is also in finance and works on Wall Street."

I scan the handsome young man in an Italian silk suit. The guy is clearly loaded. His shoes likely cost more than most people make in a couple of months. He's well put together, physically fit, and has a jawline that must make women drool. I can understand Kinsey's attraction to him.

Giovanni extends his hand with confidence and arrogance. I take it, but it isn't a friendly shake. It's reminiscent of two adversarial world leaders meeting at a summit when a handshake is expected for the cameras, but they'd rather be beating each other with clubs.

"I didn't realize Kinsey was married," he admits.

"You probably aren't used to seeing her wearing her ring. And I'm also sure you never bothered asking. You don't seem the type to care."

"Braden!" Kinsey chides as Giovanni smirks. I turn to her. "Just tell me, is this guy pre- or post-Travis?"

"Who's Travis?" he asks.

"One of the other guys she was sleeping with while we were married. I'm sure there are countless more."

I should have seen what's coming next. Even if I did, I probably would have let it happen. It's time to end the charade, and what better way to get the attention of all the elites in this gallery than a slap that reverberates through the building? Anyone who wasn't paying attention to us is now. A crowd begins to gather in the foyer as the patrons begin filtering in from adjacent rooms to take in tonight's entertainment.

Giovanni laughs. "You deserved that."

Now, it's my turn to smirk as I rub my cheek. "I suppose I did, but…."

I hold my index finger up, indicating for him to give me a moment while I slowly move it away from my body. His eyes follow it until my arm fully extends, and then I raise it over my head. Giovanni's head moves with it, tilting his chin toward the sky. My grin turns to a smile.

I swing with all my might, landing my fist hard on Giovanni's face. I don't think I've ever punched anyone before. I expected to completely miss, which would have been embarrassing. But I didn't, and there's a loud popping sound when my fist makes contact with his nose. I was aiming for his jaw, but this had the desired effect. To my chagrin, he doesn't go down. It's time for plan B.

Giovanni is cupping his hands under his nose to catch the blood, not that it hasn't already ruined his pricey designer shirt. I slam my foot down on his instep in a self-defense move that women are taught. Men like to fight like boxers because it's the manly thing to do. I won't win a fistfight against this guy, or anyone, really. So, I'm going to fight dirty.

He raises his foot and hops in pain. Then he makes his next mistake – he rotates and turns his back to me. It's a good thing, too, because I had no idea what to do next. Now I do. I bring my foot up and kick out, landing it on the small of his back. Giovanni careens forward, off-balance, and can't stop his momentum before crashing into the buffet table set up with appetizers and refreshments. Silver platters crash to the ground as he topples over the table and lands on his back on the other side.

"Oh, my God!" Kinsey shouts, rushing to Giovanni's side as he lies on the ground clutching his shattered nose and reacting in horror at the sight of his blood. He pushes her hands away from him. "Braden! What the hell is wrong with you?"

"Oh, no," I say sarcastically. "Did I ruin his pretty suit?"

"Why did you do that?"

"I'm just scratching an itch."

Using one of Lyla's lines is the icing on the cake. I turn and head for the door. There's no need to be here any longer. Unfortunately, Arden knows where I'm going and is positioned to cut me off.

"Where do you think you're going!"

"Home, Arden. I'm going home."

He grabs my arm to stop me as I reach for the door. There's anger in his eyes, and his jaw is so tense that I expect it to break off his face under the stress.

"We have a deal."

"We *had* a deal. I might have been able to stomach working for you, but staying married? That's not going to happen. Your daughter's a whore. No amount of money is worth tolerating that."

I remove my wedding band from my finger and flip it to my stunned boss. The double meaning isn't lost on him – the marriage is over, and so is our agreement. There will be consequences to that. Right now, I'm beyond caring what they are.

Chapter Sixty

Russian Roulette

The phone call wasn't surprising, but the timing was. Fortunately, The Cossack was ready to jump into action. In fact, he was already downtown when his cell phone rang. It became a race to get here, and he won it. There was no chance that Braden would go home like he told Arden. There is nothing for him there. He only needs to make one stop before disappearing, and since he has no storage units or friends and wouldn't go to the office, this is the likely place he would come.

It took only fifteen seconds to find the bag he had stashed. All that's in there is a change of clothes, some cash, and a passport. Most of the items are khakis and shorts, an extra pair of boat shoes, and short-sleeved shirts. Wherever he's planning on going, it's warm there. Nobody dresses like this in the mountains. That means the Caribbean or South America, probably the northern countries on the continent. He supposes the South Pacific or Indochina could also be an option, but not as likely.

Now, the moment has arrived. The Cossack can hear the key in the lock from his spot in the upstairs loft. He watches from above as Braden strides across the apartment into the living room below. He checks the spot near the sofa to find his bag isn't there. He starts to look around as The Cossack watches from the loft bedroom before moving to the top of the stairs and flipping on the light.

"Looking for this?" The Cossack asks, holding up the medium-sized duffel bag. "You were clever for hiding this here, Braden. Travis paid his rent in advance for the year, so there was no reason to believe anyone would ever find this. But you forgot that I'm not anyone, so maybe you weren't so clever after all."

"Arden called you," Braden deadpans, his voice devoid of surprise or any other emotion.

The Cossack slowly descends the stairs, toting the duffel. If there is one thing he admires about Braden, it's that the man puts things together quickly. Maybe it was obvious that Arden would make that call but not fast enough to do anything that could interrupt a well-planned escape.

"He did. You put on quite the show at the gallery from the sound of it."

"The asshole deserved it."

"Giovanni Conti. Did you know that his last name means 'count' in Italian? He walks around like he is one. If there was a picture in the Wikipedia entry for wealthy GQ Eurotrash, it'd be him."

The Cossack did a fair amount of digging into the man's background. "He's a playboy. He has money, looks, and status, making it easy to get women. And he has gotten a lot of them. For whatever reason, he has taken a special interest in Kinsey Davenport Fox. Her feminine wiles must be a challenge for him."

"You knew about their affair?"

"I learned about all her affairs, eventually. Travis and Giovanni aren't her only indiscretions, only her most recent. It seems your wife has a long history of not being able to keep her legs closed."

"No kidding," Braden mumbles.

"Your history of bad decisions is much shorter, but you made a grave one tonight, Mr. Fox."

"We all have our faults. I know you're into theatrics, but spare me the drama. If you're going to shoot me, go ahead and get it over with. Don't bother with the Travis treatment. I'm not in the mood for it."

The corner of the Russian's mouth curls. He doesn't give a damn what Braden Fox is or is not in the mood for. He walks around the living room floor, pausing under the loft and looking at the railing above.

"That's where it happened, you know. It's where your best friend met his untimely end. I tied the rope off that railing, and the chair was right about here. He put the noose around his own neck."

"I'm sure the gun you were holding helped him make that decision."

The Cossack laughs. "Yes, it sure did, but that's not what I meant. In reality, he put the noose around his neck the moment he gave into Kinsey's advances. He knew what the consequences of a tryst with the boss's daughter would be. He was a weak man who thought he was smarter than everyone else."

"And because of that, he thought you wouldn't kill him. His relationship was leverage that he didn't realize made no difference until he was dangling by his neck over nothing but air."

The Cossack wags a finger at Braden. "I like you, Mr. Fox. You're very sharp. I wish I had known you when you were at Princeton. You could have come to work for me instead of Arden. A man with your talents and vision would have been immensely valuable."

"Poaching my talent, are you?" Arden says from the door.

The old man strolls into the apartment, taking the time to look around before reaching the duo in the living room. The Cossack wonders if Arden is pondering how many times his daughter got laid in this apartment. It'd be a sick thing to think about, but the founder of American Outreach is already a few glasses shy of a full bottle.

"I'm just stating a fact, Mr. Davenport. You chose your people very well."

"Did I?" Arden asks, turning to his employee. "Did I choose well, Braden?"

"I'd like to think so."

"So would I, but then you caused a scene in front of some of the Tri-State's wealthiest residents. As upset as I am about you tainting my donor pool, I'm more distraught at your reneging on our deal."

Braden nods. "You knew I could never stay with Kinsey."

"I thought I gave you a compelling reason to," Arden says, causing Braden to glance at The Cossack. "He knows about our arrangement. I explained the whole thing to him after you left the gallery. After tonight, my Russian friend is going to get a sizable paycheck and never have to work again if he doesn't want to."

"How nice for you," Braden says with a sneer.

The Cossack shrugs. "It's a living."

"Forcing you to stay with Kinsey wasn't punishment. It was the ultimate test of loyalty, and you failed it. That means you took other measures to ensure your getaway. I know you didn't download any information. No matter how careful you were, it would have shown up in the logs. That means you built a backdoor to access my off-site servers."

"I didn't."

"Oh, you did. We both know it's the only leverage you have. I could almost forgive you for leaving Kinsey. She's my daughter, but like you, I find her completely insufferable. But betraying American Outreach…betraying me…I'm sorry, but that's unforgivable."

Everyone in the room knows what's going to happen. There is zero chance that Braden lives to see the next sunrise. The Cossack expects him to start whining or pleading for his life. He doesn't. This is the end for him, and he's accepted it. There is a degree of honor and nobility in that. Of all the people the Russian has killed, only a handful have garnered the respect he has for the soon-to-be-deceased American Outreach employee. People don't know how to die well anymore.

On the other hand, Arden is surprised at Braden's silence. He waits for him to say something…anything. He *wants* him to beg for his life or ask for mercy. No words come, and so more prompting is necessary.

"You were my most valued asset, Braden. It's going to be tragic to lose you."

"What about Kinsey? Will it be tragic to lose your own daughter?"

Arden grins. "Not as much."

"You don't know how tickled I am to hear you say that," Kinsey says from the door.

Her arrival isn't surprising to the Cossack. He was expecting her, although not with this degree of perfect timing. From the looks on their faces, Braden and Arden never expected the missus to be standing at the threshold of this apartment. That's not the most shocking part for them, though. They sure as hell never expected her to have a gun pointed at them.

Chapter Sixty-One
The Final Betrayal

I never served in the military, but I did take a military history class while I was at Princeton. The instructor was a former paratrooper who served in the infantry with the 82nd Airborne. Yes, he was one of the rare military veterans teaching at the Ivy League School. He loved quoting Murphy's Laws of Combat, and I was surprised at how well those maxims translate to the civilian world. The one that stuck with me most is, "No plan ever survives first contact with the enemy intact." That couldn't be truer.

My quick getaway is anything but one. My genius idea to stash my stuff in Travis's apartment ended up being predictable and foolish. I shouldn't have bothered and just should have bought new clothes when I got where I was going. The thought that I could come here, retrieve my bag and passport, and slip out of the city was a complete bust. I should have known better.

Not only was The Cossack here to greet me, but then Arden showed up. My fate was already sealed, but Kinsey's arrival adds yet another wrinkle. The only person more surprised than me to see her holding a gun is Arden. The Cossack doesn't look shocked at all. That doesn't bode well. I have a bad feeling that I know what happens next if Braus's information is accurate.

"Kinsey?" Arden asks, the sound of surprise dripping off his tongue. "Wh-what are you doing here?"

"You didn't think I would miss out on all the fun, did you, Father?"

Kinsey has a strange definition of what "fun" is. Now I suddenly feel like I'm playing the children's game Monkey in the Middle. The three people in this room hate me. I betrayed Arden, despise Kinsey, and abhor The Cossack because he'll do whatever Arden instructs him to. I wonder if they'll draw straws to see who gets to finish me.

"Put the gun down, Kinsey."

"Mmm, nah, that's not going to happen."

Arden looks at The Cossack. The son of a bitch looks amused. "Aren't you going to do something about this?"

He shakes his head. "*Nyet.* I don't get involved in family affairs."

That's not entirely true since Arden and I are related by marriage, but I'm not about to correct him. This isn't the time for me to open my mouth. She is pointing her weapon at her father, not me. I'll count that as a small miracle.

"Kinsey—"

"How does it feel to be powerless? You've been the revered chess master since you founded American Outreach. You're so used to using leverage to get what you want that you've forgotten that it can be turned and used against you."

"Is that what this is about? Are you mad I didn't buy you a pony when you were a child?"

I wince. Arden's daughter hates him…and she has a gun pointed at his abdomen. This isn't a time for mockery or sarcasm, and Arden should recognize that. Kinsey's evil chuckle is enough to drive home that point.

"You taught me a few things when you were threatening me," she says with a smile on her face. "The most important is that turnabout is fair play."

Arden is getting the picture. His eyes dart between his daughter and The Cossack. "You're working with the man who sexually assaulted you?"

That's news to me, but I don't need or want an explanation.

"On your orders, as it turns out. You've been abusing me my whole life. Now, it's my turn."

Kinsey closes the distance between her and her father. It's beginning to dawn on him that this is more serious than he thought. His eyes plead with the Russian, who stands there emotionless. Desperation quickly turns to panic.

"I pay you to take care of things for me!"

"You do," The Cossack says evenly. "But why settle for a measly five million dollars when I can have all thirty million of them?"

Realization. It's the result of realizing, which is when something is made real or becomes a reality. That's the definition. The exercise is purely cognitive but manifests in a physical look that everybody knows but can't accurately describe. I can't either, but I see it on Arden's face. It's the look that will be forever etched on his face after Kinsey raises her gun and pulls the trigger. The suppressed weapon burps, and the bullet punches through his forehead, leaving a clean circle right in the middle of it. The same can't be said for the back of his head.

Arden falls backward. He's dead before he hits the ground. Kinsey takes a couple of steps forward and stands over his corpse, and I begin to think that she's going to empty the rest of the magazine into his chest. Instead, Kinsey smiles. It's the most cold-hearted thing I have ever seen.

Kinsey lowers her weapon and stares at me. "I can't tell you how long I've wanted to do that."

"Bravo, Kinsey, bravo," The Cossack says, clapping as well as he can while holding his own weapon. "That was a nice shot!"

She nods in appreciation as the Cossack lowers his gun to his side. He doesn't need to hold it on me because Kinsey has already taken care of that. She levels her suppressed weapon at my chest.

"I can't believe you called me a whore in front of all those people. That wasn't very nice."

I shrug. "Neither is sleeping around when you're married."

"Touché."

"I'm impressed that the two of you cooked this up," I say before being offered the chance to utter any last words.

The Russian smiles at the compliment, not that I really meant it as one. "Arden told me about the money, but what he didn't know is that Kinsey told me about it weeks ago. It was just a matter of time. Your rash behavior at the gala accelerated things a little. So, can you guess what happens next?"

"The money transfers over to me upon notification of Arden's death. It won't matter that I'll be found dead sometime later, in which case it goes to my grieving widow along with the rest of my estate."

"Braden, I meant what I said," The Cossack says, covering his heart with his free hand. "You should have worked for me. You're spot-on."

"So, you're splitting the money?"

"Not exactly. Kinsey gets to exact the revenge she has so desperately wanted and will inherit her father's estate. I get the thirty million all to myself. See? Win-win. Except for you, I'm afraid. You'll be implicated in Arden's death, then be found dead, having killed yourself out of guilt…or whatever. Not that it matters. You can't serve jail time if you're not breathing."

"Lucky me."

"Go ahead, love. End this so we can start collecting our fortunes."

The Cossack encourages her by gesturing at me with his hand. Kinsey straightens her arm. I think about rushing her but will never make it. Bullets move a lot faster than I do, and she doesn't need to be a marksman to hit me, given the distance between us.

This isn't how I want it to end. I'm not okay with dying, but it'd be better from a big Russian assassin than a philandering wife. It's the way the world works. Getting shot by Kinsey is adding insult to already considerable injury.

"My father put a premium on loyalty. Consider this the final betrayal. How does the line go? Until death do us part?"

Kinsey moves her finger to the trigger. I close my eyes, and visions of Lyla fill my head. The only regret will be never seeing her again. She will never know what happened to me. If she does learn about it by happenstance, I will be long since dead and buried.

I hear the gunshot but don't feel anything. There is no pain at all. No blood is gushing from my chest. My life doesn't flash before my eyes. Instead, I hear the Russian grunting in agony. I open my eyes and turn to look at him. The Cossack is already on the ground, clutching his shoulder. What the hell?

Chapter Sixty-Two

Iron Doublecross

In the movies, they're called silencers. There's nothing silent about them because nothing can completely erase the sound of gunpowder exploding and creating enough pressure to push a bullet down a cylinder at almost supersonic speeds. The real name for the device is a suppressor. The cylindrical barrel screwed into the muzzle reduces the volume of a shot but cannot eradicate it.

Braus moves around the corner after he hears the weapon fire. He could hear the voices clearly and knew what was going on. He knew who the target was going to be. Now, he needs to make sure there is no retribution. Wild animals are the most dangerous when they're wounded, and The Cossack is a wild animal. There is no telling what he's capable of.

Braden is staring at his wife with eyes the size of saucers. "Okay, I didn't see that coming."

"What can I say, honey? I'm full of surprises."

"So I see, but why did you do that?"

Kinsey nods at the room's newest visitor. The German strides over and steps on the gun as The Cossack reaches to retrieve it. Blood is oozing from a wound to his right shoulder. He stares up at his underling with hate-filled eyes. He knows he's been betrayed and mutters something in Russian.

"Shh," Braus hushes him, placing a finger over his lips as he turns to Kinsey. "You didn't have to be so dramatic."

Kinsey smiles. "Don't take my fun."

Braus scoffs before picking up The Cossack's weapon and tucking his own into the holster at the small of his back. He turns to Braden, who is as confused as he's ever seen the man.

"Did you miss me?"

"I thought you were overseas on an assignment."

Braus smirks. "That's where I'm supposed to be. Thank God you made the move when you did. I wouldn't have been able to keep my absence from The Cossack for long. He's a connected man. Learning that I never arrived wouldn't have been difficult."

"You bastard," the Russian mutters, clutching his shoulder as he fights the pain.

"Stop your whining. You're a Russian. You're supposed to be tougher than this."

The Cossack grunts but takes his advice and leans his head back on the ground as he slowly bleeds out. Grasping at his entry wound isn't doing anything to stop the blood from gushing out of the exit wound. Kinsey must have nicked an artery. A medical degree isn't needed to know his life can only be measured in minutes without immediate medical care. Not that it matters.

"You're working with Kinsey?" Braden asks.

"Surprise," she says. "You should have seen the look on your face."

"I'm glad you're amused. You're still a whore."

She smiles even more broadly. "And I'm still holding a gun and have shot two people tonight. Don't give me a reason to make it three."

That's a fair point, and Braus watches as Braden turns to him. "You had this planned out when you came to see me."

"Most of it. The gallery visit was my idea. I saw the painting when we were all in Paris. It's absolutely beautiful. I knew it would trigger you if you saw it again, so I found out when the showing was scheduled and arranged for Kinsey to take you. It was my idea, not Arden's. When she told me about Giovanni, I raised the stakes by having him show up. I needed to be certain you would have a meltdown. I figured that guy would have the desired effect. He's a sleaze, by the way."

Kinsey doesn't react to the slight. "He had his uses."

"You manipulated me," Braden says.

"Yeah, I did. Call it payback for making me chase you around the world."

"I'm going to kill you for this, Braus. You're a dead man!" The Cossack says through clenched teeth.

The German stares down at his old boss. "No, I don't think so. That's not how this works. That's the beauty of the iron doublecross – it takes no prisoners."

He changes his stance alongside The Cossack and fires two rounds into the center of his chest. Eyes filled with hatred soften to the hollow stare only found in death. I won't miss the big Russian. I doubt anyone else will, either.

Braus sighs. "Messy, messy, messy."

He turns his attention to Kinsey and holds his gloved hand out. She stares at it for a long moment before returning his stare.

"We have a deal."

"One I have every intention of honoring."

She hands him her weapon, and he puts it in The Cossack's hand. He takes the other gun and puts it in Arden's hand. Braus doubts the police will think they shot each other, but it will confuse them for the time that's needed.

"What deal?" Braden asks.

Braus slides his hand into his jacket and produces an envelope. She riffles through it after he hands it to her.

"Passport, driver's license, social security card, traveling money, credit cards…a whole new identity that's clean and verifiable. You'll have no problem stepping into your new life. The picture is a match, but I will suggest you get some plastic surgery. I included the name of a man who's as discreet as he is skilled. I also suggest you dye your hair once you're out of the city. Redheads attract attention, usually not in a good way when you want to remain unnoticed."

"Thanks for the tip."

"You're leaving?" Braden asks.

Kinsey nods. "It's what I've always wanted – to disappear and never look back. You aren't the only one who wants a fresh start. Take care, Braden."

She goes to leave and makes it as far as the kitchen before stopping. "For what it's worth, I hope you and Lyla end up with a happily ever after. You're a good man. You deserve it."

Braus studies her soon-to-be-ex-husband's face. He has mixed emotions as he watches her disappear through the door. It's not sadness. That woman deserves none of that for everything she did to him. It's like coming to the end of a good novel. You're happy at the result but sad that you have to move on to the sequel, even if you're looking forward to reading it. Before that happens, Braus knows he has some explaining to do.

"You have a lot of questions, I'm sure," he says, beating Braden to the punch, "but time is short. You'll want to know why I arranged this, and my answer is that I told you I wasn't a monster. I just work with them."

"This could have gone horribly wrong."

"Yeah. I only gave this whole thing a one-in-five chance of working the way I planned. You're living a charmed life, Braden. I was standing outside in case it went wrong early. The only thing I couldn't control was whether The Cossack would shoot you immediately. I didn't think he would. He liked theatrics, as you know."

"One in five? That's reassuring."

Braus claps him on the arm. "No risk, no reward."

"So, what happens now?"

"You need to get out of the city like you planned. The money will transfer to an offshore account in the morning, per Arden's last written instructions." He pulls out another envelope from a different pocket. "The account details in the Cayman Islands are in here, along with your new identity. That will be good enough for you to run a low profile. Try not to get arrested overseas. If they take your prints, the game is over."

"That's it?"

Braus picks up the duffle off the floor and hands it to Braden. "Not exactly. The NYPD will want to question you about the suddenly deceased Arden and your soon-to-be-missing wife. You'll be a person of interest in all this for the rest of your life. Of course, with thirty million dollars, you can pretty much live anywhere you want. I strongly suggest it is outside of the country. Say goodbye to the United States, and don't ever come back. Perhaps you should head to South America. If you're curious, that's where Lyla is."

His mouth softens into a smile. Somehow, he survived this. Braden is free of Kinsey and no longer under the thumb of Arden Davenport. Braus doesn't need to chase him. He's free to find the love of his life and do the same for her if that's his choice. Braus is willing to bet it is.

"It's a big continent. Can you be more specific?"

He grins. "Fate brought you together once. If it's meant to be, you'll find her again."

"Thank you, Braus. I have one more question: What was in this for you?"

"A reason to go home. I inherit The Cossack's empire, but I can run it from anywhere. As far as everyone knows, this was an assignment that went wrong. Now, get out of here. Someone will have heard the shots and already dialed 9-1-1. The police have a slow response time, but they'll be here eventually."

Braden nods at him.

"Oh, and before you leave the U.S., I strongly suggest you swing by Key West."

He cocks his head. "Why?"

The German claps him on the arm again and smiles. "Just stay sober while you're at the Drunken Lobster this time. Goodbye, Braden."

Chapter Sixty-Three

Smoke & Mirrors

I drive past the green metal sign with white letters that reads, "MILE 0." A couple of tourists are already standing there, taking a picture with it and the US Route 1 sign. This is the end of the road, almost literally, and thus, a photo opportunity for countless families and travelers. The iconic route that begins at Fort Kent along the country's northern border with Canada finishes here after a journey of two thousand three hundred seventy miles.

I like Key West, not that I remember much from my time here. I spent most of it completely hammered or with the worst hangovers imaginable. I do remember leaving it, though. That might have something to do with the nervous energy generated from knowing that Braus was hunting me. It feels like an eon ago, even if the calendar says differently.

The town hasn't changed at all, not that I expected it to be radically different. I steer the rental car into the lot I fled from at the beginning of this journey and park. The sunshine beats on my face, and my nostrils fill with salty air as I walk along the edge of the marina. The boat I was staying on is gone. Otherwise, everything is as it should be, including Steve preparing The Drunken Lobster for the tourists who should start arriving soon. I lean against the bar and take off my sunglasses when he looks up.

"Braden Fox. As I live and breathe," he says, shaking his head.

"I'm a little surprised you remember me."

"Are you kidding? Who could forget? You're the best tipper I've ever seen, and the night you left has become something of a legend in this place. Then I got my ass kicked by your friend the next morning. That was memorable."

"He wasn't my friend."

"Whatever, man."

Steve is a hard-working guy who is likely considered a workaholic in a laid-back town like Key West. He's seen it all but might still hold a grudge over what happened that day. I know I would. Braus and I might have left each other on good terms, but he never slammed my face against the bar and held a gun to my head. Things like that sour relationships.

"Am I still banned from this place?"

Steve wipes the already clean bar with a wet rag. "That depends. Will your friend who's not a friend be back to visit?"

"No," I reassure him.

"Good. You still have money?"

"It's as green as everyone else's."

"Then I suppose you're welcome until you give me a reason to toss you out on your ass again."

Cash is king, and having it here translates into forgiveness. At least, it does for Steve. I look around the bar a bit. It also hasn't changed.

"Speaking of throwing me out of here, the old man – the one I was talking to that last night I was here – does he still come around? He called himself the Engineer."

Steve starts laughing so hard he doubles over, needing to support himself with the edge of the bar. The question isn't meant to be a joke, so his reaction is a little puzzling.

"All right, what's so damn funny?"

"You don't remember nothin' from that night, do ya?" Steve asks between laughs.

In fairness, I don't. I remember parts of the conversation but have no idea how I ended up in the surf on the other side of the island. I absolutely recall the words the Engineer used that led to a crazy bet on the roll of the dice that landed me in South America, where I stumbled into a dance hall and met Lyla…it goes on.

"I remember talking to him for a while over there in the corner."

I fold my arms with impatience as Steve starts laughing again, fighting to compose himself before pointing. "Well, it's your lucky day. He never left. In fact, he's in the corner right now. Go see for yourself."

The corner of the bar is empty. I offer the bartender a confused look. He drapes the towel over his shoulder and waves for me to follow him as he continues chuckling. We walk to the spot next to the bathroom door, and he points at an old framed photograph hanging on the wall. The grizzled, weathered old man is immediately recognizable. He's the Engineer.

"You were as drunk that night as I've ever seen a human being. I remember you stumbling outta the bathroom and sittin' right here," Steve says, grabbing the back of a chair and shaking it. "You started talkin' to that picture like you'd known him for years. Carried on quite the conversation. The whole bar was watching you."

Almost every inch of available wall space in the bar is covered with pictures, expressions, money, and even women's bras. My eyes don't have to travel far to see how events actually transpired that night. To the left of the picture is a framed photo of an old Western steam train with a man waving out its cab. The engineer. Above the train photo, a rusting metal sign reads: "Being alive and actually living are not the same." Next to that is another that reads: "Be Curious."

The memory comes rushing back. *You don't want to leave,* the Engineer said. *"You're curious and haven't asked me what you want to know."*

My eyes dart to a white porcelain mug on a hook. In black letters, it professes that "If it can be taken from you, it was never really yours, was it?" Words the Engineer used, written literally in black and white. Not far on the wall from that is another aging sign that serves as an old marketing advertisement for Key West. A boat is at sea under a blazing sun, and emblazoned over it are the words: experiences, adventures, memories, and love.

"All the things you should value," I utter, quoting the words I heard from the Engineer that night.

"What?" Steve asks.

"Nothing," I say.

"All right. I'll leave you here to get reacquainted," the barman says before returning to his post.

I take a deep breath and check the other wall that makes up the corner. It's also chock full of artifacts and musings about love, life, and fishing. My eyes settle on an hourglass. The top glass is etched with "past," and the bottom has "future." The bases of the device are made from thick wood and have engraved gold plates affixed to them. The top reads, "forget," and the bottom states, "focus."

"You must forget your past and focus on the future," I mumble. *"Once you do, you'll get your life back."*

I shake my head. This can't be real. Screwed to the wall next to that is a six-inch wooden figurine of the devil with a pair of fuzzy dice draped around its neck. I shake my head in disbelief again as the memory of what he said pops into my mind with vivid clarity.

"Face your demons as men do," the Engineer advises. *"You can roll the dice and let fate decide if you don't know your path. Or you can trust yourself to find your way. Live your life, Braden. Stop expecting to begin living at some random future date that may never come. That's the change you must make to get your life back."*

It's all coming together now – all except what caused me to conjure up this imaginary conversation in the first place. Then it dawns on me. I rush to the wooden door that leads to the men's room and jerk it open. I don't need to take a leak. I do feel like I'm going to throw up, though. This was not what I expected.

I immediately move to the urinal. I remember squinting, trying to read something scrawled on it. My mind was swimming in a vat of bourbon, so nothing was coming easy that night. I don't remember what was written there. I stare at the words penned in permanent black magic marker: "We never live. We are always in the expectation of living -- Voltaire."

I take a few steps back and run my hand through my hair. This can't be happening. I slowly turn and walk out of the men's room, taking a seat in the same chair I did months ago. I shake my head in mild disbelief. The conversation that sent me on the most incredible journey of my life never happened. It was all in my mind. It was all smoke and mirrors. I made the whole thing up.

"Forget your past to get your life back," I mumble.

That was a scream from my subconscious to make a change. I did this. I gave myself the advice I needed. I put myself on the path. I close my eyes at the shock of the realization. I had the power inside me all along.

Chapter Sixty-Four

Memory Lane

I wander back to the bar and sit down on the stool in front of the bourbon that Steve already has waiting for me. He must have known that I needed it, and he was right. I do.

I pull out my wallet to retrieve the money to pay for it and see the edge of the photo sticking out. I had forgotten this was still in here. I slide it out of the pocket it's tucked into and unfold it. I used to look at this as a happier time that I was desperate to return to. It's amazing how things change. The beautiful, smart, elegant boss's daughter I felt privileged to be married to was nothing more than a philandering, deceitful murderer. Go figure.

Fate has a twisted sense of humor. Kinsey was replaced by a more beautiful, intelligent, artsy woman of the world – one who happens to be shadowed by one of the foremost intelligence agencies in the world as penance for her father's and grandfather's sins. Everybody has a past, and that includes me. It's what we do with our futures that matters. If I learned anything from my imaginary conversation with the Engineer, it's that. The capability to change is within us all. It is only a matter of taking that first step and following it with another.

I drop the photo on the bar. Part of me is tempted to use it as a coaster.

"Did you enjoy your second chat with the wall?" Steve asks with a chuckle after returning to the bar.

"Yeah, it was a revelation for sure. I'm glad you're having so much fun at my expense."

"Sorry about that. A bartender's life can get dull. I need to have my fun when I can. You still have that picture?" Steve asks, pointing at the photo on the bar. "Who is she, anyway?"

"Dead to me."

"Ah. Well, I have something for you. While you were taking your stroll down memory lane, I went rummaging through the back office to find something for you. I had almost forgotten about it."

Steve holds up a plain white envelope. He hands it to me as I give him a puzzled look.

"What is this? My bar tab?"

"Nah, that would have been much thicker. Some woman dropped this off for you a couple of months back. She insisted that you'd be by sooner or later to get it. I argued that it wouldn't happen, but she made me take it. Never in a million years did I think you'd be back here to collect it. But I kept it, so here you go."

"Why'd you take it if you didn't think I'd return?"

"Honestly? When a woman that beautiful asks for a favor, only a fool keeps arguing."

I study it for a long moment. My hands begin to shake as I peel open the sealed envelope and withdraw the single piece of tri-folded paper. The elegant script is written in black ink, and I begin to read it quietly to myself as Steve moves off.

My Dearest Braden,

Mere words cannot express how sorry I am for the way I left New York. I wanted to say goodbye, but you probably know the reasons I didn't by now. I also cannot leave things unsaid between us, so I hope when this letter finds you, it finds you well and willing to listen.

I could not have imagined on that dance floor in Buenos Aires what impact you would have on my life. You were torn and conflicted, and I was alone. I took a risk inviting you into my life because I was sincerely afraid that my past would catch up to me. After what happened in Paris, I swore that I would never get involved in another relationship. There was too much at stake, and it wasn't fair to subject someone to my demons.

What happened was a realization of my fears - as our friendship grew, so did my feelings for you. We danced, had great adventures in foreign lands, slept under the stars, and experienced the best that life has to offer. And with each moment, I fell more in love with you, fully knowing that I shouldn't. You had a past you were hiding, and so did I.

For one magical moment in Venice, I summoned the courage to let my guard down. I don't regret a minute of it. I imagined a future together, and that scared me. That's why I wanted to return to Paris. I needed familiarity to understand what I wanted, and I realized it was you.

I knew that we were Eurydice and Orpheus and that our story could only end in tragedy. When Kinsey appeared at our hotel, I knew the end was near. When Braus told me of your ordeals and how he was aware of mine, I knew for sure. Now, I have lost you forever and am left with a shattered and broken heart. I am back to wandering the world, as alone and afraid as I was the day you found me.

The stars may have determined that our paths can never intersect again, but know that I regret nothing about the path we traveled together other than wishing it could have been a longer journey. The time spent with you has been the happiest of my life. I will forever miss your presence by my side. Know that I still love you, Braden, and always will.

Forever Yours in this Life and the Next,

Lyla

Tears well up in my eyes as I finish reading. A single drop breaks free and streams down my cheek as I refold the letter and tuck it back into the envelope. I hold it against my lips as I try to compose myself.

In Greek mythology, Eurydice was one of Apollo's daughters who married Orpheus, a legendary musician and poet. After their marriage, Eurydice was pursued by Aristaeus and, in an effort to evade him, stepped on a snake. She was bitten and subsequently died, leaving a devastated Orpheus to play such a mournful melody that the gods themselves wept in anguish. They advised him to search for Eurydice in the Underworld and bring her back, so that's what he did. Now, that's what I need to do.

I fold the envelope and stuff it into my shirt pocket before slugging down the bourbon and sliding the twenty across the bar. "Thanks for everything, Steve."

"Wait! Where are ya goin'?"

I smile as I slide off the stool. "Dancing. I just need to find my partner first."

"The girl who gave me the letter? Lucky guy. How are ya going to do that?"

"I have to figure out where it itches."

"I don't know what that means, but good luck, buddy. Don't forget your picture."

Steve holds up the photo of Kinsey and me in Central Park. It wasn't just a lifetime ago. It was another life, and one I'm eager to finally put behind me. I need to forget my past to get my life back. That's what I intend to do.

"Chuck it, Steve. I don't need it anymore."

I slide my sunglasses on and head out into the bright Key West sunshine with big plans to make. I took my first step toward freedom the last time I left this bar. Now, I'm about to take the second.

Chapter Sixty-Five

Every Stop is a Place to Start

The arrangements took two days to make. This is Key West. It's a town full of sailors. It was just a matter of finding a captain who was going in my direction. Then I found one.

I checked out of the hotel and grabbed my stuff before heading to the marina. Arrangements were made for the rental car to be picked up. I would abandon it, but since it's listed under my alias, I decided that paying a few hundred dollars is worth keeping me out of trouble. I get to leave Florida without a guilty conscience.

The sailboat is beautiful and even bigger than the one I was staying on during my first trip here. The older couple are as nice as can be. This is an annual pilgrimage for the retirees, but I think they're happy to have some additional company besides their two crewmen contracted for the trip.

After I get settled in, we cast off. I have no issue working as a deckhand despite being a paying customer. It actually feels good doing some manual labor, even if that wasn't part of the deal. My hosts are appreciative. Sailing can be labor-intensive, and the larger the crew, the easier the work. Before long, we are in the open ocean, or gulf, to be more precise.

There's something romantic about riding the wind across an expanse of water in a sailboat on a beautiful, sunny day. There isn't another vessel on the water as far as the eye can see. The world feels like it belongs only to us.

"Hey, Braden!"

"Yes, Captain?"

"Why don't you come back here and take the wheel? I need to go below decks and help the missus with lunch."

I move from the bow to the wheel located near the stern. The man shifts over to make room, and I take the big wooden wheel. I have no idea what I'm doing.

"Are you sure? I mean, I've never driven a boat."

"We're not on I-95, son," the man says with a smile. "You're not driving…you're sailing. Now, look in front of you out at the horizon and tell me what you see."

"Water."

"That's right. If you hit another boat out here, you've accomplished something. Just keep her on this course right here," the captain says, pointing at the compass.

"What if I see another boat?" I ask.

He looks at me like it's the dumbest question he's ever heard.

"Don't hit it."

"Aye, aye."

The man claps me on the shoulder, just like Braus was fond of doing. That brings back some memories. Even if the German wanted to find him, he never could out here. That's the beauty of the sea – it's vast, empty, and anonymous.

I hold my face up against the breeze, savoring the feeling of it. For my entire life, I was incapable of being in the present. I had no idea how to enjoy the moment. That's the problem with always focusing on the future – you miss everything that makes life worth living.

The first novel about my life has drawn to a close. Now, it's time for the sequel. It will be a new adventure, with new characters and an ending yet to be written. That's the fun of it. I have no idea what to expect, and for the first time in my life, I'm okay with that.

This sailboat will get me where I need to go. Then, the hard part begins. South America is the fourth-largest continent at nearly seven million square miles. Lyla won't be in the Andes Mountains or in the Amazon rainforest, so that reduces the number of square miles I need to search. As if that's going to help.

More than four hundred million people live in South America. I would start in the cities, but Lyla also likes the countryside. Her fondest memories were in places off the beaten path. There is a decent chance she won't be in any of the major metropolitan areas. They are big and expensive. She would prefer something smaller. But where?

I have an entire voyage to think about what to do when we arrive in port. It's going to be like playing Marco Polo in a pool when the other person doesn't respond. It's an almost impossible task, but my thoughts don't dwell on not finding her, as likely as that seems. I wonder what I will say when I do. I wonder what she will say. Will she fall into my arms, or will it be as awkward as it was when we first met? Time will tell, and I look forward to finding out. But not today.

At this moment, I'm content knowing what I need to do with the rest of my life. I'm going to enjoy the feeling of the breeze and the sailboat gliding across the water. I'm going to listen to the enchanting melodies of Jimmy Buffett playing over the sailboat's sound system. I feel the pressure and stress of a lifetime of fulfilling someone else's expectations melt away as I listen to "Son of a Sailor," "Margaritaville," "Fins," and "A Pirate Looks at Forty." They are all great songs. When "La Vie Dansante" comes on, I can't help but smile.

"I'm on my way, Lyla. I'm on my way."

A Note from the Author

I have no idea where the concept of this book came from. I do know how it developed into the novel you just read. In too many political thrillers, I find the characters very underbaked. I wanted to write a book that gave the protagonists something to do other than run for their lives – something like falling in love.

I also wanted there to be different shades to the antagonists. Was Arden the real bad guy? The Cossack? Travis? Kinsey? Everyone will have a different opinion. Even Braus, a man who had no problem putting guns to people's heads or roughing them up to get what he wanted, showed a different side by the end of the story.

The name was inspired by the Jimmy Buffet song "La Vie Dansante," for sure. I wrote it as a screenplay almost twenty years ago and had Braden doing a lot of dumb things in the movie. It didn't work, and the Braden you just read about is far different than that character. Some things carried over. He did win on a hop bet at the craps table in both works.

As for the theme, there are a lot of books and movies about men saving women and an increasing number of works where women save men. I wanted to write a series where they save each other, sometimes in more ways than one. The Dancing Trilogy is my attempt at that.

So, is this a romance or a political thriller? I call it a polythrillmance. I have no idea how it will be received – there isn't an extraordinary amount of crossover for readers who enjoy those two genres. If nothing else, it's going to be interesting to see what my readers think it is.

I hear horror stories about dating in the modern age and I wanted to spin a tale where a couple keeps some dark secrets from each other. What would that do to a relationship? Would it matter in the long run if they truly love each other? You'll have to find out in the next novel.

Braus was not in the screenplay. The German enforcer's name comes from a funny story. My mother had a toe amputated, so I told her that her new mafia name was "Nine Toe Nancy." Then, she had her eyebrows colored, and I started calling her "Brows." Before they lightened up (she's a blonde), they got even darker, and Brows became Braus - my mother, the German assassin.

Before anyone questions how I could say that to my mother, we are very close and she would wonder what was wrong if I didn't razz her about things like that. Don't worry, it's reciprocated.

I am a horrible dancer. Okay, maybe not horrible, but definitely not good. My wife wanted to surprise our guests on our wedding day with a choreographed dance that was mostly a Viennese Waltz. I agreed, and we took lessons for about eight months under one condition: It had to be danced to a slowed-down version of the Game of Thrones theme. Clearly, that was before season eight came out. It had the desired effect on our friends and family.

The places Lyla and Braden travel to in the novel are either cities I've visited or ones on my bucket list. I have been to Key West, Vienna, Monaco, Venice, and Paris. I don't live far from New York City and have been there hundreds of times. I have gambled in Monte Carlo and taken a gondola ride in Venice. The other places, especially Rio, Buenos Aires, and Lucerne, are high on my list. And I have always wanted to run with the bulls, but odds are my stay in the hospital will be longer than Braden's was.

To answer the question I know is coming, yes, there will be a sequel. Two, actually. This is a planned trilogy, and I am already working on the second book. Will Braden and Lyla find happiness when their story finally ends? You will have to wait and see, partly because I'm not sure myself, yet.

Acknowledgments

I am going to start where this began. A good friend and former Army buddy of mine read "La Vie Dansante" when it was a screenplay. He was so furious about the ending that he refused to read anything more of mine until a sequel was written. That was nearly twenty years ago.

Well, you're getting your wish, Bill. And once the sequel comes out, I have eighteen more books as of this writing for you to catch up on. Happy reading!

Thank you to all my readers, especially the ones who participated in the advance reader copy program for this novel. For anyone who has not joined my newsletter, please visit my website at www.mikaelcarlson.com. I offer free novels from time to time, and there will be many more incentives coming in the future.

I warned my editor that this would be different than many of my previous novels. I'm pretty sure that piqued his interest, but he still made an inordinate amount of grammar changes that made me question the English language. Thanks to Mike from Sticks & Stones Editing for another fantastic job!

When I contacted the cover designer and told him I wanted a pink cover, I'm fairly certain he questioned my sanity. It happens to be my wife's favorite color, and she doesn't like almost any of my other covers. It isn't because JD&J doesn't do fantastic work because they do. She thinks they're either too violent or too manly. Well, yeah, I'm a thriller writer, and that's not the reality television genre she enjoys.

So, I had JD&J create a cover that I knew she would love, and they succeeded. Now I have a pink cover that is going to look very weird next to the others on my wall. Thank you, Dave, for making my wife's dream come true.

Speaking of my beautiful wife, I like changing up where she lands in these acknowledgments because I know she reads them first. I toyed with the idea of leaving her out of them once, but my couch isn't *that* comfortable. Thank you, Michele, for all your love and support.

I would also be remiss to leave out my family, extended family, and friends, many of whom are my most avid supporters and readers. A special shout out to my mother, Nancy, who let me borrow her newest nickname, Braus, for this book. Unfortunately, she will be rooting for him the whole way.

www.ingramcontent.com/pod-product-compliance
Lightning Source LLC
Chambersburg PA
CBHW060706190726
48289CB00002B/567